THE RINGMASTER

The Ringmaster

MORRIS WEST

HEINEMANN : LONDON

William Heinemann Ltd
Michelin House, 81 Fulham Road, London SW3 6RB
LONDON   MELBOURNE   AUCKLAND

First published 1991
Copyright © Melaleuka Investments Pty Ltd 1991

A CIP catalogue record for this book
is held by the British Library
ISBN 0 434 85898 6

Phototypeset by Deltatype Limited, Ellesmere Port

Printed in Great Britain by
Clays Ltd, St Ives plc

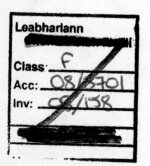

For PHYL
with gratitude and affection

Circus. A place where horses, ponies
and elephants are permitted to see men,
women and children acting the fool.

The Devil's Dictionary
Ambrose Bierce
(1881–1911)

Acknowledgments

This book could not have been written without the help and advice of many friends in the international communities of diplomacy and finance. These are sensitive professions, so my informants have preferred to remain anonymous.

One benefactor I can name, however, is my dear friend David Ashley-Wilson, boon companion on my last working visit to Malaysia, Indonesia, Thailand and Japan. My thanks to him and to all the others who offered the courtesy of their houses and the gifts of their experience.

M.L.W.

One

It was not the best of times. The Iraqis had taken over Kuwait. The Americans had begun pouring troops and armour into Saudi Arabia. There was an odds-on chance of full scale war in the immediate future. The Nikkei Index had dropped through the floor. The shockwaves of recession were being transmitted to every stockmarket in the world. For the moment, however, I was far removed from these harsh realities.

I was a guest at Kenji Tanaka's country house, in the uplands of Nagano province, an old princely estate, cradled inside the rim of an ancient volcano. The morning after my arrival my host handed me a thick document written in Japanese, then took off for Tokyo in his helicopter. I settled myself in the old tea-house by the lake and began to work through the papers.

It was the season called maples-in-flame. The sky was ice-blue, flecked with wisps of cloud against which the crags of the crater rim rose black and threatening. Among the high peaks the air was cold; but in the deep hollow of the basin it was warm and still. The lake, girdled by garden plots and stubble land, lay mirror-smooth, gleaming like old lacquer. Along the footpath that led from the lake to the dwelling, the colours of the maples flowed russet and gold and crimson, a runnel of fire through the dark thickets of the pinewoods. After the ant-heap scurry of Tokyo and Osaka, the solitude was a balm to the spirit.

There had always been for me a curious melancholy about the Japanese landscape, a melancholy heightened by the tortured formalism of life and custom; but here in this hidden valley, the sadness seemed less. Even the black cloud which had settled over me since my wife's death lifted a little, to show at the fringes a faint gleam of silver.

All my friends, even my children, in their own grief, had promised me that time would heal the heart and work would dull the heartache. But I had found all too soon that time dragged and work was a drug that left me in the end with a long, red-eyed hangover. Nonetheless,

1

Tanaka's document was more than work. It was – at least, it could be – the challenge of a lifetime. By lunchtime I had still only digested the preamble. By late afternoon I had skimmed the whole document – dense, closely reasoned and heavily qualified in Japanese corporate style – and was convinced that the notion was hugely exciting. I was still trying to come to terms with the stretch and scope of it when I heard the clatter of rotors. Tanaka's helicopter was spiralling slowly round the funnel of the crater to land on the beach at the head of the lake.

Kenji Tanaka got out and turned away, crouch-backed, from the swirl of the rotor blades. Then he straightened up, waved off the pilot and stood watching until the machine had cleared the crater rim and turned westward back to Tokyo.

He was tall for a Japanese. His hair was grey, but his skin was as smooth as old ivory and he carried himself like an athlete: supple, sparing of gesture but poised always to move swiftly. He was dressed in a business suit and overcoat, both tailored in London. His fur hat was a gift from colleagues in Moscow. He carried neither luggage nor briefcase. Whatever he needed was here, waiting for him in the old house hidden among the trees, in the small temple shrine where his father's ashes were honoured.

There were servants to attend him day and night but no one came to greet him. Even I, his waiting guest, did not approach him. In this place he required that the rituals of his comings and goings should remain private to himself. So, I watched him through the moon-window of the tea-house.

He squatted by the lake's edge and, with great care, gathered a handful of flat pebbles, testing each one for size and weight. Then be began skimming them across the water, measuring the distances against an old mooring pile to which the gardener tethered his punt. However, the sequence of the throws was more important than the distance. First he skimmed eight pebbles, then uttered a small explosive, 'Ya!' Next he counted off nine, 'Ku!' And finally, three, 'Sa!' I knew what he was doing because sometimes on our walks we had played the game together.

The numbers were the most dreaded sequence in the old flower-card game called *hanafuda*, which the cardsharps used to play in the country inns to fleece the yokels. They added up to twenty and the final zero made it the worst possible score. He had learned the game here, as a small boy. He had learned also that when you threw away the same numbers you could distance yourself from bad luck. The numbers had other meanings, too; but these had been revealed later in his life and were not related to this primitive ritual of childhood.

He clapped his hands together, dusted off the sand, then turned away from the lake and began walking steadily down the avenue of maples-in-flame. I followed at a respectful distance, but he seemed – or chose to seem – unaware of my presence. A hundred paces brought him to a small pagoda set in a garden of white pebbles and black rocks. The pagoda was very old, built of hand-hewn pine, fastened with wooden dowels. Its roof was of green ceramic tiles, still bright after the lapse of centuries.

Outside the entrance, hung by leather straps in a teakwood frame, was a bronze gong, as tall as a man, with a wooden striker. Inside was a single image of the Lord Buddha, carved in wood in the Amida style and painted with antique gold. Flanking the image were two small alcoves where the ashes of his father and his grandfather were kept, with their funerary histories recorded on hanging scrolls.

He made obeisance to the Buddha and to the ancestors. He lit incense sticks and planted them in the sand-pot. Then he closed his eyes and stood very still, reliving the experience that Hiroshi Teraro, the scholar monk, had taught him in his boyhood: 'Close yourself in silence. Stand still as an ancient rock. Let the river of life flow round you and over you.'

I had known him long enough to understand that this bare, timeworn place was the fountainhead of the life-current of Kenji Tanaka, whom even his closest colleagues called the Stone Man. He had come here when he was ten years old, in the days of the Great Defeat, just after the annihilation of Hiroshima and Nagasaki. His father was in hiding, threatened with assassination by the militarists because of his pleas to cabinet and to the Emperor to end the hopeless struggle. To protect his wife he had divorced her and sent her back to her family. Then he had fled with his son to this secret valley, last relic of an old family fiefdom.

He had placed the child in the care of the country family who managed the small estate and under the tutelage of Hiroshi Teraro, who had been a soldier and was now a poet, a calligrapher and adept in the disciplines of Zen.

It was in this shrine that all three of them had sat to listen to the Emperor's speech of surrender. For the first and last time he had seen his father weep. Then he had heard the words that drummed in his

3

skull-case for half a century: 'We were fools and cowards, gulled by criminals. We wallowed in cruelty and called it the honour of warriors. We locked ourselves in a madhouse and threw away the key. So, we became the first victims of the atomic plague which now threatens all mankind. At last we have been given a chance – a small one but, yes, a chance! – to build a new Japan, even perhaps a new world. But this time we dare not fail . . . You, my son, will have your part to play, but you must make yourself ready for it. For a while you will stay here and study with your master. Then you will go abroad, to Europe, to England, to the United States. You will learn the languages and the skills of other peoples. Afterwards you will come back here and take the place I will have prepared for you and for which you will have prepared yourself.'

As his father had prophesied, so it had come to pass. Today, Kenji Tanaka was President of the Tanaka Group, a giant conglomeration of banks, insurance companies, trading corporations and manufacturing enterprises, with interests in every country on the planet. He was Chairman of the small élite consortium who controlled the economic policies of the nation. He had just been appointed personal counsellor to the Emperor. He was rich beyond his dreams. He had risen as high as any man might aspire. But he was still a debtor, to his father, to his ancestors, to the whole complex of the society in which he moved. This was *giri*, the silken cord that would hold him in bondage until the day he died. It was *giri* that drew him back always to this childhood refuge to share the triumph with his father, even though he knew there was nothing to share but silence, no one to share it with but phantoms – and me who, being a *gaijin*, an outside man, did not count.

The incense sticks continued to smoke as he bowed himself out of the shrine. He put on his shoes, then stood by the gong, drumming on it lightly with his fingertips, feeling the old metal stir into a barely audible resonance. He lifted the wooden striker. He had told me how heavy it had seemed to him as a child, how Hiroshi Teraro always admonished him: 'You do not beat the gong. You strike it just hard enough to set the particles moving within the metal and make their own harmonies. When we sit down tonight with the brushes and ink I will show you how to draw the music so that what you see on the paper will make echoes in your ears . . .'

So now, measuring and timing the strokes as carefully as if the old master were watching him, he struck the gong once, twice, and again. The sound rolled in waves through the woodland, rose and echoed

4

round the bowl of the crater. In the old house they would have heard the gong and already they would be making ready to greet him with the ceremonies due to a homecoming master.

Kenji Tanaka smiled, set the striker back in its rest and walked out of the stone garden, back to the path. He showed no surprise when I stepped out of the shadows of the shrubbery, fell into step beside him and walked, in silence, friend with friend, the last fifty paces to the house.

In the house among the autumn trees, Kenji Tanaka and I were received, with feudal respect, by the guardians of the hidden domain. There was a small tribe of them: the estate steward, the farmer, the farmer's wife, their two sons with their wives and children, the gardener, the cook, the housemaids, and Miko, whom he called his country wife, although she was neither a wife nor, properly speaking, a mistress, because she came or stayed by her own choice, at his request sometimes, but never at his command.

The farm people, usually closed and resentful of strangers, accepted her without question as the chatelaine. The young girls adored her like an elder and more beautiful sister, who came always with exciting presents and left to tearful farewells. She was coming up to forty now, but the years had left few marks on her. She lived in an aura of extraordinary calm, beyond the reach of rage or malice. Tanaka's relationship with her was the most satisfying of his life. Here in the tribal enclave she seemed the embodiment of all the traditional virtues of Japanese woman; outside she was a pilot who guided him wordlessly through the shoals and tide races of an alien ocean. As she steered him calmly through the homecoming ceremonies, I remembered what he had told me of their first encounter in Los Angeles.

In the early seventies, when the Tanaka Group was making its first big investments in the United States, he learned that a young Nisei woman was offering a range of expensive but very efficient services to visiting Japanese businessmen. The services were advertised in a brochure, designed by a famous wood-block artist, produced in Tokyo and circulated only to high-ranking executives of major corporations. That was the first surprise: her knowledge of the intricate structures of Japanese business. The second was that she was offering commercial services: bilingual secretaries, interpreters, temporary office accommodation, limousine hire, travel arrangements, lists of attorneys and accountants familiar with Japanese business. In addition, she offered conference facilities and small scale entertainment, luncheons and dinners, at her house, a discreet mansion in Holmby Hills.

Kenji Tanaka was impressed by the brochure, but sceptical of the promises. His education had made him mistrustful of American exaggeration. Also, he knew the habits of Japanese businessmen at home and abroad and he could not believe that sexual services were excluded from the menu. So he inquired of old Okawa at Sumitomo who, he knew, was as randy as a billygoat and always eager for contacts in a new city. Much to his surprise, Okawa offered high recommendation.

'This woman is very good. Whatever she promises, she delivers. Also, she knows how the town works. She explains that whores and drugs are gangster territory, as they are in Japan . . . So she refuses to embroil herself. She does have contacts in the police, in case any of her clients get into trouble; but she insists that she is not interested in salesmen's antics and noisy conventions. We are using her more and more. Her performance as a hostess is old style and very polished. The staff she supplies are well trained. I have found it pays to ask her advice. Why don't you meet her and judge for yourself?'

So Kenji Tanaka had made his first appointment at the house in Holmby Hills. He had begun by interviewing Miko, in the condescending style of man to woman, employer to eager applicant. In the end it was he who found himself under scrutiny, asked to supply references, warned that he would be held responsible for the conduct of people he recommended. And yet in some subtle fashion his pride – the uneasy pride of every Japanese male – had been saved and he had left prickling with a young man's desire to possess this exotic creature, so graceful and yet so aloof.

It took nearly a year to persuade her to become his lover. Even then it was not a conquest, but a treaty. There was no talk of marriage. Tanaka already had a wife and three children, two girls and a boy. There was no way either that Miko would consent to become a traditional mistress, maintained in high style as an ornament and evidence of the great man's success. She could not, would not, accept the role traditional to women in Japan. Her business was a success, she had money of her own. She was born American. She desired greatly to discover her ancestral roots. She reserved the right to choose the times and places of her sojourn.

When he brought her to the valley for the first time she fell in love

6

with the place. She wrapped it about herself, as the crater walls wrapped themselves around the lake and held it calm while the mountain storms raged high above.

It was here that she fell pregnant, here that she stayed to recover after the stillbirth of a son. She was back now because Tanaka had sent her the same message as he had sent to me: 'Please come. Important things are happening. I need your support.'

The welcome ceremony over, Miko led Tanaka to their private quarters, to prepare him for the bath in the great wooden tub that smelt still of pine-sap and upland flowers. It was expected that I join them later. It was equally expected that they be left alone for a decent interval.

I knew that this was the kind of body service Kenji Tanaka craved – one that satisfied his deepest and most secret yearning, to float secure as an unborn child in amniotic fluid, surrounded by mother-flesh, responding to the rhythm of a maternal heartbeat. Deprived in childhood of his own mother, living in a surrogate family, urged always to male excellence by a tutor and a father, his fantasy life had focused more and more on the lost mother image, even as his career became more emphatically that of the imperious adventurer in commerce.

The real nature of the bond between Miko and himself was expressed exactly by the Japanese verb *amaeru*, to presume totally on a mother's love, to depend as a child depends. For Miko his dependence was a guarantee against domestic tyranny. He knew that her love could be instantly withdrawn, so that her every absence was an unspoken threat. Even in play there was the tiny prick of steel, the traditional threat wrapped up in love-talk. *Okachan wa kirai yo*: Mother does not love you any more!

I understood these things because I had known him much longer than Miko, because he was my partner in business and we had played together in the floating world where, since I spoke its language and knew its customs, I was not wholly a stranger, but an amusing hybrid, an unexpected dash of colour in a garden of grey rocks and raked pebbles.

When I make a statement like that – and my children tell me I make them all too often – there is usually an awkward pause while people wait for some explanation of who I am, what I do and why I find myself in odd situations: like sitting wrapped in a *yukata* waiting for the maid to attend me so that Tanaka and I can relax and talk business while we stew like chickens in near-boiling water.

7

Who am I? I'm Gilbert Anselm Langton, fifty-odd years old and feeling much older. I'm a publisher, a major shareholder of an international group called Polyglot Press which was founded in Sydney, Australia and now has branches or affiliates all over the world. My father – God rest his scholar's soul – had held for a quarter of a century the Chair of Comparative Languages at the university and it was he who helped me frame the plan, endowed me with enough capital to seed the enterprise, fed me all the encouragement I needed and more ideas than I could use in a lifetime.

But before all that, he had given me the gift of tongues. My mother died very early in my life and my father devoted every moment of his leisure life to making me, as he put it, 'apt for a gypsy life on a shrinking planet'. He buried his grief so deep that I glimpsed it only at rare moments. All he allowed me to see was the joy of things, the challenge of new places, new people, old history relived, new history in the making. A polyglot himself, he gave me the key to the Tower of Babel where the world's languages echo in hopeless confusion. He taught me how to decipher them, remember them, turn them into the currency of daily commerce. He told me tales of the great philologers, Pallas and Bakmeister and Joseph Justin Scaliger and the greatest of them all, Joseph Caspar Cardinal Mezzofanti, who was born in Bologna in 1774 and died in Rome in 1849.

I remember how we climbed the Janiculum hill to visit his tomb in the Church of Sant Onofrio, where my father told me that I could 'accept with reasonable certainty' that the little cleric had spoken and written thirty languages with 'rare excellence' and could 'manage creditably in forty or fifty more'. Even today the phrases ring in my head! More importantly, he showed me the trick to it: a good visual and oral memory, an understanding of tribal and lingual families, a daily drilling with the native-born. In my own lifetime Australia had become a haven for migrants from all over the globe – Greeks, Turks, Vietnamese, Chinese, Ethiopians, the whole gamut of races – so practice partners were not hard to find.

I am not yet a Mezzofanti, but you can trust me in twenty three major languages and be confident I won't lead you too far astray in fifteen or twenty others. My father, however, taught me another essential lesson: a man can be a fool in as many languages as he speaks. So he insisted I read law and economics and learn business administration. That meant I had to work like a dog for nine months of every year and get my reward

8

when he and I took off for three months of gypsy travel in Asia, Europe or the South Americas.

He taught me more than language. He taught me a mannerly silence and the deference appropriate to a stranger who is invited to share the tribal fire. He taught me about women, too, because he loved them and courted them, and they prized his friendship.

So as my publishing activities extended, I found myself gradually co-opted into a new role, that of consultant or mediator in international commerce. It was not a free service. I was paid well for it. But those who understood what I could offer were able to save a mint of money in lawyers' fees and executive time. More than half the cost of international business is used up in dialogues of the deaf, between people who are totally ignorant of each other's laws, customs and business dialect.

Understand something: I am not a professional interpreter. They are highly skilled people with a precise function. They must translate and not comment. They must present a proposition bald and unglossed, otherwise they betray their trust. I can do that, but I have no taste for it. In fact, my function as mediator is exactly the opposite. I supply the tonalities of the dialogue. I explain the concepts which underlie the language. I say what is left unsaid, perhaps the unsayable. Not all of that is done in public assembly. Much of it is transmitted in private talk with the parties. However, in the end they must be convinced, not only of my competence but my integrity.

And that – God love the man! – was the best lesson my father ever taught me: 'Son, you're not God. You're not expected to know everything. So say what you do know loud and clear; but never refuse to confess ignorance or innocence.'

I was already a year into my association with Kenji Tanaka before I understood the full import of that advice. The Tokyo connection was very important to us, not only because of the Japanese market for our publications, but because we could print and produce there for other markets. The quality was excellent, the prices were highly competitive. There were no labour problems.

Then, on one of my visits, Kenji Tanaka tabled a proposition: a merger with a manufacturer of comic books and cartoon novels for which there is a huge market in Japan. The comic books are gaudy, gory and highly erotic, with emphasis on mutilation and debasement of women. Everyone reads them – commuters in trains, school children

9

waiting for buses, typists munching sushi during their lunch breaks. It is a huge and profitable industry. I could not for the life of me see why they needed our small outfit. I could, however, see that they might want our international distribution, which was functioning better every year. I knew something else for certain: these particular comic book publishers were part owned by a Godfather of *Yamaguchi-gumi*, one of the biggest crime syndicates in Japan. Its connection with Tanaka was no secret. Every great corporation in Japan has a symbiotic relationship with the underworld organisations who run the entertainment, the gambling business and the woman trade. It is as traditional as the feudal system in England. Kenji Tanaka had explained it to me many times. Now he was trying to persuade me to make the deal.

'It's big money, Gil, safe money. They'll pay a premium to come in. They'll inject new capital whenever you need it. Why are you making such a problem?'

'It's not a problem. It's a simple decision. I don't like the people. I don't like the product. I won't handle it.'

Kenji Tanaka took it very calmly. He even managed a regretful smile. 'Have you not forgotten one figure in the equation: the Tanaka interest?'

'I do not believe that will be served by such an association.'

'But surely I am the best judge of that?'

'So who arbitrates the issue?'

'I think' said Tanaka gently 'that our interest has to prevail. We can demonstrate the large financial advantages which will accrue to all shareholders. We can require you legally to act in our common interest.'

It was a clear threat, and no idle one. Litigation with a Japanese in a Japanese court is a fool's pastime. Even if you win, you lose. The network of family and business relationships is so large that, if you fall out of the net, you're finished, in business and in private life as well. So now I was under test. I could not back down, even had I wanted to do so. I could not indulge in anger or invective because that would brand me a barbarian.

I sat for a few moments pondering the dilemma. Then I asked for paper and a calligrapher's brush. Tanaka was nonplussed but he pushed the ink block and the paper across the table to me. I paused a moment to steady myself, then wrote in cursive *hiragana* an offer to sell all my stock in the Japanese company to Kenji Tanaka, at a fair price to be determined by him. I signed it and passed it back across the desk.

10

He read it slowly, mouthing the syllables as if he were checking it for errors. Then he said: 'Are you quite sure you know what this means?'

'Quite sure.'

'You are trusting me to set my own purchase price on all your Japanese stock.'

'That's right. You know what it's worth. You won't cheat me.'

'How long is the offer open?'

'You decide now!'

'And if I decline?'

'I am then entitled to offer it elsewhere. Either way, I'm out. I'll probably talk to Sumitomo. I'm sorry Kenji. You and I have had a good run together; but I'm not going to quarrel with you. I have no hard feelings, just irreconcilable differences. I'll be flying out of Tokyo tonight. Until then you can call me at the hotel.'

I stood up and held out my hand. Tanaka crumpled the paper and slapped it into my palm. His tone was harsh and peremptory.

'No deal! You're right. Who needs these shits anyway? Tradition hangs them round our necks like carrion . . . You trust me not to cheat you. I should at least trust you to run the business you know. Cancel your flight. Tonight you and I need to get drunk together . . .'

My reverie was interrupted as the door slid open and the maidservant bowed and summoned me to the bath-house, where her master awaited my company.

Miko had already taken her bath and left. I sensed that Tanaka was too jealous of his exotic prize to expose her to another man's appraisal.

The servant-girl scrubbed me down. Then Tanaka and I sat in the great pinewood tub, which was fed steadily with steaming water, the overflow of which poured into runnels on the old stone floor and served to feed the ornamental stream in the garden. Through the half-opened screen we watched the last daylight fade slowly on the russet and gold of the maples and the twisted boles of the cypresses, luminous as old pewter. It was an interlude of pure physical pleasure. No words were needed to embellish it. Tanaka waited until the last light had died. Then he asked, as was his habit, a peremptory opening question.

'Have you read all the material I left with you?'

It was a style that always made my hackles rise. My answer was terse. 'I have.'

'Any comment?'

'None, until I've heard you explain it to me.'

11

He settled himself comfortably in a corner of the tub, supporting himself with arms outstretched along the rim. 'Why are you always such a hardhead, Gil?'

'Because, my dear Kenji, every time you start talking business, you bark like a character out of the *Forty Seven Ronin*.'

'I do not mean to offend you, Gil.'

'In this matter, you do. I'm your friend, not one of your junior executives.'

He gave me a sidelong look and just half a smile. He asked what seemed an irrelevant question. 'Have I ever told you the story of the two monks and the young girl?'

'No, but I'm sure it will be instructive.'

'I hope so. I heard it first from my old master, Hiroshi Teraro. Two monks, one young, the other much older, set out from Tenryu-ji to walk to a distant shrine of the Lord Buddha. They came to a stream. Just as they were tucking up their robes to step into the water, a beautiful young woman appeared and begged them to help her across. Mindful of his vow to have no contact with women, the young monk refused. The older one, however, hoisted her on his back and, with obvious enjoyment, carried her across the water. She thanked them and left. The two monks continued their journey. The younger man, however, was in a black humour. Finally he could contain himself no longer. He demanded to know why, in defiance of all propriety, his companion had carried the young woman on his back. To which the older monk replied: "But my dear brother, what is the difference between us? you have been carrying her ever since we left the river." '

It was a perfect Zen parable and, like all such tales, it demanded a moment's reflection before its meaning was clear. In spite of the fact that I spoke and read Tanaka's language almost as well as he did, I still could not come to terms with the conventions which were as much a part of his identity as the shape of his face and the colour of his eyes. It was a real barrier to full friendship and I was the one who, in the end, would have to overleap it.

I made a slightly exaggerated gesture of apology and submission and told him: 'It's a good story. I'm sure I'll remember it.'

Tanaka brightened then. The awkward moment was past. Face was saved for both of us. He made a bald announcement. 'I bring bad news, Gil. In Iraq fighting could begin at any moment. We are being pressed to contribute to the war chest of the Americans and the combined Arab

12

forces. Our government has agreed to do that. Now we are being urged to commit armed personnel. I am against it. I believe the people are against it too. But politically . . .' He gave a small despairing shrug. 'We are hurt whatever we do. My real concern is that a war in the Middle East will cut our oil supplies and put an unbearable strain on our economy. So the project for which I invited you here assumes a new urgency, a prime importance.'

He paused for a moment, then launched into his exposition. 'Six months ago I had a visit from Carl Albert Leibig. His firm is one of the oldest German trading companies in Japan. It was founded in 1859 just six years after the arrival of Perry and his black ships. The same family controls it still. Their headquarters are in Hamburg, and they have active branches in China, Hong Kong, Taiwan, the Philippines, Korea and the United States. Their present specialty is what you in the West call turnkey operations. If you want a printing press, a food processing plant or a robot assembly line, they'll design it, build it, train your operatives and even arrange your financing. They're very solid and, in a discreet fashion, very influential in commercial politics in Europe and Asia.

'Carl Leibig told me he'd had an approach from someone high in the Kremlin. Things are desperate there, as you know. The whole Soviet economy is on the verge of collapse. The Union of Soviet Socialist Republics is breaking up. The only hope for the leadership is to show an early and visible improvement in the standard of living. Leibig was asked to come up with a pilot plan for food processing and distribution operations which could be applied quickly to the key regions of the Eurasian landmass.

'It's a daunting project; but, based on modular constructions and standardised plants, its outlines are simple, as you have seen in the documents. Leibig and I have put together a syndicate of potential investors and contractors. We are all meeting in Bangkok next week. The Soviets will be there with a team of bankers, economists and engineers. We've given ourselves two weeks to hammer out an agreement.'

'That's not very long!'

'We all know that. Our best hope is to act under the pressure of necessity and sort out the difficulties as they arise on the ground. That's why we need a mediator, to damp down political debate and encourage everyone to practical action. You're good at that, very good!'

'You flatter me Kenji; but the politics won't just go away. The Americans are offering massive funds as the price of Soviet intervention in the Persion Gulf. The Germans are paying something like five billion marks as the price for Moscow's non-intervention in the reunification of East and West. Japan is holding out for the return of the Kuril Islands, taken by Russia after the war. A settlement will take time and rough bargaining.'

'Exactly! What is needed now is private enterprise, accelerated by the profit motive. The Soviets don't want to become vassals of American capital. Germany is their natural bridgehead into Europe. Japan is their natural springboard into Asia.'

'It's ironic, isn't it?' I could not hold back the comment. 'Fifty years down the track the Russians themselves want to revive the Berlin/Tokyo Axis.'

Tanaka frowned in obvious distaste. 'The last thing we need, Gil, is a political label on this! It's pure commerce. We're asked to come up with a plan for the import, storage, processing, preservation and distribution of essential foodstuffs across the landmass of the Soviet Union. It's a huge undertaking. The climate works against it. The transport and distribution system is fifty years out of date. The armed forces have the only half-way efficient transport organisation. A large percentage of perishable foodstuffs is lost in storage or transit. Even in the grain-belt there have never been enough silos . . . Already people are tightening their belts for a hard winter. The folk in the Kremlin are having nightmares about food riots. Once we get this agreement through there will need to be massive propaganda on television and in the press and an interim programme of food imports to bridge the gap.'

'And you hope to finalise the agreement at the Bangkok meeting?'

'We must. There can be no "ifs" or "maybes". All the delegates are coming with full authority to sign or reject without reference. Our best hope is to act under the pressure of necessity and then sort out difficulties as they arise on the ground. That's why your role is so important: to damp down debate and hasten decision.'

'Do all the other parties understand that role?'

'They say they do. They have been informed of your record. They accept your presence. Naturally, each delegate will be bringing his own staff of advisers and interpreters, so you'll have a certain amount of critical competition.'

'That's no problem, provided I have daily access to all principals.'

14

'That, too, has been made clear.'

'One more question. Why Bangkok?'

Tanaka grinned like a cat with milk all over its whiskers. 'Because I like the place and the people. I'm always comfortable in the Oriental hotel. Their conference facilities are good and their security is tight. It's also a convenient one-leg flight from Moscow, London, Frankfurt and Tokyo. The delegates don't have to touch down in Mediterranean airports or overfly the trouble-spots in the Gulf. Also, thanks to our excellent relations with the Thai military and police forces, we are able to guarantee safe and healthy entertainment for all our colleagues.'

He was expecting me to rise to the bait; but I was not going to give him that satisfaction. His excellent relations in Thailand were maintained in part by the Yakuza, who did a thriving business importing Thai girls for Japanese clubs and entertainment circuits. They had other links, too, to the amphetamine traffic and the arms rackets; but they still functioned freely within a set of unwritten rules and guidelines. One of the richest men in the country was still Ryoichi Sasakawa, Godfather of Godfathers, who even went jogging with Jimmy Carter and contributed to his presidential library at Emory University. I have no tolerance for thuggery. I have seen too many people hurt by underworld exploiters. I have no patience left for historical justifications of their necessary role in society. As for the safe and healthy entertainment guaranteed by Tanaka – in Bangkok of all places! – I would not bet a dollar on it, let alone my life. One of the closest conspiracies in Thailand is the attempt to keep the massive proliferation of AIDS out of the tourist news. However, I was invited as a commercial mediator, not as a censor of morals, so I held my peace.

As if he had read my thoughts, Tanaka said 'We have provided you with a large two-bedroomed suite at the Oriental. You will need work and conference space, but there will be room for a lady friend, if you care to bring one.'

'I'll bring a secretary and her assistant. So far I have no other arrangements. When do you want me in Bangkok?'

'Ten days from now, Sunday 16th. We convene at nine on the Monday morning.'

'How long do you expect the conference to last?'

'Two weeks. After all the groundwork we've done, if we can't conclude a basic agreement in that time, Leibig and I will walk away. So you see, you carry a heavy responsibility, Gil.'

'You know how I work, Kenji. I don't guarantee success, only an even-handed mediation.'

'We expect no more and no less.' He waited a moment, framing the phrases with great care. 'Do you remember the day when you challenged me to buy you out and set my own price on your Japanese shares?'

'I remember it very well. That was the moment when I believe we became true friends.'

'I suppose it was.' He did not sound very certain. He had another thought in his mind. 'You didn't know it then, Gil, but the whole thing turned out to be a joke with a double meaning. In the Yakuza, when a man makes a mistake, he cuts off a finger joint to show regret and make amends to his *oyabun*, his father-chief. I made a mistake with you. I thought I could guarantee your co-operation. That mistake cost me more than a finger joint. I lost twenty million dollars . . . No matter! If this project works, I shall recoup it a hundred times over. So you see, my dear friend, I am relying very much on your skills as a negotiator . . . Now let's dry off and have some dinner!'

I was halfway to my room when the true import of the words hit me. In Tanaka's eyes, in the value system to which he had been bred, I was his debtor. He had made a concession to me which had cost him dearly. Now it was time for me to acknowledge the debt and pay it. I should do that by changing my role at the conference from independent mediator to partisan promoter of Tanaka's interests.

The strange and difficult part was that Tanaka saw it as the most natural thing in the world. He was not threatening me. He was not bargaining. He was doing nothing dishonourable. He was simply reminding me that, as one to whom a service had been rendered, I was bound by *on* – an obligation which might be deferred but could never be abrogated. Tanaka and I were using the same language; each of us was locked into a different system of logic. I might rage, protest, resign from the conference; but none of it would make any sense at all to him.

The bitterest irony of all was that I could play Judas to myself and no one would ever know. If the conference failed, no one would blame me. If it succeeded, no one would remember whether I had delivered an honest plea or a partisan one. I felt suddenly sick with anger and frustration. There was a taste of bile in my gullet. It took me another ten minutes to compose myself and put on a smiling face for dinner.

That night Miko ate with us, while the maids served our meal. I noted with wry admiration how well she played the complex role which she had accepted in Tanaka's life. She was instant with small services, pouring his liquor, feeding him choice morsels, giggling behind her hand at his jokes. She was also a skilled raconteur and she spun out a whole series of pungent observations about business and politics and public officials in Washington and Hawaii.

For me, the male guest, she had another kind of attention, a teasing interest in the details of my sex life, my girlfriends, my relations with my secretary and my children. It was all very skilful, the sort of act which geisha spend all their girlhood learning. But this one was no geisha. She was like a grafted plant who had reverted, in a magical transformation, to the original Japanese rootstock.

Tanaka doted on her. I liked and admired her. I think she found me agreeable enough. I knew she was observing me closely and that her judgments would be passed later to Kenji Tanaka. So, I took pains to be an entertaining guest. I opened my grab-bag of memories: my boyhood travels with my father, my first encounters with the upland tribes of New Guinea, who worshipped a pig-god and believed that their magicians could change themselves into cassowary birds and travel as fast as the wind from village to village. I told them of the voodoo rites we had witnessed in the favelas of Rio and the day we stood in a back street in Tunis and watched a bored workman excavate rows of little urns, the ashes of first-born sacrificed in the fiery belly of Baal.

It was, I confess, a carefully calculated performance, designed to charm Miko and impress Tanaka. I could not come within a shout of his wealth, his power, even his mobility. His private jet could whisk him at any moment to the ends of the earth. But every Japanese, however widely travelled, lives always encapsulated in his own history, his own culture, his own language. There is, in fact, a whole sub-species of modern literature called *nihon-jinron* – Japanese look at themselves. It is pulp magazine stuff for the most part, which emphasises the racial uniqueness and superiority of the Japanese people. Naturally enough, the conviction of uniqueness and superiority provokes a counter-current, a sense of isolation and inferiority. This was the only weapon on which I could call if my relations with Tanaka turned hostile.

It was not at all impossible. Before we concluded our deal to set up a Japanese branch of Polyglot Press, I had sat through days of haggling with him and his senior staff. He knew every trick in the book. He could be as rough as sandpaper, as smooth as lacquer. Whenever he felt an argument running against him he would make a sudden display of anger, swift and threatening as a swordsman's lunge. I learned that I should never recoil from it, but move in close, body to body, blade on blade, for the parry. It was too early to know whether we would come to battle during the Bangkok conference; but I had to be prepared.

By the time the meal was over, however, we were both mellow with liquor and Tanaka was listing a little when Miko helped him to his feet. I had noticed in other encounters that he had a poor head for liquor. He rarely drank heavily except in private.

When he bade me goodnight he was loquacious and affectionate: 'Sleep well, Gil. I am very fond of you. You are a good friend and a very clever man. Your only problem is you work too hard and don't play enough . . . I work hard, but I know how to enjoy myself. Ask Miko here. Do I not enjoy myself? Do we not have fun together. . . ? Even now, when there may be war at any moment, we are preparing for a great adventure. You are like my German friend, Carl Leibig; very stiff, very correct. Which reminds me, you must see him before you leave Tokyo. Telephone him in the morning. I know you will get along together very well . . . Oh, and one last warning, Gil. Don't walk in the garden in the moonlight. That's when the fox-woman prowls. Tell him about the fox-woman, Miko. No, don't laugh. Fox-women look like beautiful maidens but they bring death and disaster. One of them seduced the Emperor Hansoku and on her account he murdered a thousand of his most loyal samurai. We know one of them lives in this garden; but you don't have to worry. She will never come inside unless you invite her. So go to bed, my friend. Pull the covers over your head and dream happy dreams . . .'

Finally, Miko managed to coax him away. I stood and watched her supporting him all the way to their bedroom.

For me, sleep was long coming. I tossed restlessly on the futon and lapsed in and out of shallow sleep. Twenty minutes after midnight I woke to a moment of pure terror. A woman's face, moon-pale, was suspended in the darkness above my head. It was Miko, dressed in a black *yukata*, her dark hair unbound and trailing to her waist. I swore in English.

'For Christ's sake, woman. What is this?'

She sealed my lips with her fingertips and answered in English. 'Don't worry. Kenji was quite drunk tonight. He will sleep for hours yet. I must talk with you.'

'Can't it wait?'

'No. The helicopter is picking us up at nine. This is the only chance I'll have to talk to you.'

'About what?'

'Kenji believes you are angry with him.'

'I was. I'm not now.'

'If it's about the conference . . .'

'Listen to me, Miko! With Kenji, I work one to one, no go-betweens, no hidden agenda. If he has questions, he asks them himself. Did he send you to me?'

'God, no! He would hate me if he knew.'

'I might tell him. Have you thought of that?'

'You won't. You're not that sort of man.'

'Don't bet on it. So Kenji knows I was angry with him. He must know why.'

'He does. He's too proud to explain himself to . . .'

'To a *gaijin*?'

'To a friend who may misunderstand. So will you listen to me please? Don't interrupt, don't argue. Just let me say it and I'll be gone. Please?'

'Go ahead.'

'Kenji is a sick man. The doctors here and in Europe have diagnosed leukaemia. You know what that means in terms of treatment. He will not face that. I know he will decide at some moment to end his life rather than submit to the indignities of this illness. So our conference has become very important to him. It represents a limited goal which he knows he can achieve before he declines too far. Rightly or wrongly, he believes that it can lead to an early treaty for the return of the Kuril Islands to Japan. That he sees as the crowning of a life work, a tribute to the memory of his father and the ancestors, a gift to the Emperor and the nation. I can understand how he feels. It would help if you could understand it too.'

'I do. You must believe that. I've always read it as one of his goals. I don't oppose it. I can, and probably will, plead the case eloquently in the conference. But what I can't do, will not do, is assume the role of exclusive advocate for Kenji Tanaka. My task, my clearly stated function for which I accept money, is to help work out a deal acceptable to all parties. To do that I must be seen to be acting even-handedly and in good faith. Kenji knows that, has always known it. I was angry today because I felt he was trying to manipulate me into another position.

19

There's a name for it in Japanese: *Shiso zendo* – thought guidance. I don't blame him for trying; but there's no rule that says I have to like it. So what more is there to say?'

'Nothing. Except that Kenji finds it hard to understand your special kind of morality.'

'What's so strange in that? He has his own thought guidance: the ancestors, the Emperor, the social contract. I don't subscribe to them myself, but I have no difficulty in understanding them.'

'You're a hard man, Gil.'

'And Kenji is not?'

'Not always, and never with me. I love him, Gil. Old-fashioned Western style, I love him!'

'And he loves you?'

'In his own fashion, yes. I am the comfortable corner, the playroom of his life. He is happy to confess that, as he did tonight; but at the same time he resents it as weakness. In the end, I know he will find dependence intolerable and he will begin to practise the cruelties that will force me to leave him. Then, I am sure, he will kill himself.' She gave a small rueful laugh. 'As you have already discovered, Gil, we Japanese are a very complicated people. Do you know what Kenji most admires about you?'

'I haven't given any thought to it.'

'He says you have a certain primitive simplicity, which he admires greatly.'

'And that's a compliment?'

'He means it so. Though I don't agree with him. I think that you are a very complex man.'

'Go to bed, Miko, for God's sake!'

'I'm going. Thank you for listening.'

She touched her fingers to her lips, then laid them, light as a butterfly touch, on my mouth. The next moment she was gone.

Sleep was impossible now. I got up and slid back the *shoji* screen that opened on to the garden. Above the crater rim the moon was riding high, a silver boat on a dark sea dotted with stars. In the garden, the light on the leaftips was sparse and cold. The shadows under the shrubbery were dark, the sound of the stream thin and tremulous. Then, loud and clear and very close, I heard the ghostly screech of a vixen in heat.

Two

Carl Albert Leibig surprised me. I do not know why, but I had expected an ageing man, sturdy, chunky and grim of visage, the perfect stereotype of an old-time Baltic trader. Instead, the man I received in my office was a trim, blond, athletic fellow in his late thirties, beautifully tailored, with a cheerful smile, a firm handshake and impeccable manners. He greeted me in German and our conversation continued in that language.

We exchanged cards and courtesies. I found he was much better briefed on my activities than I was on his. He was even able to make intelligent conversation on my latest Japanese publishing venture, an illustrated, multilingual guide to traditional craftsmen in modern Japan – painters, sculptors, designers of brocades, wood-block printmakers and the like.

We discussed the technicalities of the job and he promised to send my editor a list of little known masters from the northern provinces. He also gave me valuable information on a new colour printing plant which his company had just installed in Seoul. He told me the Koreans were looking for start-up business and I might well be able to strike an advantageous deal.

' . . . Especially as you speak and write the language. However, you will need to exercise rigid quality control in the beginning of your relationship. Our company has been established there since 1886, so we have what you might call mature connections. You have not yet begun publishing there, I think.'

'Not yet. We have licensed certain titles: science textbooks, economic surveys, that sort of thing. We've had a few problems, mostly in the accounting area.'

He laughed and quoted in Korean a piece of bawdy doggerel about a *kisaeng* girl and a tourist from America. He gave a grin of approval when I rendered it in Reeperbahn slang.

21

I knew that he was putting me through my paces, testing what Tanaka had told him about me. I did not blame him. I gave him full marks for style and effort. After all, he had set the whole project in motion. He had to be sure I would not fumble my part of it.

We talked about Tanaka's conviction that a Middle East war was imminent. Leibig was more hopeful: 'I believe that there can be a bottom line compromise. Unfortunately the risks of war increase daily. However, precisely because of the danger our project assumes a very special importance . . . Historically, you see, German involvement in Russian trade goes back to the twelfth century, which was about the time the Hanseatic League began to come into existence. The north Germans controlled all the Baltic trade in the East. In the West, the Rhinelanders were dominant in the Low Countries and England. Gradually their interests merged. They began to co-operate to suppress piracy, to provide navigational aids like beacons and lighthouses, buoys and pilots. They agreed a common code of trading practice which came to be known as the "Law of Lübeck", because Lübeck was the key city of the Baltic network which included Visby, Novgorod, Riga, Tallinn and Gdansk. By the close of the thirteenth century, all North German towns and their trading bases abroad were joined in the League. The old word *hanse* means just that: an association of those with like interests. My family were originally Lübeckers, but one of my ancestors moved to Hamburg . . . I'm very proud of that tradition. Every young man in those days had to do a term of service at a *kontor*, an overseas trading post of the League. All the buildings were corporately owned. The traders lived under the "Law of Lübeck" and if they broke the discipline were kicked out, excommunicated. They even had a word for it: "unhansing" . . . It was this tradition, you see, which enabled us to settle so easily into Japan in the Meiji period. We weren't just merchant adventurers, we weren't colonisers; we were old-style Baltic traders, keeping ourselves to ourselves . . . I hope I'm not boring you, Mr Langton.'

'On the contrary. You're giving me fresh insights which I badly need.'

'There's much that people have forgotten. For example, who except the historians remembers that after the Russian revolution there was an autonomous German Volga Republic in the Soviet Union? Nearly seventy per cent of its inhabitants were of German stock, descendants of the original settlers invited by the Empress Catherine. The Republic lasted until 1941, when Stalin abolished it, split the territory between Saratov and Stalingrad and deported the German inhabitants to Siberia. However, the real point is that the ethnic and psychological links are already established. Our new Germany is the natural begetter of industrial and commercial reform in Russia . . .'

'So why have you chosen to make this a joint exercise with Japan?'

'Commonsense, Mr Langton.' He was quite precise about it. 'Common interest – and the simple facts of geography. The line of communication between Moscow and Vladivostok is too long, too vulnerable to climatic and ethnic influences. So we cut the distance in half.'

'And divide the spoils?'

He was obviously angry, but he controlled himself very well. 'I'm not sure I understand your meaning, Mr Langton. The word you use, *beute*, has an ugly sound. In English you would call it "booty", "plunder", would you not? We are not talking war. We are discussing a commercial proposition equitable to all parties.'

'I'm glad to hear it, because that's the situation I've agreed to mediate. I just have to be sure we're all working from the same text . . . Please! I don't mean to be offensive; but you're testing me; you can't blame me for giving you the same treatment.'

He thought about that for a moment and then relaxed again into good humour. 'Clearly you have some reservations either about your role or the matter of the conference itself. Can you tell me what they are?'

'Let's not even call them reservations. Let's just say I'm a born sceptic, and I know there is no such thing as a free lunch. You, Tanaka and the other members of the consortium are supplying the meal – a huge technical infrastructure of production and processing, a new transport system, road, rail and air, and even retail outlets. It's a wonderful scheme. It could revolutionise the social and political life of the country, but who's picking up the tab?'

'In the beginning it's external funding. We've undertaken to raise all the capital for the first two years of operation.'

'Against what security? Who pays the interest on the funds? What tenure do you have? What tax arrangements? Who is your guarantor of last resort?'

'All these matters are covered in the outline report. Tanaka assured me he had put it in your hands and that you had read it.'

'True. However, the report Tanaka gave me was in Japanese.'

'Which I understand you speak, read and write fluently.'

'True again. That's where my problem begins. I'm very conscious of nuances and qualifications in the language which may not be apparent to others. What was the original language of the document?'

'German. I wrote the first draft myself and did the final editing before it went to print.'

'And who did the translation into Japanese?'

'Tanaka arranged that. My Japanese is good, but I was not prepared to rely on it in legal matters. We had the translation checked and certified by a linguist on our Embassy staff. Are you suggesting . . . ?'

'I'm not suggesting anything. I'm doing with you what I did with Tanaka, insisting on a verbal rundown, which will express your intentions more clearly than the briefing document. We can address ourselves to the text itself after lunch.'

'Good. I'd like that. I have to tell you, Mr Langton, although my company has been trading here for a hundred and thirty years, we learn something new every day.'

'Has Tanaka made his intentions clear to you?'

'I believe,' Leibig answered with a certain hesitation, 'I believe I'm interpreting them correctly. He needs sources of raw materials – timber, minerals, foodstuffs. He needs markets for his manufactured goods. He wants, as if they were the fabled city of gold, the return of the Kuril Islands. That issue sticks like a fishbone in his throat. Personally, I think he'd be crazy to insist too hard just at this moment.'

'Perhaps not so crazy.'

His head came up like that of a snake ready to strike. 'Why do you say that?'

'Because his peers in the *keiretsu*, the big family of bankers and industrialists, are scared of a commitment to the Soviets. They know it could be a bottomless pit, devouring money. However, if the Kuril Islands were handed back as part of the deal, Tanaka would become a national hero overnight.'

'A triumph which he might not live to enjoy. You know he's a sick man?'

'I learned it only last night.'

'He told you?'

'No. Miko did.'

A gleam of appreciative lechery showed in Leibig's blue eyes. He

24

nodded approval. 'Now, that's quite a lady. I've been tempted more than once to bid for her.'

'Why didn't you?'

'I couldn't afford it, my friend! I'd have a war on two fronts. Tanaka would chop me off at the ankles. My own people would have my head!' He gave an open, happy laugh. 'I like Oriental women. But not enough to die for! I'm still a Lübecker, remember. The old rule of the *kontor* was that members could have local concubines, but they could not marry without the consent of the group. Our family always observed that rule. Children born on the wrong side of the blanket – and there were a few of those! – were supported, educated and offered jobs in the company. But marriage, never! Which reminds me, I've taken the liberty of arranging a lunch at my home. You will meet a few of the people with whom you'll be working in Bangkok. I suggest we walk. It's quicker on foot than in a taxi.'

My office was two blocks off the Ginza. The building was owned by Tanaka, so I got the lease at a discount rate, which would still have sent me broke in London or Manhattan. However, I did have space and light and an airy stretch of studio where my designers and layout people could work in comfort. The surrounding area abounded in small restaurants, sushi joints and clubbish bars. The Ginza was its weekday self: a throng and press of earnest people – the genus salary-man and his dutiful handmaidens – busy as ants about company business. Among them we blue-eyed, long-nosed foreigners stood out like a pair of sore thumbs.

As we jostled our way through the surge of bodies, I wondered what strange stew would be cooked out of the exotic ingredients of the Bangkok conference. Leibig, Tanaka and myself were already an odd enough combination. I was a man from Australia, the last continent before the penguins at the South Pole, a vast emptiness with a population of only seventeen million people, an unstable blend of European migrant tribes, Asians and a remnant of aboriginal peoples. We were avid tourists and hustling carpetbaggers, sitting on enormous untapped mineral wealth and piles of unsold grain and wool, while above us the teeming millions of South-East Asia sweated out subsistence and their traders bargained hard for a larger and larger foothold on our shores.

The history of our aboriginal people was shrouded in the mists of time – forty, fifty thousand years at least. It was recorded only in the memories of those tribal elders who were called the Keepers of the Dreaming. They could not, would not, share it with us, the late-comers, the spoilers, the genocides.

Our own history on the continent was pitiably short. For the oldest families, it was a bare two hundred years. For the newest, the post-war Europeans, the boat people from Vietnam and Cambodia, the refugee students from China, it was shorter yet. They were alien seed, putting down fragile roots in a darkling, hostile forest. Their psychic existence was a daily crisis.

I was lucky because my father had endowed me with a talisman that made nonsense of time and frontiers. On the other hand Carl Leibig was a European, born during the age of Aquarius in the resurgent Germany. For him the ruffian triumphs of the thousand-year Reich, the horrors of the Holocaust, the ruinous twilight of defeat, were tribal histories he refused to share. He had not been born then. He did not believe in guilt by inheritance. The only tradition he embraced wholeheartedly was that of the old traders, who lived in the *kontor* on foreign soil, leaving the paladins to make war at home. Even so he discovered very early that, while he could happily abdicate the unshared past, his rivals in commerce were always ready to remind him of it.

This was Tanaka's dilemma too. His country and his family had survived the ignominy of defeat and occupation. In a swift reversal of history they had colonised their conquerors and turned them into economic allies or financial vassals. Yet they had still not succeeded in laying the ghosts of Nanking and Manchuria and the Burma railway and the Bataan death-march. The 'soft, moist people' of popular Japanese fiction were still remembered abroad as the heartless warriors who walked the way of the samurai, glorifying death in life.

Now, we three were called to be midwives at the birth of a prodigy – a capitalist economy wrenched from the worn-out womb of Russia's socialist revolution. Like all midwives, we were summoned for our skills; but we could give no guarantees on what we might deliver: a stillbirth, a monster, a wonder-child. Whatever the outcome, we would demand to be paid. It was perhaps too much to hope that we might earn a blessing as well.

Leibig's house was a surprise. The entrance was at street level: a heavy wooden door between a bookstore and a small hotel of the kind frequented by salary-men who spent their working days in Tokyo and returned to their families only at weekends. The door was lined with steel plate and fitted with an electric dead-lock, opened by a push-button code.

Behind the door was a narrow alley which opened on to a classic Japanese garden, contrived with rocks and waterfalls, dwarf trees and flowering shrubs. The greenery almost concealed a large traditional Japanese house, which had been cunningly modernised, with air-conditioning, central heating and fire protection. The interior was a careful combination of European comfort and Japanese decorative economy.

The only visible help was a young and very spruce German manservant, who served us drinks and informed us that we had about twenty minutes before the other guests arrived. It was clear that Leibig wanted as much private time with me as he could get; I, too, needed to inform myself a little more about the self-possessed Lübecker. I asked him how all this protected space could exist in modern Tokyo, where land values were an astronomical madness. He explained with obvious satisfaction.

'This place and the blocks which front the street were a grant, made to my family during the Meiji period in recognition of our contribution to Japan's industrial development. After the war, we were put under great pressure by one of the big banking houses to sell or to develop. We declined for a long time. Then, the usual pattern, we began to be harassed by a local Yakuza group. Finally, we compromised. We retained title to the land. We reserved this rear portion, with the existing dwelling, for ourselves; and we sold a seventy-five year development lease to the bankers. We have the best of the bargain, of course. This place is an oasis of sanity in an urban madhouse. However, since nobody sees us anymore, nobody gets jealous. Very Japanese, wouldn't you say?'

There it was again: the sudden thrust of the probe, the unspoken assumption that I would somehow side with the Europeans against the Asians. However, this was not the time for confrontations. I smiled and shrugged. 'The game's the same everywhere. Only the tactics change. The Americans try to bully you into a boiler-plate contract; the British have raised incoherence to a fine art; the Chinese make you walk ten miles to advance one. That's what I'm paid to deal with.'

He gave me a sidelong quizzical look and said, 'You haven't mentioned how we Germans do business.'

'That's because I'm waiting for you to instruct me. After all, you are one of my principals.'

'Always the diplomat, eh, Gil?'

'My father used to say that the best diplomat is the one who knows how to tell the truth – and who knows when the other fellow is lying.'

At that moment the first of his luncheon guests was announced: a big, untidy fellow in his mid-sixties, with a wide smile and shrewd, unblinking eyes. I recognised him instantly: Sir Pavel Laszlo, Hungarian by birth, Australian by nationality, principal shareholder of a national airline, and an international freight and transport group already solidly established in the United States and the Western and Eastern zones of Europe. I had worked with him twice before, the first time at a pan-Pacific tourist conference, the second at a seminar on airport safety in Jakarta. Our conversation was in German because, as he announced shamelessly, 'The Germans have never bothered to learn Hungarian and we mustn't be rude to our host . . .' Then he plunged straight into business: 'How much briefing have they given you?'

'I've had all the Japanese papers. Carl is giving me his original German copy. However, the outline plan is clear. I'd like to hear your end of it.'

'It's all summed up in one word – transport. This is a vast and ambitious plan to feed three hundred million people before they take to the streets in hunger riots. My job is to help to plan an adequate transportation system for the whole of the Soviet continent. The present network – road, rail and air – is obsolescent and quite inefficient. We have to reorganise existing resources and pump in new ones as fast as possible . . . The first job, as I see it, is to make a deal with the military so that their manpower, rolling stock and aircraft can be used for civilian needs. That's a high policy matter. I'm trying to persuade Carl here that we should have an armed forces transport specialist with us in Bangkok. At the moment all he can think about is bankers.'

'Because without money we can't move.' Leibig was suddenly defensive. 'Even Tanaka is finding problems with his colleagues. They'll let him risk his own funds. They're very reluctant to commit theirs.'

'So we'll have to persuade them, won't we?' Sir Pavel Laszlo had the soul of a dreamer and the nerve of a riverboat gambler. 'Have the Soviets announced their delegation yet?'

'They have not. Nor will they, until we can assure them that the primary funds are in place.'

'Nonsense!' Sir Pavel waved away the objection like smoke. 'They'll make any deal that gets them moving. They need something they can dress up on a television screen so that it looks like Moses feeding the Israelites in the desert. And as far as your bankers are concerned Carl, they too have to learn the facts of life in Eastern Europe. The British and the Americans both missed the chance to finance the Bolshevik revolution and bring the Soviets into full communion with the West. Now they've got another chance. If they miss it, God help us all!'

'It's easy for you to talk.' Carl Leibig was irritated. 'We're deep in recession. The Americans are up to their ears in debt . . . the money-men are scared out of their wits . . .'

'And here is a whole retarded continent waiting to be brought up to scale in production of minerals, natural gas, oil, foodstuffs, tourism. God damn it, man! The bankers are paper men, always have been. We're the ones who have to show them how to turn paper into real wealth.'

The contrast between the two men intrigued me. Laszlo was a Hungarian Jew who had fled the Holocaust to make a life and a future for himself in Australia. Leibig was old Prussian stock, conscious or unconscious heir to centuries of anti-semitism. Yet the lure of trade had made them stronger allies than any treaty could have done. They were still arguing volubly when the rest of the guests were announced, two men and a woman. Leibig presented them in his formal fashion.

'Doctor Rudi Forster, from the Swiss Banking Union, engineer Mauno Leino from Leino Corporation, Chicago, Buenos Aires and Finland, Professor Marta Boysen late of the Food and Agriculture Organisation . . . Doctor Forster's presence explains itself. He is here to set the Japanese and other Oriental elements of the banking syndicate. Engineer Leino has had twenty years experience in engineering design for all branches of the food processing industry in the United States, in the South Americas and in Europe. He has just completed an eight-month study of processing plants in the Republics of the Soviet Union. Moscow gave him full access, so he is able to report accurately on needs and problems. Professor Marta Boysen is a specialist in the history of geopolitics and its application to modern economics, a subject which, I hasten to add, is much more complex than it sounds, and of great importance to our plans . . .'

While the first tentative conversations were beginning, I tried to work out the pattern of Carl Leibig's strategy. The banker was the first essential element. Money talked all languages, and had no smell at all. What was significant was the choice of the Swiss and the Japanese to launch the syndicate, instead of the British or the Americans. In the sacred world of money the position on the 'tombstone', the advertisement of the underwriting group, was like the orb and sceptre, an unmistakable symbol of primacy. Certain great houses used to make it a rule that they would not participate unless they headed the tombstone list. The choice of a Finnish engineer also made sense in a certain historic context – the old Hanseatic League, and the post-war working relationship between the Finns and the Russians. The Finns knew how the Soviet system worked. They knew all its defects, they had learned how to work them to their own advantage.

The wild card in the pack was Professor Marta Boysen, late of the World Health Organisation. I could understand the value of her specialist information. I could not see why, at so early a stage, she had been co-opted into this group of hard-nosed financial manipulators, intent on colonising the old Marxist empire with Western capitalists. At that moment, she was standing opposite me making animated talk with Sir Pavel Laszlo, known in both hemispheres as a connoisseur of pretty women. I judged her to be about the same age as Carl Leibig, mid-to late-thirties perhaps, but beautifully kept and groomed with expensive discretion. No dowdy bluestocking this one. She had a thoroughbred's body, a classic bone structure in the face, a complexion as clear as fine porcelain, deep blue eyes and corn-gold hair caught back in a ponytail, held with a black butterfly bow. She wore no wedding band, but her rings and her bracelet and the sunburst brooch on her lapel were all fine Italianate work. And if you want to know how a bookish fellow like me, past his prime and too long a widower, could see so much so quickly, the credit goes to my scholarly father, who taught me very early to recognise good lines in a woman and a craftsman's skill in art.

Unfortunately, I was buttonholed by the Finn, who had been briefed to test me in his native language. I had to remind myself that this was the penalty of all polyglots. People regarded them as a kind of circus act, like a singing dog or a counting horse. In the mid-nineteenth century every scholar and pedant and tourist snob in Europe felt obliged to seek out the ageing Cardinal Mezzofanti to test him in Coptic or Urdu or some obscure Uralian dialect. According to his biographer, the old man was always willing to oblige, as an act of Christian charity to the ungodly. I was not so agreeable; I was being paid handsomely to be polite and to indulge my lecheries, if any, in private.

Promptly at one o'clock, luncheon was announced. If you are expecting me to describe some kind of banquet, an opulent gesture from the Nordic knight to his band of adventurers, forget it! This was strictly a working meal, Tokyo style. The table was laid on three sides only, so that all the guests had a full view of the large computer display screen against the wall. The food was a standard Japanese boxed lunch brought in from a nearby restaurant, laid on a tray in front of each guest. No liquor was served, only tea or mineral water. We were not there to be seduced into a deal, but set to work by our young leader. Only Laszlo had the gall to comment on the Spartan arrangements.

'You give me great confidence Carl. You're never going to send us broke with entertainment bills!'

Leibig had the good grace to blush. 'If the food is not to your liking, we can always send out for something else. Personally I find I cannot work efficiently after a big midday meal.'

'Oh, it wasn't a complaint.' Laszlo was as bland as honey. 'Just a comment. Of course we'll have to do things more stylishly in Bangkok where we're actually soliciting business.'

'You may be sure that we will, Sir Pavel.'

Leibig dismissed the subject and waved us to our places. I was seated with Marta Boysen on my right and Forster the Swiss banker on my left. He put the question which I had hesitated to ask.

'So, Professor Boysen, what precisely is your role in the Leibig enterprise?'

'In the most precise terms, my dear Doctor,' her smile was sunny and guileless, 'my role is a negative one: to ensure that funds and effort are not wasted on avoidable mistakes. Example: you will remember that some time ago powdered milk and condensed milk were sent to depressed areas in India as part of a relief operation. One of your biggest Swiss companies was involved. What was intended as a gift of life became a lethal weapon. Peasant women mixed the tinned milk with polluted water and fed it to their babies who promptly died of enteric infections. That's an extreme case. Here, however, we are talking of a commercial enterprise to supply the dietary needs of three hundred million people across a huge continent. Always it is the women who buy and prepare the food; it is to their requirements that we must first

31

address ourselves. Our engineer friend from Finland has devised a system – a very efficient system, by the way – for the robotic butchering of cattle and sheep and the packing of meat into household portions. Immediate questions arise. How will the housewife recognise the unfamiliar portions? How will they fit her family circumstances and her budget? How will she cook them? How will she preserve them in a country where there are few domestic deep freeze units, and small practice in their economic use? How long will it take, how much will it cost, to change domestic conditions, eating habits, culinary skills, in so many ethnic enclaves? That was the thrust of my work at the Food and Agriculture Organisation. That's why Carl Leibig invited me to join you.'

Doctor Rudi Forster took a little time to digest the idea. Then he delivered his verdict.

'It seems, then, we may all be taking too simple a view of a very fragmented question.'

From the other end of the table Carl Leibig intervened curtly. 'We are dealing first with major pilot projects in areas of high-density population. In other words, with large and reasonably homogeneous consumer needs. It is our own fault if we let the project fragment itself. Nobody in any country has yet devised a safety net for every single citizen or even every minority group.'

Forster was not so easily mollified. 'Even so, Carl, every distortion of the pattern increases the financial risk.'

'This is risk banking, Rudi. That's why you get over-riders on your fees and commissions. But,' he spread his hands in a gesture of resignation, 'if you can't stand the heat, get out of the kitchen.'

'And talking of risks,' Laszlo gave everyone his best Hungarian smile, 'remember the basis of the deal will be the issue of sovereign bonds by the Soviets. That's a long way more secure than much of the Wall Street junk paper that's been circulating lately.'

'That's a presumption we can't make yet.' Forster was on the attack now. 'All the Soviet Republics are moving fast towards independence or, at least, towards a very loose Federation. So who's going to be issuing the bonds? The union itself or individual republics? And what's going to be the differential between the credit ratings of the Russ, the Kazaks, the Uzbeks, the Mongols?'

'There is a very simple answer to that question,' said Leibig. 'But I should like to hear our mediator respond to it.'

'In what language Carl? You're conducting the examination.'

That raised a laugh around the table; but Leibig was a fast learner. He apologised instantly.

'Forgive me. I did not mean to sound peremptory. Since we are all speaking German perhaps you would be good enough to respond in that language.'

'Very well. The position paper which I have read indicates that your financing will be backed by what you call three acceptable elements: sovereign bonds, equity participation in each individual enterprise, barter arrangements involving certain key commodities – timber, minerals, natural gas, chemicals and so on. My guess is that the Soviet offer will be sound enough, but that you will have to face certain shortfalls and extensions of time while they organise themselves. Until they present their counter-offer in Bangkok there's not much more you can do. It's a waiting game.'

'Thank you, Gil. My own answer to Doctor Forster would have been exactly the same.'

'Then why waste time needling the man.' Laszlo was suddenly testy. 'We're all adults here. Let's get down to business.'

'By all means. I invite your attention to the display screen. The diagrams you will see are an attempt to simplify the outline plan and to test it in open discussions with our mediator present.'

'One question before we start, Carl. Has Tanaka seen the diagrams?'

'Not yet.'

'Any reason?'

'We may decide after our discussions that they need refining. Objections?'

'None, only a caution. My job is to find the common ground between all parties, to serve as best I can their common interest. I'm your counsellor, not your servant. If you're wise you'll give me all the relevant facts. If there's something you don't want to disclose, then say so. But never, never try to mislead me. If that happens, I'm out. I hope that's clear to everyone.'

There was a brief murmur of assent, then Leibig punched up the first image on the screen. It was a map of the world, compressed into an elongated oval like a football, with the Eurasian continent as the centrepiece and the eastern and western coasts of the Americas at either end, separated from Eurasia by the Atlantic and the Pacific oceans. Carl Leibig's voice delivered the commentary.

'Geography, my friends! The prime determinant of our destiny. Do we freeze on the tundra? Do we die of hunger and thirst in the desert? Do we grow fat in the fertile plains, the envy and ultimately the prey of the less fortunate? Modern communications modify the effect of geography. They do not change its essential influence. Focus now on the Eurasian landmass itself . . .'

The following frames showed the full stretch of Eurasia from the British Isles to the Bering Sea. The divisions of the landmass were shown not as borders, but as economic groupings: the European Community, Central Europe, the Baltic States, the various productive blocs within the Soviet Union itself, China, India, the oil basins of the Middle East; and Japan itself, linked to its trading partners in the South Pacific and South-East Asia in the modern version of the old Greater South-East Asia Co-prosperity Sphere. Leibig's commentary continued.

'In the West, Germany is the natural land bridge, the natural route of trade and culture between the European Community, Central Europe and Russia itself. Our newly united Germany is the focus around which the old elements of the Austro-Hungarian empire will coalesce for mutual trade and tourism. They will solve their tribal problems in their own way; but for commerce they will constitute a highly flexible unity with reunited Germany.'

Suddenly it hit me. I had heard all this before. I had seen the maps, too, a long time ago, in a whole series of variations. I was still trying to pinpoint the reference when Professor Marta Boysen passed me a note scrawled on her napkin. 'You and I must talk about this later . . . M.B.' I crumpled the note and shoved it into my pocket, then reached out to touch her hand in acknowledgment. Her answering smile gave me an absurd boyish pleasure. Now the screen was illustrating the distribution of Soviet prime resources and the sorry state of their rundown industries. Carl Leibig was waxing eloquent.

'The Russians have discovered, as the Romans and the British and the Spaniards and, indeed, we Germans discovered, that the cost of empire is ruinous. The cost of disengagement will also be high; but if it succeeds without violence, the rewards will be enormous. Trade with Eastern Europe will no longer be a barter of junk for junk but an exchange of needed goods for negotiable currency. The economies of Middle Europe will revive, as they have already done in Hungary, as they will do in Poland, the Baltic satellites and even in Bulgaria and the

Balkans. Instead of being stagnant sumps, manned by listless turnkeys, these nations will become active conduits of production, trade and hard currency tourism from the émigré communities in the United States and elsewhere. We know it can be done. We know how to do it . . . We are working at the express invitation of Moscow at a time when Europe is in the ascendant and the American economy is in deep recession. I submit that we simply cannot fail.'

It was a bravura effort and it should have earned him some polite applause; instead the group went to work on him with hatchets. Rudi Forster led the attack.

'I think the diagrams should not be displayed and this kind of speech should not be delivered in public. Together they give a political colour to what should be a pragmatic business proposition.'

'I'd put it even more strongly,' Laszlo was clearly angered. 'You made my flesh crawl, Carl, with all this claptrap about Western and Middle Europe and the old Austro-Hungarian Empire. Of course there are common threads of interest. There are also deep wells of shared hatred which you would do well to remember every day! You yourself didn't create the hatred but, by God, you'd better be aware that it exists and festers. We're setting out to do business, big business, we hope. We'll have enough opposition in the normal course of affairs. Let's not make any more by trying to rewrite history.'

Leino, the Finn, was equally emphatic. 'Those charts and that sort of rhetoric will make you a lot of enemies in the United States and in England, not to mention France. Like it or not, we're going to need their co-operation and very probably their investment. Besides, Germany is herself a member of the EC. You have to bend over backwards not to give offence. Another thing. Your Japanese partners are not going to thank you for reminding the Chinese and the Koreans and the Filipinos about the kind of co-prosperity they enjoyed under the Japanese army. I'm surprised to find you so naive, Carl. I'd certainly like to hear Mr Langton's opinion.'

There was no way in the world I could duck the issue. I tried to be very calm and polite. 'I understand what you are saying, Carl. It may in fact be a very natural development; but if I were a Soviet negotiator I would read your intention as an attempt at economic encirclement by Germany and Japan – the old Berlin/Tokyo Axis in fact. Who prepared that presentation, Carl?'

'I myself prepared the outline. The detailed work and the charts were prepared by our advertising agents in Hamburg. They are reputable, very skilful people.'

'They made a hell of a mistake this time. Where did they dig up the charts and the maps?'

'I presume they designed them in their own studios, to meet the specifications I had laid down.'

'More accurately' said Professor Marta Boysen quietly, 'they re-designed them. They are based on the works of Major-General Professor Dr Karl Haushofer, formerly professor of geography and military science at the University of Munich. He was introduced by Rudolf Hess to Adolf Hitler for whom, according to reliable report, he wrote the famous chapter sixteen of *Mein Kampf*, the one which deals with *lebensraum*: living space for the German people.'

Carl Leibig was suddenly pale as death. He seemed to be choking on the words. 'I did not know that. Truly, I did not know it.'

'You know now,' said Sir Pavel Laszlo firmly. 'The matter has been dealt with in club. No damage has been done outside. My motion is that you wipe all this stuff out of the computer and confine yourself to the brief we have all agreed – no rhetoric, no public statements unless they be cleared by Gil here. All in favour?'

All hands were raised around the table. Then Laszlo, oldest and canniest of us all, got Leibig off the hook. 'Don't fret about it, Carl. We all make asses of ourselves. We're lucky if it happens among friends. Now, I for one could use a stiff drink.'

While the drinks were being poured, Carl Leibig cornered me and asked with a certain desperation.

'Are you going to report this to Tanaka?'

'He'll ask me about the meeting. I'll have to respond. Why don't you call him first?'

'What do I tell him?'

'The truth. You made a presentation. It was not well received. It was decided to rest on the original text. When he questions me I'll confirm that. I'm sure Laszlo will offer the same report.'

'You mean he'll be communicating directly with Tanaka?'

'Come on, Carl! What's got into you? Tanaka and Laszlo are in contact every month of every year. They have big tourist investments together in Australia – hotels, golf courses, reef islands. But they are in the club, your club! They're not going to sell you down the river. But for God's sake take note of the advice you got here today.'

36

'I will, believe me. Excuse me, I must talk to Forster and Laszlo.'

The moment he left, Professor Marta Boysen was at my side. She wasted no time in small talk but asked 'Will you take me to dinner tonight? We must talk.'

'I'd be delighted. Where are you staying?'

'At the Okura hotel.'

'I'll pick you up at seven.'

'Thank you. I may have a surprise for you.'

'A pleasant one, I hope.'

'I'm not sure. You have disappointed me, Mr Langton.'

'How? Why?'

'I'll tell you at dinner. I must go now. Sir Pavel has offered me a lift back to the hotel.'

As always, the old rogue had the last word. We were walking through the rock-garden and down the alley to the street when he drew me aside from the group and murmured a piece of advice in Hungarian.

'That's a bright woman, Gil. If I were staying here I'd whip her away from under your nose. But I'm leaving tonight, so she's all yours – if you can catch her!'

'Go to hell, you old goat!'

'Another thing, more important. Did you believe Carl's protestations of innocence?'

'Not a word of them. He was frightened, yes, but only because he misjudged the mind of the meeting. If you want the truth, I don't like the man. I think he's arrogant and politically naive. That's a dangerous combination. I'm thinking seriously of bowing out.'

'For God's sake, don't do that! You've got to stay in place until we see where Tanaka stands in all this. You're the only one close enough to him to make a sound judgment.'

'I don't think Tanaka will want any part of Leibig's political pretensions.'

'I'm not so sure.' His tone was sombre. 'I'm wondering, in fact, whether Tanaka encouraged them. The Japanese have always been very clever at kite-flying.'

Three

After an indifferent lunch and a contentious conference, the thoughts I took back to my office were gloomy ones. I had been long enough in business to know that every deal, large or small, brings out a little more of the bad in people; greed, anger, ambition, envy. Even the conventional deceits of the bargaining table – the concealments, the half-truths, the downright lies – erode the foundations of public and private morality. In politics there is no morality anyway. The nature of the game precludes it. A politician's career depends upon the fickle wind of public opinion. He is forced to trim his conscience to catch every shift of the breeze. It was an ironic coincidence that the day's motto on my desk pad was a quotation from that amiable cleric, Sydney Smith; 'No man, I fear, can effect great benefits to his country without some sacrifice of the minor virtues.' I had sacrificed a few in my time, so I could not plead pristine innocence.

If Laszlo's suspicions were correct, then I was taking very large money to serve two very dubious masters. On the other hand, Laszlo himself was no plaster saint. One of his well-known techniques was to spread suspicion and dismay in the barnyard, and then buy the eggs and the chickens and the farm itself at a discount. Besides, there was in Carl Leibig a certain pardonable simplicity, the arrogance of a successful young man who had inherited a prosperous business and now was anxious to see how far his own legs would carry him. He was suffering, as Tanaka had suffered, as we all do to some degree, from selective education and selective social amnesia. History is always written by the victors, and the defeated create a new set of myths to explain the past and gild the future. Still, I could not spend a whole afternoon scratching an itchy conscience. There was work piled on my desk: colour proofs to be checked, contracts to be studied, an editorial conference to consider three new projects. It was nearly five thirty before I was able to talk to Kenji Tanaka on his private line. He was brisk and businesslike.

'Carl Leibig called. He told me you did not like his presentation.'

'None of us did.'

'He told me that, too. He has sent me a tape recording of the conference.'

'The sonofabitch!'

'I beg your pardon.'

'I said he was a sonofabitch. I meant it. Nobody records a meeting without the knowledge and consent of the participants.'

'And he did not request it?'

'He did not.'

'Then when he is made aware of his mistake, I am sure he will apologise.'

'And he should either erase the tape or send authentic copies to all parties.'

'I shall suggest he does that.'

'Does Laszlo know about this?'

'Probably not. He spoke with me before Carl Leibig called.'

'Then I believe you should call him at his hotel before he leaves for the airport. He of all of us is the most vulnerable to press gossip and misreport.'

'I shall. I cannot tell you, Gil, how much this has upset me.'

'It's upset me too Kenji. I'm not sure I can work with Mr Leibig. I'm thinking quite seriously of quitting.'

'Please Gil, don't do that! At least give me the chance to persuade you to stay. I am sure Carl Leibig meant no harm, no insult. He is a young blood with dreams of glory in his head. Believe me, I shall intervene very strongly to ensure that nothing like this happens again. Promise that you will talk to me before you decide.'

'All right. We'll talk.'

'Thank you my friend. When next we meet – which I suggest should be tomorrow morning at eight in my office – I shall provide you with a complete history of the Leibig enterprises. My research people have discovered that they had connections with my family back in Meiji times. Interesting, no?'

Interesting? Hell! It was downright unbelievable that Tanaka was only now making discoveries about a company to which he was committing so much. In fact it made a nonsense until you put it into Japanese. Then you had to use two words: '*tatemae*' which means the way things *should* look and '*honne*' the way things *are*. In these terms, truth is relative and not absolute. By consenting to accept the relative, you absolve yourself from any charge of lying. You are simply arranging 'a correct image', an acceptable definition of an unacceptable contradiction. In short, my friend Tanaka was doing a snow job on me. So I gave up the debate for the day and thought about my dinner date with Marta Boysen.

I do not keep an apartment in Tokyo. City rents are so high and my visits so widely spaced that it is more convenient to take a suite at the Seiyo Ginza. They treat me like a prince, and charge me accordingly; but the service is impeccable and the chef an international master, so I wallow in the luxury and write it off to the business.

At six thirty my driver met me at the entrance and we set off to pick up Marta Boysen at the Okura. The traffic was, as usual, a nightmare. I used the car phone to call Marta and tell her I might be fifteen minutes late. On an impulse I asked whether Laszlo was staying in the same hotel. She told me she had just had a drink with him. He was checking out at eight o'clock for the night flight to Sydney.

I called again and was lucky enough to find him still in his room. I told him of my call to Tanaka. He told me that Tanaka had called him a second time to report our conversation. Laszlo sounded worn out. For an overweight hypertensive in his mid-sixties he drove himself dangerously hard.

'I tell you, Gil, I'm getting too old for these capers. Long-haul flights play hell with my metabolism. I run a damned good airline, but if I could spare the time I'd travel by ship . . . I know! You want to talk about Leibig and Tanaka. Let me give you a quick reading. Leibig has a strong business in the Orient and in South Africa. In America he's a token presence. In Germany he's small compared with the giants, but the company is highly respected because of its long family tradition. What is important is that he's got a big idea, the one he borrowed from Haushofer: Germany and Japan as bookends to European and Asiatic Russia. Tanaka seized on it because it was something he could sell to all the big boys in the *keiretsu*. It fits their historic fictions as well as it does those of the Germans. I bought it because I don't give a damn about politics, only about business. Sooner or later we traders own the politicians because we're the ones who make the tax-money and keep the proletariat working. Tanaka knows that. You know it, too, because you have a sense of history and this extraordinary gift of tongues. Tanaka wants to keep us both. As for Leibig, he's young, he's arrogant and he's got a ramrod up his arse. But in the end Tanaka will bend him or break him. He'll make his apologies. You can afford to be generous. Pat his hand, take him out to play – though I'm still not sure what games he likes. Maybe he'll tell you. You're a very persuasive fellow. The lady is very taken with you.'

'You haven't told me where she fits in.'

'I'm sure she's bursting to tell you herself. Good luck, Gil. See you in Bangkok.'

He cut the connection. We continued to crawl at a snail's pace through the traffic towards the Okura hotel.

There are two ways to cope with business life in Japan. You can scurry about like all the other ants, frantic and industrious. Or, like the ancient sage, you can hide yourself in a cloud of unknowing, sink yourself so deep in contemplation that the ants will swarm around you and over you and you will not feel them. In the legend, of course, the sage was totally devoured by the little beasts and no trace of him was left at all. I had no intention of being eaten alive, but on that slow-motion trip to pick up Marta Boysen I thought deeply about what Laszlo had told me.

Of all the tribes in the world, the Hungarians were the most adept in the art of survival, smelling the winds of change, reading the cloud patterns, sensing the shocks before the earthquakes began. Pavel Laszlo had money invested in transport systems all round the world. There was no way he was going to stay out of Russia. Already he was standing on the doorstep. If Carl Leibig or Kenji Tanaka could lift him over the threshold and get his planes and his heavy transports moving, fine. If the devil was prepared to be a gentleman there was no reason to banish him from the dinner table. You just had to be sure you had the longer spoon.

Conclusion for Gilbert Anselm Langton? If he stayed, he would be on the game like everyone else. He would be a whore; but he had set a high price and listed all the things he would not do. All that was left was to make sure he got the money before the client got near the bed.

It was a sour and cynical thought, a poor prelude to an evening with a beautiful woman. I tried to dismiss it. I was twenty minutes late. Marta Boysen was waiting in the foyer, dressed in a very simple, very expensive black cocktail dress with a shawl to shield her bare shoulders against the autumn cold. I apologised for being late. She hushed me with a finger laid against my lips. She assured me it would be quicker going back to

41

the Ginza, and besides, we had the whole evening ahead of us. She was not making theatre of it. She was simply cordial, warm, welcoming.

I did not ask myself why, even in my head, I used three adjectives to describe a woman I was taking to dinner. I was a widower married now to business. I took a lot of women to dinner. Sometimes I took them to bed. But I did not sing paeans about them. Paeans are hymns of praise, joy and exultation, and it was a long time since I had been lifted so high.

We had run out of small talk before we reached the hotel. We ordered cocktails while we studied the menu. As soon as the waiter had taken our orders I dived, head-first, into deep water.

'Let's get the bad news over. You said you were disappointed in me. Why?'

'Because you didn't remember me.'

'My dear Marta, until today I'd never seen you in my life.'

'Are you sure of that?'

'Absolutely.'

She gave me a small, mocking smile, opened her handbag and took out an envelope. It contained a series of faded snapshots, all taken with an old-fashioned Rolleiflex camera. There were four people in each picture; a woman who might have passed for Marta herself, my father as I remembered him in his vigorous forties, a tiny flaxen haired girl, and myself as a gangling young man. We were all dressed in holiday clothes, the woman and the child in dirndl, my father and I in slacks, woodsmen's shirts and heavy walking boots.

The scenes were the outside of a stuberl in Grinzing, the entrance to the Burgtheater in Vienna and a couple of woodland settings, obviously in the Wienerwald. The legends on the backs of the photographs were written in a woman's hand in German. 'Anna and Anselm, Marta and Gil. Summer 1957.'

I felt a sudden odd sensation of detachment, as though I were looking at myself looking at the photographs. From somewhere very far away I heard Marta's voice asking: 'Do you remember now?'

'Some of it. Yes. That was the year I went up to Oxford. My father took me to Austria for a walking vacation. He said he had a friend there, a singer. He took me to see her at the Burgtheater. While in Vienna we went out on picnics together.'

'And when I got tired you carried me on your shoulders. I was four years old at the time.'

'So Anna was your mother.'

42

'Still is. She's in her mid-sixties now. Still vigorous. She teaches singing in Salzburg.'

'And your father?'

'He was a singer too, a baritone. He was killed in a skiing accident the year after I was born. You will laugh at this, but after your visit I used to dream about having you as my big brother. After that summer, you could have been. My mother and your father became lovers. They corresponded for years, almost up to the time of his death. My mother has kept all his letters. It's strange you didn't find hers among your father's papers.'

'Not so strange. In the last months of his illness he burned all his private correspondence. All that he kept were his scholarly papers, which he left to me. I knew he had a lot of women friends but he never gossiped about his affairs. He was a man who loved women and needed them in his life. He wasn't secretive about it. In a way he shared them with me, as surrogate aunts or big sisters. He used to say that what lovers shared was a precious and private currency. One shouldn't debase it by public commerce . . . Well, what do I say? Thank you for the memory! But your mother's name wasn't Boysen.'

'No. It was Lovins-Gruber. Boysen is my married name. My husband and I divorced seven years ago. I kept my married name because all my academic honours are recorded in it.'

She pushed the photographs towards me. 'My mother and I thought you might like to have these.'

'I would. My thanks to you both.'

At that moment I felt a sudden surge of grief and loss. I was very near to tears. Marta Boysen reached out to touch my hand.

'I didn't mean to upset you. It was supposed to be a pleasant surprise.'

'It was, I promise.' I made a poor attempt at a joke. 'It gives me the opera without the boring bits in the overture. My father, your mother, all those years ago! Now perhaps you can tell me how you came to be working with Leibig?'

'That's another story altogether.' She was obviously happy to change the subject. 'I did my doctoral thesis on the geopolitical theories of Karl Haushofer. I had access to all the archives which are preserved in Koblenz. The curator became a personal friend. It was he who told me of Leibig's interest in the subject, and who passed my name on to Leibig as an expert. He contacted me at the FAO in Rome and offered me a part in this project. Leibig mentioned your name as one of the people involved. So here we are!' The waiter laid the first course in front of us. 'Good appetite, *schatzi!*'

The endearment slipped casually from her lips. I raised my glass in a nostalgic toast.

'To absent lovers. *Prost!*'

After that, we were content to be comfortable together, savouring the wine and the food, each filling out for the other the blank pages of our biographies. She had travelled widely with the FAO. She had worked in Russia itself after the Chernobyl disaster. She had found distant relatives among the surviving German stock in the Ukraine. It pleased me that she seemed to have a compassionate understanding of the human condition and the wit to know how many of its miseries were incurable. Of her marriage she said simply:

'It was disaster for both of us. He had an old name, and old money. He farmed his estates in Carinthia, collected antiques and hated to be more than one day's journey from home. I was ambitious, mobile, hellbent on a career. There wasn't enough love or understanding to hold us together. Fortunately we had no family. The divorce was less painful than the marriage. Do you have children, Gil?'

'Three. Two boys and a girl. She's married and expecting her first child. Both boys work in the company, one in London, the other in New York. They're good kids. They look out for each other, and for the old man.'

'Don't you ever get lonely?'

'Who doesn't? We're all pretty primitive and tribal. We go out to hunt among the predators. Afterwards we need the cave and familiar bodies round firelight and the magical drawings on the walls.'

'That's how I feel tonight. I have to say I found this afternoon a rather shocking experience. It was so calculated, so harshly commercial and political. Carl Leibig's performance troubled me very much. When I first met him I liked him. Today he was like a cruel young prince suddenly confronted by bullies stronger than himself.'

'And I was one of them?'

'I didn't think you were bullying him. I thought you were trying very hard to be polite. But he was lying. You know that.'

'I suspected it. I'm not sure I can or want to prove it.'

'I can, and since you're the mediator I think you should at least have the proof in your hands. The day may come when you'll need to use it.'

Suddenly, this was another Marta, the one who had scribbled the imperative note, who had commanded me to dinner, who had taken possession of me by the oldest magic of all – my image held in her hands. As we ate I questioned her closely.

'Assume I know nothing about Haushofer and his theories. Instruct me. Show me where a military scholar, long dead, fits into our enterprise.'

She was all professional. She marshalled the information quickly and delivered it briskly. 'Karl Haushofer was born in Munich in 1869, the son of a civil servant. He enlisted as a career officer in the Bavarian army and became a lecturer at the Academy of War. In 1909 he was sent to Japan as an artillery instructor to the Japanese army. You will remember that the Meiji emperors enlisted the Germans to teach them trade, war and the legal systems of the West. But mark the year, Gil, 1909. That was when Prince Ito was assassinated by a Korean nationalist and the Japanese established a military dictatorship over Korea. Note something else, too. In the small foreign community it was the most natural thing in the world for the Leibig family to welcome Haushofer into the house. It was equally natural for Haushofer to establish a professional friendship with Tanaka's grandfather, who was a senior officer on the general staff. Now do you see how it begins to come together?'

'How long have Tanaka and Leibig known of these old connections with Haushofer?'

'It's at least six months since I supplied Leibig with the documents. He told me he had passed them on immediately to Tanaka.'

'So when you challenged Leibig at the meeting this morning, he knew you were calling him a liar.'

'He certainly did.'

'But he's your boss, the man who's paying your salary. Why call him out in public?'

'Because, like you, I'm not on salary. I'm paid a fee to provide information and counsel. Like you, I guarantee a true bill of goods. I will not have it falsified in my presence. You made exactly the same point, in different words.'

'In spite of that, they want us to stay with the project. How do you explain that?'

'Let's talk about it later, Gil.' She shrugged off the question as if it had little importance. 'I want to finish the Haushofer story, otherwise the rest of this won't make sense.'

'Please! I didn't mean to interrupt.'

'Haushofer was a natural polyglot. He spoke Chinese, Korean, Japanese, Russian, French and English. As a military academician he had a passion for history and geography. In the First World War he served as a brigade commander. His personal aide was Rudolf Hess, who introduced him to Hitler. When Hitler was imprisoned in Landsberg, Haushofer visited him often and the rumour that he had written that crucial chapter sixteen of *Mein Kampf* began from those encounters. When Hitler came to power he appointed Haushofer to the presidency of the Germany Academy. He also confirmed, by special decree, that Haushofer's part-Jewish wife and their two sons were Aryan. From that period onward Haushofer became the fountainhead of German geopolitical theory and an important reference point for worldwide Nazi intelligence. When the war ended, he was investigated, though not indicted, as a war criminal. He and his wife committed suicide. The bitter irony was that his son Albrecht, who held the chair of political geography in Berlin and also worked at the Foreign Office, had joined the July plot against Hitler. He was arrested in 1944 and shot in April 1945 while being transferred from Moabit prison.'

She broke off and sipped her wine, watching me over the rim of her glass. Finally she said thoughtfully: 'You listen. You say nothing. Don't you have any questions?'

'I'm waiting to hear exactly what Haushofer's theories were and why they are being given so much importance in our project.'

'Let's be clear. They weren't all Haushofer's ideas. He borrowed them from an Englishman, Sir Halford Mackinder, who expounded them to the Royal Geographical Society in April 1904. Mackinder summed up his theory as follows: "Who rules Eastern Europe commands the heartland," Russia. "Who rules the heartland commands the World Island," Eurasia. "Who rules the World Island commands the World." Leibig's new maps and charts were intended to illustrate that thesis, except that they translated the old-fashioned ideas of military domination into modern economic terms. You don't fight your way into a country, you trade your way in. You don't have to make armed threats, you hold the purse-strings, because you're the banker. You control the trade, because you're a major buyer of exports.'

'And you think the Russians don't see that?'

'Of course they see it. They're not stupid. They know that they're faced with a short term choice between two economic tyrannies, that of the Americans or that of the German-Japanese Alliance. There's a third option, of course: they go shopping for aid and technology in the European open market. There they can find the money perhaps, but not all the technology. So they have to choose between Scylla and Charybdis – the rock and the whirlpool.'

'So why should they choose the Germans and the Japanese, with the Haushofer theory written so plainly over the deal?'

'Because they'll discount the theory for the practical short-term gain. Look, Gil, they've just thrown all the sacred dogmas of Marxism out the window! They've junked their own socialist revolution and opened the front door and the back and every window to the capitalists. Do you think they're going to be stopped by an almost unreadable German theoretician? I've studied him line by line and Major-General Professor Doctor Karl Haushofer makes damned hard reading. However, I can give you a couple of very good reasons why the Russians will bargain with Leibig and Tanaka.'

'That's what I need to know.'

'I'm sure you know it already. First, America is out of favour with the Muslim world. The Soviets have to live with it inside and outside their frontiers. Second, Japan is now the leader in the microchip industry, key to all industrial progress in the twenty-first century. That's not the whole story and . . .'

'Only time will show whether the general argument holds good; now tell me truly, why you? Why me? What is our contribution intended to be? I want your personal reading.'

'That's the easiest of all to answer. Both Tanaka and Leibig would like us to be special pleaders for their case. They know we won't be. So they'll present me as an unbiased counsellor and you as the un-prejudiced mediator.'

'Which is only true in part; because we'll be seen to be sitting on their side of the table. The presumption of our virtue favours them.'

'So, the reason we're talking now, the final question for each of us, Gil; do we stay or quit?'

'I've decided to stay. Laszlo half convinced me and your argument convinces me wholly. The Soviets will discount the theory; so I don't have to lie about it. I do what I am paid for, try to achieve a workable compromise that gets the Soviet economy moving with our people as prime traders. And you? Where do you stand?'

Before she had time to answer, the waiter approached the table with a telephone: 'A call for you, Mr Langton. The operator says it's urgent.'

The caller was Kenji Tanaka. He made a ritual apology. 'Forgive me for disturbing you, Gil.'

'How did you know where to find me?'

'Simple. You live there. I called the restaurant to ask whether you were dining in tonight.'

'What can I do for you?'

'Something important has come up. We must talk.'

'We're meeting at eight in the morning. Isn't that soon enough?'

'Unfortunately, no. There are calls I have to make as soon as business opens in New York and on the West Coast. Miko and I are only a few blocks away. Why don't we join you for coffee?'

'Kenji, I'm entertaining a lady.'

'I know. Laszlo told me. I promise you I won't take too much of your time. Miko can entertain her while you and I talk. Shall we say fifteen minutes?'

'If you must.'

'I am in your debt, Gil.'

I put down the receiver and wished him to hell. Marta was amused.

'Don't worry about it, Gil. I'll be interested to meet him and his girlfriend.'

'I was hoping . . .'

'I know; but you and I hardly need to rush our fences do we?'

The quiet caution silenced me. I signalled the waiter and asked him to set coffee for four. Then it was my turn to issue a warning.

'Be careful with Miko. She's very clever and Tanaka depends on her more than he'll admit. The less you tell her the better.'

The admonition seemed to trouble her. She was silent for a long moment, then she said gravely: 'I don't like this, Gil. I took this appointment, as you seem to have done, with a certain enthusiasm, even a kind of idealism. It looked like a great adventure, to take some part in the reconstruction of a whole continent, to make trade and commerce the basis for a whole new era. In a way, that's what started me reading Haushofer and Mackinder; and Kjellen the Swede who was working along the same lines at the same time . . . But now, suddenly, it's all changed. I feel like a conspirator, sordid and venal. I don't think I can live with that.'

I knew how she felt. I had felt it myself many times, as I travelled the world setting up the various local corporations in the global network of Polyglot Press. In the beginning, wherever I might be, I always felt at home and welcome. People were flattered that I spoke their language with ease and elegance. I was flattered by their admiration. But always, sooner or later, I became the stranger again, the outsider, the huckster from over the frontier. At first I was affronted, then slowly I came to realise that this was, and always would be, the rule of the game. Every tribe in the world had its own version of the scapegoat, marked for exile or persecution when the homefolk needed to purge themselves of their own guilts. Only the trader himself could decide whether the game was worth the risk. I tried to explain the experience to Marta.

'In my second year at Oxford my father rented a small house just south of Olbia in Sardinia. It was a fisherman's cottage, right on the beach, fronting a tiny islet across the water where we used to dive for artefacts, pottery and amulets. The islet used to be a Phoenician trading post. They would come up from Carthage when the south winds started to blow. They would trade with the local Sards for tin and oil and slaves and bronzeware and sheep hides. Then, when the north winds began they would head back to Africa, leaving a tiny group to man the outpost until the next trading season. They kept a small shrine from which they sold sacred oil and amulets. They bought fish and fruit and goat's meat and charcoal to sustain themselves. So, while they were always regarded with suspicion – and sometimes with awe – they were never molested. Little outposts like that became the colonial cities from which the Phoenicians traded as far north as Ireland and the Hebrides. My father used to liken them to the wandering scholars who later peddled knowledge around Europe and colonised the barbarians with monasteries and institutions of learning. They, too, were the outsiders of the day, but little by little they changed the face of the world. If it weren't for people like us – and the Leibigs and the Marco Polos and Commander Perry and all the assorted rogues, scholars and hucksters down the centuries – the Japanese would still be wearing kimonos and samurai topknots and slicing up commoners in the alleys of Edo.'

It was a familiar theme, which I suspected my father had embroidered to justify his scholar-gypsy existence after my mother's death. In my youth I embraced it with passion. Later it became a maxim – or an excuse – for my own career as an ageing widower and a publisher who knew how to be a bachelor in twenty three major languages.

Its effect on Marta Boysen startled me. Her control cracked like a sheet of glass. Her eyes filled with tears. Her lips trembled. Her voice issued in an angry undertone. 'God! I wish I'd heard that story ten years ago. It might have saved me a lot of heartache and humiliation. That was the theme my husband harped on all the time: "You have no roots! You have no sense of permanence! How could you have presumed to make a marriage? I will not make children with you and see them brought up as gypsies . . ." ' She fought hard to control herself and managed half a smile. 'Damn you, Gil Langton! You're too dangerous to be let loose! I never break up like this, never! You'll have to excuse me. I need to make some repairs before the coffee guests arrive! May I use your suite?'

I handed her the key, and she hurried out. Five minutes later she was back, polished and shining like a piece of Dresden porcelain, every hair in place, her smile a permanent miracle. A moment later Tanaka arrived with Miko. He was dressed in a new Savile Row suit with the miniature of an Imperial order on his lapel. Miko was resplendent in a kimono and *obi* which, even to my untutored eyes, were worth a fortune. It was a three-bow occasion. Miko excelled herself in ceremonious humility. Tanaka paid princely deference to Marta, who responded with all the respect due from a female to a distinquished gentleman of Japan. I caught in Miko's veiled eyes a gleam of surprise and approval. Then, before we had a chance to seat ourselves, Marta spoke to Miko.

'Mr Langton has kindly given us the use of his suite while Mr Tanaka and he have their conference. You and I will take coffee there. Excuse us, gentlemen.'

Before anyone had time to protest, she was shepherding Miko out of the dining room, through the lounge and towards the elevators. It was a beautifully executed manoeuvre. No one, man or woman, was going to dismiss Marta Boysen, or suggest that she absent herself from grown-up company. Tanaka and I settled ourselves at the table. Tanaka nodded a restrained approval.

'So. That is the distinguished Professor Marta Boysen. There was no need for her to leave so quickly. They could have taken their coffee in the lounge.'

'I explained that you're pressed for time, Kenji. It's coming up to nine thirty am in New York.'

'You and I have to talk first. I must know whether you will stay with the project.'

'I have certain reservations about the way things are being conducted. I believe, however, they can be dealt with. So, yes, I'll stay.'

'Thank you. Events are moving much faster than I expected. I need all the help I can get. I gave a small dinner party this evening for certain members of the Cabinet and for two of my most senior colleagues in Japanese business. The government refused absolutely to send Japanese Service personnel to the Gulf. Such a move would utterly dishonour the neutrality and anti-militarist policy to which we are pledged. Members of the self-defence forces would be functioning as military personnel on foreign soil. The consequences would be larger than anyone dreams. Old ghosts would walk again. However, the final announcement of our refusal is being deferred so as not to embarrass the Americans.'

'Any reaction from the Russians?'

'I have already had a brief conversation with the Ambassador. They are to this point ambivalent. They, too, have been under heavy pressure from the Americans to participate in the Gulf blockade. The Americans have made it a matter of money and technology, oil technology, which the Russians desperately need. So, they understand our position.'

'And the Germans?'

'They are being very generous, offering to send all their outmoded East German armaments, which they would have to scrap anyway.'

'Does our conference in Bangkok go ahead?'

'With special urgency now. Moscow has been told that we need swift contact with members of their delegation to get preparations moving. But clearly, all our strategy now must be to emphasise the practical advantages of our proposals and de-emphasise any strategic implications which may be drawn from them.'

'In other words, bury the Haushofer theory, and make sure Mr Carl Leibig is gagged.'

'If you want to put it that way, yes.' Tanaka was nettled. 'I believe he has learned his lesson.'

'Have you learned yours, my friend?'

'I don't know what you mean.'

'I believe you do. All the Haushofer information and all the conclusions, good and bad, that might have been drawn from it, were in your hands six months ago. You chose, for very good reasons, no doubt, to conceal that fact from me. The result? Yesterday's embarrassing confrontation and the very real possibility of a later leak to the press at a bad moment. All that stuff is still on file in an advertising agency in Hamburg.'

'And in Professor Boysen's own files. Carl Leibig thinks she may well be the weakest link in our security chain. He has decided to pay her a generous fee and dispense with her services. I think he's probably right.'

The waiter was at his elbow refilling his coffee cup. Tanaka's momentary distraction gave me the chance to control myself and assume the mask of polite indifference, so necessary in every Oriental business transaction. I waited for Tanaka to deliver more information. Instead he challenged me with a question.

'You don't agree with Leibig's decision?'

'It doesn't matter whether I agree or not. I have no standing in the matter. Marta Boysen is a professional in her own right. She doesn't ask my advice about her career.'

'Carl is very angry about her conduct yesterday. He claims she made him look foolish and deceitful.'

'She did and he was. We were all witnesses, remember? Laszlo, Forster, Leino, myself.'

'So you don't think he should dismiss her?'

'I repeat, what Leibig does is his own business. My private opinion is that he's acting like a spoilt child. However, if Professor Boysen does become free, I'll offer her a job on our team. My contract provides that I have the choice of my own staff. Marta Boysen could be a valuable colleague. I'm not sure she'll accept, but its worth a try.'

'Are you sure, Gil?' He was very cool and deliberate. 'Are you quite sure this is a good move? I know she's attractive. I know she has a splendid academic record, but what do you really know of her? You met her only this morning.'

'My dear Kenji, I've known her since she was a child.'

He gaped at me, speechless. I took from my pocket the photographs which Marta Boysen had given me and spread the fading prints on the table in front of him.

'These were taken in Austria in 1957. That's my father, the woman is Marta's mother. That handsome beanpole is me. The child is Marta.'

Tanaka shook his head in disbelief, then a slow smile twitched at the corners of his mouth. 'I should always listen to Miko. She keeps telling me that you are not half as simple as you look.'

'That's kind of her.'

'There's more. She says that in dealing with you I have to bet on your telling me the truth, even if it is a truth I do not wish to hear.'

'Your Miko is a very clever woman. You should heed her advice.'

'And will you heed mine?'

'Friend to friend, yes.'

'Then, Gil – my dear friend Gil – listen to me carefully. For all of us the hour of maximum danger is very near. I am talking of the whole global pattern of which our enterprise is a small part. We are coming up to earthquake time – and we Japanese know about earthquakes – when the great rock plates shift and slide and buckle against each other and all our frail human edifices come tumbling down. In the Gulf an upstart dictator straddles a quarter of the world's oil supply. If he cannot be squeezed out by blockade there will be war, the wild beasts let loose again. Even so, we must still keep planning and building in hope, co-operating as best we can, even when our confidence in one another is eroding as ours is now. You are a lucky man, Gil. You have been given a gift which enables you to see the world as an astronaut sees it, with its rivers and seas and forests and mountains and its cities all reduced to miniature. But you have paid a price for that gift. You have forgotten how things look at ground level. To me, for instance, a man enclosed in a capsule of language, customs, relationships from which I can never escape. You and I live on different planes; we are measured on different grids. The accommodations we make one to the other are not matters of right and wrong, but of possibility, of what is achievable between us at any given moment . . . Even tonight, one of my colleagues, perhaps the most powerful banker in Japan with assets all round the world, was saying that, since a partial rearmament is being forced upon us, we should possibly go the whole way, reconstitute the military forces and even create our own atomic arsenal. I told him the people would never stand for it. He laughed in my face. He said that with a saturation campaign in all media we could change national thinking in a month. I knew he was right and I was horrified. I saw how far I had been led down the same road by the revival of the Haushofer theories. For this very reason, Gil, you are very important to me. Even when I disagree with you, I recognise that you give me a different norm of judgment. You are my *sensei*, my teacher and counsellor in the ways of a different world . . . To others, however, you are exactly what my banker friend called you: Tanaka's tame *gaijin*. In short, Gil, you are making enemies, not because of what you do, but simply because of what you are. You have to know that one day even I could be your enemy. If one or other of my historic obligations conflicts with our friendship, I have no choice. The dice are loaded against you. Do you understand what I am trying to say?'

'I understand it. I respect you for telling me. I still pray we may never be enemies.'

'I too, Gil.' He gave a small despairing shrug. 'But circumstances change so swiftly. I was told tonight that an American/British group may bid for Carl Leibig's companies.'

'Would he or his family sell?'

'I don't know how the shares are held. But since everyone has a price, we have to be prepared for the possibility.'

'What happens then to the Tanaka/Leibig alliance?'

For the first time Tanaka relaxed and laughed. 'Then I mount a counter-bid with another German partner, who is already in place if we need him. But you see, Gil, nothing is quite as simple as it looks. When the earthquake comes and the great plates grind together, people get hurt. You could get hurt, Gil. I don't want that to happen. On the other hand, I may not be able to prevent it.'

It was the old, old problem: he was saying much less than he meant. I had to decipher the message for myself. I thanked him for the warning. He acknowledged my thanks. Then I faced him with the one question to which he had to give a straight answer.

'Do you have any objection to my employing Marta Boysen?'

'In your publishing business? None at all. On this project? Yes, I have objections. We still have to work with Carl Leibig. On the other hand,' he chose the words with a certain care, 'if you have a personal need of her, take her. Enjoy her. She's a well-educated, beautiful woman. You're getting too old to be catting around the alleys.'

It was an equivocal answer, heavy with sexual innuendo and traditional chauvinism, both of which I chose to ignore. I wished only that I could be a fly on the wall of Tanaka's bedroom when Miko reported her little chat with Marta. Now it was time to close the show. I suggested we should sum up, so that there could be no possibility of misunderstanding between us. I counted off the points.

'You want me to continue as mediator to the conference.'

'I do.'

'You will inform me as soon as there is a Russian contact available to me.'

'I shall.'

'It is agreed that the political aspects of the proposed deal are to be subordinated to its practical applications.'

'Yes.'

'You have arranged that Leibig's contentious material is to be suppressed.'

'I have.'

'My future procedures with Leibig: who makes the next contact?'

'He does. In the morning you will receive a note of apology for the unauthorised taping. He has agreed to destroy the master tape. After that your relations will continue as originally planned.'

'In that case I shall not preempt his decision on Marta Boysen. She has told me that she is very unhappy with this morning's events. I shall indicate simply that there is a place open in my company at any time she cares to consider it. For the rest,' my turn now to do a little underlining of the subtext, 'it would be unwise for anyone to make presumptions about the lady and myself simply because we have a long-standing family relationship.'

Tanaka's relief was plain. He offered me his hand across the table. I noticed that it was slack and clammy. 'Thank you, Gil. I wish I had been trained to be as direct as you; but even our language doesn't permit it.' He gave a small tired laugh. 'Perhaps it's just as well. If all the millions of these small islands decided all at once to proclaim their private convictions, we'd have a hell of a mess! Would you mind calling the ladies down? It's been a long night for me.'

While the waiter was bringing the telephone to the table he added a swift afterthought.

'Would you like us to drop Professor Boysen at her hotel? It would save another car and another trip.'

'A good idea. Thank you.'

When I called my suite Marta answered.

'Marta? Gil. Mr Tanaka is ready to leave now. He's offered to drop you back at your hotel.'

'That's very kind.' She was a woman who picked up cues quickly. 'Miko and I have had a most pleasant chat. I'll call room service and ask them to clear away the coffee things. Then we'll be right down.'

We said our brief farewells in the forecourt where Tanaka's limousine was waiting. Marta Boysen thanked me for a pleasant evening and promised to call me in the morning. I asked her to give my regards to her mother and to thank her for the photographs which I would have blown up and framed as a keepsake for her. That was the only hint I could give to prepare her for the interrogation she was sure to get on the drive back to the Okura. When Tanaka eased himself into the limousine after the women, I noticed that he was pale and sweating profusely.

As I stood on the kerb watching them drive away I felt a surge of relief that the long day was over. I was dizzy with fatigue and deeply troubled by Tanaka's obvious anxieties. I was glad that I had been spared a private farewell with Marta Boysen. I was strongly attracted to her. She had been disarmingly warm and open with me. But I was in no mood to begin a new affair, or risk making a fool of myself on a first encounter. Of course, that was only half the truth. The rest of it was less comfortable to contemplate. I was not a youth any more. I was getting middle-aged and crotchety. I had other things on my mind than pillow-talk and love-games.

When I got back to my suite I found an envelope pinned to my pillow. The note inside it was written in Japanese:

'I like your Marta Boysen; but Carl Leibig is going to fire her, because she made him look bad in the meeting. Kenji will not interfere because he is under a lot of other pressures. News of his illness has leaked out among the family of big companies. I think his doctor sold the secret. So now a power struggle is beginning in the *keiretsu*. It is complicated by the problems in the Gulf and the effect on the stock markets around the world. Kenji needs your support and your friendship. Especially he needs this Russian project to go smoothly, though he will never tell you how great is the need. I can tell you because I trust you and I am very fond of you although I cannot share myself with you as I might sometimes wish to do. Please destroy this letter and do not speak of it to anyone. You will do what your friendship tells you. Miko.'

It was written in haste on hotel stationery. The script was awkward, the language less than polished; but the message was clear and, I believed, authentic. It told me in a woman's way what Tanaka failed to convey with twice the eloquence. He was ill and in trouble. The vultures were assembling in the treetops.

To understand the dimension of the drama, you have to have some grasp of the complexity of Japanese business organisation. Most of the big firms in Japan belong to half a dozen even bigger groups, vertical and horizontal organisations like Mitsubishi, Sumitomo, Sanwa and Mitsui. Each of these groups has its own banks, its own insurance companies, its trading houses, its estate agencies and share brokers. All the units within it hold interlocking shares and have interlocking directors. The biggest groups are similarly hooked in one to the other. The total effect is rather like that of a huge, all embracing net whose strands are impossible to follow. There is another effect, too, even more potent, a set of unwritten rules under which both risks and decisions are shared and any rule-breaker gets very short shrift indeed. The system is a marvellous shock-absorber against the ups and downs of world markets. However, the rivalries within it and the pressures on ailing or failing members are enormous and occasionally lethal.

Tanaka's metaphor of the earthquake was absolutely accurate. Woe betide any hapless creature who became trapped between the grinding plates, upon which the whole intricate structure rested. In the context of financial instability the illness of a man like Tanaka could spell catastrophe, especially if he refused to step down at the prudent urging of his peers. If he became incapacitated, or if his reputation were damaged by too many mistakes, he would have to be insulated first and then quite possibly eliminated.

The Russian deal was an enormous risk. Therefore the other members of the big groups were holding back until the risks were shown to be acceptable. The effect of the political context, the hark-back to Haushofer and his theories, was paradoxical. The big men of the big houses saw them as positive elements. They pointed to a renewal of historic alliances that had almost succeeded and this time could very possibly succeed. If they led to a return of lost territories – more, if they gave Japan a foothold back on the mainland, trading presences in Siberia, in Manchuria – ah, then the whole equation would be different.

So Gil Langton, the tame *gaijin*, was begged not to rock the boat. Gil Langton could roister himself silly with wine, women and song, all on a very large expense sheet, but he must not meddle in the big game staged by and for the big players. Truth to tell, Gil Langton had no intention of doing anything so silly. He would fulfil his contract to the letter: best efforts, candid discussion, no polemics, no politics. Then he would go about his business of spreading enlightenment through the printed word to Arab and Greek and Armenian and Uncle Tom Cobbley and all! Gil Langton was a very sleepy boy. He was already launched into a dream of fair women.

I had not been asleep five minutes when the telephone shrilled in my ear. Marta Boysen was on the line, bright as spring sunshine.

'I just wanted to tell you I enjoyed myself very much. I hated having to hurry away like that, but it was difficult to refuse.'

'I suppose Tanaka bombarded you with questions.'

'As a matter of fact, no. He wasn't very well. Miko had the chauffeur drive to his apartment first, then take me on to the hotel.'

'We might just as well have gone in my car.'

'I know. Never mind. There'll be other times. However, when I got back there was a letter waiting for me from Carl Leibig.'

'Oh. What does it say?'

'Nothing much. He asks me to be at his office at nine-thirty in the morning to discuss a matter of mutual importance. He is sending his car to pick me up. What do you think it means?'

'More importantly, what do you think it means?'

'It could be he wants to get rid of me, which is what I've been thinking about all day. If that's what he has in mind, I'd rather resign.'

'Don't be a fool, woman!'

'What do you mean?'

'If you resign it costs him nothing. If he fires you he has to pay severance, transport home, whatever else is stipulated in your contract.'

'I hadn't thought of that.'

'Keep thinking of it. Pride's a costly indulgence. Call me after you've spoken to him. I'll be in my office.'

'Is that the best you can do, Gil Langton?'

'There's one more thing.'

'Do tell me.'

'If you're out of a job in the morning, I'll offer you one with Polyglot Press. The money's good. And I'm much easier to get on with than Carl Leibig. Think it over.'

'That's very kind of you Gil, but . . .'

'No buts, please! I'm dead in the water. Call me tomorrow. Golden dreams, *schatzi*.'

'And to hell with you too, Gil Langton!'

I called the operator and asked her to put a block on my phone until seven in the morning. After that I remember nothing, not even the dream of fair women. Obviously I had lost it.

Four

Every Friday in Tokyo I became a company president, Japanese style. I sat at the head of the boardroom table with Yukio Tanizaki, my chief executive, on the right and Junichiro Oshima, my financial controller, on the left. On either side of the table, in descending order, were the executives of Polyglot Press Japan Incorporated – editorial, illustrations, production, sales, promotion – each with a label, each with a precise place in the hierarchy.

I was not expected to do anything or say anything. I was Number One, he who sat, silent and awesome, on the throne of power. It was Tanizaki who ran the meeting. He snapped out the questions, made critical comments on the answers, meted out praise or blame and ended always with a tirade: however well things had been done, they could always be done better; if they had been badly done, it was a collective responsibility to see that mistakes were not repeated. He was as merciless as a master sergeant in boot camp.

When I had first seen the ritual performed I had been shocked. People should not be treated like that. There had to be better ways of motivating a team than by public abuse and humiliation. This was old-fashioned hype for the football jocks in the locker room. It had nothing to do with the making and selling of books.

Tanizaki and Oshima took me to lunch and told me, very respectfully, the facts of business life in Japan. If I wanted to be a nice guy that was fine, but nice guys always ran last in the rat race. If I did not care enough about performance and profits, my staff would not care either. If they were not bullied enough they would feel rejected, inferior to their colleagues in other publishing houses. When I answered that I wanted to show appreciation for good work, Tanizaki told me that I could do it at bonus time. Even then, a certain restraint was advisable. The employee had to respond with a gift to the boss; and the proportion of one to the other was critical.

So I learned silence and the company prospered. We held our staff and the work got done and our bills were paid on time. The Friday ceremony became a feature of my visits, a parade ground ceremony. Once I had met everybody and exchanged bows and compliments I became as redundant as a fifth leg on a donkey. The astral form I left behind in the chair would still dominate the meeting.

Nevertheless I liked to be there, watching how this one and that answered the quite brutal challenges of Tanizaki, the meticulous probing of Oshima into costs, sales projections, discount sales and the rest. I never asked questions directly, I put them through Tanizaki or Oshima. The staff were prepared for their interrogations. Mine, coming out of high heaven, would most certainly have embarrassed them.

Just before midday I was called out of the meeting to take a call from Marta Boysen. Her news was a complete surprise.

'Rejoice with me, Gil. I'm the prodigal daughter, kissed on both cheeks and welcomed back into the family.'

'How the hell did that happen?'

'My mother did it.'

'Come on. Don't tease me, I'm busy. What happened?'

'Well, after we talked last night I lay awake for hours thinking. I didn't want to lose this job. I'd put a lot of work into it and the possibilities are still enormously exciting. I thought about your offer, which was more than kind. I'd love to work with you, but I couldn't work for you. Then I remembered the exercise which my mother imposes on all her students, especially those who are just beginning to get professional engagements. She calls it "reviewing the performance" and she takes the artist phrase by phrase through the piece, with criticisms and notes for improvement. So, when you hung up on me last night, that's exactly what I did. I went over my performance at Leibig's meeting and I decided that he had a perfect right to fire me. I had acted quite arrogantly and left him no line of retreat from all the quite valid criticisms which the rest of you had made. I could and should have remained silent. So I took the initiative, apologised very humbly and offered my resignation.'

'Which he promptly refused.'

'Not promptly. He had to go through a little song and dance first, for the benefit of the young man who appears to be his senior aide. Then, having delivered his reproof, he relented. He did not want to lose me.

He did not agree that the Haushofer material was a dead letter. There was still enormous value in it. All that was needed was to reshape the argument, and who better to do that than Marta Boysen, now that she had learned discretion. So there you are! Tonight I'll buy the champagne; unless you have another Friday woman?'

'I'll have to check my diary, but I think I'm probably free. Why don't you pass by my office at six and let me show you what you missed? Then, maybe we can talk about plans for the weekend.'

'I'd like that, very much.'

'And I'm glad we still have you with us. Tanaka will be pleased too.'

That was a tactical error and she picked it up immediately. 'You mean he knew I was going to be fired?'

'Yes.'

'Miko, too?'

'Yes.'

'That was in the note she left for you?'

'Yes.'

'But none of you told me. And neither you nor Tanaka intervened with Leibig?'

'No. We agreed it would be impolitic to do so.'

'But you at least could have warned me.'

'You were already expecting it. I offered you a job, wasn't that warning enough?'

'Why couldn't you be open with me? I'm a friend, a colleague. I'm not a pawn on a chessboard!'

'Then before we meet tonight, I'll follow your mother's precept and review my performance. Meantime I'm glad things turned out well with Leibig. See you at six.'

This time it was she who broke the connection. I picked up the phone again and dialled Tanaka's private number. He answered immediately.

'Kenji, this is Gil. How are you feeling this morning? You looked very tired last night.'

'A momentary indisposition. I am much better, thank you.'

I told him of Marta's telephone call. He did not seem surprised. 'That's a satisfactory outcome. It also speaks well for Professor Boysen's commonsense. I regret that I disturbed your evening.'

'No matter. There will be others.'

'Other evenings or other women?'

'I am open to all possibilities.'

It was an old Zen phrase and he gave me the response to it.

'But not all possibilities are open to you! Now I have news for you, Gil, good news. I made a number of calls last night. Our banking arrangements are promising enough for us to proceed with confidence. Nothing is signed yet. Everything depends on the final shape of the document we produce in Bangkok. However, the climate is markedly better. The best news of all is that the Russians are sending their facilitator immediately. He will arrive, with his assistant, in Tokyo on Monday morning. His name – just a moment while I look it up – his name is Vannikov.'

'What's his given name?'

'Boris. Why do you ask?'

'Boris Vannikov was an important man in the early nuclear programmes in the USSR. His eldest son, who was named for him, was trained as an academic economist, then moved into publishing. I sold him rights to a number of scientific works and introduced a couple of his regional authors into German and British Commonwealth lists. Then he was co-opted on to Gorbachev's personal staff. If this is the same man, we at least begin on first name terms.'

'That would be a great advantage. But as yet I have no dossier. In the normal course that would be sent to Leibig first.'

'Do you want me to meet him at the airport?'

'No. The protocols are already in place. He and his aide, who, I understand, is a woman, though I do not have her name, will be met at the airport by the commercial attaché for the Soviet Embassy, where they will spend twenty four hours. Then Carl has arranged to fly them to Nara. The Leibig company has an estate there. They use it for company seminars and sales promotions. It is remote, private and well-staffed. There is a helicopter pad and security is easy to maintain. By the way, have you received Leibig's letter yet?'

'It's on my desk. I haven't read it. I've been in a meeting all the morning.'

'Do me a favour, Gil. Read it now and telephone him.'

'As soon as we've finished this call. When are we scheduled for Nara?'

'Wednesday and Thursday of next week. On the Sunday we must be in Bangkok. The conference begins Monday morning at nine.'

'But we still don't have the list of Russian delegates.'

'Vannikov is bringing it with him.'

'Let's hope he's brought more than that. The more ground we can cover before we get into conference the better.'

'I agree. Have you made any plans for the weekend?'

'I was thinking of taking Marta Boysen out into the country. And you?'

'I am visiting my son and my grandchildren in Kyoto. Miko is flying back to the Coast. She will meet us in Bangkok.'

'Travel safely, my friend.'

'You too, Gil. Today all the news is good. We should hope it continues so.'

After that I read Carl Leibig's letter.

Please accept my apologies for the unauthorised recording of our discussions. I beg you to believe there was no malicious intent. It was, in fact, a simple oversight on my part. In the flurry of preparations Franz, my personal assistant, asked whether the proceedings should be taped. I told him I thought it would be a good idea. He made the arrangements. I completely forgot the essential courtesy of asking the consent of the meeting. I beg you to forgive the lapse and not to let it damage the co-operation upon which the success of our enterprise depends. We are all a little edgy, I think. Natural enough, is it not, since we are assisting to shape a whole new order on the vast Eurasian continent . . ?

Once again I had to give him full marks for style and to revise my hasty judgments of him as an arrogant young upstart. Obviously Tanaka had put him under pressure, but he had still managed to extricate himself with dignity from a very awkward situation. I called him immediately and we had a comfortable chat during which I made an admission of my own.

'I agree with you, Carl. There's a lot at stake and we were all very edgy at the meeting. The good things are that the team is still intact and we have all blown off a little steam. By the time we get to Bangkok we should be able to present a very sound proposal.'

He thanked me for my confidence and then told me he had just received from Moscow a faxed copy of Vannikov's curriculum vitae. I asked him to read me a few lines of it. Ten seconds later I was able to give him the good news that Vannikov was indeed my former publishing colleague. Leibig was delighted. Then it occurred to me to ask whether the Soviets had asked for dossiers on our team.

'Oh, yes, indeed. They went off weeks ago.'

'But the only Soviet dossier we have is Vannikov's.'

'So far. I'm told Vannikov is bringing the others with him. But you obviously have a question.'

'Not a question, just a comment. Vannikov's presence is not a coincidence. Even after heavy doses of *perestroika* and *glasnost*, the Russian bureaucracy still works. Vannikov's name and mine are linked in the files.'

'Is that a good omen?'

'I think so. We know each other's style. That's an advantage to both sides.'

'And how would you describe him, Gil?'

'He's urbane. He's literate. He's fluent in French, English and German, and he also has some Latvian and Armenian. I know he doesn't speak or read Japanese, so his aide will probably be an interpreter from the Ministry of Foreign Affairs. He has an eye for good paintings and pretty women. He's an ardent soccer fan. He's also a tough bargainer who can squeeze the last fraction of value out of a dollar bill and the last drop of blood and patience out of a negotiator.'

'You will have hard work ahead of you. I wish you luck. I'll call you Monday as soon as I've made contact with Vannikov. Maybe we could all have a drink together before we leave for Nara?'

'I'm at your disposal, Carl. Have a pleasant weekend.'

I got back to the boardroom in time to close the meeting and take Tanizaki and Oshima to lunch, along with those three executives whose departments had turned in the best performance of the week. The criteria by which Tanizaki judged them were arcane and complicated, but I asked no questions, offered the appropriate compliments and bought them an expensive meal at a place called the Silver Tower which has a Korean owner, a French chef and a reputation for serving the best fillets of Kobe beef in Tokyo. After that it was a downhill run until five, when I showered, shaved and changed in my office bathroom, picked up a manuscript and sat waiting for Marta Boysen to arrive.

The manuscript was dull. After five minutes I tossed it aside, leaned back in my chair and tried to focus on the questions of where and how to entertain Marta Boysen at the weekend. The where was not a problem. There were half a dozen beautiful country inns within two hours of Tokyo. The autumn gardens and the temple precincts would be in full

64

flush. There were galleries and the workshops of local craftsmen, carvers, potters, printmakers, some of whom were friends of mine. I made a couple of calls and settled on a place just outside Kamakura which offered two adjoining rooms that gave on to a private garden.

That took care of the 'where'. The 'how' was the nub of the problem. How did she want, how did I want, the weekend to develop – as a pleasant touristic interlude, as a brief affair, or a love-match such as our parents had made? Already both of us had been acting out the prelude, alternately advancing and retreating, smiling and then rasping at each other. The rules of the game demanded that I make the next move. Hard-won experience suggested that I ought at least to figure out how the game should develop afterwards. I had loved my wife desperately. When she died, something in me died too, not the old Adam, who could still rise up rampant and roaring to be bedded, but the sense of permanence, the belief that the experience of love which we had shared could ever be renewed with another woman. Slowly I had come to understand the lesson my father had taught me one summer evening when we strolled down the little dock on the island of Lesbos.

We were sailing that year in a thirty footer we had chartered in Athens: to the Cyclades, the Dodecanese, the Dorian coast of Turkey and north to Ephesus. My father had a pedant's habit of picking an English word out of the air then asking me to translate it into a series of languages, while he commented on the change in colour from one tongue to another. The word he picked this time was 'dalliance' and the choice was prompted by the sight of a pair of lovers perched on a bollard, kissing passionately, while the local policeman stood with his hands in his trouser pockets lusting vicariously.

Dalliance is a very old-fashioned word. It can mean to amuse oneself, to toy amorously with someone, to be evasive, to make sport. The Germans call it *tandelei* or *liebelei*. The Italians make a mouthful of it as *amoraggiamento*. The Spanish call it *retozo*. The Japanese say it is to play at love *uwaki suru*. My father thought the French made the best of it. They called it *badinage* and he made that the burden of the lesson, which he used, I think, to explain himself to me.

'You can play whatever games you like with a woman, provided you both find them agreeable; but you don't play games with love. "*On ne badine pas avec l'amour.*" '

There is a sting in the tail of that one, too. If you are past fifty and you

65

know what love is, but you are not sure you can face the risks of finding it again, then you are in a very bad way indeed. My father always knew what he wanted but, since he could not call my mother back, he settled for what he could get – a warm welcome, a friendly goodbye and an open door if he passed that way again. What I did not know, of course, and what I was only now beginning to learn, was how much it had cost him to accept the compromise and the long stretches of solitude between the lovings.

All my soul searching came to an abrupt end when at exactly six o'clock the telephone rang. Marta Boysen was on the line, very much the Frau Professor Doktor, offering a formal apology.

'I'm sorry, Gil. I'm not going to be able to keep our dinner date. I'm really not up to it. As for the weekend in the country, it was a kind thought, but in all the circumstances it could be the wrong move, for both of us.'

'Are you sick?'

'No. I just feel that . . .'

'Then shut up and listen to me. I'll be at your hotel at seven-thirty. Be packed for a casual weekend. You'll need something warm; the nights are cool.'

'Gil, don't you understand? I'm not coming. You can't bully me into . . .'

Suddenly, as if from a far place in another time frame, I heard myself shouting in very vulgar German. 'Bully you? For Christ's sake! You're the one who sought me out, brought me the family snapshots, handed me that line of schmaltz about wanting me for a big brother. Well I'm not your brother! I'm my father's son and I'd like to make love to your mother's daughter on a futon in a country inn. If you don't want that, I won't press it. I booked two rooms anyway, so you'd have the option to say no. But you did promise to come, remember? You're a big girl now and you're supposed to be a sophisticated scholar. If you're still pouting over an imagined slight – which was really an attempt to save face for you – then you'll be boring company anyway. So, I'll meet you at seven-thirty in the bar. You offered to buy me champagne to celebrate your kiss-and-be-friends with Carl Leibig. If you're not coming, we'll call it a farewell drink and afterwards we'll stop being friends and be sober, courteous colleagues. No less, no more.'

There was a long silence then, calm as bedamned, in her best Hochdeutsch she announced: 'You're right Mr Langton. I did offer champagne. I'll expect you at seven-thirty. I'll even give you twenty minutes' grace in case the traffic is bad. Please drive carefully.'

I arrived on time. She did offer champagne, but it was still in the bottle and the bottle was in her overnight bag and she was dressed and ready for the road. Defying all Japanese decencies, I took her in my arms and kissed her and we set off, singing lustily, on the highway to Kamakura.

As the snarl of traffic enveloped us, we stopped singing and I listened as Marta Boysen began, hesitantly at first, then with increasing urgency, to talk herself out of the corner to which she had retreated.

'Every so often I feel besieged, hedged about by people who refuse to let me be myself, but want to bend me by force or guile to their own purposes. Some of it dates from my marriage. Some of it goes further back still, to my childhood when I travelled with my mother . . . She kept me with her most of the time. I give her full credit for all the love she put into that; but there were always other people managing my life – a nurse, a nanny, a tutor-companion. I couldn't become attached to one place. There was always a manager, a producer, stepping through the door waving a piece of paper and bidding us to move on.

'You will laugh at this, but one of the things that attracted me to an academic career was the enormous authority and independence of the Herr Professor. You know how it is in Germany, even now. The professor is Jove dispensing thunder and lightning. Of course, that's an illusion, too, as you well know, but it drove me hard enough and far enough to launch me on my career. Looking back, I suppose one of my more vivid memories of your father and you was the sense of freedom that swept into the house with you. Anything was possible. Any place in the world was only a hop and a skip away. My world was exciting enough, God knows, but yours was . . . oh, infinitely extended. Later, it reinforced my conviction that scholarship itself was a liberator.

'Then I threw all my freedom out the window and shackled myself to a *gutsherr* from Carinthia. How? Why? It's such a damn silly story I'm almost ashamed to tell it. My mother was singing at the Burgtheater in Vienna. The management staged a reception for her. He was there, dolled up and dashing, handsome as Lucifer. I was tired and bored after a long arid year of study. We started going about together. He showed me off like one of his prize mares. I loved it. I was ripe and ready for breeding anyway. We were married before summer was out. By autumn's end, while I was trying to cope with my courses again, the marriage was already in ruins. He wasn't a bad man, just stupid, with a streak of childish cruelty in his nature. He was madly jealous of everything I was or wanted to be. He wouldn't share my interests, but he wouldn't let me be private either. I had to build a fence around my professional life so that he wouldn't come trampling through it like an old fashioned Junker, kicking up mud, slashing about with his riding crop. Then he became cunning, setting little traps, playing games to disrupt my schedules or taint my friendships . . . That was a horrible time. I needed counselling to get me through it, and I still get bad dreams. What happened this morning seemed exactly like one of those dreams. I felt I'd been set up for something and you were part of the nasty prank. Even after the reconciliation with Leibig I couldn't shake off the resentment. In the end I panicked and tried to call off our date.'

I had no comment, because just at that moment a suicidal maniac nearly ran us into the guard-rail, trying to squeeze into the traffic ahead of us. Behind, a big transport rammed on his airbrakes and, for one dizzy moment, I thought we were going to end up as meat sandwich in the middle of the highway. My first coherent utterance was a torrent of obscenities in Japanese and outback Australian.

We were both badly scared so, at the first opportunity, we turned off the highway and on to a side road that wound through a string of villages to our destination; a traditional Japanese *ryokan* secluded in its own garden, with stone lanterns dotted among the trees, a carp stream spanned by a graceful bridge, and a tranquility so carefully contrived that we might have stepped back a hundred years.

The moment we slipped off our shoes and were bowed into the magic square of our living space, our world changed and we were changed with it. Two smiling maids disposed of our meagre baggage. The screen wall was slid back to reveal a bathroom with the great wooden tub already filling with steaming water. Once it was clear that we were sleeping together – not that there had been any question asked, but I had booked two rooms – then one chamber was set for our sleeping, and the other for our eating and our contemplation of the garden when the moon rose or daylight came.

The ceremonies of welcome and comfort seemed interminable, but finally the maid gave us a small conspirator's smile, pointed to the handbell that would summon our dinner service, and left us to take our bath.

And there we were at last, two very adult people, staring at each other in wonderment across two metres of tatami floor. Then we were laughing and kissing and fumbling with fastenings until we collapsed together on the futon and made love desperately as if the next moment the world might end.

A long time afterwards we began the ritual of the bath. Marta sat naked on a pinewood stool while I ladled water over her from a wooden bucket and soaped her, head to toe, exploring her slowly, playing the love games I had dreamed in lonely nights and rehearsed sometimes in loveless rooms. Then she did the same for me, slowly and skilfully, until the tension became unbearable and we coupled again on the warm wet tiles of the floor.

Then we were in the bath, languid and playful as seals, rapt in each other's company, careless of the dangers that lurked in the black deeps beyond. We spoke little. What was there to utter except the small sudden words of pleasure and the long, sensuous sighs of relief and relaxation?

Came then the comedy of trying to dry ourselves with those ridiculously tiny wash-cloths which became sodden in a moment, and must be continually squeezed to dry the next patch of skin. At last, wrapped in *yukata*, we rang the bell and, with surprising appetite, worked our way through a dinner which the old merchant travellers to Edo would have been happy to share.

Afterwards, what is left to say about the afterwards? We folded ourselves together on the futon and played again, slowly and tenderly, until we slept from sheer exhaustion.

Somewhere in the small hours I woke. The room was full of moonlight and the sound of the night wind searching through the woodland. Marta was lying on her side, her face turned towards me, her hair streaming back across the low pillow. She was deep in sleep, every muscle relaxed, her breathing slow and regular. I wanted to kiss her, but it would have been a cruelty to wake her. Instead I watched her, studying the contours of her face, her shoulders, her breasts, noting the first faint tracemarks of time and experience. I was grateful for those. They assured me I was not some ageing fool, breathlessly chasing his youth among the yearling fillies. I remembered something she had said to me as we floated in the bathtub.

'Isn't it wonderful to do happy, silly things and not feel foolish?'

For her it was a heartcry against the frustrations of her marriage. For me it was like the rising of a new moon, a promise, a hope at least of change and renewal. For a travelling bachelor like myself, the world is full of opportunities for sexual folly. They are provided in infinite variety, by professionals. If you have the money, and a certain monomanic dedication to erotic practice, you can access them all by telephone and credit card. Even if you discount the risks, which get higher every year, you are still faced with the age-old questions: what the hell do you say to them afterwards, and how many times can you bear to say it? I remembered the old Chinese proverb which my father used to quote: 'When one talks to the girls in the tea-houses, one should leave one's heart at home!'

This time, it seemed I had brought my heart with me and the girl in the tea-house was not a girl, but a passionate, companionable woman who could give or withhold the key to her own private domain. The question now was reversed. What would she say to me afterwards, in the first grey light of morning?

She stirred, opened her eyes and smiled drowsily when she saw me bending over her. She took my face in her hands and drew me down to kiss her. Then I cradled her in the crook of my arm, her head against my heart. After a while she spoke, so softly that the rising wind almost carried the words away.

'I can't tell you how afraid I was. You made it all so simple. I hope we can keep it like this.'

'No reason why we shouldn't.'

'Here and now, no.'

'Here and now is all we've got. We were damn near killed tonight. Remember?'

'I know.' She began to giggle. 'And if that wasn't enough, we nearly killed each other. It was nice though, wasn't it? Like the first romp in the meadow after the snows have gone and the spring flowers are out. We make good playmates, don't we, Gil?'

'We do, schatzi. We do.'

'And what are we going to do in the morning?'

'It's morning now.'

'I know; but when it's daytime.'

'Let's see. We make love, we get up, we have breakfast – they'll make us coffee and toast if we ask for it. After that we'll stroll in the garden. I'll give you the botanical tour. Then we'll walk into the village to meet two old friends of mine, one is a *sumi* painter who is rated one of the great masters of the art. The other is a very old man, a famous maker of wood-block prints. He has a large studio where he trains young men to the art. There is fierce competition for admission, but he gives preference to those from poorer families. I arranged his first exhibition outside Japan and published two volumes of his prints in the United States and Europe. We'll spend a little time with him, then we'll visit a family pottery where the craft has been handed down for generations. The whole tribe is involved: grandparents, uncles, aunts, even the children. When they come home from school, they . . .'

She had not heard the half of it. She was already asleep again and smiling at some pleasant dream.

The day dawned cold and clear. The wind had dropped and there was a thin rime of frost on the moss banks in the garden. As we walked, each wrapped in the heavy *yukata* with which the hotel had supplied us, our breaths mingled in little plumes of mist. Marta had undergone a small psychic shock when, sated with early morning loving, we stepped out of the warm room into the autumn chill of an alien landscape. She shivered and drew close to me, thrusting her hand into my pocket, twining her fingers in mine for reassurance.

I knew what she felt: a human presence imposing itself on the most primitive natural elements, rocks and plants and water, a kind of meticulous tyranny which transformed a wasteland into a subtle but quite unique formality. Even though I had complete verbal and visual communication in Japan, I very often found the impression of imposed order strong and disturbing. We walked for a while in silence then, just as she had done on the drive down, Marta began a monologue, as if she were picking up a conversation that had lapsed only a moment before.

'You said we have only today. That's not quite true. We also have yesterday, all the inescapable memories of yesterdays. Until last night I wore mine like a prisoner's shackles. You struck them off. You made love to me and set me free. For that I love you, Gil. Here and now in this garden, I love you.'

'Here and now in this garden, I love you too, Marta Boysen.'

Even as I uttered the words I could hear a ghostly cricket-voice chirping in my ear: '*On ne badine pas avec l'amour*': You don't play games with love. It was too late. The words were already floating in front of us, little puffs of white vapour. They could be recalled and quoted again at any time. They could also be extended into a pact, a treaty, a contract of companionship or marriage. 'Here and now in this garden, I love you. I want to have you and hold you and love you for always.' Was that what she wanted? Was that what I wanted? There was only one way to find out. When we stopped on the little bridge to watch the carp circling lazily in the sunlight, I asked her.

'Just suppose, Frau Professor, pure hypothesis this, just suppose we both of us are offered a tomorrow, a succession of tomorrows perhaps, what will we say then?'

She gave me a small, enigmatic smile and shook her head. 'No, Gil. Let's take each day, each night as they present themselves. Perhaps they will lie always like separate pearls on a jeweller's black velvet mat. Perhaps they will be so perfectly matched that we will want to make them into a necklace that has no end. For you and me I think it would be an arrogance to plan too far ahead. It would be like saying we have a right to what is, in fact, a wonderful gift. Today in this garden we love each other. *Das ist genug und über*. That is more than enough.'

So, I had my answer, and an unsought absolution from any uneasy thought that I might be playing games with love – or the lady. I felt a new lightness in our step as we walked arm-in-arm out of the garden, to pay our respects to the master craftsmen in the village.

Taisei, the master of brush-painting, was already at his table, with the simple materials of his craft laid out before him: the grinding stone, the inkstick, the brushes, the white porcelain dishes, the cotton wads, the water jars, the scroll of paper held firm with a metal bar. Having determined first that Marta spoke no Japanese, he asked me to translate a compliment and a welcome, and then proceeded in mime to give her a first lesson on the classic procedures: the grinding and dilution of the ink, the holding of the brush vertically to the paper, the grip high or low according to the strokes. He showed her how to achieve line and tone and an economy of form. He drew a bamboo, a bird on a twig, a horse, a crab. Then he asked her to sit for him; and while he was studying her, he explained that the aim of ink brush portraiture was not the likeness of the subject, but the expression of life itself as exemplified in that person.

It was a metaphysical point of view which appealed to her German spirit and she asked me to translate a series of questions to the master and interpret his answers to her. Taisei was delighted. Already the three-cornered conversation was a segment of life in action. Finally he held up his hand for silence, picked up his brush and in a couple of minutes had produced a beautiful line and tone sketch of Marta. She was delighted. I was surprised at how much of her he had caught with so few strokes.

While the sketch was drying we drank tea and talked. I told him we were going to visit Mikami, the print-maker. He advised me against it. The old man was failing rapidly. His daughter was caring for him and her husband, who had been one of his pupils, was running the studio. If he knew I was in the house the old man would insist on entertaining me and he had all too little strength. If I wanted to write him a note, Taisei would see that it was delivered. He brought me paper and a brush and a seal and nodded a qualified approval of my calligraphy. Then he rolled up Marta's picture, put it in a cardboard tube and presented it to her with his compliments.

As we made our farewells, he grinned at me and said: 'You always had a good eye, my friend. It seems to get better every time we meet.' It was not quite the compliment it sounds in English. Had Marta been my wife, he would never have made so frivolous a comment. But a mistress, a girlfriend? These belonged to the floating world. They were a possession, a badge of male honour, a matter of envy if you were lucky, of contempt if your woman made a fool of you.

The pottery was some distance away so we walked briskly, watching the village life unfold before us. It was a tiny, rural enclave in a huge industrialised area but, like so many such places in modern Japan, it seemed to preserve a resolute attachment to a more rustic way of life. Behind the line of stores there were still rice fields and vegetable plots, hand farmed by family groups. There were crafts people, weavers of straw and workers in wood and metal, repair shops for automobiles and machinery. The big city was here, too, an inescapable octopus whose tentacles encircled the banks, the local insurers, the wholesale suppliers; and even the bond sellers, men and women who peddled the big mutual funds and the stocks in new enterprises that the bankers wanted to get off the ground with the minimum of risk.

The pottery was a long, low building set back from the street with finished wares displayed in front and, behind, the ovens and the claypits which the family had owned for more than two hundred years. As we came near I explained to Marta that this was a place where I always bought something. The business was old, respected, but still marginal for so large a family group. They would press a token gift upon us, but we should buy first. Their goods were of fine quality. I sent them as Christmas presents to family and friends. They would pack and insure and send all over the world.

Marta pressed my hand and said with gentle mockery: 'Why do you have to appoint yourself a custodian of everyone's interests?'

73

'Do I do that?'

'Yes, you do. Even mine. When we came together last night I wasn't just a consenting party. I wanted you. I was stumbling around trying to get to you, tripping over all my past on the way, but I wanted you at all costs. You think because you've broken through the language barriers you've breached all the others too. Let go, Gil! Let me be responsible for me. Let them be responsible for themselves. Enjoy for a change. Your father did. That was what my mother loved about him, she told me so over and over. "This man," she said, "has joy in him. If he comes, if he goes, if he stays, I don't care. He carries joy!" '

'And what do I carry?'

'Other people's burdens, I think.'

'Obviously a very bad habit. I'll have to change my ways. Let's go meet my friends.'

It was a happy, hugger-mugger kind of reunion, with much bowing and smiling and inquiries about everyone's health and well-being. Then, for Marta's benefit, we took the full tour: the claypits, the ovens, the workshops, the drying racks, the paint rooms where the glazes were applied and, finally, into the store itself, where the wares were displayed for sale.

Marta, I discovered, had an eye for quality and some knowledge of the craft itself. She asked me to explain that in her student days she had worked as an apprentice decorator at the Nymphenberg porcelain works near Munich. Immediately a bond was established and she embarked on a spending spree that made my eyes pop. My own purchases were more modest, a couple of sets of sake cups for my sons, a fine bowl for my daughter.

Since credit cards are not common currency in rural Japan, I paid in cash, while Marta offered Deutschmark travellers' cheques. This involved much frantic figuring and a telephone call to the local bank to establish a rate.

Then came the long business of writing address labels and Customs declarations to be fixed to each separate package.

Marta was perched awkwardly on a stool in front of a bench. Her handbag was open beside her. Spread in front of her were a book of travellers' cheques, an address book, a holder for visiting cards and a small notebook with perforated pages. I offered to help with the paperwork but, no, it would be quicker and easier if she did it herself. She waved me away and the gesture sent the notebook flying to the

74

floor. As I bent to retrieve it, I noticed that a card had slipped out from between the pages and was lying half a pace away from the book itself. It was a rectangle of plain white pasteboard, the size of a business card. One side was blank. The other carried a two-line message written in English: 'Leave Vannikov arrangements to me. Will pick you up 1500 hours. You will be back in time for dinner date. M.'

On pure impulse I slipped the card into my pocket and laid the notebook on the bench in front of Marta. She thanked me absently and went on transcribing addresses on to despatch labels. I wandered round the room fingering the merchandise. I thought it strange that nothing was broken – because the roof had just fallen in on top of me.

Five

Once upon a time, for my own amusement, I wrote a pompous little parody on the talents essential to a good negotiator. Among them I listed a smiling countenance and an unshakeable composure. Then I went on to qualify the terms. The composure must not be the white-knuckled restraint that betrays fear or anger: the fear denotes a victim, the anger an enemy. It must not be the hard-eyed wariness of the professional gambler, counting the odds in his head, wondering always if the cards are marked. That immediately makes him an adversary. The composure that is needed is an attitude of total relaxation which says, more eloquently than words: 'My friends, we seek truth, not contention. We seek justice, not partisan advantage. We understand your difficulties. We are prepared to be patient.' That is why the smile is important, even critical. It must be open and agreeable. It cannot be condescending, evasive, contemptuous, vacant, servile, or twisted as if you have just sucked on a very sour lemon.

On the other hand the smile is not only what you put on your face, but what the viewer reads into it. And that is where the skill comes in. You cannot work out the right smile by numbers, or by time and motion studies. You have to reason yourself into it; and the simplest reason is generally the best one: you look better if your mouth turns up at the corners than if it is dragged down into a permanent scowl.

As I walked with Marta from the pottery to the rustic restaurant where we were to have lunch, I needed all my composure and all my muscular control to keep the smile on my face. Marta was delighted with her morning. Her portrait would frame beautifully. The glazes on the stoneware she had bought were almost miraculous. And the intimacy of it all! She could not understand a word of Japanese, but because of me – only because of me – she seemed to absorb the meaning by osmosis.

At the restaurant she was still riding high on a rush of adrenalin. I had to explain every dish on the menu – fortunately there were not very many – describe the ingredients, how they were cooked, thus and thus, until I almost gagged at the thought of eating. To this day I cannot remember one dish from that meal. The whole day had a curse on it now. As for the night, I could not bear to think about it. I had no idea how I was going to get through it without shame or disaster.

I was suddenly reminded of Tanaka's drunken warning about the fox-woman, who looked like a beautiful maiden, but who brought death and disaster to any man who bedded with her. I recalled his sober report that Carl Leibig regarded Marta Boysen as the weakest link in his security chain, and Tanaka's own refusal to let me employ her on his team. I remembered also that news of Vannikov's arrival had reached Tanaka and myself just before midday and that his faxed dossier had reached Leibig's desk just before my lunchtime call at twelve thirty. I needed a whole series of answers to questions which I did not yet know how to frame or dare to ask.

Of all the dangers which threatened the project the two greatest were premature disclosure and straight out sabotage. Premature disclosure would make headlines round the world and set the ghosts of the wartime atrocities in Europe and Asia wailing and walking abroad. Every one of us would be tagged with a political label and a whole plan of economic rescue could collapse into confusion and disaster. Sabotage was a constant possibility. Huge money was involved and intense commercial rivalries, right across the board. One could never discount the possibility of treachery or mere venality among any of the parties. That, obviously, had been the burden of Tanaka's warning to me and it was perfectly feasible that Leibig had retained Marta Boysen in order to insulate her within the group, instead of risking her as hostile witness outside it. All this was pure speculation, but there was no speculation about my own position. If Marta Boysen was tainted, I was tainted too, my reputation damaged beyond repair. No one would dare accuse me. No one would say a word of blame, but the small ship that carried the Langton house flag round the world – and carried it proudly, by God! – would be blown clean out of the water.

At that moment I must have been in a state of acute schizophrenia, because I was still smiling and making some kind of conversation about *haniwa* clay figures. Then Marta stopped me in mid sentence.

'Gil, what's the matter with you? Your mind's a million miles away.'

'I'm sorry. That wasn't very polite. To tell you the truth I was thinking about Vannikov.'

77

'Vannikov?' Her eyes were mirrors of limpid innocence. 'Who's he?'

'He's the Soviet facilitator for the Bangkok meeting. We heard about his appointment only yesterday. I wonder Carl Leibig didn't tell you?'

She gave a small embarrassed laugh. 'He was probably too busy with his disciplinary lecture to me. But tell me more about Vannikov. And why, suddenly, is he having lunch with you and me?'

'A trick of association, I guess. Vannikov collects paintings. He would have enjoyed this morning.'

'You know him then?' For the first time there was the faintest hint of uneasiness in her tone.

'Quite well. His father was one of the important nuclear planners in the Soviet Union. He himself was an economist turned publisher, but he was always well placed within the establishment. He and I did some business together. As a matter of fact one of the last publications we did was a book on the Chernobyl disaster. You told me, I think, that you went in just afterwards with a team from the FAO.'

'That's right. We were trying to assess radiation damage to essential agricultural products. Tell me, is this Vannikov a pleasant man?'

'Very. You'll meet him anyway. He arrives in Tokyo on Monday. On Wednesday and Thursday we go out to Leibig's place at Nara for a shakedown discussion before Bangkok.'

'I hadn't heard.' Suddenly she was irritated. 'Carl Leibig isn't very good at communication.'

I tried to shrug off the complaint. 'He's frayed, like everyone else. This is a big event. There's a lot of work behind it, and a lot of good to come if it succeeds. He told me himself he was feeling edgy.'

'Did he say anything about me?'

'No. Why should he?'

'No reason, I suppose.'

The little white card was burning a hole in my pocket. I wanted to slap it on the table in front of her and challenge her to explain it; but that would buy me nothing but more deception. My father was a devoted reader of Browning and he had a whole anthology of quotations which he would trot out at a flip of a hat brim. One of them popped into my head at that moment. It was from 'My Last Duchess':

Oh Sir, she smiled no doubt, when e'er I passed her;
But who passed without much the same smile?

Hard on the heels of that one came a very sour thought. How could I face another night of lovemaking, of Judas kisses and couplings driven by anger instead of love? Then the chirping cricket-voice spoke again in my head, this time with an inspiration. The lady did not understand Japanese. I could say whatever I liked and it would sound like chatter from outer space. I made an instant little drama.

'My God! I'd clean forgotten. My sales people had a big meeting last night with important clients. I promised to phone to see how it went off. Excuse me. I shan't be more than five minutes.'

There was a phone near the cashier's desk. I used it to call Yukio Tanizaki at his apartment in Tokyo. Fortunately he was at home, nursing a hangover from a night on the town with a group of booksellers from Kyushu. I told him what I wanted. He promised to attend to it immediately. He was rather amused by the notion. In the floating world which he frequented on the expense sheet, amorous intrigue is the spice of life. Good fellows have to stick together, because sooner or later everyone gets caught in the Venus flytrap.

We took our time walking back to the hotel. We turned into a narrow alley where, years before, I had discovered a fusty-looking bookshop, run by an ancient gnome-like scholar who dealt in antiquarian materials. We exchanged bows and courtesies. I explained that Professor Marta Boysen was a distinquished scholar from Germany. We browsed for twenty minutes and then he came up with a set of early illustrations of German officers training Japanese troops in cavalry and artillery manoeuvres. I pointed out to Marta the connection with Haushofer's early history. I suggested it might make a diplomatic gift for Carl Leibig, or an interesting exhibit when she was called upon to speak in conference. She thanked me for the thought and then added an astringent little postscript.

'You never stop, do you, Gil? You're always one move ahead of the game.' Again there was that faint tone of unease and challenge.

I tried to placate her with a shrug and a grin. 'It only looks like that. Take yourself as an example. In your own profession, in your own country, you control the situation, because you're at home in the idiom. Here, you're disadvantaged. It's like playing unfamiliar music with a new conductor, whose tempi you don't know, whose language you don't understand. I look clever only because I've read the score, and I've worked with the conductor. I can anticipate his beat and understand what he's asking me to do. That, of course, has its own problems. It's very easy to become over confident and careless.'

'I can't imagine your ever getting careless. Even when you seem most relaxed, I can hear the little gears clicking inside your head.'

The tension was rising in her. She was spoiling for a quarrel. I was old enough and versed enough in women's ways to sidle away from it. 'Japanese girls say: man who think too much, no good in bed.'

She gave a small, strained laugh. 'There was nothing wrong with your performance last night; but I'm not so sure of you today. Or am I missing something?'

The little gnome finished wrapping the package and presented it to Marta. I paid. We thanked him and left. As we were turning into the grounds of the hotel Marta repeated the question.

'Am I missing something, Gil? Is anything wrong?'

'Nothing that I know of, but you sound a bit edgy yourself. Why don't you take a nap or sit in the garden and watch the carp? We've had a big morning. No one can absorb too many impressions at once. You have to give yourself space and time to let them sink in.'

Instantly she was on the attack. 'There you go again! I know you mean to be kind, but you are not responsible for me. I can arrange my own life, thank you.'

I accepted the snub in silence. For my purposes it could not have been more timely or useful. As we entered the hotel, I was presented with a faxed message from Tanizaki. It was in English. I scanned it in silence, and handed it to Marta.

Good news and bad news. The president of the Kyushu group has made a substantial offer for full and exclusive distribution rights to our list in their province. The offer is well within parameters agreed in the Board memorandum signed by you and Mr Tanaka. I have accepted, subject to contract details. Bad news is that said president is spending the weekend in Tokyo and desires social contacts with you to establish personal relations. Of course you can still decline, but I advise against it. I have committed you to a nine o'clock rendezvous at Fuji Club tonight and to Sunday golf at your club where I have booked eleven o'clock tee-off time. Deeply regret this intrusion, but it has taken us two years to develop this Kyushu contract. Your readiness to interrupt private weekend would be gracious compliment to new and important client.

Marta handed the paper back to me. She was obviously put out, but she made no fuss. 'You have to go, of course.'

80

'I'm afraid so. There's no such thing as a sacred weekend in Japanese business. Also, my people have big commissions riding on the deal. I can't let them down.'

'When do you want to leave?'

'As soon as we can, before the afternoon traffic gets too heavy.'

'Give me ten minutes and I'll be ready for the road.'

'I'm truly sorry.'

'Don't be.' She kissed me lightly and headed for the bathroom. 'What we had was wonderful. I can't thank you enough.'

As soon as I heard the water running I opened her handbag and slipped the white card back into her notebook. It was the last act of a sordid little drama. It absolved me, for the moment at least, from any compulsion to judge or intervene. I could not accuse Marta to our colleagues, because I had nothing to depose against her. I could not confront her without revealing myself as a sad Paul Pry fumbling through a woman's handbag. Whatever the secret, small or large, behind the handwritten message, I was not the only one who knew that it existed. The truth might be trivial. It might be highly sinister. In that case, whatever inquiries had to be made, I would have to make them. Whatever action had to be taken, I would have to devise it. For whatever followed, farce, intrigue or tragedy, I would be responsible. All I could think of for the moment, however, was getting the hell out of that bedroom and on the road to Tokyo.

Marta was very tense when we left the hotel but, as the highway opened up before us, she relaxed and lapsed into sleep, her head pillowed on my shoulder. She woke as we were crawling the last half-mile to the Okura. She gave a long, relaxed yawn and said: 'That was a nice sleep. A happy dream, too.'

'I hope I was in it.'

'Yes. You were the ogre who was chasing me. The prince who rescued me was someone else.'

'That's a hell of a note to end our weekend.'

'It's ended for me. For you, it's only beginning. The Fuji Club, golf tomorrow . . .'

'Have you been to the Fuji Club?'

'Nobody's invited me yet.'

'And they're not likely to. It's all house girls and outsiders are definitely unwelcome. For me, it's going to be a late and expensive night, and my golf is going to be shot to hell in the morning. How is Monday for you? We could have dinner perhaps?'

'Monday? No, that's out. I'm sorry, I have a date.'

'What sort of date?'

'The usual, a man.'

'Do you mind telling me his name?'

'Not at all. He's a friend from my Roman days, Max Wylie. He used to work at the US Embassy. Now he's attached here in Tokyo. I cabled to tell him I was coming. He invited me to dinner.'

'Well, at least he's respectable competition.'

'Very respectable. Just about your age, good-looking, well-dressed. Sings baritone like my father.'

'And he's an Olympic athlete in bed.'

'I wouldn't know. We've never slept together. He has a young wife and he dotes on her.'

'What does he do in the Embassy?'

'I think he's in the Consular section. Anything else you'd like to know?'

'No, that about covers it. I'm sorry for the foul-up. I'll make it up to you, if not here, then in Bangkok. The rest of this week is going to be hectic for all of us.'

'It was hectic in the country, too, but much more fun. I'm sorry if I was snappish. We did have a big night. And I still love you, *schatzi*.'

'I love you, too, Marta Boysen.'

We sealed the declaration with a long Judas kiss. I left her in the care of the doorman at the Okura and drove back to my own place with the taste of ashes in my mouth. I rang Tanizaki to thank him for his comradely service and found he had done more than duty demanded.

'About tonight, Gil-san. I wasn't sure. I signed you in to the Fuji Club. They've booked Naomi and she will take calls for you. If you don't show by eleven, it costs you two hours of her time. Tomorrow's golf booking is real, just in case anyone's checking up on you. You're listed for a foursome with Mr Taoka of Merrill Lynch, Mr Takemato of Daikyo and Mr Philip Fromkess of the American Embassy. If you want to cancel, of course, it can be done; but you pay for the round.'

'No. I'll play. Thank you, Yukio. You've done me a big service.'

'Small service for a good friend. I hope the problem is not serious.'

'Not too serious, Yukio. Nice woman, but I'm getting lazy. I don't like hard work.'

82

'Women are always hard work, Gil-san, even when you're paying them to do the work for you. But there is also good news. We did get the Kyushu contract.'

'Congratulations!'

'Thank you. I get the hangover. You just pay the bill. Now, please, I am going to take a bath and a massage and sleep ten hours.'

It sounded like a wise prescription for me, too. There was no way in the world I was going to face a raucous evening under the strobe lights of the Fuji Club. Nobody would miss me, least of all Naomi, to whose tender if costly care we recommended all our out-of-town playboys. She amused them, kept them out of trouble, did not pad the cheques too much, and put them in a taxi afterwards to make sure they were not rolled on the way back to their lodgings. The next day, by some labyrinthine Yakuza network, the bill was delivered to our office. Tanizaki checked it. Oshima passed the payment, and a safe and necessary social facility was kept open for the use of Polyglot Press and its valued clients.

The golf date was a different matter. We paid a mint of money for corporate membership and my senior executives had most of the fun. The thought of a few hours in the open air was very seductive. I felt as though I had spent the last days trapped in a timewarp of salon politics and boudoir intrigue – a state of mind which in Japan can grow quickly into an obsession unless you jerk yourself out of it. Again, it is the old problem: nothing is quite what it seems, the words never mean what they say. Before very long you find yourself hedging your own life with the same evasions.

Marta had lied to me by disclaiming any knowledge of Vannikov. I had lied, just as blatantly, by my subterfuge with Tanizaki. Whether she was lying about her embassy friend, Max Wylie, was still subject to proof. The name, Max, certainly matched the initial with which the card had been signed, but the text itself seemed to indicate an existing connection between the writer and Vannikov. If not, how did he know of Vannikov's arrival, and what was his interest anyway?

The logic of the situation was, to say the least, highly suggestive. In political terms, a German-Japanese plan to bail out the Soviets was a high-priority US Intelligence matter. In financial and commercial terms it was a critical one. With the Gulf situation deteriorating more and more quickly towards war, the strategic considerations were of enormous importance. In any conflict in the Gulf, America had to rely on Soviet co-operation and at least a limited military involvement. The price was already offered: massive funding for reconstruction and access to high technology. But after the mess in Afghanistan, it would be hard to sell the people another foreign war; so if there were other funds on offer, without the price tag of armed intervention, then the American position would be drastically weakened.

And where did Professor Marta Boysen fit into that very threatening scenario? In a strange fashion, her role was similar to that of old Haushofer himself. She was the repository, the codifier, the interpreter in modern terms, of his geopolitical ideas. Those ideas could be used by either side. The Americans could use them as a powerful piece of propaganda against the formation of a new Berlin/Tokyo axis. The Germans and the Japanese could use them in exactly the opposite sense. Geography made history; Germany, Russia and Japan made a natural continuum with the landmass of Eurasia.

And if you ask why Gilbert Anselm Langton, publisher, professional polyglot and paid negotiator, should concern himself with these high matters, then you should know that in my own country I have been used sometimes as a point of reference in Intelligence affairs. That, precisely, was the nub of my position, the danger about which Tanaka had warned me.

In fact, and in conscience, too, I was exactly what I was paid to be: an honest broker, an even-handed interpreter of conflicting views, a mediator of compromise settlements. In fact, also, I could quickly be painted in different colours: a venal servant, a false advocate, a double agent of commercial interests or of foreign powers. My company functioned around the world in a series of partnerships with local investors. Even my talents as a polyglot made me suspect, because I dealt directly with principals without having to invoke the aid of government agencies or professional fixers. So, in the very nature of things, I was vulnerable. My brief bedding with Marta Boysen had made me more vulnerable yet.

It was still early to go to sleep. I took myself out for a stroll and finished the evening in a small bar off the Ginza, where I drank beer and ate sushi and exchanged gossip with a pair of transvestites who dropped in for a snack. They were very pretty boys and their clothes were expensive. Business was slow, they said; but it always was at this hour. So many salary-men went home to their families at the weekend. If I were interested there was a pleasant love-hotel just round the next

84

corner. I thanked them for the offer. I told them I was just filling in time before a late date. They understood perfectly. They paid me a compliment on my Japanese. They gave me a card, in case I needed their services at any time. I thanked them and left. Half way home I tore up the card and threw the scraps in a trash bin. Things like that can be a trap for the unwary. You never know who may find them. And long after the event, how do you explain them: 'There's this little sushi place. I just dropped in for a beer and a snack . . .' And so to bed, as Sam Pepys used to say. I hoped I would not have nightmares.

Sunday dawned cool and clear. My driver took me out to the golf course so that, if I had drinks after the game, I would not be arrested on the way home. The fairways and the greens were beautifully manicured. The little caddy-girls were amiable if not beautiful. The long procession of players was managed like a military operation.

Let me tell you the truth and shame the devil. I am not a good golfer. In Japan I play for business; elsewhere I play for pleasure. I have a hard won handicap of sixteen; but my performance is patchy and, if you are looking to win money in a foursome match, you should never depend on Gilbert Anselm Langton.

My only merit, which all my friends acknowledge, is that I am a good-tempered loser and modest about my occasional runs of good luck. The cynics, of course, point out that I have much to be modest about and that there is no profit in anger for a man with a poor short game and an incurable tendency to shank with a long iron.

However, this was one of my better days. We drew straws for partners. Fromkess and I were matched against the two Japanese, who were handicapped at ten and twelve. They spoke good English and played in that do-it-by-the-numbers, head-down, steady-the-stance style created by local professionals. We were taller, rangier and much less controlled. Nevertheless we hit form, squared the outward nine and finished two holes up in the home stretch. In the bar afterwards we bought the drinks and then, while our partners drifted off to talk business with their peers, Fromkess and I sat quietly in a corner and talked about the situation in the Gulf. He was pessimistic. He thought there was a better than even chance of war.

'We've got a quarter of a million troops there, Gil, and another hundred and twenty thousand on the way. Hussein is reinforcing all his border troops in Kuwait. There's no way you can hold a stalemate like that, in desert conditions, in a Muslim country. I think we can win the war, but we'll have a hell of a job winning the peace. And the way the Israelis are behaving – that bloody massacre at the mosque! I'm a Jew, Gil. I've got cousins and an uncle in Israel; but my gut turns over when I see what's going on. From all I hear, you're betting heavily on the red numbers . . .'

'What exactly do you hear, Phil?'

'That you've been hired to mediate economic discussions between the Germans, the Japanese and the Russians.'

'And who gave you that piece of news?'

'A couple of our spooks – pardon me, our Intelligence analysts – were discussing it. Nothing derogatory, of course, nothing hostile. I got the impression they'd like to have you on our side.'

'I'm not quite sure what your side is, Phil.'

His face clouded and he pursed his lips in distaste. 'At this moment I'm not so sure either. Let's just say I serve the Administration as best I can. I don't agree with all its policies.'

'Do you know a guy at the embassy named Max Wylie? I believe he works in the Consular section.'

'Sure, I know Max. Came here from Rome about twelve months ago. What's your interest in him?'

'None. A woman I know was talking about him yesterday. Apparently she knew him in Rome. That's it. Just small talk.'

'An odd coincidence though.'

'Why so?'

'He was the one who brought up your name in the discussion. He said he'd like to meet you some time. I didn't mention that I knew you. He's a pretty pushy guy, one of the good ole boys, a real piss-and-vinegar patriot.'

'He sounds a real pain in the arse.'

'He is, but he's got a very pretty wife – the second or third, I'm not sure which.'

'How much clout does he have?'

'How do you ever know with a spook? I have to say I get very tired of them, Gil. They tramp over everything with treacle on their boots. But what the hell! You played good golf today, maestro. It's my pleasure to buy you another Scotch . . .'

I arrived back in Tokyo mellow and relaxed. I talked with my daughter in Australia and called one son in London. The other in New York was, presumably, in bed and sleeping. I read the messages that had been laid on my desk. In the Seiyo, messages were never pushed under a door, but delivered ceremoniously even in an empty room. There was a note from Marta, sent by messenger: 'Thanks for the night, the day, the portrait, the book, and you. I called my mother. She sends her love. Mine comes with it. Marta.'

There was another, more cryptic, with a Kyoto telephone number. 'Call me. Tanaka.'

I knew in my bones what he was going to ask me: How was your weekend? How was the lady? Did you learn anything useful? I knew with equal certainty that I was not yet ready to answer. So I called the operator and asked her to hold all phone calls and send a masseuse to my room. She arrived ten minutes later, a square, chunky, unsmiling, Korean matron, with washboard hands and strength enough to subdue a welterweight. She bowed a silent greeting. She handed me her workslip, which I signed. I stretched myself out on the bed. She rubbed, kneaded, stretched and pummelled me for fifty minutes and then bowed herself out, leaving me limp as a rag doll, with only a towel covering my nakedness. Fifteen minutes later I had recovered enough to call Tanaka in Kyoto. His opening gambit was a series of bald statements.

'The Russian peace initiatives in Iraq have broken down. The Germans have interrupted talks on trade and tariffs with the rest of the European Community. They want them deferred. Arab newspapers are now peddling the idea of a swift strike and a war that could be ended before the feast of Ramadan in March. All the signs are bad, Gil. A war can only exacerbate the needs and problems of the Soviets. I talked to their Ambassador a couple of hours ago. He is most anxious that our conference should succeed, especially because the Americans and the rest of the Europeans want to defer decisions on aid until the German position is clarified. You see how it works?'

'Very clearly. What news on Vannikov?'

'He arrives tomorrow as planned. We start with him on Tuesday: luncheon at the embassy, Leibig, you and me. I'll pick you up at your office at twelve fifteen. We should arrive and leave together.'

'I've made a note of it.'

Then, just when I thought I had escaped, the questions began. 'How was your weekend?'

'We only had part of it. I played golf on Sunday.'

'How was the lady?'

'No comment.'

'Did you learn anything useful?'

'Useful, no. Disturbing, yes.'

'Tell me.'

I gave him a curt and colourless narration to which he listened in silence. Then he asked: 'Have you told Leibig about this?'

'No.'

'Why not?'

'We are talking only about suspicion. I share it with you, because there is friendship and duty between us. *Wakatte kudasai* – understand please! Don't push me any further. Not yet.'

'I am not prepared to risk this whole enterprise on a woman – any woman!'

'Nor am I.'

'Have you not already done so?'

This was the old Kenji, he of the swift anger and the sudden lethal lunge. Instantly I braced for the close encounter.

'Kenji, you're out of line! You asked me in. You can tell me to withdraw at any moment. There'll be no backlash, no hard feelings. I respect your privacy. You respect mine. I do not require that you confide everything to me, only what touches our work together; but you have not been wholly open with me.'

'I don't know what you're talking about.'

'If you like, I can give you a shopping list of things you should have told me but didn't. However, try this one. You're under siege from the *keiretsu* because it is known that you are a sick man.'

There was a long silence out of which a flat toneless voice asked. 'Where did you hear that?'

'It doesn't matter. It is known. It is talked. You should not suffer in silence, or fight alone. Whatever the others may say, I am not your tame *gaijin*; I am your friend. In this deal I am also the paid guardian of your interests. You have to trust me or fire me. For the moment let me deal with Marta Boysen. I promise to keep you informed. If a situation arises that I can't handle I'll give you fair warning. Agreed?'

'That doesn't dispose of Carl Leibig. His interests are ours. He cannot be left in the dark.'

'Then leave it to me to find a formula that alerts him without damaging Marta Boysen before she has been proven guilty. Leave it to me to make my own investigation of what she's doing or not doing.'

'We have to know before we begin our shakedown talks in Nara, or she has to be gone before then.'

'That gives me only Monday and Tuesday.'

'It's all we can afford.'

'I'll do my best.'

'One more question, Gil. If it comes to a choice of loyalties in this matter . . .'

'There is none. There can be none. I told you, it was a very short weekend.'

And there we left it. I climbed into bed with a new courtroom thriller which my son had just sent me from New York. My attention waned quickly and I found myself drifting off into a half-world of memory.

We were in Spain that year, my father and I, hitch-hiking or riding on public transport while I brushed up on the fine points and the vulgarities of the language, and he divided his time between correcting my accent, drenching me with history, and instructing me in the manners of woman-hunting on the Iberian peninsula.

We were drinking in a bodega near Navarra, right in the heart of the Basque country, because he had insisted I break my brains on the Basque language, which is still one of those I have never wholly mastered. My father was emphatic in his belief that Basques came from somewhere in the Caucasus during the bronze age, so emphatic indeed that if I had had a bronze axe I might have beaten him on the head with it.

The only thing that stopped the flow of his eloquence was a quarrel at the next table, where two youngish couples were drinking up a storm in local brandy. The quarrel was about a supposed insult offered to one of the women. Blows were exchanged. Glasses were smashed. One of the men pulled a fisherman's knife from his belt. With a speed and a strength I could not believe, my father felled him with a back-handed blow to the side of his jaw, and stamped his foot on the knife. The fellow was still prone on the floor when, in his gentlest and courtliest Spanish, with a Navarrese accent that he summoned up from no place, my father apologised for interfering. Every man had the right to settle his own quarrel, but this one was getting a little out of hand and one or other of the ladies might have been hurt. He hoped he had not hurt the gentleman too much. He hauled him to his feet, still groggy. He handed him back the knife, hilt first, put money on the table to pay the score, and presented me to the gathering as 'my son, an Oxford scholar, here to study your language, Eskuera, the most ancient language in Europe.' He walked me out of the place to a round of applause, then hurried me away form the neighbourhood as fast as we could run. Later, in a more sedate drinking place, he read me his homily.

'All that happened because some country oaf was insisting on *pundonor*, the point of honour. He'd have killed for it and gone to prison for life. Crazy!'

When I reminded him that he, too, could have been killed for meddling, he simply grinned and raised his glass in a toast.

'First rule of existence, my boy: learn the arts of survival, most of which involve combat in one form or another, against man, animal or the elements. Second rule, which old Cicero wrote most elegantly: "Expediency and honour never conflict." '

I could hear myself remonstrating that he did not believe that, could not possibly believe it.

'Think back, my boy. I apologised to a bully. I hammed up a speech that would have had me hissed off any amateur stage, and I ran like hell so we wouldn't get beaten up in an alley. That's expediency! The honour resides in the fact that I'm ready to admit it. Now, back to the language. What is the nominative plural of *harri*, a stone . . ?'

By the time we got to that part, I was long over the border into dreamtime, but I slept as soundly as I had on that faraway night when the old man and I curled up in a hayloft and woke at cock-crow to hit the gypsy road again.

The morning papers were delivered with my breakfast tray. Every one of them confirmed what Tanaka had told me: the Gulf was on the brink of war; Europe was in disarray over trade policies and farm subsidies; Gorbachev was still grandstanding his way round Europe trying to drum up ready-cash aid, while the Union was breaking up and troops were being called in to quell insurrection in the southern provinces.

In America the Republicans were beating the war drums, the Democrats were recalling Vietnam, the military were underscoring the obvious: inaction corrupts fighting men, war machines will not work unless they are used regularly.

In Japan there were rumblings of protest against any form of military intervention. The Pakistanis had at least the elements of an atom bomb. And China, the giant, was ominously silent.

My own big, empty country was in dire straits, with three years'

90

wool-clip in store, no market for her grain and company after company sliding into bankruptcy because of profligate spending of borrowed money and usurious interest rates.

All in all it was not the happiest of seasons. I had a thought, however, that I might be able to offer a constructive idea to our people, if they cared to study the opportunities offered by the Tanaka/Leibig plan. We had food running out of our ears. We were shooting sheep. The mice were nibbling at the wheat in the silos. If credits could be provided to ship the stuff to Russia, we might jump-start a programme that would leave the Americans and the Europeans gasping. Laszlo had the same thought, and the clout, if not the money, to sell it to our politicians and bureaucrats. I was, unfortunately, regarded as an expatriate. My strongest influence was abroad. At least it was worth a try. The Bangkok conference was no longer a diplomatic secret. I called the Australian Embassy and asked for an urgent meeting with the Ambassador. He was surprised, but co-operative. He would see me at noon.

At nine-thirty, I presented myself unannounced at Carl Leibig's office, having first established that he was in but not available. Although he was obviously irritated, he had no option but to receive me. His assistant Franz hovered in the background. I had to ask that he absent himself. The business under discussion was for principals only. Refreshed after a good night's sleep and a communion with my nearest ancestor, I had worked out a crabwise approach to the problem of Marta Boysen. The logic was simple, old-fashioned medicine: you tap the patient's knee to make sure his reflexes are working; you make him stick out his tongue, which embarrasses him; then you ask him all sorts of questions about his bowel movements, his sexual habits, his water-works. After that you have him totally at your mercy.

First, I made an apology for coming unannounced. Then I explained it. 'Certain matters came up during the weekend. I spoke with Tanaka late on Sunday night. He thought it was imperative that you and I confer. Do you mind if I ask some questions, just to set the ball rolling?'

'Please.' It was a reluctant concession.

'Did you know I spent part of the weekend with Marta Boysen?'

'I didn't know.' A faint smile twitched at his tight lips. 'I guessed it might happen sooner or later. I trust you had a pleasant time?'

'Pleasant enough, yes. Let's say it helped to define our future roles as co-operative business colleagues.'

'I'm glad to hear that.'

'Next question. It had been your declared intention to fire Marta. Why did you change your mind?'

'She made a very gracious apology for her indiscretion at the meeting. I felt she deserved a second chance.'

'According to Tanaka you considered her a possible security risk. Have you changed your mind?'

'No. I happen to think that, for the moment, she is safer inside our net than outside it.'

'Did you tell her about Vannikov's appointment or arrival?'

'No, I did not; because at the time of our meeting I did not know about them. Why do you ask?'

'Please, bear with me a moment. Did she ever tell you that she had an American friend in Tokyo, an official at the Embassy?'

'Now that you mention it, yes. It came up quite casually. I had offered to introduce her to some German friends who would entertain her during her stay in Tokyo.'

'How exactly, why exactly, did you see her as a security risk to the project?'

He hesitated for a moment, then excused himself and went into the outer office. A few moments later he was back with a letter in his hand. He did not offer to demonstrate it to me, but explained: 'This is the letter of recommendation written to me by the curator of the Haushofer archives. It is full of praise for Marta Boysen and her academic qualifications. Then he says, "She is an acute and accurate observer of the economic and political scene and has on occasion provided valuable information and advice to certain senior ministers in Bonn." '

'In other words she supplied Intelligence information?'

'It would seem so.'

'But surely that would be an added recommendation?'

'For some, yes. For me, no. Intelligence is a trade which often leaves dirty marks on men and women. It is also very hard to escape from old associates. Besides I have a healthy mistrust of governments, all governments. Even in the old days we lived under our own law.'

'But you still hired Marta Boysen. What decided you?'

'She had a unique combination of sound historical research and a wide background in strategic economics.'

'Did you, do you now, have any grounds for suspicion that she might be betraying business confidences?'

'No.'

92

'But you gave the opposite impression to Tanaka.'

'What I told him was that she was the weakest link in our security chain. If I conveyed more it was because my anger betrayed me into overstatement. Now perhaps you will tell me the reason for this interrogation?'

'It's a piece of information which you and I have to assess. I played golf on Sunday with a friend from the American embassy. I discovered three things: our project is under discussion, Vannikov's arrival is known, and Marta Boysen's friend is a spook, CIA probably.'

'Have you told her?'

'No.'

'What does Tanaka say?'

'He wanted you to be told. I've done that. He wants Marta Boysen cleared or fired in forty eight hours, before we go into session in Nara.'

'And you, Gil? What do you recommend?'

'I'm a tainted witness, Carl. There's a very old connection between us. My father and her mother were lovers. Marta and I are, well, I'm not quite sure what we are at this moment.'

'And you're not quite sure what she is either?'

He said it with surprising gentleness and no hint at all of malice or triumph. He did not wait for an answer. It was written all over my face. Instead he had another question.

'Is there anything you haven't told us, that you think we should know? I know bedroom dramas are embarrassing to describe. I've had more than a few myself.'

'This didn't happen in the bedroom, Carl, it just slammed the door. However, before I say anything, I have to insist that as a piece of evidence it's quite inconclusive.'

'We're not in court, Gil. The rules of evidence don't apply. Tell me what's on your mind.'

I told him about the card, the message signed 'M' and the fact that Marta had denied any previous knowledge of Vannikov. I told him why I had not pressed the question. He nodded absently and leaned back in his chair, closing his eyes. He looked suddenly a great deal older than his years. Finally, he opened his eyes again and faced me across the desk. He said deliberately: 'Marta Boysen is contracted to me. It is my responsibility to deal with what you have told me. I shall consult with Tanaka, of course, but the decision is mine. I know these disclosures have been painful and embarrassing for you. From this moment I want you to step right back. Observe all the social courtesies with Marta Boysen but for the rest, do nothing, say nothing. The issue is out of your hands. I'm sure Tanaka will endorse what I am saying.'

'That's all?'

'That's all. It's finished, done. You have much more important things to occupy you. I hope one day to express my thanks more eloquently.'

As an afterthought, I told him of my appointment with the ambassador. He nodded approval. His mind was obviously on other things. Mine was suddenly invaded by the dream-image of my father declaiming into his brandy the second rule of existence: 'Expediency and honour never conflict.' I hoped to God he was right, because at that moment I felt as though I'd been sawn down the middle by one of Leino's robotic butchers.

Six

Andrew Kealey, our Australian Ambassador to Japan, was one of the new breed: language-trained, culture-conditioned, committee-modified. I respected him. I liked him. I understood at least some of his problems as the representative of a small but vocal Pacific nation occupying a huge landmass, the envy of Asia with its teeming millions and diminishing physical resources.

He was doing well or badly, according to your point of view. Japanese capital was still flowing in. Our real estate was still being alienated; our coal and iron and timber were still being stripped out; golf courses were still being built to attract Japanese tourists; megacities were being planned to accommodate their aged and infirm; while our wheat farmers and pastoralists and tourist operators went down like dominoes, month after month. It was not his fault. Nobody seemed to understand that, finally, we had become one world. The only surprise was that we were not all brothers and sisters, but still tribal packs, preying on each other.

Kealey's welcome was warm. He asked whether I would mind having two or three of the staff in on our discussion. He confessed, with a certain ingenuous charm, that it would save time and paperwork, since they were the ones who would ultimately process my submissions. I told him that I was not making submissions, but offering suggestions from which I stood to profit not at all. However, by all means, wheel in the auditors.

There were three of them. The First Secretary, the Commercial Attaché and someone called Arnold whose surname and appointment seemed to lose themselves in the shifting air. It is a familiar phenomenon in diplomatic circles. You either insist on a repeat or you ignore the ploy altogether. Since I had nothing to sell, I chose to ignore it. My private guess was that Arnold – whoever, whatever – was a special category man like, for example, Max Wylie.

We talked about Australia first. We were in a hell of a mess. The international tariff agreements had broken down. Our farm products were priced out of the market by US and European subsidies. Our value-added industries could not compete against low-cost Asian labour. Since our frigates were helping to blockade the Gulf, the Iraqis were not paying for the wheat we had shipped and we certainly were not shipping any more. Australian citizens were being held hostage in Baghdad. We went through the whole litany of grief and came to the inevitable questions: where do we go from here, what are you offering us, Mr Langton?

'I'm offering nothing. I'm pointing to a window of opportunity. We have food in abundance. We want to sell it, raw, part-processed, fully processed. The Russians need it, because they do not have year-round production as we have, nor adequate means of conservation and distribution, which is what this enterprise is about. If the German/ Japanese consortium puts in the plants, if our own Pavel Laszlo gets to organise the distribution system, Australia can become a natural source of supply, Sydney to Vladivostok by sea, for example.'

We kicked that idea around the floor for a while and then Arnold Whoever made a sudden very aggressive entry into the talk.

'Why didn't you come to us with this idea in the first place?'

'Because it isn't my idea. It isn't my project. I come to you by indulgence of my principals. Besides, the overall cost is far beyond our national resources. This is exactly what I said it was, a window of opportunity. I can't climb through it for you.'

The Ambassador waved a calming hand over the troubled waters.

'We all understand that, Gil. I think Arnold is aware of the importance of your suggestion. Our problem is very clear. We're fighting a trade war about agricultural subsidies. We can't destroy our case by introducing subsidies ourselves. They'd ruin us!'

'We're damn near ruined anyway,' said the First Secretary. 'My family have been on the land since the year dot. Now they're all vassals and villeins of the banks.'

'There are still options.' The Commercial Attaché was suddenly there, bristling and combative. 'Government to government credits, barter deals, you can trade anything if you set your mind to it and skip a few pages in the book of rules. I'd like to follow this thought with my people in Canberra.'

'I have another thought, which I must express.' Arnold Whoever was

96

back again; milder now but, for that reason, more threatening. 'It's not a criticism, you understand, rather a question of clarification. You're an Australian citizen. You're an international publisher.'

'Who brings ten million a year net income into the Common-wealth.'

'Of course. So you'll understand we see a certain anomaly in your function as a paid mediator between three foreign corporations, which . . .'

'Which once were our enemies. That's the nub of the question, isn't it?'

'If you like to put it that way, yes.'

I looked around at the small audience. The First Secretary and the Commercial Attaché were studying the sunspots on the back of their hands. Arnold Whoever was doing his best to face me down. The Ambassador was hoping I would exercise my right of reply.

'I'm a free citizen who travels and works abroad. I have a talent which, like the talent of a musician, a painter, an inventor, I negotiate in a world market. When my own country has chosen to employ that talent I have offered it freely. But I think I hear familiar echoes in this room. Could I be right, Andy?'

'Echoes of what, Gil?'

'I'm sure you read the weekend press and your own Intelligence summaries. The Uruguay round of talks on tariffs and trade have broken down. Europe is split over farm subsidies. American farmers have lost their markets in the Middle East. So, Australia is carrying the can. We're committed to a pro-America line in foreign relations, but Washington is cutting our throats with subsidised foreign trade. They're compounding that by a not too subtle smear campaign against competitors. It's a short-sighted policy and our friend here seems to be aiding and abetting it. I leave you with a practical suggestion, Andy. Call your minister, have him talk to Sir Pavel Laszlo before he leaves for Bangkok at the weekend. He's a much more lively advocate than I am. Thank you for your time, and yours, gentlemen.'

I stood up to leave. Kealey pressed me to stay for a few moments. The staff filed out with polite murmurs and handshakes. Arnold Whoever was the last to go. His exit line was a classic.

'I'm sure you know there was nothing personal in my remarks, Mr Langton. It's just part of the dialectic, you know, the clash of contraries.'

I did not say anything. This was a good ole boy, Australian style, impervious to reason or experience. Andy Kealey held me back for a few final words.

'Your guess is right, Gil. We are collecting flak from the Yanks and we're tossing tin cans over their fence, too. They've got themselves into a hell of a mess: the Gulf, a European trade bloc in 1992, and still no enlightened policy for the Pacific rim. Your name is being bandied about in the present context, because you're painted as some kind of golden-tongued demagogue, leading the ungodly against the faithful. You have to understand it, Gil. Folk memory is long and vivid. We're a very insular lot, suspicious of all foreigners. But you're right. This is a window of opportunity for us. I'll try to keep it open. Take care now!'

It hit me as the Ambassador walked me out to my car. I had just heard, in Australian vernacular, a repeat of Kenji Tanaka's earthquake warning. Watch out! The earth plates are shifting. The pillars of the world are rocking. The roof beams are creaking. Any minute now they may fall in and bury you.

This was an experience for which all my father's love and counsel and companionship had not prepared me – the loneliness and hostility of the gypsy road. I was beginning to learn how poignantly he had experienced it, with what extraordinary love he had tried to protect me against it. And yet, and yet . . . Here I was, rich, respected, with work to do around the world, a talisman of language to walk me across every frontier and into most tribal enclaves. Yet suddenly I was a threat, a maker of alien magic.

Which recalled another fragment of our days among the Basques in Navarra, when my father retold the terrible tale of the witches of Labourd and the campaign of extermination waged against them by the magistrate Pierre de Lancre in the seventeenth century. Even today the country folk will tell you that the Basque women practise sorcery. It was Kenji Tanaka, a very civilised man, who warned me against the fox-women of Japan. And my own compatriot, a Down-Under pragmatist if ever there was one, had lapsed unconsciously into his own Celtic yesterdays, when he admitted that my talent for languages made me – how did he put it? – a golden-tongued demagogue leading the ungodly against the faithful.

I could not call it superstition or bigotry. I was conscious of certain mysterious elements in myself and in the talents I exercised. To this day I cannot tell you precisely how or why the trick of language works for

98

me. Of course, I am trained and drilled in all the logic of the process, all the rules and all the variables. But the final step into understanding does not work like that. It is as if I am standing, staring at a high blank wall and suddenly I know, with total conviction, that I can walk through the wall and that what is on the other side of it will be familiar to me.

There is another aspect of the phenomenon which still gives me the occasional shiver of apprehension. When we are speaking our own language among foreigners we assume that it is a cloak of invisibility, keeping us private from all viewers. As a young man – sadly it does not happen now – I have sat listening to gaggles of girls, Arab, Thai, Greek, Swiss, making bawdy talk about what I looked like, what I might look like without clothes, how I might perform in bed. I learned very quickly not to reveal too abruptly that I understood their talk. The cloak of invisibility is not a matador's cape. You do not make bravura passes with it, otherwise you are likely to be gored.

It was lunchtime when I got back to my office. I hoped to spend a quiet hour dealing with my own affairs. Instead, I was handed an urgent message: Tanaka and Leibig were lunching at the Bankers' Club. I should call Tanaka immediately. His response was relaxed and cordial.

'We are discussing the problem of the lady. Have you heard from her this morning?'

'No. I've just got back to the office. Have you made any decisions yet?'

'Carl proposes to call her in for a quiet chat. Your name will not be mentioned. We are both grateful for your frankness. We are hoping that there may be a quite reasonable explanation which will enable us to continue her services, in isolation from the crucial discussions. However, what is more important is that the Soviet ambassador called me just on lunchtime. Vannikov has arrived. He is resting for a few hours, but he wants you to call him about three and set a private meeting before the end of the day.'

'That's a surprise.'

'We were surprised, too. Then, on reflection, it seemed to make sense. It is his responsibility and yours to prepare the ground for the principals in the discussion.'

'Do you have any objections to our meeting?'

'None.'

'Tomorrow's luncheon at the Embassy?'

'Is confirmed.'

'Then I'll call Vannikov in an hour and suggest we meet for drinks or dinner tonight.'

'Call me at home after you've met.'

'If it's dinner it could be quite late.'

'At any hour. How did your meeting go with the Australians?'

'They have an obvious interest, and even more obvious financial problems. They did, however, tell me that there is overt opposition in Washington to our project and that I am being cited as a potential troublemaker.'

'I warned you this would happen, Gil.'

'I'm not worried.'

'Carl and I are concerned for you. We have decided on certain security precautions, both here and in Bangkok.'

'That's not necessary.'

'Don't argue, Gil. We're carrying heavy insurance on you. The policy requires we give you adequate protection. Good luck with Vannikov.'

The message from Vannikov troubled me. Tanaka's easy agreement to our meeting troubled me even more. I did not for one moment accept that the protocol was normal. The Vannikov I had known was an agreeable companion, but I had never seen him yield an inch of financial or psychological advantage. In the jealous ranks of the Soviet *apparat* he was more vulnerable than I to mistakes, misjudgments and the malice of colleagues.

Moreover, after my weekend episode with Marta I, too, was gun shy. There are always two versions of a private dialogue and each can be made to sound as improbable as the other. If Vannikov brought a witness, in the shape of his female assistant, I would have to bring one too. I could not use Marta Boysen. I could not introduce an outsider into the circle. I need not have bothered. Vannikov's needs were very simple.

'A quiet night, Gil. A good dinner. Friendly talk, someone to drive me home if I drink too much sake.'

'You've got it, Boris. Do you want to bring anyone? Your assistant perhaps?'

'Thank you, no. Tanya's good at her work, and in bed. But she's starting to nag me like a wife. We need a rest from each other. I'll come alone. What time?'

'I'll call for you at seven. Leave a note at the guardhouse so that I can drive in and pick you up.'

'Thanks, Gil. I've been beating my brains out for weeks. I can't tell you how much I need a quiet night.'

When I put down the phone, I called a place which I used very rarely because it was so damned expensive. It was, and is still, an old-fashioned tea-house where the most powerful men in Tokyo meet to entertain their favoured guests. I have privileged entrance because I am a friend of Tanaka, but also because, in the faraway days of the occupation, my father, who was then interpreting at the Japanese war crime trials, used to come here in his off-duty hours. He paid the score with food and liquor bought at the PX, and the o-kami-san, who was then a girl serving food in the private rooms, worshipped the ground he walked on. Tonight she promised me a good room and the two best girls in the house to serve our dinner.

After that, it was all work time for Polyglot Press. When I left the office to bathe and change, there was still no word from Marta Boysen. I wondered how she and Max Wylie would be spending the evening.

The name of the tea-house was Bird in Plum Blossom Tree. It was one of those exotic enclaves which still survive, by miracles of money and influence, in the devouring megalopolis of Tokyo. To the street it presented only a high brick wall, pierced by a narrow wooden gate which opened to a push-button code given to the guest when he made his reservation. Once past the gate you found yourself in a traditional garden, so convoluted that it seemed twice as large as it actually was and so cunningly lit and shadowed that the garish neon world of Tokyo was instantly obliterated from the memory. The timbers of the tea-house were dark and luminous with age. The tatami was smooth under our stockinged feet. The only sounds inside our private world were the thin thread of samisen music that trailed like vapour in the air and the rustle of the girls' kimonos as they laid the table before us. I had ordered the food and the liquor in advance so that there would be the least possible intrusion into our talk.

Vannikov's appearance shocked me deeply. I remembered him as an elegant, vigorous fellow with a ready smile and a swift, passionate reaction to whatever pleased or displeased him. The man I saw that night was grey and haggard, seeming to hold himself together by sheer strength of will. When I commented on the change he made a weary gesture of resignation.

'I know. I look terrible. I feel terrible after that bastard of a flight from Moscow. Aeroflot is an exponential disaster. I had a medical checkup before I left. My doctor says I'm still organically sound but dangerously overworked. But who isn't these days? That's really why I need your first reading on Bangkok. If it's going to turn into a dog fight, I don't think I'm up to it. I'll have to call for reinforcements.'

I gave him full marks for the opening gambit and a nice, frank answer to reward him.

'So far as I'm concerned, Boris, I've been given an open brief: get the heads of agreement as quickly as possible and sort out the difficulties later. You know, and I know, it's never as easy as that; but I'm not going to be turning this into a dog fight or a chess game. The way things are in the Gulf, we're all at five minutes to midnight. We can't afford to waste time or goodwill.'

'Thank Christ for that!'

He tossed off his sake at a gulp and washed it down with a beer. While the girl refilled his cup and glass he palmed his eyes as if to rub away the vestiges of a bad dream.

'Your brief is simpler than mine, of course, because you're answerable only to your two principals and both are autonomous. I've got to cope with a dozen different groups of *apparatchiks*. But you can take it that my approach will be the same as yours – to clear the road, not put up new obstacles.'

'Did you bring a list of your delegates?'

'I did, but I left it at the Embassy. I'm sorry. I'll have it tomorrow at lunch.'

'Then give me some idea how your team is constituted . . .'

Before he had time to begin, the first course was laid in front of us: thin strips of tuna and whitefish and turtle meat, with a sauce to marinate them to our taste. As we ate and drank, Vannikov brightened somewhat. The colour seeped back into his cheeks and there was more vigour in his voice.

'You're right, Gil. Time is running against us. In Moscow they're trying to do what Lenin did in 1921: construct a new economic policy. Our problem is that we don't have the tools any more. It's like starting nuclear age technology with the stone axe. I know, I exaggerate, I always do. But look, we've had seventy years of centralism. Two hundred and fifty million diverse peoples governed from the top of a pyramid. We know literally nothing about the simplest mechanics of the democratic or the capitalist systems: local autonomy, market pricing, floating interest rates, joint stock companies, competitive agriculture. It's not only that we don't know about them, we're scared even to handle them or adapt them to our purposes. It's as if we were tossing about live hand grenades, and, in a way, we are. Sure, we can put space stations into orbit, but on the ground it's dog-eat-dog. All you hear in your world is *glasnost* and *perestroika*; what I see is *uravnilovka*, our niggardly spirit that says cut everybody down to ground level, let's all be miserable bastards together. That's the strongest force against us today. And half the folk in the *apparat* love it that way, because it protects the privilege they've built up over the decades . . .'

He broke off, picked up the last piece of fish, dipped it in the sauce, popped it into his mouth and washed it down with sake and beer. The tension in him subsided again. He pointed his chopsticks at me and said with a grin: 'Now you tell me your troubles, Gil. How is your love life?'

'Non-existent.'

'Sex?'

'In this city, always available.'

'Safe?'

'There are few guarantees.'

'And the publishing business?'

'That prospers for us. I can't speak for the rest of the trade; but we seem to have hit a good line: reasonable risks, adequate profits, no big exposures.'

'That's good to hear.'

'And you? Are you out of the game altogether?'

'I still consult. I draw fees and bonus payments. But, yes, it's over for me. I had to make a decision: scrabble about in the market place or go to work for a man I believe in. I do believe in him, Gil! I know he's made a hell of a lot of mistakes, but who else would have dared so much and done so much? I'll tell you a secret, Gil. My family has always been part of the *apparat*; but now, for the first time in my life, I feel like a patriot. I must be getting drunk. That's the first time I've used that word to anyone.'

He was a little drunk with fatigue and liquor. I murmured to the girls to bring hot towels and serve the food more quickly and hold back on the liquor. Meantime I tried to keep him talking. If I was not getting the truth, or something near it, my name was not Gilbert Anselm Langton. I asked him: 'Do you think your man can win?'

'I don't know. Some days I feel we're at the walls of Jericho. All we need is one last trumpet-blast, the walls will fall down and we'll go marching in triumph into the Promised Land. Other days I feel the whole system is going to collapse and we're going to die of hunger and violence in a new Winter Revolution. This new mood in Europe, the deferment of decisions on aid to the Soviets, is ruinous to us. If there's war in the Gulf and we're called on for troops, we could have mutiny and insurrection among the Muslim republics. Now, you tell me some good news for a change.'

'Fine. Here's the good news. What you need is available: technology, organisation, training, finance, speedy input in all areas. The bad news? Unsettled questions at your end: land tenure, export of profits, convertible currency, access to exploitable raw materials in the country . . .'

'Your people must know we're working on those things.'

'They do, but they're bloody bankers. They want the securities in place. And so far as the Japanese are concerned, there's the question of the return of the Kuril Islands.'

'Oh God.' He groaned and slapped his forehead with his palm. 'I knew we'd trip over them sooner or later. Have you ever seen 'em? Godforsaken rock piles where even the seals are miserable. If we get a head-to-head confrontation on that issue, we'll never get through the agenda.'

'That's where you and I come in, Boris. We have to be clever little messenger boys, carrying the right messages from room to room.'

'You're in a much better position to do that than I am, Gil.'

'How so?'

'Unlike me, you're not obliged to succeed. You're not the owner of the restaurant. You're a waiter – a goddam good waiter, I grant you, but still you fetch and carry. The cook hands you a plate of shit. You put it in front of the customer and wish him a good appetite. But you don't have to eat it. I do.'

'Even so, we both have to go through the same motions.'

'Not quite, my friend. To whom will you report at the conference?'

'Leibig and Tanaka.'

'Now let me read you my team list: the commission for economic alternatives, which reports to Gorbachev, who reports to the presidential council; the academy of economics of the USSR, which reports to the council of ministers, which represents the state committee and fifty-seven ministries, which report to the supreme soviet of five hundred and forty-two deputies, and the congress of peoples' deputies, which has two thousand, two hundred and fifty members!'

'You should be glad they're not all coming to Bangkok.'

'You laugh, Gil, but somehow or other they've all got to be placated, if not convinced. Sure, the President can make the decision, but if it's the wrong one they'll roast him and serve him for dinner with an apple in his mouth. That's why you've got to help me, old friend.'

He was not half as far gone as he seemed to be. There was a pressure play coming. I waited for him to spell it out.

'Help me and you help yourself, Gil. You must know you've got heavy competition in this deal.'

'Tell me about it.'

'The Americans want front running in any reconstruction plans. They're afraid of what will happen with a united Europe in 1992. So they're offering a lot of seed money, oil search technology, a whole inventory of projects.'

'For which they want your forces in the Gulf and favoured-nation access to your import and export markets. You'll have a ring through your nose for the next half century.'

'What do you think the Japanese and the Germans want? Economic encirclement. They've even spelled it out in a thesis by a very clever lady called Marta Boysen. It's the Nazi geopolitics updated into modern economic jargon.'

'I haven't seen it.' That at least was true. I hoped to God he would not question me further. 'And as for adopting it as a political programme, I'm sure that's not the case, otherwise I would have been informed. Where can I get a copy of the document?'

'I brought one with me. I'll give it to you tomorrow at lunch, with our list of delegates. Talking of which, I haven't seen your list yet.'

'That's odd. We were talking about it on Friday. Leibig assured me our list had been sent to Moscow some time ago.'

'It could have been.' He shrugged it off as a matter of small importance. 'Our procedures are getting as slack as everything else. It could even be that it came to my desk and Tanya simply put it in my work file; I'm drowned in paper these days. No matter, it will turn up. But to come back to Boysen's thesis. It is very clever. You can read it as a blueprint for economic and political stability right across Eurasia, or as a subtext for a twenty-year squeeze on our divided nation.'

'How did you come by the document?'

'Our copy came with the compliments of the United States Embassy in Moscow. That should signify something to you, yes?'

'What can I say, until I've read it? But what does it change? Your people approached Leibig and asked him to put this consortium together. Yes or no?'

'Yes.'

'Have you gone cold on the idea?'

'No, but the Boysen argument will influence certain people who are totally opposed to a German/Japanese intervention.'

'Which is precisely what the Americans intended it should do, yes?'

'Probably.'

'It could, on your own showing, be equally an argument for the project.'

'I'm not sure of anything any more. Our whole situation is like a Chinese puzzle: one ball within another. Anyway, enough of business. We came here to relax. Talk to me about women, Gil. Tell me how a fellow like you arranges himself in Tokyo or Bangkok.'

It was after one in the morning when I delivered him back at the Embassy. His speech was slurred and he was rocking a little, but he pulled himself together and marched up the steps like a grenadier. I drove back to my hotel, soaked myself in a hot bath and then made my promised call to Tanaka. It was Miko who picked up the phone.

'He's asleep. He came home looking very grey. I insisted he go to bed. I told him I'd wait up for your call.'

'There's nothing to report that can't wait until the morning. I dined with Vannikov. I'm convinced that the Soviets want to do business and that Vannikov and I can work constructively together. On the other hand, there are real problems, which we should discuss before our lunch tomorrow.'

'Kenji suggests nine in the morning at his office. Does that suit you?'

'I'll be there. Anything else?'

'I called Marta this afternoon. We had tea together at Takashimaya.'

'I hope you enjoyed yourselves.'

'We did. I told you, Gil, I like her. Now I'll tell you something else. She's in love with you, head over heels.'

'That's not the message I was getting.'

'Maybe because she knew you wouldn't want to hear it.'

'Please, Miko. It's way past my bedtime.'

'And you're sleeping alone, which is exactly what you deserve.'

'At this moment it's exactly what I want. Now stop annoying me and get off the line.'

'I haven't finished yet. This evening Kenji told me about your weekend with Marta.'

'I hope to God you didn't discuss that over the teacups.'

'How could I? I didn't know then. But frankly, I'm shocked. You acted like some goddam secret policeman. You didn't give the woman a chance to answer for herself. Japan is bad for you, Gil. It's making you devious. You're picking up all our bad habits and none of our good ones. I see it, because I live in two worlds, and if I didn't have Kenji I might be making a play for you myself. There now, I've said my piece. You can go to bed. I wish you happy dreams.'

I was tempted, then and there, to ring Marta Boysen. Prudence and cowardice counselled me against it. After all, if a woman is wakened at two-thirty in the morning the least she should expect is happy news or love-talk. I had only troubling questions and my Judas tongue would stammer over any word of love. I spent a restless night. The liquor made me wakeful. My fitful sleep was haunted by a serial nightmare.

I was in Venice. My father had challenged me to explore the city at night, alone *andando per le fodere* as the Venetians say: 'going through the linings', the underside of the city, its silent alleys, its black reeking canals, its deserted hostile squares.

It was a sinister assignment, but the real horror of the dream was that my father had never been a sinister figure in my life. I could not understand how or why he had changed so suddenly. Nevertheless, I set out on my journey, ready to meet all the grandees and grotesques to whom over the years he had introduced me as familiar acquaintances: Byron, with his screaming women and his menagerie of raucous animals; Mocenigo, who hired the scholar Bruno to teach him magic and, when he could not, sold him to the Inquisition; the three luckless traitors buried heads down in the Piazzetta with their feet sticking up above the paving stones; Paolo Sarpi, the Servite monk who defended the rights of the Serenissima against the exactions of Rome; the courtesans with masked faces and bare nipples, celebrated through all Europe for their beauty and the high cost of their services.

I searched and searched, but found none of them. On every bridge, at every alley's end, at every lighted window, standing in every black gondola, I saw only the accusing image of my father, his hand out-thrust in rejection, his lips framing his constant jibe against respectable traitors: 'From the man I trust, may God defend me. From the man I mistrust, I can defend myself.'

I woke, trembling and sweating, afraid to sleep again. I got up, shaved, showered and dressed, then worked through meaningless papers from five in the morning until breakfast.

By then, my hangover of liquor and guilt had subsided. Common-sense and courtesy prevailed. Before I left the hotel I called Marta. To my surprise, she seemed genuinely pleased to hear from me.

'I know you've been very busy, so I didn't expect a call. But, just the same, I missed you.'

'I missed you, too. Today is going to be rough; but we could meet for dinner if you'd like.'

'Of course, but I'd like to keep it simple, something light sent up to the suite. We have to talk, Gil. I've felt very uneasy ever since Saturday. I feel as though I've said or done something to offend you. I know I was tense and tired. When that happens I get these mood swings . . .'

'There's nothing to worry about, *schatzi*. I'll send the car for you at seven. We'll have an easy domestic evening. Have you spoken to Carl Leibig?'

'Yes. We met briefly after lunch yesterday. He's come up with an interesting suggestion, which I'll tell you about tonight. Oh, and I had afternoon tea with Miko. She's a fascinating woman.'

'And how did your evening go with Max Wylie?'

'It was very pleasant. We dined at his apartment. His wife's an excellent cook. They have a two-year-old daughter, a beautiful child. You'd like them, Gil. He was telling me . . .'

'Sorry, *schatzi*. You'll have to save it for this evening. I have to run. There's an early meeting at Tanaka's office.'

'Off you go then. I love you, Gil Langton.'

'And I you, Marta Boysen.'

What did you expect me to say? Let us have no talk of love, madam? Let us be civilised and formal; let us call each other dear colleague, kiss hands without passion and never linger over a parting? I learned a closer, warmer kind of converse; I could not be expected to forget it overnight. Besides, was I not doing exactly what had been asked of me: observing all the courtesies, stepping back from all arguments? Was I not Gilbert Anselm Langton, the perfect diplomat, making the rough paths smooth, the crooked lanes straight, clearing the way for the money-men, the new Lords of Creation?

Seven

At nine o'clock to the minute, Tanaka, Leibig and I met in the huge penthouse office, whose glass walls opened on to an elaborate roof garden, a small hidden world high above the canyons of the city. I made my report and summed up with three propositions.

'The Soviets want the deal; they want it fast. The Americans are dead against it and we may expect a public confrontation very soon. If there's a political price-tag – like the immediate return of the Kuril Islands – the whole project will collapse.'

There was a longish silence. Then, with surprising mildness, Tanaka opened the discussion.

'How close are the Soviets to determining such matters as freehold, leasehold, percentage of foreign ownership, all the matters, in fact, which are essential to our proposals?'

'Progress is patchy. My reading is that once a ground of agreement is established, there will be a presidential intervention. Vannikov is a trusted man. He knows how the *apparat* works, but he has direct access to Gorbachev. I impressed upon him most firmly that this was, first and foremost, a banking operation. Their people had to have the agreed securities in place.'

'Let's talk about the Americans.' Carl Leibig seemed ill at ease. His curt Junker certainties had deserted him. There was puzzlement and anxiety in his voice. 'I understand why they're opposed to our project. We're natural commercial rivals. On your evidence, Gil, they're planning a highly incendiary campaign, based on the Haushofer material and executed round the world at embassy level. Is that correct?'

'That's what it looks like. The other side of the coin is that the Soviets don't want a witch hunt or a ghost hunt. They'll do business with the Devil if they can get quick and tangible results. Which brings me to an important point. Our case would be enormously strong if we were able to say today at the luncheon or tomorrow in Nara that our funds are in place and we are prepared to move as soon as an agreement is signed. Can we do that?'

'Before I answer,' Tanaka was carefully obstructive, 'explain why it is important to make such an announcement.'

'Because both Europe and America have said there will be delays in their commitments, at least until December. With money on the table, I believe we could strike our deal in Bangkok and be on the planning board before Christmas.'

Carl Leibig was obviously unhappy that I had tabled the issue. He prompted Tanaka: 'You know that our commitment, part German, part British, Scandinavian and European, is already in place, subject, of course, to documents and appropriate agreements on the Soviet side. What is the Japanese position?'

'The Tanaka Group is already committed. At this moment, other Japanese investment from major houses depends upon a settlement of the Kuril question.'

'But Gil has made it very clear; that question will not be settled in Bangkok or, indeed, for a long time after.'

'So there will be a large shortfall in Japanese commitment.'

'Which leaves the rest of us naked in a snowdrift.' Carl Leibig was bitterly disappointed. 'We cannot, we dare not, proceed. The risks are too great.'

For the first time, Tanaka smiled. He locked his hands behind his head and leaned back in his chair, the image of relaxation and good humour.

'My dear Carl, you lose heart too easily. You jump to false conclusions. I told you there will be a shortfall in Japanese investment. I did not say there would be a shortfall in the funding I have promised. I can tell you now that everything I pledged to provide is in place and available on demand.'

'That's wonderful!' Leibig was like a schoolboy suddenly given a day's vacation. 'Who are these fairy godmothers?'

'No names, Carl.' Tanaka's refusal was emphatic. 'Not yet. That is the wish of our investors. I agree with it. Secrecy is our best weapon against hostile political intervention or propaganda by American interests. I ask you simply to accept my word that the funds are committed and in place with hard cash.'

'So, we can announce at the luncheon today that we are fully funded? I can give my colleagues the same news?'

'Of course.' Tanaka heaved himself out of his chair and stood challenging us both. 'But we still do not abate our demand for the return of the Kurils to Japan. We can divorce it from these proceedings because we now have time and space to negotiate. However, once our deal is signed, then every week, every month, we tighten the screws until we get back what was taken from us.'

It was my turn to intervene in the argument. Come lunchtime I had to be fully briefed, I had no intention of making an ass of myself in the first encounter. 'Now that the money situation is settled, I'd like to discuss the problem of the Americans. Their Embassy in Moscow sent Vannikov a copy of Marta Boysen's thesis. He recognised it as a provocative gesture which said that they knew exactly what was happening and were ready to muddy the waters when they chose to do so. Now we have the direct connection between Marta Boysen and Max Wylie in Tokyo. You spoke with her yesterday, Carl.'

'How did you know that?'

'She told me. We talked this morning. She said that she would give me her account of your meeting this evening.'

Instantly Tanaka became the interrogator. 'You still propose to maintain the association with her?'

'I'm doing exactly what Carl requested me to do: observe all the social courtesies. Your very words, Carl, yes?'

'Yes.'

'So I need a full briefing on what passed between you and Marta. And from you, Kenji, I'd like to hear why Miko was entertaining her to tea at Takashimaya. Clearly she would not have done that without your knowledge and permission.'

Tanaka made a small dismissive gesture and sat down at his desk. He said curtly: 'Explain to him, Carl. I am bored with this part of the business.'

I rounded on him then. 'Don't get too bored, Kenji. There are lots of trip wires around. You need as many friendly spotters as you can get! Go ahead, Carl. Tell me everything that happened with Marta.'

'First, we three had agreed that your name would be kept out of the discussion, yes?'

'Yes.'

'Next, we were all of the opinion that – provided she were not actively conspiring against us – it would be better to isolate her within our group than have her as a hostile element outside it.'

'Yes.'

'So, I approached our meeting with these two reservations clearly defined. I recalled to her our earlier discussions about the effect of the Haushofer thesis on our negotiations. I told her that it was now our opinion, and yours, that the Americans could and would use it as a propaganda weapon against us. I told her that with a carefully revised presentation it could equally well be made to work to our advantage, as an exposition of economic co-operation instead of hostile military strategy. I then asked her whether, in the short time available to us, she could work up such an exposition.'

'And she agreed to do that, of course.'

'Yes. I then asked her about her own associations with Americans, in academic life, at FAO and in her personal relations.'

'She didn't object to that line of questioning?'

'Not at all. I had already explained that it was relevant to our project.'

'Relevant in what sense?'

'Once our conference begins in Bangkok, we shall be besieged by the international press. We have decided, therefore, to set up a press and public relations office – in co-operation with the Soviets, if they will agree – to provide daily information to the international media. I proposed to Marta Boysen that she could most usefully serve in that area.'

'Her reaction?'

'She agreed, without hesitation. She said, in effect: "I think I'd prefer it. I'm not sure I like the atmosphere of big business." '

'I'm not sure I like the way you're doing business either, Carl. I'm supposed to be negotiating for you and nobody has even bothered to mention this notion of a press office in Bangkok. I don't disagree with it. I think it's a damned good idea; but since I'm going to have to clean up any mess that it makes, don't you think, both of you, that I should have been informed and consulted about its functions?'

'Alongside all the other things, it's a mere detail, Gil.' Tanaka was sedulously casual. 'Of course you would have been informed and consulted. But there is a question of priorities.'

'Don't give me that crap, Kenji!' I was furious now. Discretion was out the window. 'You're already in the middle of a trade war. Your own colleagues in the *keiretsu* are standing on the sidelines waiting for you to be cut down. Propaganda's a war weapon and you'd better be damned sure yours is in working order. Who's going to explain to the world press about your mysterious unnamed investors? Who's going to direct Marta Boysen? She's a damned good academic, but she knows nothing about media manipulation. Come on, man! You're playing games here. I don't like it. I've warned you before. You can make my excuses at the Embassy. I'm not prepared to make a fool of myself because you've handed me a bad brief. You'll have my formal resignation within the hour. Good day, gentlemen!'

I walked out, seething with anger. I did not give a hoot in hell any more about protocols and politesse and losing face. I was tired of getting egg all over mine. I was sick of evasions and half-truths and distorted images. I loathed being manipulated in the name of friendship.

I rode down alone in the elevator; but the moment it stopped, two young men in business suits stepped inside, barring my exit. Before I could open my mouth to protest one of them punched the buttons, the doors closed and we were riding up again, express to the top floor.

The second man bowed and explained courteously: 'Mr Tanaka regrets that your conversation was interrupted. He will not take up too much of your time.'

I could have objected, but it would have meant nothing. Push come to shove, these two young bucks would have immobilised me in an instant and dumped me like a sack of rice on the floor. So I went with them in silence and stood, mute and angry, in front of Tanaka's desk, while Carl Leibig, a pale and shaken spectator, sat huddled in his chair. Tanaka made a gesture of dismissal. The bodyguards bowed to him and to me, then withdrew.

Tanaka picked up a paperknife, made like a miniature sword, unsheathed it and began toying with the naked blade. I knew he wanted me to sit down, so that we could treat at eye level, yet he would not invite me to do so for fear I might refuse. So, he avoided eye contact altogether and focused on the small, shining blade in his hands. His tone was studiously formal, as if he were a pupil reciting a lesson to his master.

'I know I have offended you, my friend. It was not my intention to do so, but it is certainly my fault that it has happened. I am not sure how I can make amends.' He put his left hand flat on the desk with the fingers splayed and laid the blade of the knife, like a guillotine, across the small finger. 'I can do the traditional thing, of course, and offer you a finger joint; but that would simply be painful to me and embarrassing to you. So I ask you, what amends do I have to make to keep your friendship and respect?'

Once again, he had outplayed me. The words and the gesture conveyed regret and self-accusation. In fact, they were a challenge to prove myself as magnanimous as the great Tanaka who, a moment before, had sent his minions to deliver me, by force if necessary, into his presence. What he had failed to understand was that I had lost heart for the game. What had looked like a match of champions was now a shabby, sand-lot scramble, played behind a dust-screen, and I could make no sense or pattern of what was going on. My only hope was to take time out.

I told Tanaka: 'I'm very angry. Whatever I do or say now I shall regret later.' Tanaka looked up. Now at least we were in eye contact. I went on. 'So, I am not coming to lunch. I shall call the Embassy and excuse myself formally. You will hear what is said. You and Carl are fully briefed to handle the meeting with Vannikov and the Ambassador. You will make your own judgments, for or against the report I have given you this morning. Later, you will call me at the hotel. You will tell me whether you still wish me to continue. I will tell you whether and on what terms I can do so. If we part, at least we can continue as friends.'

Tanaka leaned back in his chair. His eyes were hooded. He was still making mesmeric little passes with the paperknife. He asked: 'How will you explain your absence from lunch?'

'Very simply. A diplomatic illness. You will hear what is said.'

'I do not speak Russian. Do you, Carl?'

'Not well enough for a business dialogue.'

'Then we'll speak English. Vannikov is very fluent. You have an amplifier on the phone, Kenji?'

'Of course.'

'Then would you be good enough to call the Embassy and tell them I want to speak urgently with Boris Vannikov.'

Two minutes later, Vannikov was on the line. I greeted him in Russian. He thanked me for a pleasant evening, cursed me for his hangover and begged to know what he could do for me. I explained that I was in the office of my principals and that, for courtesy's sake, we should converse in English. I introduced Tanaka and Leibig. Boris slipped immediately into his best conference mode.

'Good morning, my friends. This is Boris Vannikov. I am at your service.'

'Boris, I'm sorry to tell you I can't make our lunch meeting. Mr

Tanaka and Mr Leibig will be there. Unfortunately I have to see my doctor.'

'Nothing serious I hope.'

'I hope so, too. This morning when I got up, my blood pressure was dangerously high. It may be that I'm just getting too old for these gaudy nights. Anyway, I wanted you to know that Mr Tanaka and Mr Leibig are fully briefed on our conversations last night. They are as hopeful as I am that a good solution can be found. It is possible that Mr Tanaka may release some very good news at the luncheon. On the other hand, he may decide to defer the announcement until a more public moment. However, there is good news. I expect to be back at my hotel about three-thirty this afternoon. You can call me there if you wish. My apologies to His Excellency.'

'Of course. Tanya will be disappointed, too. I had promised to introduce her to you.' Then, for a brief moment, he slipped into Russian. 'Are you sure you're all right, Gil? No snags, no personal problems?'

'None, I promise you. I should know better than to drink late with a Muscovite! Have a pleasant lunch.'

I put down the phone and faced Tanaka once more. 'That's all, I think. You heard the conversation?'

'Everything but the opening and the close.'

'They were courtesies only.' Leibig assured him hastily. 'I thought Gil handled it very well. It may even be an advantage that our first talks are held without his intervention.'

'It may. It may not.' Tanaka was terse. 'I'll call you Gil, before I leave the office this evening. If you decide to continue with us, I shall arrange for you to be picked up and taken to the heliport in the morning. I hope, I truly hope, we may still work together.'

'That is my hope, too,' said Carl Leibig fervently. 'We need you, Gil.'

I was not at all hopeful. Something had gone grievously wrong and, for the moment at least, I could not define what it was. I felt like a man drowning in a bath of feathers.

One thing was clear: Tanaka's colleagues in the *keiretsu* had declined to support his project. They had stepped back, leaving him three choices: to submit to the counsel of the group, to find his funds elsewhere, or ruin himself with a solo bid. He claimed to have found other partners. Who were they? If the United States was actively hostile, as it seemed to be, then the funds were not flowing through Wall Street. Carl Leibig had already tapped the European market through his Swiss connection. So where was the money coming from?

The funds in question amounted to something like five billion dollars. Assuming that Tanaka picked up his original commitment of one billion – and even that would hurt him if he had no market support outside his own admittedly strong structures – that left four billion, which he claimed to have available, on call, in cash, from unnamed sources.

I could not conceive that he had lied about it. That would have been a suicidal folly. Miko had said that he was contemplating suicide when his life became less than tolerable; but that was in another context and involved a retreat from dishonour rather than an expiation of it. All my experience of the man argued against his being a liar. That same experience warned me, however, that his concepts of truth, justice and the social moralities were written in different ideograms from mine and it was up to me to make sure I was reading the text and the subtext correctly.

Another anomaly: Carl Leibig, the initiator of the enterprise and a full partner in it, had been clearly taken aback by Tanaka's revelations. He, too, had been kept in the dark and forced to accept Tanaka's assurances on the one hand and the existence of anonymous partners on the other. I was not particularly fond of the man; he could be both pompous and naive. However, I believed he was honest and his business record was sound. If this project turned sour, it could set him back half a decade. Tanaka knew that and he would not scruple to enforce a flawed bargain. I remembered his warning to me: 'You have to know, Gil, that one day I could be your enemy. If one or other of my historic obligations conflicts with our friendship, I have no choice.' I wondered whether he had ever given the same warning to Carl Leibig. My guess was that he had not. He would have reasoned that Leibig was a trader whose family had been in the game long enough to teach him all the rules and all the tricks to evade them.

Even so, this enterprise was too big and too complicated for mere trickery. The risks were great, but the potential rewards were much greater. They had all been spelled out more than half a century ago by Major-General Professor Doktor Karl Haushofer. My father, too, had spelled them out in his own eccentric fashion.

We were in Alexandria, I remember. It was a Sunday morning. The city was fetid with heat and squalor. My father had insisted on dragging me to a noon Mass in a crumbling old Coptic church where, he said, the Mass was celebrated in the Bohairic dialect of the eleventh century. The liturgy was long and even longer was my father's disquisition on a manuscript of the *Song of Solomon*, proudly displayed by the priest, which he claimed dated from the fifth century and was written in the Sahidic dialect. I was drowsy and ill-tempered and I only began to revive when he fed me cold beer and peanuts in a Greek taverna far away from the church.

All of which is irrelevant, except as a prelude to my father's further lecture on the rise of empires. 'Three steps, my boy. Occupy, pacify and then crucify with taxes raised on contract by tax-farmers who pay hugely for the rights. When the taxes don't pay the running costs of the empire, screw the tax-farmers to squeeze out more money. When the people start murdering the tax-farmers, then the empire's already in dissolution. Pour me another beer like a good fellow.'

From Alexandria to Tokyo is a long hop, step and jump; but suddenly my father was there with me, a genial ghost striding along the Ginza, two steps ahead, talking back to me over his shoulder as he used to do whenever I lagged. 'Nothing changes too much. For tax-farmer read concessionaire or franchisee; for concessionaire read monopolist exploiter and you're right up to date in the twentieth century. The Emperor, the granter of the franchise, got his money up front with the best guarantee of all, the tax-farmer's life. The tax-farmer got more, but in smaller instalments. The amount depended on what he could squeeze out of the locals.'

Then I remembered a section in the Tanaka/Leibig document of proposal. It was headed 'Granting of Sub-contracts, Leases and Franchises' and it dealt with the right to farm out benefits acquired under the original arrangement. So the question narrowed itself a little: who were the most likely, the most practised, the wealthiest tax-farmers? To whom would Tanaka turn for funds when his prime colleagues turned him down?

I stepped into a phone booth and called the Okura hotel to leave a message for Marta Boysen. They told me she was still in the hotel. Her phone was busy, but if I would like to wait a moment . . ? I waited. I resisted two attempts to have me call back. Finally, she came on the line. I asked her to meet me at noon in my hotel.

'But we're meeting tonight.'

'I know. Something's come up. We have to talk.'

'I've just finished talking with Miko. We've arranged to lunch together.'

'Call her back and cancel it. Make any excuse you want, but don't mention me. I've just refused to lunch at the Soviet Embassy with Tanaka and Leibig.'

'But what's going on?'

'I'm not sure. That's why we need to talk. Please?'

'Of course. Twelve noon.'

Came then the questions: What was I going to ask? How much was I going to tell? And what could I expect to gain or lose? I looked at my watch. It showed twenty minutes past ten. I still had an hour and forty minutes to make up my mind.

The first thing I had to remember was that I had no executive authority at all. I was, in the final analysis, a private contractor, providing my linguistic skills and my practice as a negotiator to bring about an agreement between my clients and other parties. I could advise and interpret. I could not dictate what they should do. If they declined my counsel I would still be paid. Unless they were engaged in criminal activity, they could still enforce the contract against me, at least to the extent of excluding me from offering the same service in the same industry, and certainly by proceeding against me for any breach of business confidence.

Before going back to the hotel I called in at my office. There were two messages on my desk. The first was a fax from Sir Pavel Laszlo in Sydney.

Australian share market deeply depressed by new wave of big bankruptcies, high interest rates and depressed markets for primary exports. Japanese investors are curtailing both current and planned investment. Tanaka interests here are still functioning normally; however, there are rumours here of severe disagreements among financial leaders and increasing isolation of Tanaka interests. Was unable to contact Tanaka at weekend but shall try again today, Monday. Meantime, would appreciate your opinion as informed observer with Western viewpoint. Best, Laszlo.

I couldn't help chuckling at the sheer gall and *chutzpah* of the man. If he wanted something – of man or woman – he asked for it. Sometimes he would get his face slapped, most times he got at least a usable answer. This time, however, he would get nothing from me until my own problems with Tanaka had been solved. My loyalties were divided enough already.

The second message was from the Commercial Attaché at the Australian Embassy. He would like me to call him back. He had news for me.

'After our meeting yesterday, I spoke to my chief in Canberra. As I expected, he's ready to do handstands in the park if that will help to shift our agricultural surpluses. He's willing to discuss, without prejudice, any financial formulae you care to bowl up to him. Also, as you suggested, he's going to call Sir Pavel Laszlo to get his view on the situation. So, for what it's worth, I thought you should have a progress report.'

I thanked him warmly; then, being a quick learner from people like Sir Pavel, I asked him: 'What was all that crap yesterday from Arnold whatever-his-name-is? It made no sense to me. It still doesn't.'

'It doesn't make too much to me either. I try to stay well away from all spooks. I'm a businessman. I deal with imports and exports and balance of payments. It's not my business to enquire about people's sex lives or their politics. But, in answer to your question, lately we've had a spate of memos about the infiltration of foreign criminal organisations into Australian business: the Chinese Triads, the Italian and US Mafia, the Yakuza from here, certain neo-Fascist groups from Yugoslavia. It's the usual fragmentary stuff, none of it highly focused. We've been asked to try to identify any companies seeking to do business in Australia which do not have a reasonably clear history and identity. It's a formality for the most part. In these hard times you've only got to wave money around and you start the stampede of the Gadarene Swine. However, if there's anything specific you want me to check out, make it official and send me a memo. I'll deal with it promptly. They seem to like you in Canberra.'

'They damn well should. I pay 'em an arm and a leg in taxes! Thanks again. I'll be in touch.'

I put down the receiver and sat for a long time staring at the flower arrangements which my secretary Eiko placed every morning on the coffee table in the conference area. She made the arrangements herself and I was expected to compliment her on them and to listen to her explanation of their meaning. This one she had named 'autumn lake', because it was made with sedge grasses, a twig of russet maple leaves and a platform of little stones shelving into clear water.

The sight of it recalled with extraordinary vividness the picture of Tanaka standing alone by the lakeside, picking up pebbles and skimming them across the water in the magical sequence, 8-9-3. I felt a sudden shiver of apprehension, the telltale tremor which, my father used to say, always comes when someone walks over your grave. When I asked him whether he believed in ghosts, he answered me with a Sybilline riddle. 'I do and I don't; because all the vestiges of all our yesterdays are still with us and there's no such event as tomorrow. All we have is now.' It was Kenji Tanaka's Zen story in another mode. I mused on them both as I hurried to the hotel to meet Marta Boysen.

Her taxi arrived just as I was stepping out of mine. I paid off both drivers and hurried Marta towards the elevators. We rode up with two elderly Japanese couples, so we were spared the embarrassment of an embrace. I hurried her into the suite, locked the door and put on the safety-chain.

She smiled and said: 'Do you think that's really necessary?'

'It may be. You're not going to like what I'm about to tell you; but I don't want you to leave until you've heard it all. Would you like a drink?'

'No, thank you. I'd prefer a kiss.'

'You may not want that either. So let's see how you feel afterwards.'

'Gil, what in God's name has come over you? You're being positively brutal. Why?'

'Because this is the only way I can get this off my chest. Bear with me, please. Just listen to what I have to say.'

'Very well. I'm listening.'

She sat bolt upright in the chair, her hands holding tightly to the armrests. I perched myself two paces away on the edge of the small dining table. I tried to suppress all emotion and tell the story as if she and I had no real part in it. I did not succeed very well at all.

'Saturday in the country. We went first to the painter's house, then to the pottery. You made your purchases. You were sitting at the bench doing paperwork, travellers' cheques, Customs declarations, addresses. Your handbag was open. You had things spread about you. Are you with me?'

'I'm with you, but . . .'

'I offered to help. You waved me away. Your notebook fell to the floor. A card fell out of it.'

'I didn't notice.'

'I know. I read the card, put it in my pocket and later put it back in your notebook. Do you still have it, by any chance?'

'No. I tore it up.'

'Do you remember what was written on it?'

'A private message to me.'

'The message said: "Leave Vannikov arrangements to me. Will pick you up 1500 hours. You will be back in time for dinner date." And it was signed "M". Remember now?'

'It was something like that, yes.'

'Yet, later that afternoon, when we were talking about Vannikov, you implied that you had never heard of him.'

'So?'

'So you lied. I lied too. I fabricated an excuse to get back to Tokyo, because I couldn't face another night in bed, with all the love and passion I'd felt going sour inside me. Some men can turn anger into sex. I can't. I'd have been impotent and shamed us both.'

'And you're doing exactly that now, Gil.'

'I have no choice. Things are happening which may have catastrophic consequences. I have to know who wrote that note and what it means. I should tell you that both Tanaka and Leibig know about it.'

She gaped at me in disbelief and then uttered a contemptuous dismissal. 'The great Gil Langton, a common informer. I'm glad your father's dead, Gil. He deserved better, for all the love he spent on you!'

'And I deserved better of you than a whore's lie.'

After that there was a long, wintry silence. For want of anything better to do or say, I went to the liquor cabinet, poured two stiff whiskies and handed one to Marta. She accepted it without a word and sipped at it slowly. Then she put the bleak question.

'Is it worth saying anything else? Will we ever believe each other again?'

'We won't know, will we, until we're over this hurdle. Who wrote the card?'

'Miko.'

'When?'

'It was delivered by hand to the Okura on Friday morning.'

'Which means that you had discussed some of its contents the night before, in this room, while Tanaka and I were downstairs.'

'That's right.'

'Yet that was the first time you and she had met face to face?'

'Right again.'

'Nevertheless, you were discussing a name which even I didn't hear until Friday – the name of Boris Vannikov . . . What did Miko mean by "the Vannikov arrangements"? And why were they, and he, so important that you lied to me about knowing even the name?'

'Miko realised she had been indiscreet. She said that Tanaka and Leibig would be furious if they knew she'd been gossiping about business. I promised to say nothing. I kept the promise. It's that simple.'

'What did Miko mean by "the Vannikov arrangements"!'

'The question of whether or no I would be meeting him before we went to Bangkok. I sensed that, because of my open confrontation with Leibig, I was being edged away from the centre of things – which is exactly what has happened. Miko had another idea altogether: that she and I could, as she put it, "cultivate the Russians" and especially Vannikov, the negotiator. As we talked, we built it into a kind of schoolgirl joke between us.'

'Some joke!'

'Please, Gil, stop bullying me. I know it sounds too childish to believe, but it's the truth. It's also embarrassing, because the moment I met Miko there was an instant attraction between us. I'd never felt anything like it since I was a schoolgirl, a sudden, unquestioning intimacy, an immediate consent to playful conspiracy. I found myself pouring out my life story. She told me about her affairs, her business, her life with Tanaka – even the attraction she feels towards you, Gil. I asked her to explain to me how this project came into being, your part in it and your personal friendship with Tanaka. It was in that context that Vannikov's name was first mentioned. She had just seen a fax announcing his arrival. She wasn't sure Tanaka had sighted it; at least, that's what she told me. You wondered why I was so angry on Friday, why I didn't want to come away with you for the weekend. After all the confidences we'd shared, Miko still hadn't told me of my impending dismissal by Leibig. You, at least, had prepared me for it. She had said nothing.'

'Yet you still went to tea with her on Monday. You were still exchanging confidences.'

'I'd had a pleasant time with you. I felt at ease again.'

'You had also talked with Leibig.'

'That's true.'

'What did he say to you?'

This was a crucial question, because I had Carl Leibig's own account of the meeting clearly fixed in my head. Any discrepancy between that and Marta's narrative would show up immediately. Even so, the last phase of the story came as a surprise.

'He asked me about what he called "my American connections" and in particular about Max Wylie. I told him I was a scholar in my own right. I reminded him that I had come to him from an international body, the Food and Agriculture Organisation. My personal loyalties were to my own homeland and my private friendships were outside the domain of politics.'

'How did he take that?'

'Very well. He did make the point – which now I see referred to your report – that we were dealing with sensitive matters, inside an unfamiliar culture; therefore, I should be very cautious in public and private utterance. After that he suggested I move sideways into the public relations area and concentrate on working the Haushofer thesis into the framework of this specific project. Any more questions?'

'None, thank you.'

'Do you believe what I've told you?'

'Yes.'

'Now it's your turn to answer some questions for me.'

'Ask them.'

'Why do you do this kind of work?'

'I like it. I'm good at it. I've been endowed with a unique talent. This kind of thing gives me a unique opportunity to exercise it. It's a marvellous change from the desk work of publishing.'

'Does it not also give you the opportunity to exercise power without responsibility?'

'The opportunity, yes; but I find no satisfaction in the abuse of power.'

'Why are you working for Leibig and Tanaka?'

'I am working for Leibig because I accepted to assist Tanaka, who is my friend and business associate.'

'Do you trust Tanaka?'

'I don't trust anyone absolutely, even myself. In friendship, you accept the risk. In business, you calculate it. In Tanaka's case I have found the risks acceptable – so far.'

'How far do you trust Miko?'

'Not as far as I trust Tanaka.'

'Because she's a woman?'

'Because she's a woman in Tanaka's world. She has different survival rules. I don't know all those rules, only a few of them. So I try not to embroil myself in her private game. The Japanese have a word for it, *misu shobai*: water business, the whole life pattern of the floating world. What I'm saying is no discredit to Miko. I have no idea what provision a man like Tanaka will make for a woman as important to him as Miko. I wouldn't dare to ask either of them.'

'You said: "Things are happening which could have catastrophic consequences." What did you mean by that?'

'God! A whole list of things that you can read in any newspaper: the possibility of war in the Gulf before Christmas, the breakup of the Soviet Union, food rationing in Moscow, the breakdown of the General Agreement on Tariffs and Trade, which can plunge the whole bloody planet into a trade war with starvation in the midst of plenty. Our single enterprise is directly affected by all those things; but if you want it closer to home, Tanaka's most senior financial colleagues have turned away from him. He has had to look elsewhere for funds to complete his obligation to the consortium. He claims he has the funds. He may even be announcing the fact at this moment over lunch at the Embassy . . .'

'But you don't know who his other backers are?'

'No, I don't. That's why I absented myself from the lunch. I had to have time to consider my position.'

'Instead, you're spending the time with me.'

'Because you're a key element in the situation. Your thesis is a weapon that can be used for or against us. And there's still a big question mark hanging over your relationship with Max Wylie.'

'What the devil do you mean, Gil? I've told you already . . .'

'Now I'm telling you. Max Wylie is a US Intelligence agent who is working actively against the Tanaka/Leibig project. The United States do not want this kind of Euro-Japanese enterprise flourishing in the new Soviet. That's politics. That's international business. Whether you like it or not, you're caught up in it. I'm not blaming you; all I'm saying is that you can't walk around with your head in the clouds. Next question.'

'Do you suspect I am working with or for Max Wylie?'

'It is my job to look at every possibility, good or bad. In that sense, yes, I have to suspect you. I know, for instance, that my name has been raised in an Intelligence discussion by Max Wylie. You dined with him on Monday night after our aborted weekend. Was there any talk about me?'

'Of course. I had a lot of pleasant things to tell about you.'

'I believe you, *schatzi*. I do, truly, believe you. And I believe just as truly that the first note Max Wylie wrote in his diary this morning was the old cliche: "Gilbert Langton and Marta Boysen have established a sexual connection. Continued surveillance is recommended." '

'Oh God!' It was a heart-cry of frustration and anger. 'I can't believe I'm hearing this.'

'Why should it surprise you? We're key players in a big game of money and politics. The stakes are enormous. Max Wylie's on the other side. The rules don't change. It's still "woe to the conquered". That's why I had to talk to you today. You can't afford any illusions.'

'I can resign.'

'But your Haushofer thesis is still a big element in the game. You defended it before the faculty in Munich. Now you have to defend it again. You can't let the propagandists pervert it into a weapon of war.'

She thought about that for a long moment, then gave me a ghost of a smile and held out her glass. 'I could use another drink.'

While I was pouring, she asked the last question, the one with all the money riding on it.

'What about us, Gil? Where do we go from here?'

At three o'clock we were still in bed, still bathed in the fading afterglow, when Boris Vannikov called from the Embassy. The luncheon was over; the guests had departed. He was anxious to know about my health.

'I'm much better, thanks.' That was absolute truth. 'I'm resting.' That was true, too; and there was no cloud of post-coital sadness over the bed. 'My doctor tells me that men of my age who work too hard or drink too much tend to develop a labile blood-pressure. However, I'm down to normal now. How did your luncheon go?'

'Very well, I think. You had obviously briefed them accurately and they responded, without too much contention, to the exposition of our problems. The Kuril Islands still kept leaping out of the sea like sharks. I left the Ambassador and Tanaka to deal with that one. Is your doctor going to let you travel to Nara tomorrow? Tanaka said that there was some doubt about your being able to make the trip.'

'The doctor is calling in this evening. He'll decide then.'

'I hope you can make it. You and I can save everybody a lot of time and energy. By the way, the notion of a jointly controlled press office is not a bad one. We told them we'd consider it and discuss details in Nara.'

'I think it's a good idea, too, provided you and I can run it. Anyway, things went well. A good first session is important. See you in Nara, I hope.'

I put down the receiver. Marta and I folded ourselves together for a last, drowsy embrace. Once again, the phone rang. This time it was Carl Leibig.

'I know Tanaka will be calling you later, Gil. I just wanted to give you my own interim report. The meeting was cordial. The report you had given to us proved accurate in every detail. You have my thanks and my compliments.'

'Did Tanaka make his big announcement?'

'He made it; but not in a big way. In fact, he was almost casual about it: "Your Excellency understands, of course, that we are not selling noodles on a street corner. What we promise in terms of funding and expertise we can deliver the moment we have agreed documents." It was just the right note, understated but impressive.'

'And the Ambassador?'

'He was very frank. He was not yet sure of a number of positions. He recognised the need to define them swiftly. Your friend Vannikov is obviously a powerful voice . . . By the way, he heartily approves the idea of a press office in Bangkok, provided he and you control it.'

'I've been thinking about that, too, as well as your suggestion to use Marta Boysen. I myself had a long talk with her today. We've just finished, as a matter of fact. It was a very frank discussion. It had to be, because we are involved with each other on a personal basis as well as in business. She gave me a full and truthful answer to all the questions I asked. I also explained to her our concerns about her friend Max Wylie.'

'And your conclusion, Gil?'

'I believe she is a loyal servant of the enterprise and should be treated as such. Our personal relationship, which was somewhat damaged, has now been fully restored.'

'That's very good news. I hope you are going to stay with us, Gil. We have great need of you.'

'Let's wait until I've talked with Tanaka.'

'I know he wants you as much as I do; though he may not say it in the same words. He is ill. We know that. He has always been a closed man, hard to know, but these days he is even more difficult. The defection of his biggest financial colleagues has left him very isolated. Unfortunately, that is the one thing he will not discuss with a *gaijin* like me. In any case, I must leave the decision to you.'

I thanked him for his call and told him I prized his frankness. It was not an idle compliment. I was beginning to see more in him than a stuffy Baltic trader with a taste for handsome young men. I was beginning to get very tired of clannish politics and words that changed colour like chameleons. Marta smoothed out the furrows on my forehead with the tips of her fingers and chided me softly.

'I'm afraid of the dark man I see sometimes behind your eyes, the man who knows too much and trusts too little. We must be happy now, Gil. We must.'

The chirping cricket voice reiterated the warning: '*On ne badine pas avec l'amour,*' don't trifle with love; you may not get another chance to enjoy it.

Punctual as always, Tanaka telephoned at five thirty. He was still in his company mode, brusque and peremptory. Even his commendation had the same imperious ring to it.

'You did well for us, Gil. Both the Russians and we ourselves were amazed at how well the ground was prepared. I was impressed with Vannikov. He has much respect for you. The Ambassador was surprised, I think, to find us so well advanced. He has promised to put pressure on Moscow for a speedy resolution on basic issues. Now, let's talk about you . . .'

'Before we come to me, let's talk about Marta Boysen.'

'I thought Carl Leibig had settled all that.'

'Not quite. You told me you wanted her cleared or discharged before we left for Nara. I undertook that responsibility. I have spent several hours today questioning her about all the recent events which I discussed with you. I discovered that there had been a whole series of misunderstandings and one untruth which arose out of a promise to Miko not to repeat an injudicious piece of gossip. My personal relationship with her has been restored. I can recommend wholeheartedly that she be retained as a loyal member of the group.'

'Good.' Tanaka gave an audible sigh of relief. 'I cannot cope with women's chatter. I shut my ears and hope it will go away. Now, let's get back to our affairs. I need you. Are you prepared to stay with the project?'

'Subject to certain conditions, yes.'

'Name them.'

'That if a press office is set up, Vannikov and I be directly responsible for it. Any staff take directions from us.'

'Agreed.'

'That I take over the personal direction of Marta Boysen's work.'

'If the lady raises no objections – and I am sure Leibig will have none – then why not?'

'In other words, you agree.'

'I agree.'

'Finally, I am tired of complaining to you about non-disclosure of matters essential to my functioning. You must know that I cannot tolerate any surprises. I must know everything, including the names and identities of your new investors. I must also have at least an outline picture of your present relationship with your colleagues in the *keiretsu*. I know these are heavy demands, which require a high degree of trust in my integrity. If you feel that the risk is too great, just tell me. I'll retire without a murmur and we can still be friends.'

'No, Gil!' His voice was sombre. 'If you quit now, we can never be friends again.'

'Between friends there has to be trust.'

'There has also to be respect for those things which cannot be shared, our history, our ancestors, our private gods, even our women – my Miko, your Marta. You cannot take over every room in my house, Gil.'

'And you have to give me enough information to work with, Kenji.'

'I offer that; not all at once, but as you need it, when you need it.'

'I have to judge that moment, not you.'

'You're driving a very hard bargain, Gil.'

'Would it be simpler if I put a figure on it? You tell me nothing but you pay me three million dollars? You tell me something and the amount is reduced? You know that's not the issue.'

'I know.'

'So let me spell it for you, friend to friend. When I come to you and say: "For this meeting I have to know this, for this reason," will you tell me?'

'What if the telling damages me?'

'Then you say so. We reason about it.'

'And if we disagree?'

'I am free to leave. You, as principal, conduct your own business without me. That's the bottom line.'

There was a longish silence then, curt as bedamned, he answered: 'We have a deal. You will be picked up at your hotel at eight tomorrow morning and driven to the heliport. Bring your woman with you. I'm bringing mine. Nara is a beautiful place in autumn. Carl Leibig is not sufficiently grateful to the ancestors who bought the land for him. Until tomorrow, Gil. And thank you.'

As suddenly as it had begun, it was ended, like a kendo contest. The clatter of bamboo staves was suddenly silenced. The combatants were bowing to each other across the floor. I turned to see Marta walking naked out of the bathroom, towelling her damp hair.

'I know that was Tanaka, but I didn't understand a word of what you were saying.'

I told her the bottom line and promised to explain the rest between sunset and sunrise. She did not seem too eager to hear it. She was content with her own new certainties. She could hardly conceive the deep, black gulf which separated me from my friend, Kenji Tanaka.

Eight

The flight to Nara was a carefully staged exercise to impress the Soviet clients. Tanaka's people had arranged the transport: a procession of limousines to the heliport at Haneda domestic airport, a brisk division of the guests into two parties, a ceremonious welcome aboard the two helicopters, a fifty-minute flight, south along the coast and then a short leg inland to Nara, the ancient capital of Japan.

Our party was a gallery of familiar faces: Leino the Finn, Forster the Swiss banker, Boris Vannikov, Marta and myself. The second flight carried Tanaka, Miko, Vannikov's assistant, the Political Attaché from the Soviet embassy and two men I had not seen before, one Oriental, the other European. I was told that Carl Leibig and his staff would be waiting to welcome us to the estate.

As we flew in low over the city, I was amazed at the extent of urban encroachment on this once rural environment, full of ancient relics, temples, pagodas and imperial estates. On the other hand, I was vastly impressed that Carl Leibig's company had managed to retain so much of its valuable holding: fifty acres of greensward and woodland with a nine-hole golf course, a nature park for the Nara deer and a small colony of traditional guest houses, grouped about a central clubhouse and convention hall.

Here Carl Leibig himself took over. We were dispersed in golf-carts, each national group diplomatically separated from the other, the couplings, if any, left to the group-leader to determine. Each guest house was beautifully furnished and – a blessing in the sudden autumn chills – equipped with its own central heating, hot water service and bath chamber. There was a well-stocked liquor cupboard, a flower arrangement, toiletries, a cotton *yukata* for inside wear and a padded one for outside. The golf-cart with two sets of clubs was parked outside. There was a welcoming gift for each guest: for Marta, a wood-block print of a carp and iris by Koho, for me an antique sword-hilt, nestling on a silk pad in a lacquer box. Carl Leibig's card to me said, simply: 'I am happy you are here. I am happy Marta is with you.'

There was also a folder full of information. We would hold our first formal meeting from noon until one. There would be a brief introductory address, followed by a general discussion. We would lunch, buffet style, seating ourselves as we chose. The afternoon would be spent in informal discussions, either on the golf course, strolling about the grounds or meeting privately in our lodgings. Cocktails would be served at six, dinner at seven. The whole of the first day was intended as a sociable prelude to the heavy schedule of the next one, when a series of specialised committees would begin at nine and finish at five. It was hoped that before we left Nara we would have identified areas of early agreement and problem issues which we hoped could be resolved in Bangkok.

There was a note from Carl Leibig attached to my schedule:

At the noon meeting I shall make a very brief address of welcome on behalf of Tanaka and myself. Then we would like you to take over and explain how you propose to work as mediator. We know that your own preference is for a mode of friendly informality. We feel also that at general meetings you should act, if not as chairman, at least as a moderator, keeping the whole show under control. There are four people to whom you have not been introduced. I have marked them on your guest list. Tanaka will supply basic biographical information.

By the time I had looked over the papers, Marta had unpacked and was going through her own folder. She drew me to her, kissed me and said: 'I have to say, *schatzi*, I find all this rather daunting.'

'You mustn't. You've been through this sort of convention a hundred times. People mill around, sniffing the air, picking up tag-ends of talk. After a while, they settle down to normal business.'

'But this business isn't normal, Gil. It isn't an academic exercise. It's billions in money and the fate of a great nation.'

'To which you can contribute, yes. For which you can, in no sense, be responsible.'

'I wish I could feel as secure as you.'

'I'm not secure, my love. I'm relaxed. I'm in the game, but I'm the referee, not a player.'

'And what am I?'

'A player; but it's the referee's job to look after the players, and I'll be keeping a very watchful eye on you.' I kissed her and held her close. 'If people ask you questions you don't want to answer, or you don't know how to answer, say just that. If they try to press you, tell 'em as politely as you can to go fly a kite.'

'It all sounds vaguely sinister.'

'With everything that's at stake, it has to be sinister; but you'll cope. Now, grab your briefcase and let's go. The performance starts in fifteen minutes.'

In the foyer of the conference hall Kenji Tanaka was waiting with Miko and the two new members of his entourage. He introduced them in English: Mr Domenico Cubeddu of the Palermitan Banking Corporation, and Mr Hoshino, president of the Pacific Littoral Development Group. Cubeddu was Sicilian from the soles of his shiny shoes to his smiling lips and his jet-black eyes. Hoshino, in spite of his Japanese name, had the look of a Korean, which made him very odd company for an old-line patrician like Tanaka. After the Japanese invasion, many Koreans had settled in Japan. Some of them had become rich. None had achieved full acceptance into Japanese society. I asked myself whether these two represented the full spread of a four billion dollar investment fund or whether they were just mannequins used to dress the window of the store. My guess was that any enquiries would reveal a whole network of corporate titles and alliances and very little hard information. So, being a polite fellow, I asked whether there were any other languages in which they felt comfortable. Surprise, surprise, Mr Cubeddu had French, Spanish, and Portuguese. Mr Hoshino had Mandarin, Cantonese, Korean and Japanese, which were more than enough to be going on with.

Then Boris Vannikov arrived with his assistant Tanya, a dark-haired Armenian with a model's figure, a Madonna smile and bright, shrewd eyes. Her Japanese was good, if formal, and her English came with the standard American accent. The political officer was a squat, smiling Georgian whose name was Lavrenti Ardaziani. He said he spoke only Russian and Georgian, which I did not believe for a moment. However, it was very clear where his interest lay.

'I'm supposed to be a watchdog over Boris. But he's already a political aberrant and beyond cure. In fact, I want to see some of your investment go to my homeland. Have you ever been to Georgia?'

I told him I had not only been there, but I had stayed a summer with my father in Tbilisi, learning the language and studying the folklore. Later, my company had published a textbook on the modern Georgian language and an English translation of the works of two Georgian poets killed in the Stalinist purges. For good measure, I quoted him a couplet from one of them, Titsian Tabidze, and wrote it in *Mkhedrule* script on a page of his notebook. He was impressed, as I had intended he should be. Georgians – with some notable exceptions, like Beria and Stalin – are generally open-hearted and convivial folk. I hoped I had made a friend. However, as a political officer – they are more difficult to read than poets – he might just as easily have been recording me as a very well-trained subversive.

In the far corner, Boris was in cheerful talk with Marta and Miko. I noted with a small pang of jealousy how happily the two women were responding to each other and were playing Boris Vannikov like a trout in a quiet pool. He, too, was enjoying the game; and the Armenian Madonna clearly was not. He looked better this morning, relaxed and rested. He had said to me on the flight: 'Thank God, we're beginning! I cannot build my life on ifs and maybes. I'm glad Lavrenti's coming. He's not a bad fellow – for a Georgian!'

Tanaka, I noticed, was in close talk with the two newcomers. His demeanour with them cast doubt on my notion that they were simply front men. A moment later he signalled me to join them. He introduced me with a slightly forced joke.

'Gentlemen, I want you to know that you can rely on Gil, both for accurate rendition of a discussion and an informed opinion on any issue. He does not expect you to agree with him. He and I have differed sharply on many issues; but I have learned to listen carefully and think hard about what he tells me. If you have problems, you may express them freely.'

Both men smiled and bowed. Then, without warning, Mr Hoshino launched into a torrent of Korean, in which he asked me to explain the separate functions of the Soviet representatives. All the time he was speaking his eyes were locked with mine to discern any flicker of doubt or uncertainty. When I gave him the answer with equal fluency, he bowed and said in English: 'Thank you, Mr Langton. I understand now why Mr Tanaka has so much confidence in you.'

I told him then, in Korean, that I was sure I could repose the same confidence in him and any of his colleagues whom it might be my later pleasure to meet. I pointed out that all parties in the deal, including the

Soviets, were working at risk and in areas of great uncertainty. Therefore, mutual confidence was very important. He agreed, with less elaboration, that it was.

Mr Cubeddu watched the exchange with a certain puzzlement, then asked me in English to explain what was going on. I told him his colleague was testing my qualifications as a linguist, and that people had the same curiosity about the accomplishment as they had about card tricks and sleight-of-hand. He gave a thin smile and a dismissive shrug. He said that money talk was the same in all languages. Which seemed to end that line of conversation.

Kenji Tanaka asked blandly whether there was anything else they needed to know. They told him they had more than enough to digest and drifted away towards the conference room. I turned to Tanaka.

'I wish you wouldn't stage these little comedies. They make me feel like a performing seal.'

'It was necessary. They had to prove what I had told them. They are hard-heads, those two. They represent very hard money.'

'I need to know a lot more about them than you've told me, Kenji.'

'No.' He was very emphatic about it. 'They are here only to display their house flags and give aid and comfort to our Soviet friends. In Bangkok you will be more fully informed. I must say, Gil, you handled them very well. I could see they were impressed.'

'I'd have done better with a little warning.'

'I doubt it.' Kenji Tanaka gave me a reluctant grin. 'Surprise is the essence of the test. You would have made a good swordsman, Gil. You're very quick on your feet.'

I had no answer for that. I was irritated with him; but I could not afford the luxury of telling him so. It was right on noon, time to get the show on the road.

The meeting itself began more smoothly than I expected. Carl Leibig's speech of welcome was felicitous. He spoke in English, which was the easiest currency for the whole group. Tanya translated the speech into Russian for the benefit of the political officer. Leibig side-stepped very adroitly the dark pools of history and talked of opportunities for constructive co-operation between private commercial corporations and whatever new trading entities emerged in the industry and agriculture of the Soviet Union. This was in no sense a bargaining session, but an exploratory meeting to discuss the documents which had been submitted at the request of Moscow.

That lobbed the ball neatly into Vannikov's court; but first I made my little spiel. I told them that, at the joint invitation of the hosts, I was presiding over this opening session, but that I should be happy to vacate the chair at any moment. I had no financial or national interest in the matters under discussion. I was being paid to mediate, interpret, facilitate, clarify. I had enjoyed good relations with Boris Vannikov, Kenji Tanaka and Carl Leibig. I hoped those relations would be improved by this exercise. So, over to you, Boris Vannikov.

Friend Boris was as sharp as a needle. He, too, offered to deliver his response in English. His political colleague had no objections – this with a sidelong grin – because he had already cleared the text in Russian and had suggested that it would sound much better in Georgian. Quietly at first, then with increasing eloquence, he delivered his statement.

'I speak to you, not as businessmen or bankers or traders, though you are all of these things, but as potential co-operators in a new and challenging enterprise. Mr Tanaka and Mr Leibig, with their colleagues, have responded to our invitation with a proposal of authentic value. We have studied it carefully and, while there is much in it that requires discussion, debate and definition, we accept it as a sound basis for the work to which we have committed ourselves in Bangkok.

'That said, however, my colleague and I are obliged to give you fair warning of the difficulties which lie ahead for you and for us. We are a nation in transition, a Union fragmenting itself. All the dogmas to which we pledged our belief are now under challenge. They were the cement which bound us together in all our diversities of race, history and traditional belief. Now the cement no longer holds. Individual republics are demanding that their separate identities be recognised. We are still trying to devise a new form of federation which will permit us, not only to co-exist, but to co-operate to a common advantage. Everything in your document' – he held it up in a dramatic gesture –'everything is predicated upon an assumption that the arrangements you offer will be made with a central authority and backed by a common pool of resources, expressed in a common currency. You have a right to expect that. You cannot, in today's world, be expected to negotiate separate trading and banking arrangements with each single republic. Equally, you have the right to know that the central authority can honour its pledges, its commercial paper, its freeholds and leaseholds and tax arrangements.

'More than this, you have to believe that the people themselves are willing to trust you and co-operate with you. They have had seventy years of socialism. Not all of it was black. They will not readily throw it away for a new capitalist illusion. Some of them are drones, only too happy to survive within a protective system. They will not change overnight into industrious, competitive workers.

'As you can read in your daily newspapers, all those matters are now in open debate in the Soviet Union. It would be as disastrous for us as for you to make agreements that could not be honoured. My country is in crisis at this moment. I believe we shall weather it. I can promise no more.

'None of us here knows what will happen in the Gulf. We all know that we are walking a razor's edge across a pit of fire. Whatever happens in the next few weeks may destroy all our hopes; but so long as there is hope ahead, we must continue walking towards it.

'So, let us talk openly. Ask me or Lavrenti here any questions you like; we shall try to answer them. Expect questions from us, too, because we are responsible to those who sent us. What more can I say? When I was a small boy I used to think it was the ringmaster who made the circus. Now I know that maybe he is afraid of bears; maybe he couldn't walk two steps on a high wire; maybe if he tried to be a clown they would pelt him with bad eggs; but the performance would not be the same without him . . . Back to you, Gil.'

It was a fine performance and it deserved the applause they gave him. I called on Tanaka to respond. Instead, he offered the floor to Domenico Cubeddu.

When he rose to speak, the Sicilian radiated an air of authority. His attitude was curiously arrogant, rather like that of a prosecuting attorney determined to impress the jury with his opening address.

'I represent a group of investors who, subject to agreed documents, have pledged financial participation in the Tanaka/Leibig consortium. So, I'm a money-man, talking money. Money isn't a hothouse plant that can only be nurtured in stable conditions. It's a weed, with a million mutations. It will grow anywhere. There's trouble in the Gulf? Sure there is! But the spot oil market is still open, the wires and the satellite channels are still open to all the stock markets. If war breaks out, business will still go on. What I want to say to Mr Vannikov and his colleagues, what I want to say to Mr Tanaka and Mr Leibig as well, is this. Total stability in the Soviet Union, in Europe, anywhere else, is a myth. For a money-man, the unstable time is opportunity time. You want the other side of the coin? Look at China, since Tiananmen Square. Very stable. So stable, it's stagnating and until things liven up I won't advise my people to invest a nickel there . . . This document, this proposal, is a good and sound one. It's conservative. It engenders confidence. But in my view it's too conservative, too hidebound. I don't think the Soviet Union is going to settle down in a month, a year, even a decade maybe, not unless you want a military coup and blood in the streets and the Lubianka working twenty-four hours a day. So what are we waiting for? Let's do business in the world we've got. If the risks are high, let's increase the risk loading on the funds. Our stakes are on the table. It's time for Moscow to ante-up and let's start cutting the cards.'

The effrontery of the man took everybody by surprise. Vannikov and his colleagues were visibly shocked. There was sound sense in what he said; but the brutality of the utterance was Wall Street at its worst, crass, vulgar and insulting. It was also totally destructive of the atmosphere we were trying to create. As a neutral mediator, I had to hold myself clear of the debate. I looked at Tanaka to bail me out of it. Instead, he indicated by a gesture that I should call the other newcomer, Mr Hoshino, who promptly sprang another surprise. He said he would prefer to speak in Japanese. He would ask me to translate it first into Russian and then paraphrase for the others. His speech was brief.

'There is much sense in what my colleague has said. My company trades all around the world. In every territory there are different conditions. There are no common laws, only customs and expedients, which each of our executives has to learn for himself. The one universal rule is respect. So long as that holds, one can do business. Without it, the pirates take control. I am older and therefore more patient than my friend Cubeddu. I am prepared to listen to any sensible proposition.'

I addressed the translation directly to Vannikov and was relieved to see him relax slowly and then nod approval to his colleagues. When I paraphrased the statement for the others, I pitched it directly to Leino and Forster, who were clearly somewhat on the fringes of the event. Even as I spoke, I was becoming more and more uneasy. Cubeddu and Hoshino had each spoken with considerable authority. In the case of Cubeddu there was something more, a high-handed despotism, as if he were totally independent, or, more likely, was the man of confidence for a very powerful group who would automatically endorse and enforce any decision he made. For the moment, there was nothing required of me except the even-handed conduct of the meeting. The political officer raised his hand and signified his desire to be heard. He asked whether he might be permitted to put questions to the delegates. Tanya would translate both questions and answers. The questions were addressed to Tanaka.

'Your document prescribes that we must reach substantive agreement over a two-week period in Bangkok.'

'Correct.'

'Then there are time limits within which the work must begin and be brought to various stages of completion?'

'Yes.'

'If these deadlines are not met, and in default of an agreed amendment to the schedule, the funds may be withdrawn?'

'Yes.'

'Is that not a very onerous condition? A very dangerous one from our point of view?'

'I agree.' Tanaka was courtesy itself. 'It is both onerous and dangerous. However, it is designed to protect us against certain uninsurable risks – like war, civil disorder or industrial disputes which we have no means to arbitrate. It is one of those things to which Mr Cubeddu referred as "a risk loading". Like everything else, however, it is negotiable. You reduce the risk, we reduce the loading.'

Nobody else noticed it but, by God, I did. It was the first time ever I had heard Tanaka link his own name with that of someone who was not at the same level of authority as he was. However, I could not dwell on the thought. The political officer was already on his next question. This one had a very sharp sting to it.

'The original intention, still stated in this document, was that the Tanaka interest would be represented by wholly Japanese capital. That is clearly not so under the present arrangements. Can you explain that, Mr Tanaka?'

'I can. Let me say first of all that there is no contradiction between the expressed intent of the document and the circumstances that exist now. Everything in the document depends upon satisfactory contractual agreements between the parties. There is a section, rather broadly worded under the heading "Freeholds, leaseholds, free ports, Customs-unions and territorial concessions". My colleagues in the Japanese banking system have made the return of the Kuril Islands a condition of any investment on their part. I disagreed. I believe that the territories should be returned as soon as possible, but I recognise also that a diplomatic negotiation will take much more time than any of us here can command. So, in order to honour my promise to Mr Leibig and my commitment to the consortium, I sought other parties of substance. Their representatives are with us today.'

'Ah yes. The Palermitan Banking Corporation and the Pacific Littoral Development Group. These are not, shall we say, prominent names in international finance.'

'Not prominent perhaps; but powerful nonetheless. Which would you rather have: big names imposing penal conditions, or big money committed to bold enterprise?'

Lavrenti gave him a big Georgian smile. 'I'm sure the money is there, Mr Tanaka. My real question is: where is it coming from?'

It was the question I myself had been dying to ask but, without translating it, I ruled it out of order.

'I'm sorry, my friend, but I cannot permit you to discriminate between the financial parties present. You might equally well ask the same question of any banker. He would certainly refuse to answer. No banker is required to reveal the source of his funds. No shareholders' names are revealed by a broker until they are inscribed on the share register. You are out of order, my friend.'

'Forgive me. I withdraw the question.'

He sat down without another word. Kenji Tanaka asked sharply: 'Why did you not translate what was said?'

'Because the question was out of order and it was withdrawn.'

I caught Carl Leibig's eye and knew that he had very well understood the drift of the question. He and I had asked it before but, sooner or later, Tanaka would be forced to answer it. We still had about ten minutes left before the luncheon break. I decided to use them to get the three parties circulating during the afternoon. It was time to let Boris Vannikov do a little work for his living. I put it to him.

'It's clear that all parties are looking for explanations rather than stalemate on prepared positions. I suggest we break now for lunch. Please take this opportunity to get to know each other and to sort yourselves into working groups. If you have any communication problems, Tanya or I will be at your disposal. The bar is open. Good health and good appetite.'

As they drifted out of the conference room and into the bar, Miko was waiting to receive them and, with singular skill, coax them into new encounters and new groupings. I was about to follow them, but Carl Leibig held me back. He was a very troubled man.

'Gil, we have to talk.'

'I'm all yours. Where and when?'

'In my office. Turn right at the end of the hall. You go first. I'll make our excuses and join you in a couple of minutes.'

'As you wish. Tell Marta I'll join her shortly.'

I walked down to his office. Franz, his assistant, was already there. He seated me and offered me a drink. Then he laid on the table a large scrapbook full of newspaper cuttings.

'Carl asked me to explain this. As you have probably guessed, Carl and I are lovers, have been for a long time. There is a deep trust between us. At weekends we usually retreat here to Nara. I have a foolish ambition. One day I want to write thrillers like the American, Raymond Chandler, whom I have admired for many years. I am interested in – what do you call it? – *das Leben der unteren Stände.*'

'Low life?'

'That's it, low life. I cut stories out of all the newspapers which I read: German, Japanese, English, American. For the plots, you know?'

'For the plots, of course.'

'This morning when you all arrived I saw for the first time this Mr Hoshino, the new associate of Mr Tanaka. I recognised him. I have him in my scrapbook.'

He opened the scrapbook and pointed to a cutting from a Japanese magazine. It showed a well dressed man raising his glass in a toast to an unseen photographer. There was no doubt at all that it was Mr Hoshino. Franz pointed to the caption: 'Hoshino Taoka, whose real name is Chong Gwon Yong, is the reputed leader of the largely Korean brotherhood known as the Association of South-East Asia Friendly Societies which, although headquartered in Tokyo, controls many offshore criminal activities in Indonesia, Thailand, the Philippines and South Korea.'

I was still staring at the page when Carl Leibig came in. He closed and locked the door behind him. He said: 'What do you say, Gil?'

'What can I say? It's the same man.'

'So who is Cubeddu?'

'More of the same, I guess. *La Fratellanza*, The Honourable Society. Mafia and Yakuza. That makes a heavy combination.'

'Why, Gil? Why would Tanaka do this? It's the act of a madman!'

'I wish I could agree with you, Carl; but no, I don't think it's a madness. Look at it from Tanaka's point of view and it even makes a wild kind of sense.'

'In God's name, how?'

'Keep your voice down, Carl.'

'Please, Carl.' Franz chided him gently. 'Try to be calm.'

'How can I be calm? Tanaka is out of control. He is playing some private game, gambling with both our lives and with this whole enterprise. I can't let him do it. I have too much at stake: a century and a half of honourable enterprise in this country. Now he wants to put me in bed with thugs and bandits.'

'He doesn't see it like that, Carl.'

'How do you know how he sees it?' He was suddenly wary as a cat.

'Because I'm his partner in business, Carl. I've known him a long time. Why do you think we had that big row before we left Tokyo? Trust me in this, please.'

'Gil is right, Carl. Listen to him carefully, I beg you.'

He was silent for a moment, then he nodded agreement. 'I do trust you, Gil. I'm upset. I'm not thinking straight. What do we do?'

'First, Franz must lock that scrapbook in the safe.'

'Immediately.' He moved to the big floor safe and began dialling the combination.

'Second, we give ourselves time to think. No hurried action is needed. We still have two weeks of conference in Bangkok before any decisions are made. Until then, we're players in the game. We'll know what is going on. We'll have the power to act. Once we're out of the game, kaput. We can do nothing. So, we put on our poker-faces and play each hand as it is dealt. Are you with me so far?'

'I'm with you.'

'Now comes the important part. You have to understand exactly what Tanaka is doing and why he is doing it.'

'Do you understand that, Gil?'

'In part, yes.'

'Then I wish to God you'd explain it to me. All I can see is a monumental folly with disaster at the end of it.'

'Let me try to run it through quickly. We'll have time to discuss it later . . . Franz, would you unlock the door please. If anybody comes we don't want this to look like a conclave of conspirators. Pick up a folder and stand close to it, so you can hear if anyone's coming down the corridor. Good. Now, here are the elements. There are long and traditional links between legitimate business and the Yakuza in Japan. You know that. Japanese banks, like banks everywhere, are stuffed with ill-gotten gains, the fruits of criminal enterprise. So long as there's no label on them, who asks? Who cares? The funds that Forster is putting together for you, are they all clean? How do you prove it, yea or nay? . . . Next element. Tanaka's a man with the mark of death on him. He's already arranged his own exit. So he can afford to gamble. His peers in the *keiretsu* have walked away from him. He has vivid memories of his own childhood, when his father had to go into hiding to avoid assassination by the militarists. But more than that, Carl – and this is his ace-in-the-hole – he knows that if a good deal is struck with the Soviets in Bangkok, every member of the *keiretsu* will be back, knocking on his door to be let in again.'

'It makes sense, Gil, but there's a line still missing in the logic. What's in it for the Yakuza and the Mafia, any criminal organisation?'

'That's the simplest question of all, Carl. What do you do with black money? You wash it clean. Whiter than white. What bigger or better washing machine than the virgin land of a new Soviet Union? What better place to exploit new deals and new concessions – drugs, amusements, pornography, gambling – than a country which has just come out of the Puritan age of Marxism? Look at it like that, Carl, and Tanaka's a genius. He's set up the perfect marriage of convenience and he can still walk away before the knot is tied.'

'One more question, Gil. What do you propose to do about this?'

'Let me answer it with another. Who is paying my fee, you or Tanaka?'

'We are splitting it down the middle.'

'So you have joint ownership of my services under the contract, equal access to my counsel and equal severance rights. I cannot serve one of you at the cost of a disservice to the other. Also, I have my own freedom of conscience and my own right of withdrawal. What am I going to do? For the moment, what I have agreed. And remember, we both work under Japanese law. It is not a crime to associate with known criminals. Yakuza clubs operate openly with the insignia over the front door. Tanaka is certainly not acting in a criminal fashion. So, my counsel is to wait and see. When in doubt, do nothing. Let's go to lunch.'

Leibig still hesitated, but Franz was totally convinced. 'He's right,

Carl. What have you got to lose by waiting? I'm sure I've got more stuff on Hoshino in my files. It shouldn't be too hard to dig up some material on Cubeddu. Let's be sure we're treading on solid ground.'

'Very well. That's how we play it, with a poker-face. Thank you, Gil. Now we should go to lunch. If Tanaka asks what we have been talking about . . .'

'We tell him the truth, or at least part of it. Lavrenti Ardaziani asked a question about the provenance of our new money. I disallowed it. You asked me how the question should be answered when it comes up again, as it inevitably will. We both invite Tanaka's opinion. Clear?'

'Absolutely. Let's go to lunch.'

The table groupings were interesting. Tanaka was seated with Forster and Cubeddu and a place had been left vacant for me. Marta was seated with Vannikov and the man from Georgia, who beckoned Carl Leibig to join them. Tanya, the interpreter, was placed with Leino the Finn, Hoshino the Korean and Miko herself.

Miko had done her work well. The Korean and the Finn were effectively insulated by the presence of the two women. Forster would give a certain legitimacy to the Sicilian. I could field awkward questions addressed to Tanaka. The Russians could, if they chose, examine Marta and Leibig on the implications of the Haushofer thesis.

This time there was no fault to find with Leibig's hospitality. His chef was a young Rhinelander, French-trained and Swiss-polished. His waiters were all young men from the hoteliers school in Nara. Franz doubled as *maître d'hôtel*, moving discreetly from group to group, directing the service, alert always to catch a significant phrase in the talk. I had a suggestion for our group.

'A round of golf after lunch . . . nine holes or eighteen, as you choose? We can talk as we go. What do you say, gentlemen?'

Cubeddu was the first taker. Forster was the second. Tanaka hesitated.

'I'm out of practice. I haven't hit a ball in three months . . . But then, why not? After Tokyo the air here is almost too clean to breathe.'

The moment that issue was settled, Cubeddu was off on another tack. 'I'm much impressed with this language trick of yours, Mr Langton. How does it work?'

'Well, it's hard to analyse in a few words, but it isn't a trick. It's a combination of disciplines: linguistics, history, geography. Take your name, for example, Domenico Cubeddu. I would guess that your family originally came from the Western end of Sicily and that you could probably dig up relatives in Sardinia as well.'

'How would you figure that out?' He was giving nothing away.

'I used to sail those coasts with my father. When we called into Cagliari in Sardinia, we used to stay with a family called Cubeddu. I believe the name is Sard and not Sicilian. There was traffic between the islands from earliest times.'

He was taken aback, but only for a moment. He laughed and threw up his hands in a gesture of mock surrender. 'You told me he was smart, Tanaka. He's right. My father came from Sardinia and married a girl from Palermo. He was a great man, my father, very cool, *molto dignitoso*. Although he was a foreigner he became a man of high confidence. He never made a promise he didn't keep. You impress me, Mr Langton. I should like to do business with you.'

It was not a prospect that pleased me; but I did not want to insult the man either. I changed the subject and asked Forster: 'Does your bank do much business with Mr Cubeddu's corporation?'

'No. I know the organisation, of course; but he is not one of our regular correspondents.'

There was a special shade of meaning to that in the jargon of international banking. Translated into bald terms, it meant they would happily deal with Cubeddu's cash, but they would not be too keen to handle his paper. I could not be sure whether Cubeddu had caught the overtone or not. He seemed bent on cross-examining me.

'How many languages do you speak?'

'Fluently and correctly, twenty three. In varying degrees, fifteen to twenty others.'

'That means you can get to talk with a lot more women than most guys.'

'The problem is' – the comic relief came from Tanaka, of all people – 'he can only screw them at the same rate as the rest of us.'

That prompted me to tell the story of my father welcoming me back to the boat after I had spent a boozy evening in the Corsican port of Calvi, where young sprouts like me were no match for the paratroops of the French Foreign Legion who trained there and monopolised the best of the fillies. I returned to the docks at two in the morning, escorted back by three rather pallid girls from Wimbledon who had not been able to cope either with the French language or the Foreign Legion paras.

144

After I had got rid of them, with three pallid kisses and some inconclusive squeezes, my father fed me a mug of coffee and some bedtime counsel: 'Remember, my son, you can't drink all the wine in the world. You can't screw all the girls in the world. It's a physical impossibility for an exceptional man, which you most emphatically are not, at least, not yet. So what do you do? You buy yourself one, maybe two bottles of good wine; you find yourself one, maybe two happy, good looking girls; and you sit quietly in a corner and enjoy them. But remember something else . . .' I had a vision of that big, professorial hand of his, upraised like a prophet's as he boomed across the harbour. 'Remember, Gil Langton! If you try to drink all the wine in the world, you'll get nothing but an almighty hangover. You try to screw all the girls in the world, you'll get no fun and all the transmissible diseases in the medical dictionary. Now, go to bed.'

I must have been talking rather more loudly than usual, because everybody in the room seemed to have picked up on the story. The laughter that went up was a welcome relief from the tension of the morning and the undercurrent of suspicion that flowed between the participants in the conference.

Carl Leibig signalled the waiters to pour more drinks. Boris Vannikov took the floor and delivered his characterisation – famous, he claimed, on four continents – of the Cossack and the fifty-rouble hooker. After that it became a very relaxed lunch party and it was three thirty in the afternoon before we teed off for our golf game. At Tanaka's request, we played two and two in separate games, he with me, Forster with Cubeddu. Thus, we had the opportunity to talk out of earshot of the others. Tanaka was tired and he looked it. He asked that we should drive the buggy instead of walking the course. He played with concentration but with little energy; all his shots were straight, but short. His talk was the same, terse and direct.

'You are angry with me, aren't you, Gil?'

'Angry, no. Disappointed, yes.'

'But you protected me today, when you disallowed the question.'

'I was protecting a position; which is more important than you are.'

'I don't understand that.'

'I know. That's the sadness.'

'The sadness for me, Gil, is that you refuse to accept my position. What have you told Carl?'

'Nothing that he didn't already know. You've called in black money – Yakuza, Mafia, all their tributaries.'

'Don't you understand why?'

'We understand; but you have shamed us, Kenji. This is not the company we choose to keep in our lives.'

'So now, what?'

'For the moment, nothing. We proceed as planned. We go to Bangkok for the full-dress performance. All the time, every moment, every day and night, we reserve our position. We give you every chance to bring off your coup, toss these fellows out and bring in legitimate money. You lose, we walk. You cheat one more time, we walk. We can't change your life for you, Kenji. We can't re-write your history. What more can you ask?'

'Understanding.'

'You have that. Otherwise, I wouldn't be talking to you like this.'

'Respect, too.'

'You've always had that. Now you have to earn some of it. Answer some questions for me.'

'I'll try.'

'Who is Cubeddu?'

'He's number one laundry man for South American cocaine money.'

'How did you contact him?'

'Miko arranged it.'

'Hoshino?'

'I've known and used him for many years. He banks with us. We invest for him. Huge monies. Girl business, show business, wrestling, sports events, pachinko parlours. A great customer for any bank. A great investor for our project because he wants clean money and he'll offer a lot better terms than the World Bank.'

'You're talking of cash terms only, of course.'

'Of course.'

'But now the relationship has changed.'

'I do not see that. They are putting up hard cash, not paper.'

'They are thieves and killers. You are handing them the keys to the house.'

'It is not my house. Let the owners look to their own security.'

That took us both to the third hole, a short eight iron shot for the green. Kenji took a seven but even then hit short, landing in the rough

146

on the forward edge of the green. I took an eight, hit too hard and too low and landed on the far edge with a steep downhill putt to the hole. Tanaka, being just off the green, had the first shot. He took a long time settling himself for it, then holed it for a birdie. I had an easier shot, but I muffed it and finished with a par.

As we drove away from the hole, Tanaka said amiably: 'Golf's a crazy game, isn't it?'

'It can drive you insane, sure enough.'

'So learn from it, Gil.' Suddenly there was a ring of steel in his voice. 'Don't write me off until I've played the last shot on the last hole! That would be a big mistake.'

'And it's my right to make it. Don't you forget that either, old friend.'

It was perhaps symbolic that we were finishing square on the last hole, when I missed a three-foot putt and lost the game and a ten thousand yen stake to Kenji Tanaka.

Nine

When I got back to the guest house, Marta had the bath running and our fresh clothes laid out on the bed. We went through the cleansing rituals and the sex play that inevitably followed them. Afterwards we sat together in the big pinewood tub, neck deep in scalding water, and talked through the day.

Marta was riding a high wave of excitement. The luncheon talk with Vannikov and the political officer had gone very well. She had to play it through again for my benefit.

'They had both read my thesis and examined me very closely on it. At first, they seemed intent on proving that it had been financed by Carl Leibig for a political purpose. I told them that was nonsense. I had done the work on my own time, with my own money. After that, the talk became much more relaxed. I pointed out that Haushofer's theories had been based on a variety of sources: Kjellen the Swede, Ratzel the German geographer and Halford Mackinder the Englishman. There was still great value in them, but they had been corrupted and confused by his association with the politics and pseudo-philosophy of the Nazis. However, I pointed out the classic Marxists had been equally wrong when they rejected any notion of interaction between a society and its environment. That started another lively argument and . . .'

'And you're going to spare me the details, Frau Professor. This natural environment is about as primitive and pleasant as you can get. I refuse to foul it up with Middle European metaphysics.'

'You're a very rude man, Gil Langton.'

'Guilty as charged. Now stop talking, close your eyes and just live through your skin for a little while.'

'I have brains too, remember!'

'I know; but mine have turned to water.'

For a while we floated together, silent and sensuous in the liquid

148

world. Then, a propos of nothing at all, Marta asked: 'Have you ever been to bed with Miko?'

'No.'

'Have you ever wanted to sleep with her?'

'No.'

'Why not?'

'Why the questions?'

'She fascinates me, that's why. She's never married. She has no children. Her life with Tanaka is very much a part-time affair. She tells me that after Bangkok she'll be going back to Los Angeles to look after her business. And yet she's a very sexy, sensual woman.'

'How would you know that?'

'The way she talks, the way she acts. The things she's told me. After lunch today, while you were playing golf, she borrowed a car from the estate and we drove out to see the Katsura temple. Then we strolled in the park and fed the deer. We were like sisters together, open and relaxed. She told me that her sex-life here is spent exclusively with Kenji Tanaka, but in Los Angeles she has other lovers, some of them women. Does that surprise you?'

'Not really. In the traditions of the floating world, sex has always been an elaborate game, in which people can play roles which in ordinary life would be forbidden to them. The game has nothing to do with love, only with the refinement of pleasure. Love, in fact, is the danger to be avoided, because it destroys the illusion and stops the game.'

'What would you say if I told you Miko had invited me to play the game with her? She used a Japanese word . . .'

'*Asobi.*'

'That's right. It was just a diversion, she said, a change of taste and flavour. You think this is very silly, don't you?'

'I find it intriguing. I wonder why you bring it up just at this moment.'

She gave a little teasing laugh and slid out of my arms. 'Because it's a sexy notion and I like to have sexy notions and sexy talk while I'm making love.'

'When I need a second woman in bed or in the bath with us, I'll let you know. You can call Miko and invite her over.'

'Now you're angry. I've always thought lovers should be able to share everything, even their fantasies.'

'They also should try to get their timing right. Just now, Miko and

Tanaka are not my favourite people. But I'll answer your question. If you need another kind of loving, you're free to go looking for it. You're an adult, intelligent woman. I, on the other hand, would not be prepared to share you, or the experience. But I'll give you a caution, *schatzi*. This is the wrong place for a Western woman to go looking for sexual adventure. I'd be very careful walking into the world of flowers and willows, hand in hand with Miko. Now, let's dry off and get dressed. It's coming up to cocktail time.'

It was one of those explosive little moments which left the smell of gunpowder in the air. It reminded me that my relationship with Frau Professor Doktor Marta Boysen was far from being a tenured one. It was complicated in a curious way by my father's relationship with her mother, the eleven years difference in our ages and her slightly incestuous perception of me as a big brother as well as a lover.

There was also more to the Miko situation than I cared to confess. From our first meeting, I had always found her an attractive and intriguing woman. I had never made a move towards her because my friendship with Tanaka forbade it and any indiscretion would have put that friendship at risk. More, my own forays into the floating world had been made under special circumstances. I was always *gaijin*, the outside man, but my command of the language was a talisman that opened many doors which would otherwise have remained sealed. I had been introduced to the dying art of *geisha asobi*, the old-fashioned and very expensive game of 'playing with geisha'. On the interminable nightclub circuit, I had learned that even the humblest girl in the floating world was an artefact and that everything that passed between her and her clients was a calculated illusion. To take it seriously was a folly. In the Takarazuka theatre, all male roles were played by women who, so long as they were with the troupe, were, and are, obliged to live the cloistered lives of vestal virgins. Comics for teenage girls tend to be full of impossibly beautiful, sexless young men. The love of young men, often romantically undeclared, was one of the traditional ideals of the samurai code.

All of which made too much of a mouthful to explain to Marta at the end of a long day. I wondered, uneasily, how much of it needed explaining, and how much of herself she was trying to explain to me. One thing, however, I did know. Miko was attempting something more than a lesbian seduction. She was carefully teasing Marta into a

150

situation where she could use her as a weapon against me, or as a counterweight to my expressed hostility to Tanaka's plans.

The threads she was weaving around Marta were tenuous as gossamer. At this moment it seemed a laugh, a sigh would blow them away; but once the web was woven I knew it would hold like steel mesh. So, before we went across to join the others for pre-dinner drinks, I made an apology for my brusqueness. She accepted it with a kiss and an embrace and made me sit down on the bed, holding my hands as she explained.

'This is the one thing that worries me, Gil. I told you how it was between my husband and myself. I was like a prisoner beating my head against iron bars. Even now, the horror of it haunts me and I have to prove to myself that I am really free, that I can do what I choose and no one can stop me. I love you, Gil. I truly love you. I'm content to perch like a bird on your open hand and sing happy songs for you all day. The moment you close your hand, you lose me. That's not a threat. I fear that moment more than I can explain. Try to understand.'

'I'll try; but you must understand something too. If you want to fly away, I won't try to hold you, even for a moment. I love you too much to deny you the freedom you want; but just make sure you don't flee from one prison and find yourself in another . . . women, I'm told, can be very brutal gaolers.'

'Has that been your experience, Gil?'

'No, thank God. I was one of the lucky ones. I've had a lot of love in my life. I've learned to be very careful of it.'

'Hold me close please, Gil. Hold me very close.'

As I drew her to me and buried my face in her fragrant hair, she began to weep quietly. It took a long time to comfort her. Finally, as she was standing at the mirror repairing her makeup, she said a strange thing.

'What will you do, I wonder, when the white crow turns to black?'

I asked her what she meant. She seemed not to hear me. Because we had had more than enough of argument, I did not press the question. I kissed her on the neck so I would not smudge her makeup. She reached up and touched my face with her fingertips. Then we drove across the compound in the golf buggy to have cocktails before dinner.

The mood of the gathering had changed since the first morning assembly. The first wariness had gone. People were smiling and chatting in a relaxed fashion. Even the outsiders, Hoshino and Cubeddu, seemed at ease, chuckling at some joke which Boris

Vannikov was telling. The language barriers had broken down somewhat and, if you listened carefully, you heard a hodge-podge of words and phrases in different tongues which, in the end, made a kind of *lingua franca*, quite acceptable for ordinary intercourse.

Among my father's papers, one of the most valuable documents was an essay which he delivered each year as a three-part lecture to new students, entitled 'Intercourse on the Frontiers'. He always let the students have their laugh when he announced the title. He always added the same little joke that sex, food, drink were a soldier's first needs when he shed his battle gear. After that, he invited the class to imagine themselves as legionaries, or camp-followers, Greek hoplites, Viking voyagers or Mongol warriors, set down on the outer limits of conquest or trade. Then he asked a series of questions. After the first bloody encounters, how did they begin to communicate with local tribes? How did languages communicate themselves from one group to another? How did the grammatical structures begin? Why did accents change? I myself had listened, spellbound, to his exposition; I had later published the manuscript in a memorial edition as a tribute to his nurturing of me.

There was another passage in the series which tonight I recalled with a certain poignant clarity. This had to do with the social changes which language itself expressed. My father's point was that alien elements were necessary catalysts to human development. Strangers, friendly or hostile, created a tension and a dynamic which kept the tribal group alert and alive. I began to wonder whether the positions I had taken with Tanaka, with Marta and in my own complacent conscience, were not already too rigid to endure.

I had the opportunity for a brief word with Carl Leibig. I told him what I had said to Tanaka. He frowned and asked: 'Was that wise, Gil?'

'I think so, Carl. The cat was already out of the bag. He knows he still has our qualified support and you and I can both make an honourable exit if things don't work out.'

'I haven't spoken to Tanaka this afternoon. Do you think I should raise the question?'

'I see no harm. You can tell him of our talk. But don't reveal that you hold incriminating material.'

'Franz has dug up some more, on both Hoshino and Cubeddu.'

'Have him copy it and give it to me before we leave for Tokyo. Also,

I'd like to use your office to make some early phone calls tomorrow morning.'

'It's yours from seven o'clock, earlier if you want. Did you have a pleasant game?'

'Very pleasant. My compliments on the greens. They're in beautiful condition. I lost, of course. It cost me money. See you later.'

As I moved away, I came face to face with Tanya, the Armenian girl, she of the dark eyes and the Madonna face. She gave me a big, reproachful smile and told me: 'You've hardly said two words to me since we arrived, Mr Langton.'

I answered her in her own language. 'Let me say them now. "Thou art dark and thou art beautiful. Thy lips are scarlet and thy cheeks pink as pomegranates." '

She blushed and then laughed. 'Where did you learn that one?'

'It's from the *Song of Solomon*.'

'I know; but where did you learn Armenian?'

'Would you believe, in Venice? You must know the place. The community of Armenian monks on the island of San Lazzaro. Byron used to visit there. Their printing press is well known around the world. My father and I were guests for three months. I still deal with them for classic works in Armenian.'

'I know of it, but I've never been there.'

'Maybe now, when things are changing so fast in the Soviet Union, you'll get the chance.'

'Why don't you put in a word for me with Boris?'

'I'd be delighted.'

'How well can you speak Armenian?'

'Try me.'

That was one of the times when I did not mind doing my parlour tricks. Tanya was a very bright young woman, with a malicious sense of humour. She enjoyed being able to indulge her mockeries in a tongue that nobody understood except herself and her two bosses, who at that moment were well out of earshot. I looked across the room and saw that Marta had been taken in tow by Miko, who was guiding her into the company of Leibig and Cubeddu. The Armenian madonna was quick to notice my momentary distraction.

'You are supposed to be concentrating on me, Mr Langton. Those other two women are old enough to look after themselves.'

'And you, my dear Tanya, are old enough to have better manners.'

Her manner changed abruptly. 'I'm sorry. That was very rude. Boris tells me I'm acting like a bitch. He's right. I'm worried about what's going on in my home place. Muslim against Christian, all the old tribal hates. My father and mother are dead now, thank God, but two of my brothers are involved. One of them has taken to the hills with the local militia. The other hates his guts, because he's a Party official with three children. I hope to God what we're doing here will mean something better for us all.'

The sudden unsought confidence touched me deeply. Because we were still in her language I was, in a special fashion, in her world, with the mists of bloody tribal history trailing about me. I tried to offer some shred of comfort.

'This is a beginning, girl. One of many beginnings by many people. Sure, they're all hard-nosed traders; but as far back as you care to go, people used to wait for the coming of caravans, the excitement they brought, the changes that followed their visit. I, too, hope that good will come of all this.'

'Boris says you are a good man, one to be trusted. He and Lavrenti want to talk to you privately. They ask if you will come to our guest house for a drink after dinner.'

'Tell them, yes. It's my job to be available to everyone. Will you be there, too?'

'Of course. Everything changes but nothing changes in Moscow. I am not merely the interpreter. I am assigned to make an independent report on all activities here. The only difference is I don't have to make such a big secret of it. Now we can laugh about such things, even though there's not much else to laugh about.'

Dinner was announced. I found myself seated with Forster the Swiss and Leino the Finn, while Miko acted as our mistress of ceremonies. The meal was a splendid Japanese feast which Miko herself had planned and supervised. She was dressed in kimono and *obi*, her collar drawn back to display the curve of her powdered neck, her hair elaborately dressed in geisha style. The perfume she wore was heady and strangely erotic.

Once again, I had to admire the skill with which she courted each one of us, with small attentions, offerings of special morsels, a hand's touch, a small intimate joke. Each man felt that she was performing for him alone. Even I, the jealous cynic, had to pay tribute to her skill in the ancient game. She was not only keeping an eye on me. She was also

154

cajoling the two conservatives, Forster and Leino, into believing that somehow the intricate illogicality of the East worked better than the cold reason of the West.

When the meal was almost done, I walked over to Tanaka's table and presented him with an envelope, suitably inscribed in *katakana*, which contained ten new thousand-yen notes. I made a mock humble speech, testifying that although the game of golf had been invented by the *gaijin*, the Yamato people looked like taking that over, too. He had beaten me. I bowed to the victor. I acknowledged the splendid advice he had given me: that the game was not over until the last shot on the last hole; and I asked him only to acknowledge that this *gaijin* always paid his debts.

It sounds perhaps a silly, low-comedy charade, but in the context of place and time and circumstance, it carried its own message. It was not an apology, it was not an abdication. It was the declaration of a truce and Tanaka's expression told me that he accepted it. He then announced that he had a speech of his own to make. It would be very brief. He would speak in Japanese. He would hand me the text and then he would ask me to interpret it in the language of each of the guests. It was important, he said, that they should receive it as pure water from an unpolluted spring.

'We have begun well today. We have each learned some truths about the others. We have agreed to walk a few steps further in each other's company. Tomorrow will be a day of close encounters, careful questioning, precise but not yet final judgments. My friend, Gil Langton, reproaches me often because I think and live and work within a Japanese system, to which Western interpretations often do not apply. He is right. But I have no choice, just as our visitors from the Soviet Union have no choice. They cannot change seventy years of socialist history. They may abjure it, but they cannot abdicate it, any more than I can get rid of the weight of the past which I carry on my shoulders.

'Down in Nara city, in a small back street, is an old-fashioned worker in wood who makes boxes for precious things: porcelain, jade and the like. The joints are so beautifully fitted that even the air will not pass between them. He does it all by hand, patiently paring away the thinnest of shavings until one surface slides like silk upon the other. That is what we have to do, tomorrow here, later in Bangkok. The wood is cheap. We can always throw away a spoiled piece. What we cannot waste is the patience and the skill and the goodwill which makes commerce possible.'

It was well said. It translated simply. It was well received. Afterwards, I told him so. At the same time, I told him the Soviet delegation wanted to talk to me and I thought it proper that I should accept their invitation.

'Of course, Gil.' He was as bland as butter. 'That's your job, to keep communications open, promote understanding. In the morning, by the way, there'll be a meeting of principals: Leibig, myself, the Soviets. You won't be needed, but I'd like you to carry a bleeper so I can call you.'

'Whenever you need.'

'Enjoy your evening. Miko and I will entertain Marta.'

'Thank you. I appreciate it.'

'Appreciate? That means to prize, does it not?'

'In one of its meanings, yes.'

'I prize you, Gil. I want you to remember that always. I prize you.'

'Do you want me to call you before I go to bed? You have a right to know what has been said.'

'No. Don't bother. I shall probably fall asleep very early. We'll talk tomorrow.'

I crossed the room to tell Marta that I would be late. She was in animated talk with Cubeddu and Leibig. She smiled, touched my hand and sent me on my way to the inquisitors.

They were very amiable. Vannikov poured the drinks: a vodka, fragrant with herbs, which had a kick like an angry mule. Lavrenti Ardaziani looked like a happy Buddha. Tanya lay on her stomach on the bed, her face cupped in her hands, watching me with shrewd amusement. Lavrenti began the interrogation.

'In your opening address, Gil, you said you were being paid "to mediate, interpret, facilitate, clarify". Do I quote correctly?'

'You do.'

'You uttered those words without reservation or qualification.'

'That's right.'

'So the first thing I'd like you to clarify is why Tanaka, who runs one of the largest and most reputable trading groups in Japan, has invited the participation of two people with known criminal associations.'

'How long have you worked in Japan, Lavrenti?'

'Four years. Why do you ask?'

'To save us all some laboured explanations. You know that the

Yakuza, the various associations of criminal groups, have a historic place in Japanese history and mythology. Films are made about them every day, as they are about the Mafia. Their links with big business are well known and documented. They also have an unwritten pact with the police. They keep order on the shady side of the street.'

'We're all familiar with those connections. Please go on.'

'In the context of the present negotiations, both Cubeddu and Hoshino represent money, the so-called black money, earned directly or indirectly from criminal activities. Every country has it, even yours, my friends. Fortunately for your government and every other in the world, money doesn't smell. Even if it's drug money, sniffer dogs don't recognise it. That's why every banker in the world is glad to take it on deposit and use it for legitimate trade. What do they do in Moscow Narodny Bank, Boris? Check every bunch of rouble notes to see if they're innocent or guilty? So let's not moralise here. You need money desperately for investment and redevelopment. Some of Tanaka's has laundry labels on it. You have to decide whether you can accept it.'

'That still doesn't answer my question, Gil. Why did Tanaka bring in Cubeddu and Hoshino?'

'First, because his colleagues in the *keiretsu*, the small family of big companies, backed away. They say investment in Soviet reconstruction is too big a risk, unless there are big concessions to go with it.'

'Like the Kuril Islands?'

'Don't you understand, they're just the symbol. This bloody country lives by symbols, by group concepts. Its businessmen work to long-term objectives: market share, access to raw materials. The cession of the Kurils would tell them that the way was open for more important access to more important resources. Tanaka thought he could deliver that, at least in a measurable time. The problem is he doesn't have time. For his colleagues, he has the smell of death on him. And you've said you can't deliver anyway, because the time isn't ripe. So what does he do? He goes to one of his biggest depositors, Hoshino, black money, sure, but available now and available in the future. Cubeddu came to him the same way, through his American and South American connections.'

'And you've known all this?'

'I've seen the whole picture only this week. I've tried to dissuade Tanaka because I'm his friend and he's my partner in the publishing enterprise. I failed to change his mind.'

'But you're still with him.'

'I'm also here with you, doing the job as it was agreed, mediating and clarifying. Tanaka knows I'm here. He'll get an accurate report of our proceedings, just as you're getting an accurate report from me.'

'I believe you.' Coming from Lavrenti that was a compliment. 'Now, tell me why Hoshino and Cubeddu are prepared to take the risks that Sumitomo or Daikyo will not?'

'Cubeddu gave you the answer in his speech. It wasn't in good taste, but he was telling you a certain truth. His money is made by taking risks. He's prepared to invest it in a risky enterprise, provided the premium is high enough.'

'And what premium do you think he and Hoshino will want?'

'Concessions, opportunities, all in the leisure and tourist business, which then turns into the gambling business and the brothel business and the drug business . . . you name it.'

'And how does your high-minded Tanaka justify that?'

'Very simply. He takes the view that if he's providing mortgage money to build a house, it's up to the owner to put in his own burglar alarms and take out his own insurance.'

'And what's your view on that, Gil?' It was Boris Vannikov who put the question.

'It's you who have to make the judgment, Boris, not I. But I'll tell you a story instead. Not so long ago, Tanaka approached me on behalf of certain clients who were ready to invest a lot of money in my business if we extended it into comic-book pornography, which is big money in Japan and could be bigger still in the export market. I refused. Tanaka and I have remained friends. We are still in business, although my refusal cost him a lot of money.'

'Which you are trying to make up to him now.' The interjection came from Tanya. Boris Vannikov snapped back instantly.

'Enough! You're out of order.'

Lavrenti Ardaziani said nothing. He watched me with cool, unblinking eyes. I shrugged and smiled at Tanya.

'Where did they teach you that trick? It's too old and shopworn for an intelligent girl like you. One question none of you has thought to ask me is where Carl Leibig stands in all this, where his bankers and backers stand, and all the experts he's going to be wheeling in to Bangkok.'

'So tell us, please,' said Boris Vannikov. 'We need some guidance here.'

'First item. Leibig is picking up half my fee. He has equal call with Tanaka on my services. Neither he nor his bankers are happy with the people Tanaka has introduced. Without them, however – or without a radical change in Soviet attitudes – the whole plan breaks down. He and I have discussed this. We have discussed it with Tanaka and made it clear that we consider ourselves free to withdraw, I from my service contract, Leibig from the consortium itself. Tanaka would like to get rid of the black money and have the *keiretsu* support him. But without a change in Soviet attitudes, that's most unlikely. So, the choice is yours really.'

'It's not much of a choice, is it?' The Georgian was sour. 'Either we accept the crooks and let 'em cut our throats afterwards, or we give back the Kurils and sign an exploiters' contract over our own natural resources.'

'Or we forget the whole thing,' said Boris Vannikov, 'and try to muddle through with what we've got.'

'Which isn't very much,' said Tanya sharply. 'Today's news is the Germans are sending us the surplus food they've had in store since we blockaded Berlin, and there's rationing in Leningrad, Moscow and other major cities. So, what's your best advice, Mr Gil Langton?'

'You heard it tonight, when I was paying my golf debt to Tanaka. I was quoting his own words: "The game isn't over until the last shot on the last hole." There's a lot of money on the table; black or white, it's money. There's a lot of open ground to be covered before either side is forced to a last ditch stand. I'd say keep talking, keep working on Moscow to offer terms and concessions that will attract more reputable investors to bolster the ones Carl Leibig has brought in. Meantime, leave the money on the table. What more can I say?'

'Nothing, I guess,' said Lavrenti.

'I think you've earned another drink,' said Boris Vannikov.

'I'll pour it.' Tanya slid off the bed and rumpled my hair as she passed. 'He looks so damn benign but he's as shrewd as an Armenian carpet peddler.'

It was after midnight and I was slightly less than sober when I got back to our guest house. The lamp on my side of the bed was turned down to low power. Marta was sound asleep, the covers half thrown back to reveal her naked breast and the curve of her thigh. Her hair made an aureole on the pillow and she was smiling as if at some pleasant dream. I undressed, went to the bathroom and made ready to slip into bed beside her.

It was then that I noticed the fragrance. Marta herself always used one with the faint, fresh smell of lemon blossom. This one was heavy and musky and it clung to the fabric of the pillow and the coverlet. I crawled carefully into bed, shivering at the cold touch of the covers. There was warmth only a hand's reach away, but I could not bring myself to seek it. Marta stirred and murmured in her sleep. I could not respond. I switched out the light and lay staring up into the darkness, lapped in the cloying fragrance of Miko's perfume.

I prayed that tomorrow would come and go quickly. I wanted no more arguments, no more discussions, no more protestations. I was too old and too cynical for the games they played in the world of flowers and willows. Besides, the fox-woman was inside the house now and I was full of fear.

At seven in the morning, while Marta was still asleep, I was in Carl Leibig's office making phone calls. The first was to Sir Pavel Laszlo in Sydney. We spoke in Hungarian, in case of leaks on the satellite channel. He listened in silence, then burst into a stream of colourful obscenities. He would meet me in Bangkok on Saturday. We would try to work up emergency plans before the others arrived. I told him I needed a first rate PR girl to administer the press office. He said he had the best in the country. He would bring her with him. Then he told me: 'Keep those two bastards out of Bangkok, even if you have to hang 'em on hooks in a cold store. If the press gets a whiff of that story, we're all dead. How's Carl Leibig behaving?'

'Very well. Much better than I expected.'

'And Marta?'

'Has developed a big crush on Miko.'

'Dear God!' Laszlo swore again, volubly. 'This we need like the Black Death.'

At seven forty-five Franz delivered me a manila envelope filled with photostats of press cuttings. I locked it in my briefcase, then went to breakfast with Leibig and Tanaka. I gave them a full account of my evening with Vannikov and the Georgian and, in response to a question from Tanaka, offered my personal conclusion.

'They're in a cleft stick. They don't like the association with Cubeddu and Hoshino. On the other hand, they need money and action very quickly. The whole situation in the Soviet Union gets worse as winter gets closer. I explained your dilemma. I was open about your hopes. I recommended that Vannikov and his team work through the conference in Bangkok and see how far Moscow will bend on the Kurils or any other concessions that might bring the *keiretsu* to your side. I believe that's the course they'll recommend to Moscow.'

'So, we have a breathing space.'

'You may get more if you handle the conference this morning the right way.'

'Which is?'

'Admit the money connection is tainted. Take the trouble to explain the problem, but lean on the fact that with their co-operation you may yet provide better allies. Meantime, I'm leaving for Tokyo in an hour.'

Tanaka gave me a swift, suspicious look. 'Why? We may need you here.'

'I don't think you realise, but no work has been done to set up the press office in Bangkok. I'll have to see to that today and tomorrow.'

'That's true, but . . .'

'Also, I think you need me out of here. So long as I hang around, I can't avoid some commerce with Cubeddu and Hoshino. That, believe me, will make a bad impression with Vannikov and his political officer, not to mention the interpreter, who is also a Moscow monitor. And one other thing: no way in the world can Cubeddu or Hoshino be seen in Bangkok. The money front must be represented by you as a Japanese banker and by Forster as lead name for the European funds. You must trust me in this.'

Carl Leibig added a persuasive voice. 'He's right, Kenji. We can't take any risks at the big event. I am still far from happy, but I would not be here with you now if Gil had not persuaded me that a change was possible.'

'Why,' asked Tanaka dramatically, 'why am I cast as the villain of the piece?'

The answer to that came tripping off my tongue. 'Because that's the way you yourself constructed the script. Carl didn't write it. I didn't. You just handed us the lines and demanded that we play them. Well, we're doing our best, but we can't work miracles.'

He gave a non-committal grunt and changed the subject. 'The helicopters won't be here until four this afternoon. How will you get back to Tokyo?'

'By train. Franz can drive me to the station.'

'Is your woman going with you?'

'No. Carl needs to work with her on her presentation for Bangkok.'

I prayed Leibig would not miss the cue. He picked it up instantly. 'That's right. She made a good impression on the Russians yesterday. I'd like to build on that. Her economic and historic arguments will take some of the curse off the Cubeddu/Hoshino provenance.'

'It's your decision, of course.' Tanaka seemed to have lost interest. 'Call me if you need me, Gil. I'm staying in Tokyo until Sunday. Otherwise, I'll see you in Bangkok.'

When he had gone, Carl Leibig poured more coffee for us both and asked: 'Woman trouble?'

'Double trouble. Miko and Marta.'

Leibig frowned unhappily and shook his head from side to side in disbelief. 'I don't understand the game Miko is playing. She likes men; she likes women; that's one thing, but here she is meddling in a ten-billion-dollar deal. I cannot believe that Tanaka doesn't see it.'

'I think he sees only one half of it. I'm sure he's been using Miko as the go-between with both the Yakuza and the Mafia. She has a whole network of contacts on the West Coast, here in Tokyo and, I suspect, in the Philippines and other places. With that she serves Tanaka's interests. But she also serves her own.'

'How?'

'What happens to her when Tanaka dies?'

'I don't know. I've never asked.'

'Whatever provision he has made, it will not equal what she has now. Once the family takes over, she is finished in the Tanaka Group. So, my guess is that she's working for Cubeddu and Hoshino as well. Her contacts, her intimacy with Tanaka, his increasing dependence on her, double her market value to them. What does the Bible say? "Make friends with the followers of Mammon, so that when you fail, they receive you into their houses."'

'And Marta? Where does she fit in?'

'One more lover, one more ally for Miko.'

'Are you sure that's all?'

'No, but for all our sakes I hope so. If there's more, we're up to our necks in a cesspool. That's why I've got to get the hell out of here and back to Tokyo. I need some other allies, and I think you do, too.'

'Who, for instance?'

'When I know, I'll tell you, Carl. That's the best I can do. I also have obligations to Tanaka. I can't abdicate those either. One question: do you trust Franz?'

'We've been together fourteen years.'

'I guess that's a good enough answer. I'll be ready to leave in thirty minutes.'

'What are you going to tell Marta?'

'I have work in Tokyo. You need her here.'

'And in Bangkok?'

'You lodge her away from me.'

'I'll see to it. This is hard for you, Gil.'

'I'm afraid it's going to be harder for her in the end. I must run. I want ten minutes with Vannikov before I pack.'

I found him just at the end of his jogging circuit round the golf course. He told me he was working off his hangover. I told him I was going back to Tokyo and I needed the answer to three questions.

'Let's hear them.'

'How badly does Moscow want this deal?'

'Almost, but not quite enough to buy the present package.'

'If it had more orthodox components, big name bankers and such?'

'Then I'm almost sure it would be agreed in Bangkok.'

'I'm going back to Tokyo to put together the elements of our press office. How many people do you want to provide?'

'Just one. I'll move Tanya in there. I'll supervise her output. What about your people?'

'We'll have Marta on the political side. Laszlo, to whom I've just spoken, is flying in his best PR girl to run the administration. I've got a meeting in Tokyo with Alex Boyko of Associated Press. I'm almost sure he'll come himself. That's all we really need: one good Bureau man with the right outlets. Are you content to let me handle that part?'

'Sure. I confess to you, Gil, I'm scared. Things are so bad at home, worse than any of the press reports. This is a ten-billion-dollar aid package with a fatal flaw in it. We need the money, God knows! We need everything else that's offered, but the thugs will strangle the deal.'

'Keep hammering that into Tanaka's head when you meet this morning. Leibig and I will be doing our best to change things.'

'Why do you care so much, Gil?'

'Because I hate being screwed by people I don't like.'

'Reason enough,' said Boris with a grin. 'And talking of screwing, you've made quite a hit with Tanya. If you'd like to take her off my hands . . .'

I answered him with a laugh I did not feel. 'Thanks, but no thanks.

I've got more than enough problems. I'll see you in Thailand, my friend.'

I left him to finish his run while I walked swiftly back to the guest house to tell Marta I was leaving. I found her naked in the bathroom, drying her hair with an electric blower. I kissed her, because I was still fool enough to desire her and cynic enough to complete the last rituals of deception. She reproached me mildly.

'Why didn't you wake me when you came in last night?'

'Be glad I didn't, *schatzi*. I wasn't exactly sober.'

'And why not this morning?'

'I hated to wake you. I've been up since six-thirty. I leave for Tokyo in thirty minutes.'

'But why? I thought today was to be the big event.'

'It still is; but my job was done last night. Now I have to organise the press office for Bangkok and set a few of my own affairs in order.'

'Can I come with you?'

'I'm afraid not. Carl wants you here.'

'That's a bore.'

'I know. I'm sorry. What did you do with yourself last night?'

'Nothing very exciting, but it was fun just the same. Tanaka wasn't well. He went to bed early. Miko came over here. She brought a pack of Japanese cards and she taught me a game called *hanafuda*. We sat up in bed like schoolgirls and played. We hoped you'd be back in time to have a drink with us. Miko left about eleven-thirty. I fell asleep. I didn't even hear you come in. What time was it?'

'About a quarter to one, I think. You'd better finish dressing. I'll pack.'

'Gil?'

'What?'

'You're not angry with me, are you?'

'About what?'

'Miko.'

'Why should I be angry? Didn't we agree yesterday that I would never try to hold you? You're still the bird on my open hand, singing happy songs; at least, I hope they're happy.'

She lifted her head in a swift defiance. 'Yes, they are. They're very, very happy.'

It was only then that I remembered to ask her the meaning of the

164

riddle she had put to me the previous day: what will you do, I wonder, when the white crow turns to black?

'Oh, that!' She gave a small, embarrassed laugh. 'It was a phrase my mother used to use. One of her producers, I remember, was a great gambler. Whenever they played in a town with a casino, he would spend the whole night at the tables. Every night he knew he was going to be lucky. Almost every night he lost. My mother used to shake her head mournfully and say: "Rudi, will you never learn? A lucky man is as rare as a white crow." You're lucky, Gil, I know you are; but I wonder what you'll be like if the luck runs out?'

I could not tell her that I was just embarking on a venture which would test my luck to the limit.

Ten

I was back in Tokyo at two in the afternoon. I went straight to my office and telephoned the Australian Ambassador. Our conversation was brief. I told him he might get a call from the Americans to check on my character and my security rating, if any. He promised to classify me A1 at Lloyds. I thanked him and told him I would try to keep him out of gaol too. Then I called Max Wylie at the United States Embassy.

'Mr Wylie, this is Gil Langton. We have a mutual friend, Marta Boysen.'

'A pleasure to hear from you, Mr Langton.'

'Thank you. I've just left Marta in Nara. She's working there with Carl Leibig's team, as she told you.'

'She did mention she might be going out of town.' I noted the instinctive caution of the reply. 'What can I do for you, Mr Langton?'

'Marta did express the thought that she would like to bring us together. I think this might be an opportune moment. Would you be free for a drink this evening? Say, five-thirty at the Seiyo Ginza. I have a suite there, we can be quite private.'

'Is this business or pleasure, Mr Langton?'

'Let's say the liquor's honest and the talk should be interesting.'

'I'll look forward to it. Five-thirty at the Seiyo Ginza.'

So, the die was cast and I was back once more in a world through which I had walked briefly but without any sense of attachment or real commitment. Strangely enough, it was my father, that most liberal and free-spirited of men, who had first introduced me into the demi-monde of spooks and snoopers and sundry intrigues and guardians of buried secrets. We were in Canberra, the Commonwealth capital of Australia. We were lunching with the Governor-General, who was an old friend of my father and who wanted to honour his retirement. I was well launched by then. Polyglot Press was making a sound profit. I had flown home from London to be with the old man for the closing ceremonies

166

of his academic career and then to take him marlin fishing among the northern stretches of the Great Barrier Reef.

Among the guests at the luncheon was another of my father's friends who turned out to be the director of the Australian Security Intelligence Service. My father, as fathers do, had made a hymn of praise about my accomplishments as a linguist. The director offered me a job. I declined. He asked me would I be open to occasional assignment; for example, as an observer or consultant to diplomatic or trade missions. That seemed innocuous enough, but my agreement led me into some strange byways. My training provided me with a certain professional status which might help in my encounter with Max Wylie.

I was just settling down to a little quiet tactical planning when Tanizaki came in almost at a gallop. Had I heard the news? What news? Matsushita had just bought out the US entertainment giant Universal-MCA with all its associated enterprises, for six point one billion dollars! This was big money in any financial language. Following on the Sony purchase of Columbia, it meant that the Japanese now had control of two of the major elements in worldwide popular entertainment. The size of the deal, which obviously had been constructed in typical style from many interlocking interests, explained the reluctance of the *keiretsu* to pour risk money into long-term development in the now unstable Soviet Union. It also made me ask how and why Tanaka's own thinking was directed westward into the heartland of Eurasia, rather than eastward to the mainland of the United States, where the Japanese *imperium* was already well established on the foundations of old-style American capitalism.

We talked for a little while; then I asked Tanizaki to bring me a copy of our presentation volume *The Gift of Tongues*. It was a handsome piece of work, a combination of all the arts of book making, ancient and modern: typography, design, binding, colour printing, paper manu- facture, photography . . . It contained a historical account of the development of Polyglot Press and examples of its work in all the languages in which we published. It had won us many awards and a lot of business and I confess I was inordinately proud of it. I was proudest of all of the epigraph which my father had chosen and which was repeated in translation in every alphabet. It was from Milton's *Areopagitica*, which may seem to you to be a very strange and English thing to preface a multilingual book, but which somehow sits well in the minds of all readers. 'A good book is the precious life-blood of a master spirit, embalmed and treasured up on purpose to a life beyond life.'

Tanizaki asked how matters were proceeding with the lady. I told him they were not proceeding well at all. Whereupon he grinned and offered me, with ironic respect, a piece of advice.

'Western women, Gil-san, are better built than Japanese ones, but they need a lot more looking after. At your age you're the one who should be getting the care. Why don't you let my mother find you a nice, attentive girl of good family . . .'

I almost threw the presentation volume at him and he retreated, hissing and chuckling, into his own domain. I decided it was time to leave and prepare myself for the cocktail encounter with Max Wylie. I put the book in my briefcase and headed back to the Seiyo Ginza.

Punctually at five-thirty, Max Wylie presented himself: six feet of Brooks Brothers tailoring, blond, blue-eyed, bronzed from daily treatment under the sunlamps, with a firm, honest-John handshake and just a hint of julep and magnolias in the voice. His drink was the same as mine, old-fashioned Bourbon on the rocks with just a touch of branch water.

We took a turn or two around the skating rink. I showed him the presentation volume to explain what I did with most of my life. I told him how Marta and I had first met. I talked of my father and his life as a scholar-gypsy. Max Wylie was a very good listener.

Finally, we finished our *pas de deux* and I asked him: 'Are you, by any chance, wired for sound?'

He had the grace to blush. I held out my hand.

'Let's have it on the table, Max. If you need to record something later, we can agree what goes on or off the record.'

I waited while he slipped off the gear, a tiny, very sophisticated recording device whose microphone was built into his tie-clip. Then we began a new dance sequence; this time I wanted to lead it.

'Before we begin, I'd like you to call the Australian Embassy and ask for the Ambassador. He will confirm that I'm kosher and that I am – how do you say? – connected.'

'That won't be necessary.'

'I'd still like you to do it, if you wouldn't mind. It will make the rest of our time together much more comfortable.'

Reluctantly he complied. When the Ambassador came on the line, there was a brief formal exchange. When he put down the phone, Wylie grinned.

'You're right. It is more comfortable. Now, where would you like to begin?'

168

'Marta Boysen. You're aware of the family connection. You know, too, that she and I became lovers a week ago.'

'How in hell would I know that?'

'She told you, over dinner on Monday night.'

'Let's say it was fairly obvious she was happy about a new friendship.'

'Let's say that, yes. Now we come to the awkward part.'

It was the awkward part for me, too. It was pure guesswork and if I was wrong, he could spit in my eye and exit laughing. I asked him: 'How long have you been running Marta?'

'Running her?' His innocence was almost too painful to bear. I worked more confidently now, affirming positively what was at best guesswork. It is an old trick and, strangely enough, the ones most vulnerable to it are professionals.

'I know it's embarrassing, Max, but this is the bullshit area and I'd like to get through it as soon as possible. I've got evidence from the Russians, the Germans, your own people and mine, that Marta Boysen has been supplying you and others with information for a long time. I quote a letter which I have seen: "She is an acute and accurate observer of the economic and political scene and has on occasion provided valuable information and advice, etcetera, etcetera . . ." You circulated copies of her thesis on Haushofer to your Embassy in Moscow. Later, she gave you an advance copy of the Tanaka/Leibig proposal. You were immediately apprised of her meeting with me. You did a check with your opposite number in our Embassy here. There's a lot more. So why don't we stipulate, off the record, that you've been running her?'

'Why don't we just say "no comment"?'

'Because all that would get you would be a farewell drink and a handshake. I can offer you a lot more than that.'

'Would you like to give me a hint?'

'Co-operation. You're on the wrong tack. I can set you straight.'

'And what does that cost me?'

'Ante-up first, Max. Off the record, you are running Marta Boysen, yes?'

'Yes.'

'Then you should know that within the Tanaka/Leibig organisation, which includes me as a paid mediator, she is already tagged as a security risk and her connection with you is known to the Russians, the Germans and the Japanese.'

'Uncomfortable for her, but not lethal for me.'

'You know best, of course; but you're fighting the wrong battle on the wrong terrain. Marta was Leibig's choice. He has lived such a large part of his life outside of Germany, he's full of the old German dreams. That's why he seized on the Haushofer geopolitical line and Marta's modernisation of it in her thesis. You seized on it too, Max, because it gave you what every Intelligence man wants, a clear focus of argument. In your case you would point to this enterprise as the forerunner of a new Berlin/Tokyo axis, the Hitler-Haushofer dream resuscitated and dressed in new clothes. That's the voodoo music you've been playing to the Russians. I know, because they've told me. And it doesn't scare them. Why? Because the core of the geopolitical theory is that the heartland of Eurasia is the pivot on which everything swings. They don't believe what you're telling them, because they see that the Trojan horse is already inside your walls and the invaders have occupied the city. You heard the news today, Matsushita and MCA?'

'I heard it,' said Max Wylie sombrely. 'It made me want to puke. We've got half a million fighting men in the Gulf waiting for a goddam desert war on alien soil, and we're selling out to another bunch of aliens! You're right. We are fighting the wrong battle on the wrong terrain. Over to you, General. What's your grand strategy?'

'To achieve the possible. In this case, to make a limited but effective contribution to stabilising the heartland, by improving the production, storage and distribution of essential foodstuffs. What that means is to get them through this winter with enough food and enough hope to stop bloodshed and anarchy. I think it makes sense. For that reason, I agreed to referee the game. I'm being well paid for the service, of which this talk with you is a part; but I have nothing to lose or gain personally from the outcome.'

'The honest broker.' There was more than a hint of mockery in his tone.

'That's right. Take it or leave it.'

'You're asking me to help you?'

'No. I'm asking you to open your mind to a new series of considerations and options.'

'So it's open, wide as a barn door. I could use some new facts – and a fresh drink.'

'Help yourself to the drink. The facts? The Soviets want the deal, but they're being a little smarter than your people, Max, or mine, for that

170

matter. They're not prepared to sell off the home farm to get it. If things get too desperate, of course, who knows? The next fact is that all the money is up. The experts are in place to implement the plans. The final decision will be made in Bangkok next week.'

'And what's the betting that the deal will go through?'

'Even money.'

I was shading the odds, because I needed to keep him in doubt as long as I could. I was beginning to get his measure now. Max Wylie was not a strategic thinker. He was a man who needed certainties. Give him one and he would go crusading with it, ignoring the wastelands he created on the way.

He said: 'Obviously there's a problem. What is it?'

'It's a double-header. The money-men want more trade concessions than the Soviets are offering. The Soviets are not happy with certain names on the money list.'

Instantly he was on the alert. 'That's the first time I've ever heard of people turning down hard cash.'

'They haven't turned it down yet. They'd like to.'

'And you?'

'I'd like to get rid of the road blocks on both sides. I believe I can negotiate satisfactory concessions, if certain offending subscribers are removed.'

'Why are they there in the first place?'

I picked up the morning paper and pointed to the headlines which announced the Matsushita-MCA deal. 'There's part of the reason. The Japanese always prefer low-risk enterprises, not easy to guarantee this winter in Moscow. So some of Tanaka's people dropped out.'

'How much money would that be?'

'Four billion, more or less.'

'But you tell me it's now back in the kitty. The subscription is full.'

'That's right. Tanaka has honoured his promises. He always does.'

'But this time he's got some smelly names. Yes?'

I handed him the envelope which Franz had given me in Nara. I told him: 'Those are just newspaper clippings. You'll probably have much fuller dossiers in your own files. Take your time reading them. There's a lot to discuss.'

I went to the bathroom to freshen up. I came back, poured myself another drink, opened a can of rice crackers and poured them into a bowl. I took an office folder from my desk and began working through the contents. Finally, Max Wylie looked up from his reading.

'We've got files as long as your arm on these two. We can't touch 'em. Even our immigration people let 'em come and go freely. As I understand it, these two represent Tanaka's black money.'

'That's right.'

'Well now. We've got legislation that permits the seizure of funds which can be shown to be the fruits of criminal activity. But once they've been through the laundromat, what can you do? Very little. Outside our own jurisdiction, even less. The best banks in the world co-operate under sufferance, because they want the deposits. It's impossible to determine, but I've often wondered how much of any international fund is black money. There's even a good argument for not inquiring, because the money's back in legitimate circulation. Which raises a question for me. Why did Tanaka feel it necessary to reveal the sources of his funding, even introduce them into this gathering in Nara? It seems such a reckless thing to do.'

'Tanaka isn't reckless, believe me. I've known him a long time. We're in business together. He thinks a long way ahead and on three levels at once. I think he's counting on one of two results: sanitizing the money or shaming his Japanese peers back into the game.'

'How can he sanitize people like Hoshino and Cubeddu?'

'Easily enough. They withdraw their offer of funding. The money pops up in a couple of different corporations in different territories, or as private placements by broking houses.'

'Why the double shuffle? Why wouldn't he have done that in the first place?'

'Because, don't you see, he's playing a very Japanese game. First, he's a magician who pulls money out of thin air. You don't like the colour of it? Hey Presto! It's gone. You want it back in a different colour? Ah, that costs you extra. That's why he's so sure of himself. He's on notice from Leibig and from me that we'll walk out rather than sit with Hoshino and Cubeddu. That doesn't faze him, because he has the whole game laid out, ready for Bangkok.'

Max Wylie was silent for a while, staring down at his manicured fingernails. Then he faced me with the question I had hoped he would ask. 'Why are you telling me all this? What's your game?'

'I told you the first part of it. I want this deal to go through. I believe it's a sensible piece of commerce and politics. I'd rather you weren't muddying the waters as you're doing now, with a very dubious premise anyhow. Tanaka's a friend with the mark of death on him. I think it's important that he's able to quit with honour.'

'Very commendable,' said Max Wylie drily. 'Now let's get to the milk in the coconut.'

'Marta Boysen. I want you to cut her loose, tonight. When we've finished here we'll go across to the Okura together and I'll witness the ceremony.'

'Surgery more like. Rough surgery. Why put yourself through it?'

'Because I want to be sure it's done and finished. This game's going to get dangerous. I want her out of it.'

'Which means you still haven't told me everything.'

'So this is where we start dealing: *quid pro quo*, tit for tat, you show me yours, I'll show you mine.'

'And what do I get for letting Marta Boysen off the hook?'

'A battle plan that gets us both out of the shit, with a little profit on both sides.'

Immediately he was wary and hostile. 'What are we talking here, friend? Bribery?'

'No way. I don't need it. You wouldn't wear it. I'm talking salvage. We're a pair of tug-masters taking a stricken vessel in tow. We've each got a line on board. We can either fight each other for sole possession or split the salvage money, kosher and legal. After all, Australia and the United States are allies and comrades in arms. Our little ships are patrolling the Gulf with your big ones, and we're both getting royally screwed out of the home farm by foreign speculators. Maybe we deserve it, because we're too fat and lazy to protest, but I don't like it. So let's start haggling. How're your nerves?'

'Level and steady. How're yours?'

'Just edgy enough to be wary, Max. There are lives on the line now. Mine is one of them.'

'I believe you,' said Max Wylie moodily. 'You've been keeping rough company. You want Marta Boysen, she's yours. No argument. What have you got for me?'

The bargaining went on for an hour and a half. It was slow at first, because we were more concerned with defending ourselves than with the issues at stake. Each of us had a personal position which we were not prepared to disclose fully for fear of losing a crucial advantage. In the end, however, the larger issues overshadowed the lesser and we found ourselves discussing them with the objectivity of professionals who each respected the limitations under which the other was forced to work. In Wylie's case, the limitation was a policy which he had, in part at least, helped to frame and the fact, which he knew very well, that the policy was inadequate. Already the governments of Poland and Czechoslovakia were preparing camps for an expected mass migration of refugees from a famine-stricken Russia. Once the exodus started, it would change the face of Europe overnight.

For my part, I was caught in a tangle of conflicting loyalties and transcultural attitudes. I was supposed to be the universal man. There were moments when I felt like a bumbling provincial on his first night out in the capital. At the end of it, however, we were still on our feet and able to toast each other with reasonable good humour.

It was only then that I felt secure enough to ask him the question that had been plaguing me. 'How the hell did you manage to seduce an intelligent woman like Marta into your grimy business?'

He laughed and threw up his hands at the sheer folly of the question. 'Easiest thing in the world. Rome in spring, young and brilliant academic just escaped from a tyrannous marriage. She was ripe for any adventure and that's what I sold her – the Great Game! We sit in the shadows and shake the pillars of the universe and watch the swallows fly out of the eaves. She was the new toast of FAO; she'd just successfully defended her doctoral thesis; so she was easy to flatter. We took the sting out of the job by calling it industrial consultancy. I don't think that mattered too much because, like so many of her generation, she worshipped at the shrine of Jeffersonian democracy. I feel sorry for what we have to do to her, but she's blown now and an embarrassment to all of us. I guess I'd better call and make sure she's home.'

He telephoned the Okura Hotel and spoke to Marta. She had just arrived back from Nara. She would be happy to see him if he could get there by eight. She had a dinner date at eight-thirty. He promised he would not detain her a moment longer than was necessary.

Our encounter began, incongruously, on a high note of pleasure. Marta's eyes lit up when she saw us both.

'Well! This is a pleasant surprise. How did you two meet?' She kissed us both before we were required to answer.

'We have interests in common.' Max Wylie's smile conveyed nothing but good humour. 'May we sit down?'

'Of course. Would you like a drink?'

174

'No thanks, Marta, this won't take long. Gil has found out you've been working for me. We've agreed that there is a gross conflict of interest between your employment by Carl Leibig and the work you have been doing for us. A continued association would be damaging to us all. So, as of now, I'm terminating you. The severance payment will be made to the usual account. There'll be no further dealings, no further contact. The secrecy provisions in your contract still apply. That's all, I think, except to say thank you. It was nice knowing you. Goodbye.'

The next instant he was gone, a ghost of a Brooks Brothers suit, fading into the silk wallpaper. Marta stood staring at me, speechless with anger. Then the storm broke. She slapped me hard across the face and said one word: 'Bastard!'

I pinioned her arms, thrust her back on the bed and held her down until her rage subsided into a frozen hatred. Then I released her and stepped back out of reach. She stared at me as if I were a loathsome creature which had just crawled out of the woodwork. She was stammering with fury.

'Who do you think you are? You have no rights in my life. I'm not a pawn on a chessboard.'

'That's exactly what you've been ever since you were seduced into the espionage game. What you are now is a blown agent, finished, used up. Once I told Wylie I knew he was running you, he couldn't get rid of you fast enough.'

'How did you find out?'

'Simple logic, Frau Professor Doktor. I've been in the game too, you see. I read the grubby finger marks, hear the little lies. But I've done you a favour. You're out clean. That's why I insisted on coming tonight with Wylie, to see and hear it done. Nobody else knows what's happened here. Nobody else will know unless you tell them, and that, believe me, would be a bad mistake. Money and politics are dangerous games. You're too naive to play them. That's good advice. Take it and be thankful.'

'I'll thank you to get the hell out of my life and stay out.'

'I'm on my way. If you're going to dinner, you'd better get cleaned up. You look a mess.'

Without another word she hurried into the bathroom and slammed the door. I walked out and took the elevator down to the lobby. As I approached the entrance I saw Miko being handed out of a limousine by Tanaka's chauffeur. I turned away and sat in a shadowy corner until she had passed. She looked stunning, in a classic kimono with an *obi* of rich brocade. I asked myself how any man in his right mind could make an enemy of so beautiful a woman.

The thought of a solitary night with only my guilts for company, was intolerable. I sat for a long while in the foyer of the Okura hotel, motionless and cataleptic, with no thrust of will or surge of adrenalin to set me in motion. It was a strange sensation, as if I were floating becalmed in dead water, surrounded by eddies and currents which I myself had created, but which now no longer moved me at all.

By some trick of imagination, my memory switched back to a summer morning in Greece, when my father and I ran a rubber dinghy up to the antique quay on the island of Delos. It was just after first light. The tourists had not yet arrived, the guardians of the islet had not yet begun to stir, yet the place was alive with light, flickering from the sea just stirring under the morning wind, shining from the white marbles and the blue sky. This was the virgin island, where no one was permitted to be born, to die or languish in illness. This was the shrine of Apollo, from whence he ruled the world.

We sat on a great block of masonry and ate our breakfast: bread and cheese and tomatoes and wine mixed with mineral water. As a kind of grace after the meal, my father stood on the block of stone and declaimed the Homeric *Hymn to Apollo*:

How shall I welcome the God,
The superb, the haughty one
Who stands in the loftiest place
Above all the gods,
Above all the people of the crowded earth?

Then we walked, following an inscription that pointed to 'the temples of the strangers'. Delos had once been a traders' town, as well as a shrine. Its tiny harbour had once been jammed with vessels from all over the Middle Sea. Apollo was a proud god, but not a jealous one. He understood that lesser folk made do with lesser deities. So every cult had its own small foothold on the sacred island.

That was the burden of my father's little discourse for the day: 'The loneliest hour comes after the loss of a loved one. The loneliest place is where all the gods are strange and there is not one to whom you can turn for hope, or even for the comfort of recognition. So, just as you are learning to pierce the veils of language, you must learn to look behind the rituals, the artefacts, the masks of all religions to the divinity they conceal. If you can do that, then you will never be lonely, because the same spirit is immanent everywhere.'

It was the burden of all his later teaching: that without some perception of unity one's world would become 'an unbearable chaos, a howling desolation scattered with shards and fragments, with no provenance, no present meaning, no hope of future restoration.'

On that night, in the Okura hotel, I found myself adrift in that place of desolation. My mind and my world were like shattered mirrors, reflecting madness in every fragment. I had ransomed one woman by putting another in jeopardy. From my shadowed corner, I watched them walk out together, chatting and laughing, the dark beauty and the fair one. I saw the chauffeur hand them into the limousine and drive away, out of my reach for always. I knew that I had lost a love and made a mortal enemy.

More, I had gambled with the trust reposed in me by Tanaka, Leibig and Vannikov. If the gamble failed, I should be forever discredited. I had bargained with a man whose trade was deception, the servant of a great nation, ruthless to its opponents, unforgiving to its competitors. If he did not keep his bargain, I had no recourse. He could kiss me off without a qualm and walk away whistling.

That was not the end of the story. Even if Max Wylie kept his bargain, any or all of my people could reject my deal and damn me for presuming to make it. Either way the cake was cut, my portion would probably choke me. So, rather than sit there, trapped in a nightmare, I got up, headed for the entrance, had the doorman whistle me a cab and set off for a bachelor evening at the Fuji Club.

It was early when I got there. Naomi was still free. I booked her for the evening. She found us a booth in one of the quieter corners far from the band, out of the direct line of the massive amplifiers and the brain-scrambling flicker of the strobe lights. I ordered champagne for Naomi, sushi for both of us and bourbon for myself. Naomi was good, protective company. She would make sure I was not hustled or disturbed. She would expect a generous tip and an over-rider for the house to make up for liquor I had not drunk. If at a certain hour it pleased me to ask her to come home with me and, more importantly, if it pleased her to agree, that was a matter for double negotiation, with the management and with the lady. There is a saying that in the floating world an honest woman is as rare as a square egg. I have to be a witness that Naomi of the Fuji Club was an honest woman. She gave value for money and always added a bonus for good manners and a gentle handling.

From our booth we had a view of the entrance, where all the guests paused for a few moments in a pool of light before being received by the head waiter and shown to their table by one of the girls of the house. Naomi gave me a biography of each newcomer, enlivened sometimes by a full sexual profile. All the time she made me conscious of her own physical presence, warm and comfortable as a kitten, huddled against me in the alcove.

After a while, the old shopworn magic began to work. I relaxed to the numbing beat of the music, the shifting pattern of lights, the air hazy with cigarette smoke, the monotone clatter of talk, the small seductive caresses of the woman beside me. I began to ask myself, with languid lechery, what the hell I was doing in this noisy place and why I did not take the girl off to a comfortable bed in the love-hotel just around the corner. The contemplation of the event was a pleasure in itself. I was too languid to interrupt it by the rituals of departure. Then, abruptly, I was jolted out of my reveries.

Three men walked into the club, Cubeddu, Vannikov and Hoshino, who was obviously the host. He was greeted with deep bows. A trio of the best girls was detailed to escort them to a large table in the most privileged corner of the room. Beside me, Naomi whispered: 'That is Number One. The big boss. He owns this place.' I could not suppress a laugh. Here was I, Gilbert Anselm Langton, not only disporting himself in the man's club, I was contributing handsomely to Yakuza income by our corporate subscriptions and our entertainment expenditures.

Naomi asked: 'What is so funny, Gil?'

'You will see in a moment. Do you have one of your message cards?'

One of the civilised customs of the Fuji Club was a supply of small cards and envelopes, which each hostess carried concealed in her *obi*. The cards were of fine quality board, embossed with the club symbol, Mount Fuji. If you wanted to send a message across the room, you could do so with grace and privacy. If you wanted to offer money, the envelope came in handy, too. I wrote a note to Hoshino in Korean.

My corporation has held a membership in the Fuji Club for a long time. I hope you will permit me to offer you and your guests a bottle of champagne to toast our venture in Bangkok. Gil Langton.

I handed the note to Naomi and asked her to order the champagne immediately and present it with my note to Hoshino. I waited with a certain trepidation for his response. He was not obliged to do anything but acknowledge the courtesy. I hoped he would invite me to join his party. The club was filling up now. It was about five minutes before Naomi returned, flushed and smiling. Mr Hoshino sent his thanks and his compliments and asked us both to join him at his table.

He had obviously prepared with some care for the reception of his guests. Both Cubeddu and Vannikov had been provided with Filipino girls who spoke English. Hoshino's own companion was a girl who had graduated from Takarazuka soubrette to the upper echelons of the nightclub circuit. Naomi herself was clearly in favour with the great man, who said: 'You are an asset to the Fuji Club, Gil. You choose my best woman and my best champagne.' I breathed a quiet prayer to the spirits of the place that I might get some value for money.

I asked about Lavrenti, the political officer. I was told he was waiting at the Embassy for the result of the Security Council vote on the use of military force in the Gulf. No one seemed to have much doubt of the outcome. The Soviets would vote yes. The Chinese would abstain; the only open question seemed to be a deadline for the Iraqi withdrawal. I asked Hoshino what he thought about military action. He had no doubts at all.

'If Hussein will not withdraw, America has to fight or be forever discredited in the Islamic world. In Islam the sword has always been the only passport to power. But it has to be a stunning victory, not a war of attrition like Vietnam. I just hope the Americans have the stomach for it. I deal with Muslim peoples all the time in Malaysia, in Indonesia, in the Philippines, in the Gulf itself, where we are suppliers of unskilled labour. I do good business because I understand them.' He turned to Vannikov. 'You have many Muslims in your Southern republics. Do you not agree with me?'

'Let's not talk about it tonight, please. I find the whole prospect too melancholy for words.' He raised his glass. 'Kampai!'

'To hell with war.' Domenico Cubeddu was aggressive even in his amusements. 'Let's make love.' He reached for his giggling partner and began kissing her.

Hoshino reminded him coolly: 'Whenever you're ready, there's a very good love-hotel just around the corner. I can recommend it, because I own it.'

'Good.' Cubeddu laughed boisterously. 'I don't believe in long engagements. Get the dowry settled, get the bride to bed. Then everyone can get back to making a buck.'

His crassness bored me. I asked Hoshino: 'How did you finish in Nara?'

'With problems.' Hoshino was surprisingly blunt. 'No discourtesy is meant to our friend Boris here; but it appears our money, Domenico's and mine, may not be acceptable currency in this deal.'

Vannikov shrugged uncomfortably. 'What can I say? We're here in your club, with your girls, drinking your liquor . . .'

'And on the other side.' Cubeddu was easily distracted from sex, he cut in harshly: 'We've got all the goddam hypocrisies of politics. Your country's broke, man! You're taking in food parcels, and from Germany, yet. But you're still looking down your nose at our investments. Come on. Every piece of tail in this room is earning money and you're here enjoying it.'

'You are out of order, my friend,' said Hoshino softly. 'Lower your voice and apologise to Boris.' For a moment I thought Cubeddu was going to protest, but he subsided and mumbled something about being tired and a little drunk.

Then, as if ashamed of his own cowardice, he added: 'But it doesn't solve the problem does it? Are we in or out? I have to know.'

'I can't tell you,' said Boris Vannikov wearily. 'I report, I advise, Moscow decides. Period. We'll have a lot more people in Bangkok. The situation at home will be more precarious and therefore, possibly, more favourable to a deal. That's the best I can say.'

The little Filipina refilled his glass and began cosseting him quietly. Cubeddu turned back to his love play. Hoshino stroked his woman like a pet cat and asked me in Korean:

'And you, man of many tongues, what do you say?'

'Do you have a private room here?'

'Of course.'

'Then I say we should talk for a while without the women.'

'We are here to relax and enjoy ourselves.'

'We may do that better after we have talked.'

Five minutes later we were sitting in a cramped circle in what Hoshino was pleased to call his office, a bare, unfriendly room with a round table and seven straight-backed chairs. He announced curtly: 'Gil has something to say to us. I have no idea what it is. He thinks it is important. Go ahead, please.'

I took a deep breath and dived into the middle of the argument.

'It's about the colour of money, gentlemen. What's dirty, what's clean. Is pachinko money dirty? Betting money? Girl money? Coke money, like Domenico's? Some people say if it buys food for hungry people it's clean anyway. Some people say it should not lie in the same wallet with money made by honest clerks and hard working shop girls and diplomats like Boris and publishers like me. But that's not the point. If the label on your money stops the flow of other and larger funds, causes the Soviet Union to lose friends at the time of its greatest need, then your money is bad money.'

'So, for Christ's sake,' Cubeddu exploded 'we take it home and invest it somewhere else. Simple, done, finished!'

'Hear the man, please.' Hoshino's tone was harsh. Boris Vannikov said nothing. His eyes were fixed on my face as though he were trying to read a subtext in my eyes. I pressed on.

'The Americans have been trying to sabotage this deal for months. They have been sold the notion that it represents a new version of the old Berlin/Tokyo axis: Germany, Russia and Japan controlling a new federation of republics from the Baltic to the Bering Sea. Carl Leibig planted the idea, Tanaka tried to sell it to the *keiretsu*, Marta Boysen codified it in modern economic terms. Presto! The Americans had this scapegoat made and ready. You two come along – Yakuza money, drug money – and they've got another shot in the locker. Moscow desperately needs the dollars, but they can't afford to alienate other and larger investors. Stalemate, impasse. Check me, Boris.'

'Check,' said Boris Vannikov glumly. 'It's a padded cell. I've walked round it a thousand times. I can't find a way out.'

'Maybe, just maybe, I've found one for you.'

'The hell you have!' Cubeddu exploded.

'Please explain it,' said Hoshino.

'I spent the afternoon in discussion with one of the men who has been running the campaign of obstruction for the United States. I convinced him, I believe, that the geopolitical argument would be

181

counterproductive for him. It might even blow up in his face if it could be shown that its source was tainted. I further convinced him, I hope, that he should not be seen to be impeding the flow of relief monies, from any source, into the Soviet Union. Which brought us slap-bang up against the first problem: dirty money? clean money? He agreed that if all the money went in clean, with the right laundry marks on it and the right controls, then the Americans might call off the diplomatic fight. Especially if they get the Soviet vote in the Security Council, as it seems likely they will.'

'Tanaka said nothing of this today.' Hoshino was watching me like a raptor ready to strike. 'Leibig didn't mention it either.'

'Because I didn't discuss it with them. They are aware of the problem. I had not yet proposed this solution. There was nothing to discuss until I had tested the ground. I can't commit any of you. My brief is only to inform you, to open your eyes to new options.'

'And what are our options here?' The question came from Cubeddu.

'The quickest and easiest way to sanitize your investment money is to get it out of your hands and into a trust, an old-fashioned discretionary trust with reputable trustees, and let the trust invest in this project.'

'That means we lose control.' Cubeddu was still kicking against the goads. 'We don't like that. We run our own business, always have, always will.'

'But this isn't your whole business.' Hoshino was mild and persuasive. 'Nor is it mine. What is important to us is our future relations with a new Union of Republics in Eurasia. Much of what you call control of our funds would depend upon our relationship with the trustees . . . I should not reject the idea too hastily. What is your opinion, Boris?'

'If you divest yourselves of visible control, then you're in the same position as any other investors, anonymous and clean. Provided, of course, that you don't parade yourselves in Bangkok. I believe that would give us all a good chance of success. Your legal identity and the provenance of the funds would be verified by documents. Yes, I think it's a very good idea.'

'Provided Tanaka and Leibig agree.' I had to underline the point. 'I'll call them both in the morning.'

'Domenico and I need to talk some more also.'

'And I'd like to discuss it with Lavrenti,' said Boris Vannikov.

'But in any case, gentlemen, you understand we have to have a clear agreement on this point before we get to Bangkok.'

'I have a couple more questions,' said Domenico Cubeddu. 'Who's this American contact of yours? And how much clout has he got?'

'I'm not going to give you his name. As for his clout, I don't know how much he has. I'm guessing that if he had influence enough to start harassing us, he's got influence enough to stop it.'

'It doesn't follow,' said Domenico Cubeddu curtly. 'It doesn't follow at all.'

After that, there did not seem much more to say, so we decided to rejoin the women in the club. As we hit the wall of noise and the reek of tainted air, Boris Vannikov held me back.

'Gil, I don't think I can take much more of this. Let's get out of here.'

'Give it ten more minutes and we'll leave.'

It was no great problem to disengage ourselves. Hoshino had his feet under his own table. Cubeddu could not wait to get the Filipina to bed. I made our apologies, paid off Naomi and walked out with Boris Vannikov into the chill of the autumn night. He was deeply depressed. Ignoring the garish neons of the pleasure quarter, he walked head down, making a kind of confession.

'When we got back from Nara, our desks were piled high with messages. This is desperation time at home, Gil. The Czechs and the Poles are already preparing reception camps for the exodus that will inevitably happen if we can't get the people through this winter. The government will just open the borders and let them go. Can you imagine what that kind of mass migration would mean in the depth of winter? Don't think I exaggerate. It's entirely possible. Already food is being flown in and the KGB has taken on the job of making as fair a distribution as possible. But the whole system is so run down that I'm not sure it can take much more strain. You gave me some courage tonight. Do you really believe you can make this work?'

'I'm not sure. I hope so.'

'What's on your mind, Gil?'

'I broke up with Marta tonight.'

'That's always rough. It's worse at our age, because we know time's running out on us. But maybe this time it's good luck in disguise.'

'What do you mean?'

'I don't know whether you can accept such things in a wife or in a lover. I know I can't. Your Marta is having an affair with Miko.'

'How did you hear of it?'

'Tanya told me. Miko invited her to dinner tonight, to celebrate what she called "the coming together of two hearts" which I suppose is a pretty thought in its own odd way.'

'Did Tanya accept?'

'I told her she should. I'd like to know what happens. It might be an enlightening experience for all of us.'

'I can do without it, Boris. I've never been one for scratching at old sores. I prefer clean surgery.'

'Which isn't always easy to get.' He said it without malice. 'We're like prisoners forced to walk in lockstep. Marta is important to Miko, Miko is important to Tanaka, Tanaka is important to all of us and what we do in Bangkok will be good or bad for millions of our people. I wish I could foresee what Cubeddu and Hoshino will decide.'

'For what it's worth, my guess is they'll accept the notion of a trust on the basis that they can in the end manipulate the trustees.'

'Could I offer you some advice, Gil?'

'I'd welcome it.'

'Tanaka's your friend and your partner. You live on the Pacific rim, so you see the stretch of Japanese power and influence. You're forgetting Europe because it's so far away, so centred on its own concerns. But Europe is strangling you to death, with agricultural subsidies that price you Australians right out of the world market. I watched you in Nara; always you lean to Tanaka as the man of power. I think you're making a big mistake. Now, Leibig is the man in whom power resides. All his funds are clean and in place. His policies and those of his government fit like hand into glove. He's the one who has assembled the technicians like Leino and the big planners like Laszlo and the sound bankers like Forster. Tanaka, on the other hand, is ill, isolated and out of favour with his peers. He's consorting with rich rogues, like those two back there. You're the best card in his hand, not because you have power, but because you're loyal and you're known to be honest. Look what you're trying to do now, the impossible. Turn a pair of international criminals into philanthropists. God knows it's a clever move and you might just get away with it and I might just help you to do it.'

'And how would you do that?'

He gave a small, unhappy laugh and did a series of intricate little dance steps on the pavement.

'I'd lie. I'd dazzle Moscow with documents. Tanya and I have cooked the books before; but that was harmless stuff, setting traps for the bureaucrats. This time it's different. Your American, Max Wylie, didn't surrender because he was scared of you, Gil. He was looking over your shoulder and seeing the red horseman of war riding across the desert and the pale horseman of hunger riding across the steppes. Hunger makes whores of us all, Gil. I'll sign papers with the Devil himself if he'll get us through this winter without famine and bloodshed.'

That was the essence of the report which I made to Tanaka and to Carl Leibig at noon the next day in the rooftop office in Tokyo. I confessed I had exceeded my brief. I told them I had met with Max Wylie. I told them of my encounter with Hoshino and Cubeddu in the Fuji Club. They asked very few questions. They offered no reproach. I was a good steward, trying to protect their interests.

I told them, only as a matter of record, that my brief love affair with Marta was at an end. They made murmurs of sympathy and changed the subject. They approved salary and expenses for Alex Boyko, who had accepted to run our press office in Thailand for two weeks.

And that was the end of it. We would meet in Bangkok and proceed according to plan. There was no excitement, no enthusiasm. The shadows of the apocalyptic horsemen seemed to rise up, dark against the pale autumn sky. Tanaka thanked us for attending and turned back to the pile of papers on his desk.

Carl Leibig and I rode down in the elevator together. He told me: 'I'm sorry to hear about you and Marta; but, believe me, it would never have worked out. I speak from personal experience. I had two engagements and one attempt at marriage. Total disaster! In the end, one has to surrender to what one is.'

'Now tell me about Miko. How do you see her?'

He shrugged and spread his hands in a gesture of helplessness. 'What can one say? She is a very clever woman who lives in two worlds. Tanaka uses her; she uses Tanaka. His dependence on her, his trust in her, raises deep resentments among his colleagues. For me, she's the original fox-woman, a mischief-maker. But, like the fox-woman, she'll probably turn into gold one day and all the bad things she's done will be forgotten – provided, of course, someone doesn't kill her beforehand. One more thing, Gil.'

'Tell me.'

'If the project doesn't work out the way we want in Bangkok, I'm going alone. Not with the whole project of course, that's impossible; but with the funding I have, I'll take the Western territories from the Urals to the Baltic. Forster has assured me the banks will go along.'

'Have you told Tanaka?'

'Sure.'

'What did he say?'

'The same thing he said to you. "The game isn't over until the last shot on the last hole!" What can one do with a man like that?'

Eleven

At three-thirty on Saturday afternoon, we were in a holding pattern over Don Muang airport. To the west lay the leprous sprawl of Bangkok, shrouded in a grey haze of smog. To the east were the green of rice paddies and tropic orchards, the gleam of lily pools and klongs, the brown serpent of the Chao Phraya river winding its way through the delta lands towards the sea.

I had been coming here now for more than a quarter of a century and I had watched the ravages which the Vietnam conflict, industrial progress, unrestrained tourism and the acquisitive society of the West had inflicted upon a rural civilisation. I remembered my first flight along the river, on a clear rainwashed day in the early sixties. The pinnacles of the *wats*, the golden cobras on their gables, were splendid in the sun. The river traffic was leisurely: great rafts of teak logs towed slowly to the down-river sawmills, the huge rice barges moving majestically in file, the market women paddling along the margins of the stream, selling their fruit and vegetables to the river people. But that, I had to remind myself, was in another time and another country, and the dear wench with whom I had shared it was dead.

Even so, some of the magic of that first arrival still survived. A pulse still stirred to the old excitement. Even in the fetid mass of modern Bangkok there remained a vestige of family and a kind of continuity. Across the river from the Oriental hotel, tucked away between the godowns of the merchants and the new blocks of high-rise apartments, was an old Thai house, lovingly restored, which housed the operations of Polyglot Press of Thailand.

It was a modest success because, for a *farang*, the art of living among the Thais is one of suavity and smiling courtesy and low profile. The President of the company was Khun Sirinart, widow of a princeling who had studied with my father in Australia and returned to take up a senior post at the university. Later he had invited my father to spend his sabbatical year as scholar in residence in the faculty of Arts and Letters.

During that year his patron died, quite suddenly. My father became tutelary spirit to the widow and her two children. He brought them to live in his house in Australia, taught them languages, procured scholarships for the children and, when their education was completed, suggested that I finance them into establishing Polyglot Press in Thailand.

Like most Thai women, Khun Sirinart had a genius for money management. Within ten years, I had a flourishing business, run by a very personable matriarch who spoke four European languages and admonished me constantly about my sloppy intonations in Thai. More importantly, we were of an age to be good and companionable friends and I had the pleasure of playing foreign uncle to a pigeon pair of exotically beautiful young people.

Sirinart was there to meet me at the Customs exit and to raise an enquiring eyebrow when she saw Eiko, my secretary, trailing one pace behind to shepherd the luggage. I told her she had nothing to worry about, but I had a lot on my mind that I would share at a more opportune time.

As the driver worked his way through the traffic and Eiko gazed in wonderment at the higgledy-piggledy life of the tropic sidewalks, Siri and I talked comfortably and intimately as old friends. Her questions were always direct: who was the young woman with me, was she only a secretary, why did I not marry again? This wandering life, chasing from office to office around the world, was not civilised. My father, that inveterate gypsy, had confessed that, in the evening of his life, he was feeling more and more lonely.

'You should think about that, Gil, before it is too late.'

I told her I had been thinking of it and that I had managed to make a sorry mess of my affair with Marta Boysen. She took my hand between her small soft palms and scolded me.

'You forget so quickly all the good things we teach you in Thailand. *Mai pen rai*! It doesn't matter. The wheel of life turns. One existence changes into another. Who knows? One day you may be reincarnated as a woman and your Marta as a man. You may be a Japanese. You may be a Burmese, or a bright bird in a tree. Everything passes. Everything changes. You cannot lose your peace of mind for one mistake. I would like to meet this Marta and judge for myself.'

188

'You shall, Siri. You'll hardly be able to avoid it. We'll be here for two weeks.'

'And are you going to be able to give me some time for business? There is much to talk about. We have been invited to propose a series of text books on European history and Asian geography for secondary students. The colour work we have had from Singapore lately is not the best quality . . .'

'I'll make time for it all, Siri. I promise. But first I have to get this circus organised. Every piece of news from the Gulf or from Eastern Europe sends a new shock wave through the groundwork we have laid.'

'And the shock waves will still be rumbling when you are in your seventh incarnation. *Mai pen rai*. You do what you can and rest tranquil like a petal on a pool. And if things get too bad, come across the river and sleep in my house. Your father's room is still there, with many of his books. The children would be happy to have you. So would I.'

This, I realised, was the memory that ran deepest in my un-conscious, the low pulse-beat, the sense of timelessness, of flatness, of vitality sapped by heat and damp and delta parasites, of emotions geared down to gentleness and accommodation. But there was another and darker side to this generous land and its smiling, pliant people. They had their cruelties and the cruelties were doubled by indifference. They were capable of sudden murderous rages and swift, brutal forays against any hint of insurrection. There were bandits in the hill country who attacked tourist buses. There were thieves in the city who burnt oleander leaves outside the windows of sleeping householders and robbed them when they succumbed to the toxic vapour. There were peddlers of drugs and cartels of traders who bought country girls and sold them to the brothels and bars of Patpong and Pattaya.

There was also the slow processional life of the paddy farmers and the boatbuilders and the weavers and the woodcarvers; and the yearly Festival of Lights, when all the sins of all the world were floated away down the river on boats of leaves, lit by tiny palm-oil lanterns. As if she had read my thoughts, Siri added a final admonition.

'Your father used to say none of us can live without forgiveness; but we have to begin by forgiving ourselves. So, before I leave you, promise me you will learn at least one lesson from the Lord Buddha. Do not desire anything so much that you cannot live without it. Call me whenever you want. Good luck.'

The car drew up outside the Oriental hotel. I took Eiko's arm and led her inside. She deserved some attention now. It was the first time she had ever been outside Japan. Suddenly all her bonds were broken. There were no rules any more. She was like a child, struck dumb with wonder.

I checked into a large corner suite on the seventh floor, while Eiko was lodged in a studio directly across the corridor, where she could set up her machine and spread her papers. I had what I needed: space and light and at least the illusion of magisterial separation from the parties who had accepted me as arbitrator.

There was a large folder, splendidly presented, which listed the members of each party, German, Japanese, Soviet, with their designated functions, their room numbers and directory extensions. There was a note of the business and tourist services provided by the hotel. There were the telephone and fax numbers of the Japanese, German, Russian and Australian embassies, with a list of doctors and dentists recommended by each. Most important of all was a schedule of the first week's meetings: an introductory gathering on Monday morning and then a series of committees working through each day to prepare for a full general meeting on the following Friday. After that, please God, we should spend the last week preparing heads of agreement and first draft documents. If not, we might just as well pack and go home, pull down the blinds and wait for the big bang in the Gulf and the last charge of the pale horsemen across the steppes.

I had just closed the folder when the telephone rang. Sir Pavel Laszlo was on the line. He had arrived on an early morning flight from Singapore. He was on the floor above me. Would I come up and have a drink? He needed a clear picture of what had transpired in Tokyo. It took the best part of an hour to respond to his rapid-fire questions and set down the story for him. Then he gave me his own, somewhat startling, rendition of related events.

'War in the Gulf? Fifty-fifty at this moment. If it comes, it will be a devastating event, its consequences far longer than anyone dares calculate. War is an act of violence that knows no bounds. The American offer of dialogue during the countdown period helps somewhat. It does not, because it cannot, pre-empt the gambler's throw of a beleaguered autocrat like Hussein. So, whatever we decide here in Bangkok has to be predicated on that risk, because our negotiations will be concluded slightly less than a month before the deadline. Effectively, there will be no start-up operations during that time, because it will be taken up with documentations, surveys, all the rest . . . Meanwhile, let's look at the Soviet scene. At the political level it's a mess, secessionists and centralists are at each other's throats. The generals are desperate to hold the army together as a force of law and order. The central distribution system simply doesn't work any more. The KGB are now the good guys, making sure relief supplies reach the needy. In this sense, the Tanaka/Leibig project is still an affair of tomorrow. It will have no plus or minus effect on food supplies for this winter. What it will do, however, is provide an enormous boost to morale and secure the co-operation of those food-rich republics which we target as sites for our factories, and which, at this moment, are actively supporting the black market to defeat the centralists. I've had this reaction from the Embassy in Canberra and it tallies with what you've told me about your talks in Tokyo. What I'm still trying to make sense of is the Japanese position in all this. Let's forget about Tanaka for a moment; let's talk Japan and the Gulf, Japan and the axis of trade and power across Eurasia. I'd like to hear your version of it.'

'OK. Japan and the Gulf? Here's a nation totally oil-dependent, totally dependent indeed on outside supplies of all commodities to keep her industries working. She's built the largest peacetime armament of any nation except America – aircraft, ships, weaponry – all devoted, by declared national policy, only to self-defence. Her lifeline to the Gulf is threatened. What's her contribution? A piddling amount of money and an absolute refusal of military or quasi-military support. Personally, I'm glad, because I don't want to see the militarists in power ever again. They're playing the old roulette game: straddle the numbers, à cheval, à quatre. You lower your winnings, but double or quadruple your chances. Also, they're trading heavily with Muslim nations Malaysia and Indonesia who supply, for example, a large part of her timber and take a huge amount of her manufactured electrical and mechanical products. She can't afford to alienate them. This is her original South-East Asia co-prosperity sphere. She's not going to hand it back on a silver dish to Singapore, Taiwan and Korea.'

'It's a dry argument,' said Laszlo with grim humour. 'I could use another drink. You?'

'Please.'

He crossed to the cabinet to refill the glasses, commanding me at the same time: 'Finish what you were saying.'

'The Japanese have built their economy on network alliances at home and aggressive acquisitions of markets and resources abroad. You yourself have been part of that process in Australia.'

'No argument. I have.'

'As a result, they've been able to make large profits, maintain a highly controlled labour force and high real estate prices, against which their entrepreneurs have borrowed to the hilt.'

'Again, no argument.'

'Now, with full-scale world recession, rocketing oil prices, contracting markets and real estate prices falling through the floor, the whole ball of string is beginning to unwind.'

'Conclusion?'

'In that context, any Japanese investment in the Soviet Union represents a very bad risk. The last thing they want is to buy a basket case.'

'But Tanaka's bought this one. I've bought it, Leibig's bought it. Why?'

'You and Leibig have bought it because you're Middle Europeans. You know you can't have a vacuum across Eurasia. Somehow the Soviets have to be kept working together in some sort of co-operative union. Otherwise the whole goddam cake will collapse – Mackinder, Kjellen, Haushofer weren't all that far wrong.'

'And you're saying Tanaka is the only Japanese bright enough to read that equation?'

'No. I don't believe that, any more than you do. But I still don't understand why he's so totally isolated, and why he's turned to the Yakuza and the Mafia as financial allies.'

Laszlo handed me my drink and raised his glass in a sardonic toast: 'To the age of enlightenment.'

We drank, with ceremony and a certain recklessness. Laszlo set down his glass and made a flourish with a silk handkerchief, dabbing at his lips, drying his fingertips. I almost expected him to launch into a psalmody: 'I will wash my hands among the blameless.' Instead, he announced flatly: 'I invest with Tanaka. I also invest with four other of his colleagues in the *keiretsu*. I use the same structures basically as they use in Japan: cross-holdings, shared counsel, shared risk. Therefore what I tell you now is what I know. Nobody, anywhere in the world, can run an international business without the intervention of the mobs: Yakuza, Mafia, the Corsicans, the Triads. I run a big fleet in the United States. I can't keep a single truck on the road unless I'm paid up with the

Teamsters. I can't clear a container in Sydney or Melbourne unless the Painters and Dockers have a hand in it. Protection is the oldest racket in the world; it's been going on since the first legionary held out his hand to the first pedlar coming through the gates of any city on the globe. I know this. You know it. We don't approve of the system, but there's no way we can argue with it and carry on legitimate trade at the same time. So, we play by the rules and pay the mulct. My haulage rates reflect their charges. Your books, a dozen eggs, a can of beans, cost that much more in the market. Are you reading me?'

'I'm reading you loud and clear.'

'Now let's talk about Tanaka or any other Japanese investor in Australia or Indonesia or the Philippines. He makes cars, he sells computers, he buys hotels, whatever. That's the straight-line operation. When you're selling you're in advertising, which is show business. When you run a hotel you deal with warm bodies, entertainment. You need a whole chain of support services to complete the circle, so that the money you fly in, flies back to you through the shops you own, the cars you rent, the liquor you dispense. That's where all the mobs come in, to run the ancillary services you can't manage, but on which you still depend. But it's not all lost money. The mobs need to have at least half of it laundered. So they buy stock in the big investments, the airlines, the banks, the haulage lines and the hotels themselves. It's as old as the notion of empire, Gil. The duke becomes a king by hiring mercenaries to topple the throne. Then he makes the mercenaries respectable with land grants and benefices. Nothing changes except the names and the mechanics. So I'm not surprised that Tanaka is calling on Hoshino for funds. That's the daimyo and his samurai, the duke and his mercenary all over again. But Cubeddu and the South American coke money, that doesn't fit. That can't be laundered in the same washing machine.'

I had told him of my belief that Miko, the woman with a foot in both worlds, was involved in the transaction. I repeated the argument. He shook his head in puzzlement.

'Only half right, Gil. Self-interest on her part, an insurance policy for Tanaka, these things I can see. The rest of it, no. It's oil and water, Gil. One more thing. I can see Hoshino putting his money on trust with Tanaka. That's basically where it is at this moment, since Tanaka is his principal banker. But Cubeddu and whoever's running him, no way will they pass over control of their own funds.'

'Tanaka keeps talking as though he'll stage some last-minute coup that will reconcile him again with his peers.'

'I wish to God I could read his mind. It could save us a lot of time and money.'

'Carl Leibig and I have both threatened a walkout. He still won't move from his position that it will be all right on the night.'

'Let's give it a week,' said Pavel Laszlo. 'A lot can happen in that time.' He grinned like a calico cat and splashed more liquor into my glass. 'Look how much happened to you, Gil. When this is over you will come to Hungary with me and . . .'

'I know. You'll find me a beautiful, caring woman.'

'I was thinking of two or three,' said Laszlo amiably. 'Hungary is full of beautiful women and they're all looking for a man to get them out of the place. I don't know why. I left with the seat out of my breeches. Now that I've set up business there, I'm coining money and even the president tells me what a patriot I am. He doesn't want me living there, of course, just driving the gravy train.'

The more I saw of Pavel Laszlo the more I liked him. He was a living paradox – a romantic without illusions, a cynic without malice, at once a dreamer and a hard-nosed pragmatist. I was convinced that he and Boris Vannikov would get along together. I told him so. He shrugged.

'I get along with anyone who doesn't try to sell me rabbit for mink. If he's prepared to bend some rules to get us started, we should return the compliment. I'm interested, by the way, to hear you've changed your opinion of Carl Leibig. I found him quite impressive.'

'Impressive enough to handle half the deal alone? That's what he's proposing if there's a split with Tanaka.'

'Yes. I think he's up to it. And the whole situation in Germany and Eastern Europe would favour him. But Tanaka still worries me. I've worked with him a long time.'

'So have I.'

'And I've never known him to go so far out on a limb before. Always he's come to the table with every element in place.'

'Hold on a moment. He's got them in place now. The funds are on the table.'

'But they're the wrong elements, the wrong funds.'

'Let's drop it for a while.'

'Why?'

'Because we're not thinking straight, or, rather, we are thinking straight, in a European mode.'

Suddenly he seemed to lose interest. He was an active man, easily bored with theories. He said: 'Pamela, my public relations woman, arrives late tonight from Sydney. She'll contact you in the morning. Just tell her what you want, she'll do it. She's long in the tooth but top of her class. And you don't have to spell the words for her.'

He did not have to spell them for me either. The meeting was over. We both had our noses against the same brick wall. I thanked him for the drink and went back to my room to shower and dress for dinner. I called Eiko. She was very happy. She had just met a very nice young salesman from the Sanyo company. He had invited her to dinner; she would like to accept, unless of course I needed her services. I told her to enjoy herself, then went down to a solitary dinner on the riverside terrace.

It was not a quiet place. The restaurant was full. The barbecue on the other side of the pool was crowded. On the river, the longboats with their great six-cylinder engines were still roaring up and down, their screws churning the murky waters and the pools of yellow light from the buildings on either bank. Yet after a few minutes the sounds seemed to blend and subside into monotone, leaving the tired mind to range free in another space and another time. It was like looking into a diviner's mirror, where images appeared and vanished, as if at the whim of some capricious conjuror.

There was the Feather Man, smiling and secretive, who had a ramshackle factory on the river front. To this place came a daily procession of peasants and housewives selling bales and baskets and cardboard boxes full of duck feathers. The feathers were dumped into a great engine which puffed and panted like an asthmatic giant, separating the heavy ones from the lightest which became the down for pillows and cushions.

Since there were a lot of ducks in Asia and a lot of people plucking them, the Feather Man became very rich. He also had a ready-made intelligence service, a whole army of little men and women pedalling around the countryside collecting duck feathers. He had a factory in Vietnam, supported by a similar army of collectors, but during the Tet offensive the Vietcong had captured him and carted him away into the jungle for a year, lodging him in deep holes in the ground. I wanted to publish his story, but I could never get him to tell more than a tiny piece of it. Now it was too late, because he died as secretively as he had lived and it was many months before his friends even heard the news.

Then there was Jack Grindlay, expatriate journalist, who ran an English-language newspaper and lived like a Renaissance duke with a house full of young Thai men who, during one orgiastic night, stabbed him to death in his own living room.

I recalled snatches of some very long and very exotic dinner parties at the house of Jim Thompson, called the silk king of Thailand, who went for a holiday with friends to the Cameron Highlands in 1967 and simply disappeared from human ken. He, too, had been in the game of secrets. He, too, had made many friends and many enemies and I for one had never been able to believe the myth that he had gone out walking and fallen into a tiger trap. His life, what was public in it at least, had been elegantly recorded in a book which had become compulsory reading for every visitor to Thailand. But when I as a publisher applied through my New York lawyers for access to Jim Thompson's military records, I was met with a blank wall of silence. My most vivid recollection was of a moment when I caught him unawares, with his white cockatoo perched on his shoulder, staring out the window at the weavers in their house across the klong. He looked tired and sad and infinitely weary. Then another image imposed itself on that handsome, ravaged face: the stone visage of the Lord Buddha, calm, passionless, sublimely indifferent to the petty preoccupations of human affairs.

I poured the last of the wine and, while I was waiting for coffee, walked over to the stone balustrade and stood staring out across the river to the buildings on the farther bank with the tufted trees between them.

The tide was coming in now, the matted islands of lily plants and river weed were floating upstream instead of down. The restaurant boats were cruising slowly against the current, their feasting passengers like actors on a movie screen. The deep-buried grief stirred again as I remembered the first night I had taken my wife to dine on the river, with half a dozen friends for company and a gypsy fiddler hired for the night from Bangkok's only Hungarian restaurant. That dream, too, was shattered when a waft of familiar perfume enclosed me and Miko's voice mocked me softly.

'Mind if I join you?'

This was Bangkok, where good mannered detachment, *choei choei*, was required of everyone. So I bade her welcome and led her back to the table for coffee. She was dressed Western style and she was speaking

English with the familiar West Coast intonation. She was still beautiful, but somehow too ordinary, too familiar to be associated with all the current dramas of our lives. I asked her: 'What are you doing here? You're not expected until tomorrow.'

'I know, but Kenji asked me to come ahead and check the arrangements. I took the flight after yours on JAL. Kenji and Carl Leibig arrive tomorrow with their staff. As you probably know, Marta's travelling with them.'

I did not know, but I chose not to say so. Instead, I told her that Laszlo had already arrived and that we had talked. She nodded indifferently.

'You and I have to talk, Gil. Kenji ordered me to explain certain things. Others I want you to hear from me.'

'Which do you want to tell me first?'

'Mine.'

I laid my palms together and bowed my head in a parody of respectful submission. 'I'm here. I'm listening.'

'Years ago, I bore Kenji a son. The child was stillborn.'

'I knew that, Kenji told me.'

'What you do not know is that my son could have become the head of the House of Tanaka.'

'You will have to explain that a little.'

'It is not a question of inheritance. Kenji's family are all fully provided for. There is nothing I could have done, or would do in the future, to challenge or upset those arrangements. This is a question of succession. Kenji's son has neither taste nor talent for the business. He is a biologist, a brilliant researcher in human genetics. Kenji is rightly proud of him but, in fact, he is without a family successor in the business. Do you know the meaning of the Japanese word *ie*?'

I knew it, but it was a concept difficult to convey in a European frame of reference. It described a social unit, a corporate family, a household continuum whose identity, relationships and responsibilities must be continued, if not by natural birthright, then by co-option, adoption, the creation of another kind of relationship, sometimes more binding than the natural one. Thus, in the old days a peasant boy could be adopted by the noble family under whose roof he lived. He could even supplant the legitimate son who had left the *ie* and no longer had accepted responsibilities within it. Slowly, I was beginning to see a new

197

contour to the relationship between Miko and Tanaka. It disposed me to be more gentle with her, if no less cautious.

'That's sad; for him and for you.'

She shook her head. She refused to acknowledge sadness. 'It changed things. I could not commit myself to another pregnancy. Kenji was left with his problem of succession.'

'Which is now more urgent than ever before.'

'It is critical. I have one new complication, with his health. He refuses to discuss it even with me. All I know is that he is a very sick man.'

'And your problem?'

'Is myself: what I am, what I do, today and tomorrow.'

'You seem to have solved part of it at least.'

'How so?'

'With Marta. I heard you were celebrating – what was it? – "the coming together of two hearts".'

Her reaction was swift and angry. 'Do you listen at keyholes too?'

'No. Little birds tell me fairytales.'

'Marta is not a solution. She is a diversion.'

'I hope you explained that to her.'

'She explained it to me. She said she hated closed doors, closed minds, closed hearts. She had to open them all, even if what she found inside was ugly. She said she had tried to tell you this, but you refused to understand.'

'I understood very well. I simply declined to live with it.'

'Or forgive and forget when it's over? Treat it like water-business: tonight enjoyed, tomorrow forgotten? Besides, what do you expect at your age? A certified virgin?'

'A private loving – and a tranquil one.'

'I wish you luck.'

I, too, was beginning to be angry; but the languid delta magic still held, *mai pen rai*. In a couple of weeks all this would be over and I would move on about my own business. I asked the waitress to bring mineral water and clean glasses. Then I tried to reason with Miko.

'I don't know why you're pushing this argument so hard. Marta and I are yesterday's lovers. For the next two weeks, we still have to work together as colleagues. With a little time and distance between us, we might even be friends again. So may we leave it at that, please.'

'Very well. Let's talk about you and me.'

'What's to say?'

'Why, suddenly, are we enemies?'

'Are we?'

'We should not play games, Gil. It's a small world. Things move fast. Thursday evening you and Max Wylie went to see Marta. The same evening in Los Angeles, which is eighteen hours behind Tokyo, two Federal agents visited my house in Holmby Hills and began questioning my assistant about my business affairs. She called my lawyer, who will protect my interests until I get back. How would you read that, Gil?'

'How does Tanaka read it?'

'He refuses to be concerned. He shrugs and says "You have done nothing wrong. They ask questions. You answer truthfully. The story will end there." '

'He's right.'

'He's not. There's the small matter of fees I've accepted for contacts and introductions and a million dollars in escrow to be paid to me if Domenico Cubeddu's company becomes part of the Tanaka/Leibig consortium.'

'Does Tanaka know about that?'

'We have always had an understanding about it.'

'Japanese style, of course. You don't tell. He doesn't know. You both understand.'

'You really are a bastard, Gil.'

'Good. That's the beginning of wisdom. Now let's take step two. I'm a lot easier to deal with than the Drug Enforcement Authority. I have commitments and loyalties to Tanaka. He wants you to talk to me. Do it. Tell me all about Domenico Cubeddu.'

'It's a long story.'

'I'd like Laszlo to hear it too.'

'Why, for God's sake?'

'Because he's older and shrewder than I am and he's a stronger ally than I can ever be and you'll trust him more because you didn't seduce his girl. Let's walk up to the foyer and we'll call his room.'

Sir Pavel Laszlo was not overly pleased by the call. The heat and the humidity were getting to him as they always did. He had just had a bath and he was sitting in his undershorts and dressing gown, reading a thriller. He was damned if he was going to get dressed again – even for the Queen of England. Nonetheless, he was too good a businessman to pass up inside information so, strictly on a take-me-as-I-am, don't-hang-about and I-hope-to-God-this-is-worth-the-energy basis, he consented to receive us. He brightened a little when he saw Miko, then composed his chubby features into an inquisitor's scowl as he began to question her about Domenico Cubeddu. Her answers were brisk and clear.

'First you have to understand that I do not work exclusively for the Tanaka Group. I supply services to many others. One of the services is preliminary research into business projects, particularly into the people who may be useful contacts, experts in various sectors. One of the subjects always under review is new timber resources. Japan is constantly criticised for over-logging in Indonesia, Brazil, the Philippines and other places. The demand is large and constant. I was asked by the Tanaka Group to find out all I could about untapped resources in South American republics. Colombia was one area of research, because it does have big stands of commercial timber: brazilwood, mahogany, walnut and the like. The other side of the picture, of course, is that the country is run by the drug barons who control the cocaine traffic into the United States. However, Japanese businessmen are very good at distancing themselves from local troublemakers. They make it very clear that they come to do business, not meddle in local affairs. When I thought I had enough information I suggested Kenji send down a couple of his experts to speak to the government and see what concessions might be made available to us. They came, they went, they reported back to Kenji. Detailed studies were set in motion. Then one day I had a telephone call from the Palermitan Banking Corporation, the President, no less, Mr Domenico Cubeddu.'

'So you met him. What did he offer?'

'Joint investment in any Colombian timber project and joint investment in any other project outside Japan or the United States in which the Tanaka Group was interested.'

'Any amount mentioned?'

'He said that up to eight billion would not be excessive, but they would prefer smaller tranches in a variety of projects, always joint ventures, of course.'

'The man's not stupid. He gets a free ride to respectability on the coat-tails of a big Japanese conglomerate. That's what a number of our high, wide and handsome promotors did in Australia; when things went sour, the Japanese ended up with the core assets. But get back to your story. Cubeddu put the proposition to you . . .'

'He asked me to act for him.'

'And you didn't see any conflict of interest in that?'

'No. That's what I told you at the beginning. I work for a whole range of Japanese companies, with sometimes opposing interests. I do not share or sell secrets from one company to another. That would be fatal to my business, and quite possibly fatal to me. Besides, I have to protect myself always. If the Tanaka Group didn't want to proceed, I had to be free to negotiate the idea elsewhere. That's understood always.'

'So you accepted a retainer. How much?'

'A hundred and fifty thousand.'

'Against what?'

'One million in escrow if the deal goes through.'

'Which deal is that?'

'This one. The timber proposal is on hold for the moment.'

'Was there any question at any time about where Cubeddu's money came from?'

'No. The only thing I had to verify was that it did exist and where. I had letters from a reputable banking corporation in Liechtenstein assuring me that the funds were available.'

'And that's all you asked?'

'No. When I inquired about the shareholders of the Palermitan Banking Corporation, I was shown a list and I was assured that the names on it were among the wealthiest and most powerful in Colombia.'

'But you knew their money was drug money?'

'I had no knowledge or proof that it was anything but what the correspondence stated "funds available for investment outside the Continental United States".'

'So you arranged the contact between Cubeddu and Tanaka.'

'Yes.'

'Where did the first meeting take place?'

'In Madrid. I was not present. After that, Tanaka told me to invite Cubeddu to Tokyo for discussions on our project.'

'Were you present at any of those discussions?'

'No. I was not.'

'Did Tanaka talk to you about them afterwards?'

'Only in the most general way. He told me they were progressing.'

'And you were satisfied with that? After all, you had a lot of money riding on the answers. You still have.'

'I wasn't satisfied, but I didn't press the matter.'

'Why?'

'Because I know Kenji. Once he saw I was anxious he would begin to tease me, as a boy might tease a puppy with a bone. That is not a game I enjoy.'

'So now we come to Nara and afterwards. According to Gil here and to Carl Leibig, Cubeddu made a poor impression. The Russians indicated that his participation could kill the deal.'

'Kenji did discuss that with me.'

'What was his opinion?'

'He said we simply needed to be patient. Things would soon be so bad in Russia that they'd rather eat with the dragon than starve.'

'What else can you tell me about Cubeddu?'

'Only that he's a hard, vulgar man. He's made some obvious passes at me, and some less obvious threats.'

'What sort of threats?'

'He hoped I understood that he had paid for results. If he didn't get results, he might have to "institute recovery proceedings".'

'And what did you say to that?'

'I laughed in his face. Then he laughed too and said it was only a joke.'

I had been silent during the interrogation, but I wanted to be done with half-truths and evasions. I said to Miko: 'There are two other things Sir Pavel should know. Do you want to tell him, or shall I?'

'You tell him.'

'According to Miko, Tanaka is much more seriously ill than he admits and he is looking for a successor to adopt into the business.'

'He's got a son.'

'The son is a genetic biologist. He does not wish to give up his career.'

'Ah!' Laszlo's smile was like a sunburst of revelation. 'Now it begins to make sense: everything I was hearing in Australia, what I am getting from Wall Street. Even your Mr Cubeddu fits into the puzzle. Where is he now, by the way?'

'I hope he's still in Tokyo. It was made very clear to him that he should not be present here in Bangkok. Hoshino understands very well, but Cubeddu is a hard-head, he doesn't want to learn.'

'He's here in Bangkok.' Miko made the bald announcement. 'He came on the same flight as I did. He's staying at the Sheraton.'

'That' said Pavel Laszlo, 'is the worst news I've heard tonight.'

'What do you think will happen?' It was Miko who asked the question. Laszlo stood up, wrapping the dressing gown about his bulging midriff.

'I am not a prophet, madam. All I know is that when you stick a match in a petrol tank it blows up. As soon as Tanaka arrives, Gil, tell him I want to talk to him. Now, why don't you two get out of here and let me read my book.'

As we walked down the corridor towards the elevators, Miko asked with an odd uncertainty: 'Will you do me a favour?'

'If I can.'

'Take me down to the bar, buy me a drink, sit with me and listen to the music for half an hour.'

'That doesn't sound too hard.'

The elevator arrived. We rode down to the ground floor, found ourselves a quiet corner in the bar and ordered our drinks. The piano player discoursed Cole Porter melodies in an easy, unobtrusive style. Miko raised her glass.

'*Kampai*! And thank you.'

'*Kampai*, and good luck. We're all going to need it.'

'Can we call a truce now, you and I?'

'If you want.'

'I do. I'm tired, Gil, tired and scared. You've set the dogs on me in California. I can't predict what's going to happen with Kenji or how he's going to act in the situation we have. He needs me desperately, but we communicate less and less freely. It's almost as though he's moved into another country. And Cubeddu frightens me. Hoshino's a monster. He would and could eliminate me without a word spoken; but he doesn't frighten me, because I'm part of the fabric of his world. I don't threaten him. He doesn't threaten me. But Cubeddu is different. There's a rage in him. He will not admit defeat. And he wasn't joking about recovering the money he has paid me.'

I judged it was time to put the question which we had all asked at one time or another. 'What happens when Kenji dies? Has he made provision for you?'

'Some, yes. I have no complaints. My business is profitable and it will continue, with or without the Tanaka Group.'

'So what more do you need?'

'The same thing as you, Gil Langton; a private loving and a tranquil one.'

'You mocked me when I told you that.'

'No. I was mocking myself, and I was jealous of you. There now. It's all told.'

'Not quite all.'

'What have I left out?'

'Marta.'

Her dark eyes stared at me, unblinking, over the rim of her glass. She was silent for a long moment, then she told me firmly: 'She's an adult woman, Gil. She can speak for herself. Why don't you ask her?'

Shortly after that we finished our drinks and went our separate ways to our separate beds. I sat up for a while, reading the newspapers which were laid out on my coffee table, topped with a posy of frangipani flowers to make the news more fragrant. On page three of the Far Eastern edition of the *Wall Street Journal* was a half-column news item with a Moscow dateline: President Gorbachev had accepted an invitation from the Japanese government to visit Tokyo in April for discussions on economic and political issues. Among the items listed on the agenda was the future of the Kuril Islands.

Which raised the interesting question as to how much prior knowledge Tanaka had of the proposed visit. He was, after all, a recently appointed personal counsellor to the Emperor. He was still Chairman of the small élite who controlled the policies of the *keiretsu*. There was a paradox here, too: the growing rumours of his alienation from his peers and his expressed confidence in the outcome of the Bangkok conference.

There was also another, smaller, mystery. Normally, during her stay in Japan, Miko was constantly at his side. She was both mistress and business confidante, which again had created problems with his colleagues. Now, when Tanaka was reported to be gravely ill, they were travelling separately and Miko was making no secret of her fears about her own future.

I slept fitfully that night, troubled by a frustration dream. I was in a bare room, facing a locked door. I knew I had the key. I could not find it in any of my pockets; I must have dropped it. As I groped about the floor, I found myself enmeshed in cobwebs, which were gradually filling the room and smothering me in grey filaments. When finally I found the key, I could not find the door.

Twelve

Sunday promised to be a straggling sort of day. The delegates from Tokyo would arrive mid-afternoon, those from Europe and Moscow in the early and late evening. None of them would feel much inclined for business. Immediately after breakfast I called Eiko and dictated a two-line memo to be handed to all delegates with their room keys. I would be at their disposal in my suite between six and eight.

Then I made contact with Laszlo's publicity expert, a big, no-nonsense redhead with a rasping humour, a wide grin and an outback Queensland accent. Her work experience was impressive: she had run more than five hundred contingents of Japanese investors and inter-national press men up, down and across the Australian continent. Her name was Pamela – call me Pam – Dalby and she made no secret of her talents and shortcomings.

'I can't write copy to save my life. Don't ask me to interpret complicated ideas, because I trip over my bottom lip. What I'm good at is pushing the right paper into the right hands, keeping the news hounds happy and smelling trouble before it breaks, like tricky TV interviewers and big-name correspondents who specialise in minefields and booby traps.'

I told her Vannikov and I would be directing the information flow, Alex Boyko would be responsible for text and distribution. Marta Boysen would be the ideologue and Tanya the interpreter in residence. We would have our first meeting immediately after the opening general session. I showed her the rooms from which we would be operating. She checked the equipment: stationery, copying machines, word-processors, telephones. I asked her if she would like to join me by the pool. She gave a big, bar-room laugh.

'Hell. Can you imagine me in a swimsuit with all these tiny-tot Asian Venuses? A masochist I'm not. I'm going shopping for silks and gemstones.'

'I can recommend a couple of reputable dealers.'

'Thanks, but I've been here before. I love the haggle and, believe it or not, I can read stones. My first lover, God rest his silly soul, was a jeweller. He taught me a lot about rubies and sapphires, but nothing about sex. Anything else you need before I go?'

'That's the lot. I'll be interested to see what you buy. Good luck.'

'Good luck to you, too. From what Pavel tells me, you're carrying a lot of weight in this exercise.'

'They're paying by weight. I can't complain.'

She was a big, loud woman from no place, but I felt better for meeting her. It was like stepping out of a small, dark room into a forty-acre paddock and hearing the shout of a country welcome.

I thought for a moment of calling Siri and inviting her across the river for lunch. Then I thought better of it. I did not really want to work at anything, even at being pleasant to people. I needed to be quiet and alone, to gather my wits and my strength for a performance that would go on eight, ten hours a day, for two weeks.

Rehearsals were over now. Tomorrow it would be showtime, with the big parade around the centre ring: the band, the elephants, the caracoling horses, the tumblers, the clowns. And, slap in the middle of the sawdust, the ringmaster, the temporary god who controlled all these wonders.

The pool attendant settled me in a shady spot with fresh towels and a big green umbrella. I smeared myself with protective lotion against the treachery of the tropic sun. The waiter brought me a coconut filled with exotic juices laced with white rum and curacao. I read the first two pages of a thriller I had bought at the bookstall, but it was pale stuff beside the dramas which had played themselves out along the river reaches in the last fifty years, dramas in whose epilogues I, Gilbert Anselm Langton, was most paradoxically involved.

In 1941 the Japanese had occupied Thailand, with the reluctant consent of its government which, with equal reluctance, declared war on the United States and Britain. In Washington, Cordell Hull refused to accept the declaration and the Ambassador who presented it immediately began to organise a resistance group called the Free Thai.

However, the Japanese were the occupying power. Their invasions of Malaya and Singapore were launched from Thai territory and the nightmare horrors of the Burma railway were enacted under the placid eyes of the Thai people. Now I, the son of a man who had interpreted at the trials of Japanese war criminals, was here in Bangkok, mediating the interests of a large Japanese corporation and a German one which had survived two world wars.

How to explain it? How to justify the shifting allegiances, the chameleon changes in the colour of human acts? Just behind me was the oldest section of the hotel, called the Authors' Residence, whose suites were named for famous visitors – Noel Coward, Joseph Conrad, Somerset Maugham. I remembered sitting in the lounge there one steamy monsoon night while Jim Thompson, the silk king, explained his continued loyalty to the wartime leader of the Free Thai, the Prime Minister Pridi, who was then in exile in Peking, suspected of complicity in the murder of King Ananda.

Pridi and Thompson had been close friends. Pridi was the fabled 'Ruth' of the Free Thai movement. Thompson had been, and still was at the time, an Intelligence man. He was also a great and theatrical teller of tales. So where did the truth lie? How closely was Thompson's own disappearance linked to his friendship with Pridi? Who could tell? And how much did it matter any more? What had been was already mythology, *mai pen rai*. Today was rolling back, hour by hour, into yesterday. Before judgment was even pronounced it was already obsolete.

Which brought me, by a round turn, back to Marta Boysen. I kept telling myself and everyone else that she was in the past, out of my life, because she was trapped in her own private mythology of domestic tyranny and a flight to freedom. The truth was that she was planted like a stone for stumbling in my present and my immediate future. I would have to meet her every day. I would have to say good morning and good night, offer her drinks, comment on the quality of her work; and still there would be unfinished business between us. It was all very well to talk about swift surgery and swift healing. Any doctor would tell you the ghost limb could still ache, years after the amputation.

However, in a strange fashion, I was more deeply troubled by the state of my relations with Kenji Tanaka. In the two short weeks since I had accepted to join the project, those relations had changed from warm friendship to bleak neutrality. The instinctive trust we had reposed in each other, both as friends and as business partners, seemed to have become a matter of calculation, if not of daily review by either party.

I had never had any illusions about the financial disparities between us. I was a modestly rich man with the luxury of indulging his scholarly interests to make money. Kenji Tanaka was massively wealthy, the President of a huge conglomerate of industries spread all around the world. Yet, in the narrow field of our common endeavours, we were equals, partners in a competitive game which we played for the pleasure of it.

The differences in our histories and our cultures were even greater than the financial ones. I still had childhood memories of the Pacific war and the barbarities perpetrated by the armies of occupation in Malaya, the Philippines and the East Indies. But the gift of tongues with which my father had endowed me, the overview of history which he saw as an instrument of healing, gave me, I had believed, a privileged entry into the world of Kenji Tanaka. He had acknowleged that more than once.

'I hear you speaking my language, Gil, and suddenly I am shocked that you do it so well and so easily. There is another thing which always surprises me: you are indifferent to the advantages you have. You have a key that opens many more doors than my money can. You teach me my own history. You recite fables which I had always thought were exclusive to my childhood. You will never know how much I resented the fact that you knew the song I used to sing as a little boy, *Umeboshi san*, Mr Pickle-plum.'

It was the resentment, so casually admitted, which troubled me now. I could understand that he might choose to exclude me from his business counsels; I found it hard to accept that he would shut me out from any sharing in the solitude of his illness. Even the ancient rituals of *seppuku* demanded the presence of a friend to make the final sword-cut which terminated the agony.

The archaic image was so vivid that it jolted me back to reality. What the hell was I making such a fuss about? A man had the right to die in his own fashion, wrapped in his own dignities. Why was I feeling rejected? Miko claimed that she, too, had been shut out, but she was following the tradition of all wise mistresses, making a blanket of banknotes to keep her warm in winter.

A shadow fell across me and I looked up to see Domenico Cubeddu standing between me and the light. He was as sleek as a male model in Ralph Lauren gear. He pointed to the vacant lounge beside me.

'Mind if I sit down?'

'Please. Be my guest.'

'I'm staying at the Sheraton. I thought I'd wander over here and see how the other half lives.'

'I thought it was agreed you wouldn't show here.'

'Last minute decision. Hoshino and I decided to pick up your idea of a trust to administer our joint interest in this project presuming, of course, it gets off the ground and the Soviets don't turn up their noses at good money. From what I hear, that's unlikely. They're rattling their begging bowls very loudly, everywhere. Anyway, the instrument's all ready, a traditional trust administered by German and Japanese bankers. Our funds go in the moment the Soviets commit to the project. You know, Langton, one way and another you're a bright guy. We could work well together.'

I doubted that, but what was the point of telling him? I acknowledged the compliment with a shrug and a question. 'Where's Hoshino?'

'He's in town, too. He owns a house on the river not far from here. I haven't been there, but he's invited me to a party before I leave. Meantime, he's showing me the town. The business he's got going here is fantastic. The police and the army are very co-operative – not cheap, mind you, but co-operative.'

I wondered why he was telling me all this, then I realised that he was caught in a familiar syndrome which the Feather Man had once called 'Oriental rapture, the East-of-Suez illusion'. He had explained it by saying that the rules of the game were so different that the foreigner believed that there were no rules at all. I could not believe that a money-man like Cubeddu, with the Colombian drug barons looking over his shoulder, could be so naive. In common humanity, I felt I owed him at least one warning, so I told him the story of my long-ago night with my father in Thonburi, kitty corner across the river from where we were sitting now.

In the old days of the Dutch traders and the French rivals, when Ayutthaya was still the capital of Siam, Thonburi was a Customs post where all shipmasters had to pay imposts on their cargoes. It soon became very rich. When my father and I first visited, with Siri and her husband, it was still a pleasant place to live, surrounded by orchards and palm plantations and rice paddies tilled by the folk who lived in the stilt houses along the klongs.

One night, Siri and her husband took us to a feast in the house of the village head man. It was, I believe, a betrothal between a young girl of good family and a *khon suk*, a youth who had served his three months as a monk and was therefore a most desirable son-in-law. It was a decorous little affair, which seemed to go on interminably. It was only at the end of it that I realised I must have consumed a large quantity of neat alcohol, because I had to be helped in and out of the longboat and put to bed by my father and Siri's husband.

But that was not the point of the story. At the same party was another young man, apparently a disappointed suitor, who, after we had left, became ill-mannered and loud and made some gross remarks to his rival. He, too, was drunk. He, too, was assisted into a longboat. Everybody witnessed his exit. A week later his bloated body was found in a backwater near a sawmill three miles down stream. His tongue had been cut out and his genitals were stuffed in his mouth. Domenico Cubeddu thought about the story for a moment, then nodded approval. 'Nothing changes, wherever you work. I tell my people: listen a lot, say little and if you think you're being screwed, which you probably are, relax and enjoy it. The payoff comes later.'

'Sound advice, especially in this part of the world.'

'Have you seen Miko?'

'Not this morning.'

'I'll call her from reception.'

'Before you do that.'

'Yes?'

'A word of advice. Miko talked to me last night. She seemed rather depressed. The impression I got – right or wrong – was that you were leaning on her, or might be leaning on her, over a matter of performance fees.'

Cubeddu was instantly angry. 'Even if I was, which I'm not, what business would that be of yours, Mr Langton?'

'Just this. Until the conference is over in two weeks' time, I'm paid to keep the peace, deal even-handedly with all parties and make sure there are no unnecessary frictions among the delegates. There's another thing you should remember, Mr Cubeddu. You're a long way from home. You're in another culture pattern that you don't understand at all. Miko is part of that pattern. The people inside it will protect her to protect themselves. I know you're a very big shot in Medellin and Barranquilla and Miami, but here you're a nobody with a lot of other people's money to spend. You come from Sicily. You understand what la famiglia means. Just do some simple multiplication and think how many other families there are from Tokyo to Thailand. If you're going into business, the last thing you want is a war over a woman. Take your own advice. If you think you're being screwed, relax and enjoy it.'

By the time I had finished speaking his anger had gone. He sat staring at me with dark, brooding eyes. Finally, he nodded a reluctant assent. 'First thing I do when I see the lady is tell her she's reading me all wrong. I'm not leaning on her. What she's got is hers, a non-returnable service fee. I should have made that clearer at the beginning. Now, do you mind if I ask you a question?'

'Go ahead.'

'You and Miko, have you ever. . .?'

'No, we haven't. And if you'll excuse me, I'm going for a swim.'

He sat watching me as I cruised up and down the long pool in a half-hour workout. After a while he got bored, waved to me and disappeared into the hotel. I could not help smiling at his uncertain exit. He controlled an astronomical amount of money. He had to be both smart and ruthless, otherwise the drug lords of Medellin would never have trusted him so far. Even so, there was a kind of engaging naivete about him, as if he had just stepped out of an old-fashioned gangster film, dressed to kill, with a fedora and spats and a knuckleduster ring.

It was, of course, the reverse effect of the Feather Man's 'Oriental rapture'. This time I was the victim of it. I knew the language. I knew the rules of the game. I even felt a certain kinship with the spirits of the place. Every morning while I was in Thailand I made my offering to them: an orchid bloom laid on the floor of the tiny gilded spirit house in the garden. From where I was, Domenico Cubeddu had the faintly ridiculous look of any stranger: off-key, out of mode, puzzled. It was a mistake, of course, a grievous misjudgment. The man was well versed in villainy. He was the appointed custodian of his proceeds. I was a fool to believe that he would bend to the advice of a middle-aged book man.

Hoshino's presence in Bangkok was another enigma. On the one hand, he had every normal business reason to be here. Bangkok was a key city in his bailiwick, which ran down through Malaysia and Indonesia, up into the Philippines and across to Hawaii and the West Coast of the United States. He travelled freely, amenable to no one, certainly not to Tanaka. Each ran his own side of the street. On the other hand, in a venture like this one where a common interest was acknowledged, Hoshino would defer to Tanaka. That was as traditional as the relationship between any Yakuza group and the agencies of law enforcement. A hit man would execute vengeance on a member of a rival gang. Rather than submit his comrades to police investigation and harassment, he would surrender himself into custody and the processes of the law would be mitigated in his favour. Conclusion, right or wrong: Cubeddu was here because he demanded to be here; Hoshino was present by agreement, minding the man who minded the Medellin money, until Tanaka made his call.

Now I had to make a decision: to demand explanations from Tanaka before the conference began, or to go in cold and play the script as it was improvised by the international cast. It was easier to do that than let Tanaka play his teasing game with me. The decision once made, I began to relax. I called the waiter and asked him to bring me a drink and a sandwich and surrendered once more to the languor of the tropic garden, the music of moving water and the high chirping of women's voices around the pool.

By two-thirty I was drunk with the sun. I took another swim and retreated to the air conditioned comfort of my suite. I showered, put on a fresh silk dressing gown and stretched out on the divan to work through the newspapers which had been delivered just before noon. There were three items of immediate interest. The haggling had begun over an Iraqi withdrawal from the Gulf. The hostages would be released, but there was a whole other shopping list: the disputed islands, the Palestinian question, Israel, Islam itself and the American infidel who now were *de facto* protectors of the sacred city of Mecca.

The second item was that the United States was committing more than a billion dollars in immediate aid to the Soviet Union. That, effectively, meant the end of direct opposition to the Tanaka/Leibig plan for industrial investment. The final piece of news was more ominous: Gorbachev had charged the KGB with the job of keeping the republics in line and suppressing local movements for secession from the Union.

It was at best a stop-gap measure; at worst, it could mark the return to a repressive dictatorial regime. However, the longer some form of political unity could be preserved, the better chance our project had of getting off the ground. For the moment, at least, a central government was the only bond-issuing authority, the sole controller of land rights. So far, it seemed, all the omens were favouring Tanaka's plans, which made another good reason for holding my peace and letting events take their natural course. I was still drowsing over that thought when the telephone rang. Carl Leibig was on the line. He was in a panic.

'Gil! Thank God you were in. We're at the airport, just through Customs. Marta is very sick.'

'What's the problem?'

'Stomach pains, severe vomiting. Shall I call an ambulance?'

'No! For Christ's sake, don't do that. It will take an hour at least to arrive and she'll end up in a public hospital. Bring her here to the hotel. I'll have a doctor waiting and we'll get her into a private clinic.'

Siri's brother Kukrit had a small but immaculate private hospital in a quiet compound behind the old Portuguese Embassy. His clients were rich. They had to be. Kukrit had his nurses trained in Australia. His Thai interns were all graduates or Australian or US medical schools. His equipment was state of the art and his standards exacting. His profits financed three out-patient clinics for the klong people, where the nurses and interns provided daily service and ran a research programme on parasitic infestations.

I called Siri. She rang back to say that Kukrit would be with me in thirty minutes. He was waiting, with an ambulance and crew, when Leibig's limousine drew up in the forecourt of the hotel. The moment Marta Boysen was helped out, she voided a bloody vomit in the gutter. Kukrit and the ambulance crew lifted her on to a gurney, wheeled her into the ambulance and sped off through the back alleys towards the clinic.

I lingered for a hurried dialogue with Leibig. He told me Marta had become ill about an hour and a half out of Bangkok – nausea, belly cramps and some bloody vomit. It was enough for me to report to Kukrit. The transport desk gave me a car and a driver to take me to the clinic and wait for me. I scribbled a note to be pinned to the door of my suite in case any new arrivals came looking for me at drinks time.

At the clinic, the receptionist handed me into the care of a brisk young Australian nurse who nodded understanding of my report and gave me the first bulletin on Marta.

'It looks like a fulminating haemorrhage. The first job is to wash out the stomach and stop the bleeding. It's called lavage. The doctor's doing that now. She's lost a fair amount of blood, but she's lucid and her blood pressure is low but holding steady. What's your blood type, by the way?'

'Type A. RH positive.'

'Full marks. Most people have no idea.'

'I'm a registered donor with Red Cross.'

'Better and better. You're the perfect match for your friend in there. I'd like you to make a donation now.'

'If it helps, sure.'

'It helps. The problem in Bangkok isn't finding donors; it's getting healthy blood. Hang on a minute, I'll find out how doctor wants to do this.'

Five minutes later, I was flat on my back with a catheter in my arm, draining blood into a plastic container. The nurse urged me to relax and think happy thoughts. I thought of Petronius Arbiter, bleeding quietly to death in his bath, to the sound of harps and pipes. Unlike Petronius, I felt faintly ridiculous. Here was I, the rejected suitor, pouring out his life's blood to save milady from the horrors of public hospital treatment. Public health in Thailand was not of the highest order and certainly it was not good for the tourist trade to publicise the pandemic incidence of AIDS among the thousands of prostitutes who served the visitors and locals.

The donation once made, I was ordered to rest for a while. The receptionist served me sweet tea and biscuits. Then Kukrit came in and gave me a report on his patient.

'She's stable now. She's out of shock. We've controlled the bleeding. She's responding lucidly enough to questions. I'll take you in to see her in a moment and watch how she responds to you. There's always the possibility of minor ischaemic damage.'

'How long will you keep her here?'

'Three days should do it. Then she can move into the hotel. She'll be on a strict diet, of course, and she'll need to take things easily for a week or two. But no doubt you'll be keeping an eye on her.'

I doubted it very much; but this was neither the time nor the place for explanations. I followed him into the small intensive care ward where Marta lay, pale and cyanosed, hooked up to drips and a cardiac monitor, while a little Thai nurse sat vigil in front of the screens. I bent down and touched my lips to her forehead and spoke in German.

'Marta, it's Gil. Can you here me?'

'I can hear you.' Her voice was weak, but the answer was clear. 'I'm sorry to be such a trouble.'

'No trouble. You'll be out of here in a few days. Doctor Kukrit is an old friend. This is a good place.'

'I know. I feel it.' She reached up and touched my cheek. 'Will you do something for me?'

214

'Anything.'

'Tell Miko to look in my handbag. She'll find the keys to my luggage. Ask her to bring me some clean night clothes and toilet things. She'll know what I need.'

'I'll do that. You sleep now.'

'Thank you, *schatzi*. Thank you . . .'

She was already on the borders of sleep.

Kukrit said: 'I don't understand German. Would you judge her responses were normal?'

'Very normal, I'd say. She asked for clean clothes and toilet gear.'

'Then we're out of the woods,' said Kukrit with a big grin. 'You go back to the hotel and have a good dinner. Take those iron tablets also, one a day for a week. You need a little restoration, too.'

'You're a prince, Kukrit!'

He laughed and made a gesture that embraced the world. 'Of course. This is the polygamous society. Everybody who is anybody is a prince at some remove or other. I've lost track of my noble cousins – but most of them show up here, sooner or later. On your way now. The lady's going to sleep the night away.'

It was nearly six by the time I got back to the hotel. I called Carl Leibig and told him about Marta. His relief was comically effusive: 'Thank God you were here, Gil. I don't know what we'd have done without you. I'm hopeless with female crises, utterly hopeless. Do you want to talk later?'

'I don't think it's necessary, Carl. We're all fully briefed. Let's give it a rest until tomorrow.'

'I agree. One should never be over-rehearsed. A nightcap in the bar maybe . . .'

'Maybe. Let's leave it open.'

After that I called Miko. I told her what had happened and asked her to put together some night clothes and toilet articles for Marta. I suggested she take them round to the clinic before dinner. Her abrupt answer shocked me.

'I'm sorry, Gil. No.'

'Why not, for Christ's sake! She's asked for you. It's a simple service, one woman to another. The hotel will send a driver with you.'

'No!'

'What's the problem?'

'I hate sickness. I hate hospitals. I can't bear to go inside them. I have enough problems without this.'

She cut the connection. I stood there like an idiot, still holding the receiver to my ear. The violence of her reaction shocked me, but the syndrome itself was all too familiar. One of my most distinguished editors, a man my own age, urbane and accomplished, had this same morbid affliction. Any hint of illness, frailty or death terrified him. When his wife fell sick or pregnant he would always invent a business excuse to flee the house. When his favourite daughter was hospitalised with peritonitis, he refused absolutely to visit her. Nothing in the world would induce him to attend the funeral of a colleague with whom he had worked for twenty years.

My own training had been exactly the reverse. My father's constant admonition was that on the gypsy road you had to care for yourself and your fellow travellers. You bound up cuts, you dispensed what he called 'salves and simples'. You cleaned up messes and kept yourself spruce and tidy. The mere fact of marrying and bringing up children had given me – as it does most parents – an extended internship in paediatric medicine. So, on the principle that it was simpler to do the thing myself than argue about it or deputise a hotel servant, I went down to reception, got the key to Marta's room and set about unpacking her clothes and making up her kit for her hospital sojourn.

Her documents and jewellery, together with money and travellers' cheques, were in her briefcase. I transferred them to her handbag, because the briefcase was too large to fit into the safe deposit boxes. While I was doing this I saw the diary, a handsome, old-fashioned volume with a gilt clasp and a leather binding, with the legend stamped in gold, gothic lettering: Marta Boysen's Daybook.

I confess I felt a strong temptation to open it and read her version of recent events. It was not virtue that stopped me, but a hoary old tag from Hamlet which popped into my head like a slice of overdone toast: 'What's Hecuba to him, or he to Hecuba?' What indeed? The affair was over, done, dead. All I was doing now was giving it a decent funeral. Bad enough that I was here in her bedroom, turning over her underthings and nightwear, packing makeup and toiletries like any house-broken husband.

Finally, with handbag, briefcase and makeup case, I went down-stairs, lodged her valuables in safe deposit and set off once more for Kukrit's clinic. That, too, was a minor madness. I could have sent the stuff round by hotel messenger. However, she was expecting Miko and in her weakened state she needed some evidence of a friendly visitation. As we drove through the narrow alleys, I composed the explanation which would serve, either verbally or in writing, at least until she was strong enough to hear the truth: the delegates were arriving in force now; Miko was required to work with Tanaka and his staff; I had volunteered to come in her place. Simple, plausible, not quite a lie, not quite the truth either.

As it turned out, it was not simple at all. Marta was still in intensive care, but awake and obviously making a good recovery. I could hardly refuse when the nurse told me I could spend a few moments with her. The prepared explanation rolled glibly off my tongue. Her documents and valuables were in safe deposit. Her clothes were unpacked. Her room was double-locked against her return. Herewith, by safe hand, night attire, dressing gown, makeup, toiletries and all her conference papers, just in case she got bored. She gave me a pale smile and thanked me, then made the flat announcement.

'Miko's not coming.'

'No, she's not.'

'Did she say why?'

'Yes. She's afraid of sickness, hospitals, all that sort of thing. There are people like that. It's another form of illness, or at least of unresolved problems. You mustn't distress yourself over it and you shouldn't blame her too much.'

'So who went through my clothes?'

'I did. That's where old married men come in handy. They're house trained. How are you feeling?'

'Weary, washed out. Rather ashamed of myself. Apparently I've been nursing this ulcer for quite a while. Doctor says he'll have to do X-rays and give me an endoscopy when I'm stronger. He says I'll have to go on a strict diet and avoid stressful situations. He asked if I'd been having any lately. I told him there had been a few.'

'And this isn't going to turn into another. You're going to settle down now. I'll pop round some time in the morning, probably just before lunch. We're going to be busy right up until then. As soon as you're out of intensive care I'll have them put in a phone for you. Would you like me to call your mother?'

'Better not. She'll only panic and keep you talking for hours. Wait until I'm out of hospital. Will you give Miko a message for me?'

'Of course.'

'Tell her I didn't believe her at first. I do now. She'll understand.'

'That's all?'

'Not quite. There's a message for you, too, Gil. I wrote it on the plane coming here. I'd only just finished it when I got sick. Would you pass me the briefcase please?'

I laid it open before her on the coverlet. She rummaged underneath the clothing and brought out the diary. She slipped the gilt catch and opened the volume to reveal, hidden between the papers, a large envelope, marked with the insignia of Thai Airlines. My name was written on the envelope. She handed it to me and said simply: 'Keep it until bedtime, when you're quiet and alone.'

'Time to go, Mr Langton,' said the little Thai nurse. 'We mustn't tire the patient. I'll take care of all her things.'

I bent and kissed Marta on the forehead. She raised her hand and brushed my cheek with her fingertips. Her skin was hot and clammy. When I turned at the door to wave to her, she was already asleep.

Back at the hotel, I stopped at the desk to pick up messages. As I turned away, I found myself facing Boris Vannikov and a tall, straight-backed fellow with an agreeable smile and cool, appraising eyes. Boris introduced him in Russian.

'Gil Langton, meet Lieutenant-General Vadim Popov, commander of the Kiev military district on secondment to our conference. He's our expert on transport. He did three tours in Afghanistan and supervised our pull-out from there.'

'My pleasure, general.'

'Mine also, Mr Langton. Friend Boris here speaks very highly of you.'

'Have you introduced the general to Sir Pavel Laszlo? He's heading our committee on transport.'

'I've read his dossier. Very impressive. Boris telephoned his room to invite him for a drink. He was not there.'

'Then let me be the host. May I suggest my suite?'

As we rode upstairs on the elevator I told Boris about Marta's sudden illness. He made sympathetic noises and a very practical request.

'Will you act as liaison for our people with the medical services here? Everybody's been duly warned about food, water and sexual hygiene, but we're bound to get a few casualties.'

'Let's establish a simple routine. I'll tell Tanya whom to call. I'll introduce her to the rostered medical officers and to Kukrit. Your people report to her. She calls me if there's a problem with language or anything else.'

'How long have you been visiting Bangkok, Mr Langton?'

'More than twenty years, General. I have a small publishing business here.'

'You speak the language?'

'Yes.'

'When I was at military school, we did a series of studies on warfare in delta country, both in tropical climates and cold ones like ours. I remember thinking then that the Siamese – I think we used to call them Siamese in those days – were very clever people. They used the monsoons for an ally as we used the great freeze in winter and the spring thaw.'

'They also divided their friendships, General, never making too large concessions to powerful nations. The building which you will see from my bedroom is the headquarters of the East Asiatic Company. It's one of the world's largest conglomerates, but it was founded and is still owned by the Danes. The Thai reversed the classic motto. Theirs was to divide the potential conquerors with courtesies and limited concessions.'

'You are something of a strategist yourself, Mr Langton?'

'On the contrary, General. I'm a communicator. I try to make strategic alignments unnecessary.'

'I wish it were possible, Mr Langton.'

Settled with drinks in our hands, looking down at the bustle of the river traffic and the misty stretch of delta lands beyond Thonburi, with yellow lights pricking out of the gathering dark, we were soon at ease with each other. As the man who had organised the massive Soviet pull-out from Afghanistan, Popov had turned what could have been a bloody retreat into an orderly withdrawal. He had imagination and curiosity and I thought he and Laszlo would make a formidable team, not merely at the conference, but afterwards.

'Afterwards is our problem.' Boris Vannikov was weary and inclined to be sombre. 'I have told Vadim I believe we can hammer out a good agreement here, but when we start to make it work at home, we have little practice in the mechanics of free enterprise and decades of bureaucratic inertia.'

'I have an idea,' said the General. 'It is too early to sell it yet to the

General Staff or to the President, because they still see the armed forces as a weapon only, an instrument of combat, an enforcer of public order. I see it differently – a training ground, a school of change. Look what the Israelis did, broke down the barriers of sex and reactionary religion and built a great fighting force at the same time. The fact that they've gone crazy now against the Arabs doesn't change the principle. At the upper end of the scale you've got the Swiss. You know the joke they have in Zurich: that the banks are run by the army. It's true. Every senior bank official has done his service time and has probably reached at least field rank with his contemporaries. Boris here thinks I'm dreaming.'

'Not so.' Vannikov was emphatic. 'You've got time on your side. You're only forty-six. You've got a shining record: Hero of the Soviet Union. You brought the boys home from the war. The whole country's on your side.'

'That's when it gets dangerous,' said Popov ruefully. 'Somebody starts a whisper about Bonaparte and I'm shunted sideways to a desk job in Sakhalin, in case I get delusions of grandeur.'

I was just about to ask him how he saw the effects of a German/Japanese economic enterprise, when the telephone rang. Tanaka was on the line. His first inquiry was about Marta, but his first concern was that I was back in the hotel and functioning. I asked him if he wanted a meeting. He told me, no. He was closeted with Sir Pavel Laszlo. I told him whom I was entertaining and suggested an early breakfast to discuss the routine of the first general meeting. We settled for seven-thirty on the river terrace. I begged time from my guests to make a brief call to Carl Leibig. He was relieved to hear the news about Marta and undertook to send flowers in the morning. Boris Vannikov laughed.

'They've got you running, Gil.'

'What do you expect? It's all new. It's a big day tomorrow. They're still trying to figure out which hand to wipe their noses with. Things will settle down tomorrow. You and I should brief the press immediately after the opening session.'

'How much are we telling the press?' General Popov was instantly alert.

'As much or as little as we choose. Do you have any special problems?'

'Some, yes. Laszlo and I are going to be discussing the initial use of army vehicles and aircraft for the transport of civilian material. No question, we'll have to do it; but I don't want pre-emptive discussion in

Moscow before we've sorted out a policy here. Besides, Laszlo's a Hungarian and a Jew. That makes another set of problems.'

'Correction, general. Laszlo is an Australian citizen who runs one of the best intercontinental transport systems in the world. The fact that he's a Jew is irrelevant.'

'For you, yes, Mr Langton. To some of my people it's a handicap, which has to be recognised.'

'Or a stigma which you, a general officer and a Hero of the Soviet Union, ought to protest in the strongest terms.'

'Are you teaching me my job, Mr Langton?'

'No. I'm doing mine. Clearing away the rubbish before you trip on it and break your neck!'

'I did warn you, Vadim,' Boris Vannikov put in his own rouble's worth. 'You shouldn't screw around with this man.'

'I like to test a weapon before I go into battle with it.' He held out his hand. 'You test well, Mr Langton. We'll get along together. Boris is taking me across the river for dinner with that young woman of his. Would you like to join us?'

'Thank you, no. I'm going to do some paper work, have a light meal and turn in. But you'll enjoy the Sala Rim Nam. You can see it from here. The food's excellent. The entertainment is interesting, first time around at least. Have a pleasant evening.'

'One question before we go.' Boris Vannikov paused at the door. 'What's happened with our two friends Hoshino and Cubeddu?'

'They've agreed, should the occasion demand it, to merge their funds in a trust managed by German and Japanese bankers. That's as much as I know. It means that they're prepared to subordinate their interests within the general pattern.'

'I'll believe it when I see it,' said Vannikov without enthusiasm.

'So will I; but I've got the feeling we're all in for some surprises before the week is over.'

'One surprise I'm dreading' said General Vadim Popov. 'The first air attack in the first desert battle against Iraq. Time's running out and reason is almost lost in the dust-storms. Take me to dinner, Boris. I need food and a pretty woman to share it.'

I was in bed early that night. I sat, propped up on the pillows, sipping mineral water and reading the letter Marta Boysen had written to me between Tokyo and Bangkok. It was written in that emphatic, cursive hand of hers, in a German whose colorations and emotional overtones were very much of the south.

My dearest Gil,

We met so joyfully, we fitted so well, like fingers in a glove. I cannot believe we have fallen so quickly into this pit of despair yet I know it was I who caused the fall. It was I who, years before, had prepared the slide on which we came to grief. Please don't misunderstand me. It was not malice. It was not conspiracy. It was simply the nature of things, the nature of me.

First, there was the me you remember, the little girl trotting happily beside you through the woods. Then there was the other me, the adolescent whom you never met but who was so powerfully drawn to your memory that you haunted her life ever after. You were the dream lover who comforted her lonely nights. You were the rival of every man who ever possessed her. You were the legendary lover gypsy, always beckoning, always waving goodbye.

It was the memory of you and your father which drove me, like a slave-master, to scholarship. The two of you seemed so free and yet so secure. You were citizens of a country which had no frontiers, yet whose passport was the most potent document in the world. My family, as you know, were theatre people, but all their insecurities were acted out in public, every day. That was the other side of me: the make-believe girl, whose mother was queen of a make-believe world, courted, indulged, manipulated, too, by producers and directors and young men who needed her patronage and old ones who wanted to lend her theirs. It was a world of endless intrigues and I was endlessly curious about them all, ready always for any invitation into a new ritual of mysteries. I felt few guilts and found much pleasure and I know that I was very lucky not to have come to harm, because sometimes I was very frightened by the dark labyrinths I saw opening in front of me.

And yet I did come to harm, because it was in a period of reaction and revulsion from a year of study and a short, silly season of dissipation in Vienna, that I married. The silly season had started with a flirtation with a woman which turned quickly ugly. I wasn't prepared for that. I was looking for mischief, but not melodrama. I fled, straight into the arms of my *gutsherr* from Carinthia.

I told you the miseries of that marriage. I did not tell you that half of them were of my own making. We had no theatre in the country. Good! I would create some! High drama, cruel comedy,

222

low farce to make the yokels blush! Our quarrels were like set-piece duets. Our silences were orchestrated with sinister drum beats and heavy undertones on strings and basses. Even in our most passionate matings – and we had those, too – there were elements of terror, of a vendetta enacted in the name of love.

It is the same old play, in a different setting. I am committing the greatest of theatrical follies: directing myself in the lead role. The only difference is that I am beginning to see and to fear the consequences of the folly.

Everything in my life has been touched by it. Even my scholarship, which is acknowledged to be sound, is vitiated by a certain raffishness which belongs more to a novelist or to a playwright than to a serious researcher. I see it, sometimes, as a corruption of that wonderful gift which your father possessed, of wearing his scholarship lightly, with humour and grace.

Even as I write, I can see you reading this, shaking your head, not understanding a word of it. Let me show you what I mean. My thesis on Haushofer's geopolitics was acclaimed as a solid piece of work. It won me my Doctorate and much respect. But what really set me doing it, what really interested me and, indeed, piqued my most morbid curiosities, was Haushofer himself.

Think back. He's a soldier of the old regime, academy trained, distinguished enough to be seconded as instructor to the Japanese army. He's intelligent and open. He immerses himself in Oriental languages and cultures. He's a fighting General in the First World War. He's already thinking in geopolitical terms – a world view. I understand his confusions and resentments after Versailles. I can even, with difficulty, understand his fascination with Hitler and often wished I could have found an eyewitness account of their first meeting in Landsberg prison, their first discussion about living room for the German people. But what fascinated me even more was the slow mystery of his seduction into the service of a vulgar, brutal, mindless movement led to power by thugs and murderers and deviates, and decent men who stayed silent while the indecencies were committed.

What was the music he danced to? Money? He was richly rewarded. Power? He became a kind of Delphic oracle, quoted all around the world; an interpreter of secrets, a prognosticator of events. Fear? That, too, I am sure, because he accepted a humiliating gift that at once denied his wife her personal identity and guaranteed her physical safety. But through it all was excitement, illusion, which endured right up to the final twilight of the gods.

How do I know this? I understood his temptations; I had succumbed to them myself, and for the same excitements and illusions. I made the same shabby bargain with Max Wylie. I didn't need the money he paid. I didn't believe a single word of all the shopworn incantations he intoned. I was there for the thrill of it. I was mocking myself and mocking the world by an act of transvestism, just as I did in my emotional and sexual life.

Then, you came along. No, that's the wrong way to say it. Suddenly, in Tokyo, you were there, sitting beside me at Carl Leibig's luncheon table. Time was rolled back. The wonder of our first meeting in my childhood was renewed. Time has dealt kindly with you, Gil. You have been a fortunate man, with much love in your life – and it shows. When I grew up my mother would sometimes reminisce about her own love affairs. I remember vividly what she said about your father. 'He handled a woman like a connoisseur, with confidence but with great care. He made you feel prized and precious and proud of yourself as a woman. That was wonderful; but when he was gone, it was hard to accept less. Once you develop a taste for fine wine, even good country vintage comes rough on the palate.'

I remembered that when you and I had our first night together, I smiled in the dark and said to myself: 'This is what Mutti talked about and it is the first time I have truly understood it.' Almost in the next instant, I found myself asking how long you could tolerate me once you saw how strangely I was put together, and how long I could tolerate you, even if you were prepared to put up with me.

There is that in me which cries out for a certain violence, a certain deviousness in any relationship. I knew I would have to test you to see how much you would take, but almost from the beginning you were testing me. I had not realised how hard it was to be devious with someone direct and simple. You see too much. You know too much. You will not play the games I like to play.

Miko, of course, is one of those games. I tried to coax you into it. You walked away. And that is where we are now. I'm sick at heart because I have lost something and someone precious to me since childhood. I have lost more: a respect for myself, a conviction, without which no actor can survive, that the audience will be forever enthralled by the brave fictions of theatre. I write this to explain and to apologise and – if you can believe it – to tell you that I love you, the more perhaps because I know I have lost you. Perhaps that was what I was trying to do, chase love, like innocence, out of my life.

I must finish now. I am beginning to feel nauseous and dizzy. Something I ate perhaps, or something I cannot bear to contemplate in the light of day.

God keep you, Gil Langton.

Marta

I must have wept a little, because when I woke the pages of the letter were spotted and smudged. I cannot describe how I felt, because all I remember was an absence of feeling. My mind, however, was very clear. I could recite faultlessly the admirable maxim of Rochefoucauld: '*Il y a plusieurs remèdes qui guérissent de l'amour, mais il n'y en a point d'infaillible*'; there are several cures for love, but none of them is infallible.

Thirteen

After a very bad night, breakfast with Kenji Tanaka was not a recommended diversion. My first mirror image had disgusted me: a gaunt, hollow-eyed fellow with down-drawn mouth and bloodless lips and greying, stringy hair. A swim and a swift toilet did something to restore me to human form, but the mirror image persisted behind my eyeballs. Kenji Tanaka, on the other hand, looked as fresh as newly boiled rice, in tailored slacks, a sports shirt of finest cotton and a pair of Gucci loafers. Whatever his ailments, none of them showed in his smooth, smiling face. He was a man reborn, calm, confident and more than a shade patronising.

He asked solicitously: 'Did you sleep well?'

'Indifferently. I had a lot on my mind.'

'Have I not told you many times, Gil? You should devote some time to Zen. You have experience of what it can do.'

'I know. It's like a sentence of execution. It concentrates the mind most wonderfully. Don't lecture me, Kenji. I'm not in shape for it. Let's talk about this morning's conference. I take it everybody's checked in?'

'Except Marta Boysen, but I'm sure we can dispense with her. How is she, by the way?'

'Recovering. She'll be back in the hotel in two or three days. Tell me about the Tanaka contingent.'

'We are twelve altogether, including myself and Miko who is, however, not a delegate, but a personal assistant to me. That means two people for each committee – Banking and Finance, Transport, Engineering, Production, Land Titles and Trade Agreements. I'll be presiding over all their activities.'

'Have you spoken with Laszlo yet? He was most anxious to talk.'

'We met.' I sensed the sudden withdrawal. It was like brushing an anemone on the reef, all the bright tentacles retracted into a protective cluster. 'He talked of his meeting with you and Miko. I was distressed that so much had been discussed outside the family.'

'Hold on a moment, Kenji. Let's be very clear. Miko told me you had ordered her – that's the word she used, ordered – to discuss matters with me.'

'That's true.' My emphatic rebuttal embarrassed him. 'I am not blaming you or Laszlo, but let us just say Miko went further than I intended.'

'Your problem. Not ours. Besides, here we are, two hours away from our opening session, and the Tanaka positions have not been made clear.'

'You're very prickly this morning, Gil.'

'Because you're still hedging. Enough now. Time's run out. I have a list of questions. I need answers before I walk into that conference room this morning.'

'A threat, Gil?'

'A reminder. My position and Leibig's were made clear to you in Tokyo. They have not changed. The Soviet position has become more and more clear, thanks to the groundwork we have put in. Unless I'm very much mistaken, Laszlo, too, has given you a warning.'

'Ask your questions, please.'

'Are you, or are you not, looking for a successor to run the Tanaka Group?'

'I was.'

'Have you found him?'

'Yes.'

'Is he acceptable to the other members of the *keiretsu*?'

'Yes.'

'Will they now support you in the Tanaka/Leibig project?'

'The decision is not yet final. I have good reason to believe they will.'

'When will that decision be made?'

'Within the next five days, during the course of the conference.'

'What will determine it?'

'The terms of the deal we can make.'

'How was your successor chosen?'

'By adoption.'

'His name? His family?'

'I cannot reveal that yet.'

'Cannot?'

'Will not.'

'Suppose the *keiretsu* decides to support you. What happens to the funds offered by Hoshino and Cubeddu?'

'They will be politely declined.'

'Hoshino's more politely than those of Cubeddu?'

He gave me a thin smile. 'Quite possibly. Are you satisfied now, Gil?'

'No. You've told me nothing. You have a successor, nameless. You may or may not get the support of your peers. You may or may not use the mob money you're offered. One more question: how long have you got to live?'

It was a calculated brutality, but I had to break through his equally calculated swordsman's game. He recoiled instantly and then snapped back.

'That is none of your business.'

'If you tell me so, fine. End of discussion.'

I poured myself coffee and went through the motions of buttering a croissant. Tanaka watched me with dark, unblinking eyes. I understood very well what Miko had told me about his teasing and I was as determined as she not to indulge him in it any longer. The teasing was simply an extension of a much larger game: the myth of inscrutability must be reinforced always because the gulf of non-understanding between the Japanese and the *gaijin* must be kept as wide as possible. It was like the 'discipline of the secret' in the earliest days of Christianity. The sacramental rites which gave the small communities their identity must never be exposed to profane eyes. Mystery was one of the props of power. Subtract the secret and you were left with a comical procession of naked courtiers led by a naked king.

It was at that moment I understood how much power I held in my own hands and how little desire I had to use it. I was the repository of everyone's secrets, confessor to the small, motley community met under an alien sky, under the threat of war and of civil disorder which could spread like the Black Death across the continent and sub-continent of Asia. I alone could hear and interpret the whispers of the servants and the cryptic asides of the principals in the debate. I felt a rush of bitter resentment that Tanaka should force me to waste so much of myself on the sterile rituals of face-saving. I ate in silence, without appetite, determined to be gone as soon as I had finished my breakfast.

But first, Tanaka had to respond to me. He had been given warning enough. There was no way I could face the delegates without a clear brief from Tanaka. I had only two options: retire myself immediately or range myself solely with Leibig and so inform the conference. Finally, Tanaka broke the silence. There was a winter sadness in his voice.

'I know what you're thinking, Gil. I have not trusted you enough. I have asked you to build a house and denied you the tools and the timber.'

'More than that, I'm afraid. Unless you are prepared to answer the questions I have put to you, not only for me, but for the conference, then you will lose all face and credibility. I am not prepared to represent you without full disclosure of those facts which, God knows! amount only to a declaration of identity: who you are now, what the Tanaka organisation may soon become. This isn't a solo game, for God's sake! It's a co-operative venture between you and Leibig and with the Soviets, if they agree to join you. This isn't simply a gainful commercial venture; it can be a stroke of true statesmanship, a blueprint for many others.'

'You think I don't understand that?'

'I'm damned sure you don't! You're still acting out the fiction that Japan is the navel of the universe, that nobody quite grasps this great and wonderful difference between you and the rest of the world. That's what saddens me, makes me angry, too. I always thought you were a big man, who saw the world steadily and whole, who read it in other terms than money and graphs of productivity and market percentages. It was that belief that drew me to you, made me your partner and, I believed, your friend. Now you've proved I was mistaken. I was not your friend, but your tame *gaijin*. Here we are at the last hour and, of all that I need to know, what have you told me? Nothing. Enough then. I'm out of the game. I'll sit through the conference, because I owe something to Carl Leibig; and I'll save what face I can for you. I'd better find Carl and explain what's happening. He has a right to be told before he walks in to face the lions.'

I signalled the waiter to bring a check. I signed it. As I was getting up to leave, Tanaka laid a detaining hand on my wrist.

'Please wait.'

I sat down again. Tanaka asked for more coffee. I ordered mineral water, because I needed cooling down after my outburst. When they were brought, Tanaka, in a flat, prosaic fashion, picked up the conversation.

'Your position, as I understand it, is that I answer you or lose you, yes?'

'Yes.'

'How long have I got to live? Four months, six with luck. More perhaps with treatment, which I am not prepared to undergo. Once my arrangements are in order, I may elect to terminate sooner. I have not yet decided. As I told you, that is my business.'

The snub was as deliberate as my attack had been, but I would not let him get away with it. I told him: 'It would have been an honour to be invited to the farewell. Unless, of course, you are thinking of a samurai end. I would be no good as a *kaishaku*, a second. I'm not a swordsman, never have been.'

'Don't deceive yourself.' Tanaka was grim. 'You cut like a surgeon, straight to the bone. Your next question, my successor. I am adopting the second son of Hisayuki Kobayashi who, in turn, is adopting my son and guaranteeing the future of his researches and the economic future of his family. The reason I have not spoken about this is simple. Two huge enterprises are coming together under a joint family arrangement. The union is an accomplished fact, but the paperwork is enormous and we are trying to cushion the economic shocks as much as possible.'

'But you felt you could not trust me with this information?'

'Rather, I would say it is customary to withhold it. So, too, with the financial commitment. We are now two houses instead of one. The news of Gorbachev's visit and his willingness to discuss the Kuril Islands has helped greatly to modify the climate.'

'What is the impediment to saying so?'

'Common commercial sense. All this is positive news. The Soviet enterprise introduces negative considerations which will tend to lower share prices, if only temporarily. Better, therefore, to withhold the news as long as possible. That, I think, covers everything you asked.'

'Not quite. There is still the question of Hoshino and Cubeddu. Obviously Hoshino is keeping a low profile. Cubeddu seems less likely to do so. There would also seem to be certain risks to Miko; but these are very clearly your business.'

'All of it, all of it is my business.' Tanaka was terse. 'Now you have to tell me how you propose to treat what I have confided to you.'

'Before we come to that, let me say that I believe Leibig should be assured of a positive outcome; how much detail are you prepared to give him?'

'What I have given to you, less if possible, but certainly no more.'

'How much have you told Laszlo?'

'Only that a positive solution is in sight.'

'Was he satisfied with that?'

'No, but we have worked together for a long time. He is more tolerant than you are. Now, you have to be plain with me. How much do you propose to tell the Soviets?'

'I'll give Vannikov the briefest summary. I'll tell him a large merger is in progress and may even be announced before the end of the conference. Because of the dangers of leaked information and share market reactions, we want the matter taken as read until a formal announcement is made.'

'Do you think he'll accept that?'

'Yes. If he has problems with his colleagues, he'll tell me. We'll deal with them as they arise.'

'So, you are satisfied now?'

'Almost. I still wonder why we had to face each other on the killing ground before we came to this.'

'Because, Gil, you have never understood, you still do not understand, the pressures that are on me to keep such things secret until the very last moment, the very last formality of consent. Even what I have just done places me in gross breach of proprieties which may seem as alien to you as a Noh drama, but which are, nonetheless, real to me. I belong to the smallest and most exclusive club in the world. I was born into it. Its rules touch the most intimate parts of my life – my attachment to Miko, my friendship with you, my relations with my son and his children. This, surely, is not altogether strange to you? I remember my father telling me about the English aristocracy of his day, the power of the ruling families, their unwritten rules, the unforgivable mistakes that could dog a good man for a lifetime. Two wars and revolutionary changes in Europe have fragmented that society. In Japan, a military defeat and an industrial renaissance have had the opposite effect. The old ways have been recast in new patterns, but they are more durable than bronze. I depend on them, Gil. I depend on the support of the club. I dare not go to war with it. Now, I have neither time nor energy. You have good reason to reproach me. I admit that. But I did warn you that if a choice had to be made, you would be the loser.'

'I know. I am the loser, because I can't take back the words I said. We're in business now. The social contracts have to be honoured.'

For the first time, a faint elusive smile of real amusement brightened his face. He stood up and laid his hand on mine, imprisoning me where I sat. Then he chided me like a schoolmaster.

'Gil, my friend. You're a scholar; you should stick to your books. I will give you a saying which I heard from a very modern Zen master: "When friends do business, there is no need of contracts. Unfortunately, there are no friends in business." '

I waited until he had disappeared into the building, then I went back to my room to telephone Carl Leibig and Boris Vannikov. To each I gave a slightly sanitized version of the same story. The financial problems were over. The Japanese consortium would come in kosher, white on white, with massive support from the big names. It was imperative, however, that no debate on the question be permitted, that the press releases be of the most general character and that no one, but no one, should rock the boat for fear the Tokyo stock market should take a dive. Clear? Clear as mountain water, Gil! Great work! We'll be eager to hear details, as soon as you're free to discuss them, of course. Meantime, the words of the day will be mum and stumm.

After that I had quick talks with Pamela Dalby, Alex Boyko and Tanya. We would meet in the press office for a first briefing after the opening general conference. No, they would not be permitted to attend any meetings until an information policy had been agreed. They were hired to do a public relations job, not to report the news. Truth, of course, was our watchword, but truth well selected, given a high gloss and packaged to appeal to a wide variety of tastes. So sharpen the pencils, tune up the prose rhythms, let us get ready to herald a brave new world from the Oriental hotel, Bangkok.

The opening session, held in one of the large function rooms of the hotel, was a model of precise presentation. Every visual technique was called into play; the key texts on the screen were in Russian, supplemented by German, Japanese and English versions in the folders supplied to each delegate. The introductory speeches were brief. The head of each group fielded questions after the visual presentation of his own sector of operations: building design, transport, finance. The materials were so well arranged and co-ordinated that my work was limited to an occasional clarification of a question or the interpretation of a technical answer.

As I watched the master plan unfold itself on the screens, I was full of admiration for the boldness of the men who had conceived it and the meticulous care that had been given to every detail of the planning.

Given the enormous stretch of the Soviet republics, the varieties of their climates and geologies, the inadequacy of the transport systems – the list of handicaps went on and on – this was a programme as complex as that of the first moon shot or the first space probe.

'If we can bring this off,' Vannikov whispered in my ear, 'then it will be a bigger miracle than the loaves and fishes. The biggest problem is to keep the patient quiet while the operation takes place.'

I knew what he meant. That same morning the news had broken that the Soviet Foreign Minister, a staunch reformist, had resigned. He claimed that constitutional changes, actual and proposed, would inevitably lead back to dictatorship. In the same breath, Vannikov bewailed the risk and prayed that the central authority would hold until our project was approved and under way. The Gulf crisis wasn't getting any better. Instead of counting off the shopping days to Christmas, the press were counting down to deadline day, 15 January. In Britain and the US medical corps reservists were being called up. The news traffic was being carefully confused with disinformation from both sides. It was against this background that the Chairman called on me to propose a motion on the reporting of the conference activities to the press.

I proposed three things. First, that the order of events be clearly stated: the Soviet Union, which occupied a great part of the Eurasian continent, had invited a German/Japanese consortium to submit proposals and plans for the production, storage, processing and distribution of foodstuffs from facilities and installations strategically sited throughout the country. The consortium had responded with a carefully prepared, though necessarily complex, plan. That plan was being considered at this conference; a decision would be made within two weeks.

Once that notion was firmly set, we could range widely over theoretical and practical aspects of the plan. Activities would be jointly controlled by Boris Vannikov for the Soviets and myself for the consortium. The conference was in favour. The motion was passed. The schedule of committee meetings was announced. The meeting broke at midday. Boris and I walked round to the press room to brief our little team of scribes.

We found them surrounded with brochures and illustrated material, eager to be about their business. Boris Vannikov delivered the briefing. He pointed out that the historic sequence was important. This was not a move by foreigners to exploit the Soviets. It was a constructive response to a forward-looking move by Moscow itself. The installations, however, would benefit every republic in which they were located. They would constitute a massive breakout from the present wasteful system of centralist management. The management and employees would be locals. The training would be standardised, so that ambitious people could look forward to mobility of employment.

I was happy to let him run. In this mood, he could charm the birds out of the trees. Alex Boyko and Pam Dalby, two hardbitten warriors, were delighted. Their first releases would be on the wires within an hour. We left them to their God-given task of enlightenment and treated ourselves to a drink in the bar.

Boris offered the first toast. 'To us, Gil. And to our masters. God give them eyes to see and ears to listen.'

'Amen!'

'I'll make a bet with you. We're going to ram through a draft agreement this week. Then we can sit back and let the lawyers and the technicians parse their way through the documents. We've got the principles right. That's clear even now. Right principles, right action. That's why they need philosophers to force them through to the heart of the matter. And here, the heart of the matter is simple human need: food, love and fantasy. What we've been getting for too long is hunger, hate and nightmares about the long winter ahead.'

Abruptly his mood changed. By the time he was halfway through his second drink, he was in a black, Slavic depression.

'The other side of the coin is what we're doing to ourselves. You saw the news this morning? Our Foreign Minister staged a public resignation, accusing the President of leading the country back into dictatorship. It was a brave gesture, but enormously risky. I watched the shots of the army chiefs laughing together in the lobbies afterwards. They were celebrating! The man who pulled the troops out of Afghanistan, who let the Berlin Wall come down and signed the arms limitation treaties was suddenly gone. Gorbachev is isolated now. I'm his man, Gil. He made me. I know he's walking a high wire without a net. This isn't just a simple issue of reactionaries and reformists, dictatorship or democracy. It's how to stop the tribal bickering and get down to the urgent business of reconstructing the country. I had breakfast with Popov this morning. He's a real soldier, Gil – helmet to bootsoles. But he knows what combat means and he knows what another civil war could do to us. He doesn't want the army running the country. Yet even he sees no easy

234

answer to this new tribalism. Look. It's not one of the things we talk about, but the birth rate in the Muslim republics is three times as high as that in the rest of the country. Think about that in terms of the divisions it creates, in the army, in politics, even in the economy. Now, with war looming in the Gulf, those divisions are going to open like rifts in the land after an earthquake. You're not listening to me, are you?'

'I'm trying, Boris. But I can't carry Mother Russia on my back every hour of every day. Besides, I've got to get to the hospital and be back in time for the committees after lunch.'

He was not offended. He was just at the low point of a low and needing a friend to share the misery.

'Give the girl my love. Tell her she has only to call and Boris Vannikov will come running. *Nastrovye!*'

He tossed off the last of the liquor. If we were not exactly comrades in arms, we were at least veterans who understood the follies and futilities of war games.

After that, I set off for the hospital. As the driver drew into the forecourt, I saw Siri coming out of the front door and heading for the parking area. I hurried across to intercept her. We sat in the front seat of her car while she explained.

'I knew you would be busy. I thought I should come and introduce myself to your Marta. It's terrible to be sick and alone in a foreign place. I brought her flowers and some European candies. We had a lovely chat.'

'Siri, I love you dearly; but when you try to play a British country matron I want to walk out and demand my money back at the box office. European candies and a lovely chat! Come, my sweet. This is Uncle Gil. Remember?'

'I remember.' She leaned back in the corner of the driver's seat and began gently raking my cheek with a long, crimson fingernail. 'I remember before you were married and during and after. I remember the night you stayed in my house and I heard noises and came to your room in the small hours and found you raging up and down, screaming silently, trying to call back the dead. I remember holding you in my arms until the tears came and all the wild words you had bottled up inside you for so long. I remember the darkness before the first light, when we walked down to the river and put a lamp in a boat of leaves and watched it float away on the ebb tide. That was how you said goodbye to your wife, Gil. With me. With Siri. So don't ask me if I remember.'

'I'm sorry.'

'It's already forgotten.'

'And thank you for coming to see Marta.'

'It was my pleasure. And of course you're right. I had to see her for myself.'

'Now we've both confessed our sins, tell me what you think.'

'About Marta or about you?'

'Either or both.'

'You, then. You're so like your father I think, sometimes, I'm seeing double. You're full of talents, as he was; and one of the best of them is a talent for friendship. That's rare and it's precious. You're generous. You care about people. They know you care. What they don't know is that you are much more self-sufficient than they. You don't depend on them the way they depend, or would like to depend, on you. Part of the reason is your father. He trained you to be self-dependent, but other-centred. The rest of it is harder to explain. When your wife died, the small secret room at the centre of you was left dark and empty. You locked the door and walked away from it, but you could never forget it for a moment. You had supported your children in their grief. You had never purged your own. I'll never forget the violence of your outburst that night in my house and how calm you were after we had floated the little lamp down the river. That was the first and last real goodbye you had said to your wife. But the little room is still there, dark, empty and locked. I'm sure nobody else notices this, but I do. You talk about your children. You talk about your father. Never about your wife.'

'I talk about her to the children.'

'But only when they ask, yes?'

'Yes.'

'So you see, Gil, to any woman who is in love with you – and Marta Boysen most certainly is – you present a big problem and a frightening challenge. Will she ever be able to coax the key out of your hands and open it for herself?'

'You make me sound like Bluebeard.'

'You are. What did he offer his bride? A long and happy life, but death if she violated the mystery.'

'Come on. That's too much!'

'Is it? Think a little, Gil. You're standing in a group, any group, with your escort of that moment. I come along, any other Oriental or Asian woman. Immediately, you switch into another identity. I know. I've

236

seen it. It's quite uncanny. I'm used to it, because I know you so well. But if I were your lover I could be very jealous and maybe very bitchy.'

'Why, for God's sake?'

'Because she's excluded from two parts of your life: the secret room and the public arena.'

'And what can I do about that?'

'You're missing the point, Gil. You're not expected to do anything. You're a free agent. You're not obliged to accept a gift just because it's been thrust into your hands. The real question is, what do you want? Is it Marta? Is it someone else? Is it simply the life you have and the friendships you enjoy now? If it's a new love or a new marriage, then for both your sakes you'll have to surrender the key to the locked room. You believe me, don't you?'

'You sound just like my father.'

She laughed and raked at my cheek again, harder this time, so that I felt the sharp edge of the fingernail.

'Your father taught me, too. What was the phrase? *On ne badine pas avec l'amour!* Men and women can play games together, but love's a serious matter. He lived by that, too. He never attached himself too closely to anyone but you. He came, he went, he brought a gift and left a good memory. I think I understood that part of him better than you do, because that is the way we conduct our own lives here. Enough, now. I'll expect you to dinner on Wednesday night. Come early. My children want time with their Uncle Gil.'

I touched my lips to her small, soft palm and folded her fingers to enclose the kiss. She gave me a smile and a gentle dismissal.

'Go talk to Marta, and be kind to her.'

'Thanks again for visiting her.'

'Just so you're prepared . . . I told her you'd asked me to see her.'

'Why did you have to do that?'

'It saved a lot of explanations.'

'What's to explain?'

'You and me, petals in the water . . . they fall from different trees, they are blown by the same wind, they drift on the same current. Even that little thing takes a time to tell. Go now. I'll see you Wednesday.'

Marta was in a small private room, which seemed to be overflowing with flowers. She was propped up in a reclining position, still hooked to a drip bottle, but she had lost the hollow, cyanosed look. There was colour in her face, a small new strength in her voice. She held out her free hand to draw me to her, then kissed me on the lips. She said simply: 'I seem to have lost the words I need. That's my thank you.'

I drew up a chair and sat beside the bed, holding her hand. 'How are you feeling?'

'Much better. They had me out of bed this morning. I was dizzy for a moment, then quite unsteady on my feet, but I walked across the room and back. It must be that good Langton blood they gave me yesterday.'

'The flowers are beautiful.'

'Those on the dressing table are from Carl. These are from Miko and the ones on the side table are from your friend Siri. That was a kind thought to have her visit me. I was feeling very low until she walked in. She's a beautiful woman, Gil. So calm and full of grace. You're fortunate to have her working for you.'

'Actually, she's my partner in the Thai company, the way Tanaka is in Tokyo. Her son and daughter are in the business, too.'

'She's invited me to visit her once I'm out of here. Doctor Kukrit says I can leave in a couple of days if I promise to take things easy and hold to the diet and the medication he'll be giving me. How did the conference go this morning?'

'Very well, I think. Leibig's presentations were splendidly done. The Soviets were impressed. On its own merits, provided there isn't a catastrophe in the Gulf, everyone believes the project can work.'

'And I'm missing all the excitement.'

'You've created enough already, thank you.'

At that point the conversation lapsed for a moment, then we came abruptly to the core of the matter. Marta announced: 'You didn't give Miko my message.'

'Oh God! I'm sorry. That was an oversight. Vannikov and General Popov buttonholed me as soon as I got back to the hotel . . .'

'She called me this morning.'

'Oh.'

'The message doesn't matter. She knows now.'

'Knows what?'

'The game's over. I can't play it any more.'

The flat statement didn't seem to call for a comment. I took refuge in a question.

'How did Miko react?'

'She took it very quietly. She apologised for not being able to visit me.

238

I told her she shouldn't distress herself, I understood. I do, too. It wasn't just politeness.'

'I believe you.'

'Did you read my letter?'

'Yes.'

'Did you believe that, too?'

'Yes.'

'All of it?'

'All of it.'

'So . . .' The word came out in a long exhalation, of relief or disappointment it was hard to say. 'So now you know the whole story. There's nothing more to be said.'

'There's a lot to be said, *schatzi*. But not now, not here. When you're stronger, when the pressures are off me, we'll talk again.'

'Why do you even care?'

'I remember a little girl trotting beside me in the woods, holding my hand tightly in case I left her behind. She didn't know then – how could she? – that in our family we always wait for the stragglers.'

'And you'll wait for me?'

'We're here for two weeks, like it or lump it. If we're still friends then, that's already something, yes?'

'Doctor Kukrit told me I could have died from this thing.'

'He's right. You could have.'

'So everything after that has to be a bonus.'

'Hang on to that thought, Frau Professor Doktor. It's the best one you've had for some time.'

'Now you're mocking me.'

'Would I dare? Now I have to leave you. I'll try to call by this evening. If not, I'll telephone. Would you like me to lower the pillows so you can sleep?'

'Yes please.'

As I settled her to rest and checked that the drip tube was functioning, she took my hand and held it against her cheek.

'Gil.'

'Yes?'

'I have to say this. There are no debts between us. We're both paid up. You know that, don't you?'

'I know it.'

'What I need now is some respect.'

'You've always had it.'

'You don't understand. I mean respect from me to me. I have to live with the woman I see in the mirror.'

'That's true for all of us. My father used to say: "Son, we come in alone; we go out alone; we'd better be damned sure we can tolerate our own company." '

'I feel very empty, Gil, tired of chasing dreams.'

'Time to close down the brain-box. You're going to rest now. I'm leaving.'

'Will you kiss me, please?'

There was no passion in the caress. It was rather a family ritual, the affirmation of a bond which, however much it might be strained, was never quite broken. The words were the most vivid memory I had of my mother: 'Sleep well, golden dreams!'

Fourteen

Back at the hotel, our small press corps had produced its first release for the world media. Vannikov had passed it. All that it needed was my imprimatur. I went over it, line by line, with Alex Boyko.

It was a sturdy, factual, optimistic piece which would not make headlines, but would certainly get solid and respectful analysis in the financial pages of major journals. Against the gathering gloom in the Gulf, it sounded a note of hope. It affirmed that funds could always be found for pragmatic solutions to problems that had been too long regarded as intractable. The sums involved were large enough to make the most hardened financiers sit up and blink. The list of international experts among the contracting companies was in itself a seal of excellence.

The question of German/Japanese co-operation was deftly handled. 'For the first time,' Alex Boyko had written, 'the economic problems raised by the vast stretch of Soviet Asia, the enormous variety of its climates and its geologies, have been fully recognised in an international plan for economic investment.' That, for the moment, seemed sufficient camouflage for Haushofer and his more tendentious theories.

The history of the Leibig company and its association with the House of Tanaka for more than a century and a half, opened up vistas of material for magazine treatments. The biographical sketches of the principal participants and the accompanying photographs rounded out a highly respectable piece of work. I scribbled my signature on the authorisation and offered a personal vote of thanks to Alex Boyko. He answered with a grin.

'That's the easy part. Now you and Vannikov have to decide who you're going to put in front of the TV cameras and at press conferences. That's what this story is going to bring us: requests for appearances on money programmes, in political slots on the news commentaries. How soon can I have your list?'

'This evening. What's Vannikov doing?'

'Same thing. Conferring and coming back to us. Tanya is putting some pressure on him. She's a firebrand, that one. I like her.'

'I do, too, but let's get down to cases. We need to prepare the people we put up. We can't afford fumblers and bumblers on camera or in a press conference. Tell me what you expect in the interrogations.'

'Let's take the financial questions first. They'll be the simplest and most direct. Who are the financial participants? How is the money being raised? How is the investment being managed? How are the funds secured? How is the problem of soft roubles and hard currencies being addressed? What trade concessions, if any, are being offered? All that sort of thing. Any of your senior bankers should be able to handle that kind of interview. However, the Russians will come under heaviest fire. They'll be questioned about all the things which are still unresolved in this debate between the centralists and the dissident republics. I told Vannikov this. He went a little green. I hope he can handle it.'

'As well as any, Alex. He's worried, of course, we all are, by the bitterness of the debates and now the possible threats of armed intervention against dissident republics. Let's talk about the politics of Germany and Japan.'

Boyko gave a small, grim laugh and reached for a cigarette. 'I can give you that one, chapter and verse. Item one: the Kuril Islands, which are still the bone in Japan's throat. Germany is restored and reunited, but there are still three hundred and fifty thousand Russian troops on German soil. Even so, Japan still remains to be satisfied. Item two: shades of Richard Sorge. The Berlin/Tokyo axis is now being rebuilt, with good commercial intent, of course, but with bad historic vibrations. Item three: China is still the sleeping Socialist giant. How does China react if, in fact, Japan negotiates favoured-nation access to Siberia and thence begins fingering back into Manchuria?'

'Who knows, Alex? I don't.'

'Neither do I, but whoever's going to be talking for the Germans and the Japanese had better be very clear and very eloquent. I hope you're not putting yourself on the witness stand, Gil.'

'Hell, no. I'm a mediator, not a persuader.'

'It's a precise distinction' said Alex Boyko. 'It will not recommend itself to the ladies and gentlemen of the press. So, I tell you as a friend, keep your head down. Which reminds me, various embassies, including the Americans, have telephoned and asked us to put them on

242

the distribution list for press releases. What do you want to do about that?'

'Let them have it; but ask them to arrange their own pick-up. Once it goes on the wire, the stuff's in public domain anyway. Any other problems?'

'Only one, Gil, and there's nothing anyone can do about it. My son's flying an F16 in the Saudi desert. I haven't prayed for years. I'm doing it now.'

'I think we're all doing it, one way and another, Alex. The problem is that the Iraqis are talking to God too. The hotline to heaven must sound awfully confused.'

'That's the mystery I've never fathomed, Gil. My God and thy God. And which one of them created us crazy human animals.'

There were messages in my room: one from Leibig asking me to stand by from two until four in case any of the committees wanted to call me; another from Tanaka, curt and imperious: 'Meeting my suite five thirty. Leibig, Laszlo will attend.'

The third message was the real surprise packet.

It was hand-written on hotel stationery.

Dear Gil,
   My wife and I are taking a week's pre-Christmas leave. We're lodged in the Writers' Wing in the Noel Coward suite. My wife would love to meet you. Suggest afternoon tea, four-ish, if your duties permit. Max Wylie.

I wished him to hell, crumpled the note and tossed it into the wastebasket. The last thing I needed was a fencing match over the teacups, with Wylie's wife as spectator. Then I had a wiser thought: it might be useful to have Wylie's updated view of the crisis in the Gulf and the waves of reaction building up inside the Soviet Union against the secessionist republics. He would not give away any secrets, but he might be willing to trade some useful items or add a gloss to those we already knew. It should not be too costly a transaction for either of us. There might even be a small profit in it. I telephoned Wylie's suite. He had just come up from the pool. I told him I hoped to be free at four o'clock.

'But don't be offended if I don't show. The arrangement is that I have to be on call for any delegate who needs me.'

'Understood, of course. We hope you can make it. How is Marta?'

'She's in hospital.'

'What!'

The surprise in his voice was genuine. I had to give him a blow-by-blow description of Marta's dramatic arrival in Bangkok. It seemed to leave him puzzled.

'What should I do, Gil? Visit her? Send flowers? Lie low and say nothing? She certainly had no idea we were coming to Bangkok.'

'A visit might be untimely. She's still weak and depressed.'

'How is she with you?'

'Well, I guess you could say we're friends again, in a tremulous fashion.'

'Is she coming back to the conference?'

'Possibly, but only possibly, for the second week. I'll be seeing her tonight. I'll mention that you're in town. If she wants to see you, she'll tell me.'

'Thanks. I appreciate that. How is the conference going?'

'It's opened well. The first press announcement went out a short while ago.'

'I know. I thought it was a very well framed document.'

'Where the hell did you get it?'

He chuckled happily. 'You know me, Gil. The eye that never sleeps; the ear that always listens; and you mustn't sully your lips with the rest of it.'

'You told me you were on holiday.'

'We are.' A new sombre note crept into his voice. 'It could be the last we get for a long while. Things don't look good, Gil.'

'I agree, Max. What's bothering me is that every day it gets harder to sort out the truth from the fictions. That's always a sinister sign.'

'I'm not getting too much fiction across my desk, Gil.'

'I guess not.'

'Anyway, when we've had tea, I'd like twenty minutes of your time. I don't talk business with Jeannine. It's safer that way and she prefers it. If you can't make teatime, I'd still like to talk.'

'If I'm detained, I'll call. Otherwise, expect me.'

'Before you hang up, Gil . . .'

'Yes?'

'Those two characters we talked about, friends of the friends . . .'

'What about them?'

244

'They're here in Bangkok.'

'I know.'

'The Drug Enforcement Authority and the Thai police have them both under surveillance. Your poolside meeting with Cubeddu was noted. I thought you should know.'

'Thanks for the information.'

'There's more, but it will keep. *Ciao* for now!'

Before I had time to digest that little morsel, there was a knock at my door. I opened it to confront Carl Leibig and Sir Pavel Laszlo. Leibig looked worried, Laszlo was furious. Before he was even seated, he launched into a tirade.

'We're not even at the end of day one and already the bastards are trying to screw us. I thought we were coming here to conclude an agreement. Now they want to tear up the position papers and start again!'

'Who wants to tear up what position papers?'

'You tell him, Carl. I'm so bloody angry I could blow a fuse!'

'Carl?'

'Before I start, Gil, let me say I don't agree entirely with Sir Pavel. I think he's taking an extreme view. But here's the problem. You know that an essential feature of the plan is the provision of transport and distribution facilities, so that the present bottlenecks are removed and there is a free flow of essential supplies across the country.'

'That was the pivot of the plan. Of course I remember it.'

'Then you'll also remember that stage one called for the use of "available military transport by road, rail and air". Check?'

'Check.'

'So this afternoon,' Laszlo thrust himself back into the discussion, 'not thirty minutes ago, General Popov announces that he has – what did he call it, Carl?'

'A difficulty of definition.'

'I said I thought the text was very clear: "available military transport". Then the sonofabitch started to hedge. He said that what might be available at start-up time could not be quantified even as broadly as we had done in the proposal. There was the problem of the Gulf, the possibility of new demands inside the country itself, the regrouping of troops to maintain order. All that dreck.'

'It wasn't all dreck, Pavel. Part of the problem was that he wasn't explaining himself very clearly.'

'It was clear enough to me, Carl! I've been watching the news. Gorbachev's being endowed with plenary powers. The military are making noises to show what big fellows they are and how much he's going to have to pay for their support. I'm sure as my name's Laszlo that the General's had a signal from Moscow telling him he can't make any commitments of military material or, if he can, they'll all be subject to *ad hoc* decisions. If I'm right, this whole thing's a futile and expensive exercise. The sooner we're out of it the better.'

Now that he had run out of steam, I was able to question him. 'Who else was at the meeting?'

'Tanya the interpreter. Two Japanese from Tanaka's staff, Carl's assistant Franz, who was an observer only, and me.'

'Vannikov wasn't there?'

'He was with me,' Carl Leibig interposed. 'We were sitting with the finance committee.'

'Did you meet any similar obstructions in that committee?'

'Obstructions, no. Vannikov is much more subtle and experienced than Popov. Much more good-humoured, too. But yes, we were getting what I would call reservations and equivocations. My reading is different from Pavel's. I think Vannikov and his people are highly embarrassed by what's going on in Moscow. Gorbachev will have an enormous concentration of constitutional power in his hands. The real question is how he can or will use it. Vannikov can't answer the question so, like a good negotiator, he's playing for time.'

'What does Tanaka say about all this?'

'Nothing!' Laszlo was angry about that, too. 'He's out of communication until our meeting this evening. I don't have this kind of time to waste. I've got a worldwide business to run and the crisis in the Gulf isn't making that one any easier. You're the mediator, Gil. What do you suggest?'

'Leave it to me for the rest of the afternoon. I'll talk to the General and to Vannikov. I'm also taking tea with Max Wylie, who just happens to show up here – on vacation, he says. He wants to talk. I think we need whatever input we can get. But let's not be too hasty. We're still only at day one.'

'By me,' said Pavel Laszlo, 'we're at five minutes to midnight. What did Churchill say? "The first casualty in war is truth." I think, right now, we're keeping the deathwatch. I could use a cup of coffee.'

'We'll have it in my room,' said Carl Leibig. 'Gil has calls to make.'

Fifteen minutes later I was closeted with Vannikov and the General. There was fresh coffee on the table and vodka and ice conspicuous on the bar. Our talk was in Russian, so that there could be no possible misunderstanding or equivocation. I tackled the General first. I set out for him Laszlo's impression of their meeting and Leibig's more mildly framed reservations. I explained carefully.

'This is where I come in: to make sure that each party fully understands the other. So, can you clarify your position on the use of military transport facilities?'

'It's so simple a child can understand it.' Popov was almost as angry as Laszlo. 'The whole country's in a state of confusion. There's a war looming up in the Gulf. We've got more than half a million troops still outside the country, in East Germany, in Czechoslovakia, Poland. There's no way we can make promises about the diversion of transport facilities for civilian use, now or in the foreseeable future.'

'According to the documents, General, the assurance had already been given by the president and the presidential council. This whole operation was predicated on that assurance.'

'Which was quite premature and should not have been given.'

'Has it been countermanded?'

'Yes.'

'By whom?'

'By my military superiors.'

'Whose orders outweigh those of the President and his council?'

'I have to assume that they have the approval of the President.'

'Was the order conveyed to you in writing?'

'Yes.'

'May I see the document?'

'No.'

I turned then to Boris Vannikov. 'Have you seen it, Boris?'

'I have.'

'Does it over-ride the authorities you have been given to bring this conference to a successful conclusion?'

'In my present view, it does not. I am seeking immediate clarification from Moscow.'

'Does this mean that you and General Popov are in conflict on the issue?'

'For the present, no.'

'General?'

'Same answer. For the present, we are not in conflict.'

'But, believe me, you are in conflict with one of the key commercial figures in this conference. He's prepared to walk out unless he can see some sense in your position. Look at it from his point of view – which, by the way, is very clearly expressed in the proposals – that this project cannot work without a complete reform of your internal transport systems. At this moment, you can't afford the rolling stock, the rail extensions, the long-haul carriers, the big transport aircraft. You're out of funds. So the plan envisaged an economical use of available resources. Now, unless that position has changed overnight, you're painting yourselves into a corner. If we lose Laszlo, it's your loss, too, a big loss. So what can you give me to take back, to keep the position open?'

Vannikov and the General looked at each other. Vannikov made a gesture, ceding the floor to Popov, who hesitated for a moment, then made a grudging concession.

'Sometimes you have to walk a long way to get fresh eggs. In theory, Boris can appeal directly to Gorbachev and have him countermand the orders I've been given. But now is not the time to do that. He's just been given a whole sack of new powers – but he's also been refused some. He doesn't want a head-on collision with the military. We believe the best move is what we're doing now: spinning out time, saying don't let's kill the goose that lays golden eggs. Laszlo, of all people, should understand that.'

'He does. But he also knows how the bureaucracy can kill the best of men by slow suffocation. He's not prepared to take that. He doesn't have to. Are you prepared to talk this through with him outside the committee?'

'Yes, I am.'

'Boris?'

'I don't think I should intervene in that discussion. But I'm all in favour of a quick resolution.'

'Le me call Laszlo now.'

Two minutes later, General Popov marched himself out to a rendezvous in Laszlo's suite, leaving me to a private dialogue with Boris Vannikov. He let out a long sigh of relief.

'Thank God that's over. There was a moment this afternoon when I thought he was digging in for another siege of Leningrad. This is one of the biggest problems we've got, Gil. We can't imagine life without the bureaucracy and the echelons of power.'

'Let's be frank. Carl Leibig has the impression that you yourself are falling victim to the same syndrome.'

'What did he say?'

'He used the word "equivocation".'

Vannikov grinned and spread his hands in a gesture of surrender. 'What can I say, Gil? I'm improvising to gain some time. There's no substantial change in our position, but there are a hell of a lot of changes going on in Moscow every day. Even to get two words with the President is a major exercise. Besides, for all its importance, this project is medium- to long-term. All that anybody in Moscow cares is that we're here and we're working. The farthest ahead they're thinking is tomorrow or next week. I know that's not very satisfactory to the investors.'

'That's putting it mildly, Boris. In any terms, you're high-risk investment. And the money-men are very short on patience. Laszlo's right. In the Gulf it's five minutes to midnight. Once the hour strikes, the coach turns into a pumpkin and the horses into white mice.'

'I'd settle for that,' said Vannikov with grim humour. 'A little girl-mouse and a warm nest in a deep cellar. I'm getting very tired of humans.'

I confess I was getting tired of them myself. There was a sour irony in the fact that, while I was, to say the least, over-equipped for human commerce across the planet, I was conscious of a growing hunger for the quieter byways of a scholar's life. I remembered that my father had suffered from the same dichotomy.

When he was in sociable mood, there was no more rumbustious chaser of picaresque company, in tavern or beer-hall or public square. His wit was dazzling, his eloquence overpowering in any language. When I protested, as I sometimes did, about the clamour and the lack of privacy, he would declaim old Samuel Johnson's damnation of the loner: 'Solitude is dangerous to reason without being favourable to virtue.' And then, with special emphasis: 'Remember that the solitary mortal is certainly luxurious, possibly superstitious and probably mad!' In his moments of remorse, however, he would, with an air of tired wisdom, proclaim the *Jeremiad*: '*Quis dabit me in solitudine diversorium viatorum*', Who will offer me a wayfarer's resting-place in the wilderness so that I may go out from my people and be quit of them. Then he would give his big belly laugh and confess, 'The truth, boy, the truth: when I'm alone I bore myself to tears. When I'm in company I can't wait to get back to me.'

A few minutes after four I was walking through the arcade which joins the Writers' Wing to the main body of the hotel. The arcade is lined with expensive boutiques selling jewellery, antiques, silks, high-fashion clothing for men and women. In one of them, Franz, the lover and personal assistant of Carl Leibig, was being measured by a young Thai tailor. He caught sight of me and beckoned me inside.

'I need help here, Gil. This boy has good hands and a beautiful smile, but he answers "yes" to everything I tell him. Will you explain to him, please, that I want the salmon-pink silk, that the jacket is for informal evening wear and while I need it to be waisted, I don't want it too snug.'

I went through the list of instructions for the tailor and translated for Franz his enquiries about such details as pocket flaps, lapel shape and cuff buttons. Franz insisted on making me a party to each decision. It was four fifteen before I could escape him. Even then, he held me back for a final chat in the arcade.

'I'm worried, Gil. Carl is worried too, although he tries to wear a brave face. That's his strength. He will not abandon an idea until its possibilities are quite exhausted. In this case, I am sure the Soviets are stalling.'

'We know they are, Franz. They admit it. The problem is not with this delegation, but in Moscow itself. The mechanisms don't function any more.'

'But the Japanese position seems to be changed, too. I sat through a whole committee meeting this afternoon and they hardly uttered a word. They were, quite deliberately, reserving all their positions.'

'That's their style, Franz. You've lived and worked long enough in the country to be aware of it.'

'I am, but this atmosphere is somehow different. I hope I'm wrong. If this negotiation does break down, I don't want the Leibig Corporation to be held responsible.'

'They won't be. My advice is to sit quietly and play out the game according to plan. You can't hurry events in Europe. There's a glacier-like inevitability about them. One thing is certain: the Western powers can't afford a general collapse in the Eastern bloc. Whatever happens, the Tanaka/Leibig group is well prepared to make appropriate moves. I presume you're getting regular briefings from the German Embassy?'

'They give us less help than you might imagine. As usual, the traders know more than the diplomats. However, they're staging a cocktail party for us at the weekend. That's why I'm treating myself to that very handsome jacket. Which reminds me. Where can I get some nice flowers?'

'There's a stall in the foyer. Give them an hour's notice and they'll prepare an arrangement for you.'

'I thought I should visit Professor Boysen this evening.'

'I'm sure she'll be delighted to see you.'

'Are you two together again? It's none of my business, but I'd better know so I don't make any gaffes.'

'Let's say we're content to be friends.'

He gave me an odd sidelong look and a nod of approval. 'Good. That's safe ground for both of you.'

'Meaning what, Franz?'

'You're the clever one, Gil. You know exactly what I mean. Our friend Marta Boysen is a very clever lady, too, but she's never been able to make up her mind which side of the fence she wants to live on. If you think you can make up her mind for her, that's fine. But you're taking a hell of a risk. I like you, Gil, and I'd rather not see you burned. Carl and I are lucky, we value what we have. We discovered each other just in time. These days,' his face puckered into a malicious pixie grin, 'these days, the love game gets more and more like Russian roulette.'

He left me then and I walked through the Writers' Lounge, where afternoon tea was in full swing: English teas in caddies, laid out in formal array on the trolley, cakes and scones and fruit conserves and cream, little knots of tourists sitting under faded photographs of old Bangkok and King Chulalongkorn with his consorts and their children, bookcases filled with the works of Conrad and Maugham and the long succession of famous authors who had sojourned here from the days of its modest beginnings to the era of its present splendour.

The ascent to the Noel Coward Suite is still made by a double staircase, designed for a more pretentious if less spacious time. The suite itself is as exotic as the man for whom it was named: peacock patterned wallpaper, cabinets of carved teak filled with celadon ware and famillerose porcelain and trinkets of beaten silver, twin canopied beds in the Thai style, painted in gold and turquoise blue. It made an appropriate setting for Max Wylie's wife Jeannine, dressed in a caftan of emerald silk embossed with gold. Her greeting was cheerful, half a step short of brash.

'So! This is the great Gil Langton. I'm delighted to meet you. Max says you're so clever you're a pain in the arse. Marta, who has poor taste in men, thinks you're wonderful.'

'And you, Mrs Wylie?'

'I'm pleasantly surprised. Welcome! How do you like your tea?'

'Lemon, no sugar, thank you. Is this your first visit to Bangkok?'

'No. We come here fairly often, mostly on Max's business. We thought of taking this vacation at home in Vermont, but since it's likely to be cut short, we came here instead. We don't do anything very much except laze by the pool or take an occasional river trip with a tame boatman Max knows. We like it though. After a few days Max becomes halfway civilised.'

'Lay off, lover.' Max Wylie gave me a shamefaced grin and a shrug of resignation. 'Jeannine's idea of a civilising mission is to slice me up like salami in front of our guests.'

'He needs it, Gil. He's so stuffed with secrets, I think sometimes he's going to burst. And it's all bullshit, like a bad movie.'

'She's right, of course.' Max Wylie was eager to embrace the proposition. 'It is mostly bullshit. The big things like plague, famine and mass destruction aren't secret at all. They happen in full view of the audience. The rest of it – who sold whom for how much, who got raped, stabbed, strangled in the back of a car – is so sordid you puke when you see it in real life. If you ever thought what goes on in the kitchen of a famous restaurant, you'd never eat there again. And you'd always gag on the price list.'

Jeannine handed me my tea and a slice of sponge cake. Now that she had made her entrance and established herself as the woman-in-residence in Max Wylie's life, she seemed calmer and more agreeable. Wylie responded to her mood.

'Jeannine's curious to know how this linguistic talent of yours actually works.'

'Not how it works, Max. What it does to Gil. I mean, how does it feel to walk into a room where a dozen languages are being spoken and understand them all?'

'It's confusing, as it would be to anyone. Not the languages themselves, but the cacophony. You have to focus on one subject, one person at a time. The rest becomes a babble until you're ready to concentrate and sort out the various elements. How shall I put it? It's like skin-diving over a tropic reef. The first impression is of enormous clarity. You see everything. You can reach out and touch everything.

You feel like a fish yourself. But suddenly you realise you're not a fish. You're an alien intruder in the fishes' world. You're an abnormality, a creature who needs mechanical aids to survive in water. You have to suppress that feeling, because it undermines your confidence. Nevertheless, it persists. I'm not sure I'm explaining myself very well, but . . .'

'You are, but I'm not asking quite the right questions.' Jeannine Wylie was brighter than she looked and sounded. 'What I really want to know is whether you have any extra perceptions that other people, even people who speak four or five languages, don't have.'

'Yes, but those perceptions are related not only to the language itself, but to all the background which I absorbed as I was learning it. My father educated me by total immersion. We *lived* the language with the people who spoke it. Each word therefore acquired a whole cluster of associations which no dictionary can ever give.'

'So what do you hear when you are listening to these terrifying speeches from the Arab leaders in the Gulf?'

'It's the high rhetoric of a god-centred people, a people with a long tradition of conquest. It's ritual speech, like the Christian liturgy or parliamentary eloquence. I'm attuned to it, because I've experienced it at first hand and as a stranger who had to survive by understanding. I'm not frightened by it but I am frightened of it, because I know how potent its emotional and spiritual appeal can be upon a people bred and rooted in Islam.'

'And meantime,' said Max Wylie, 'the bare facts and the figures tell an even more frightening story. The International Monetary Fund is just about to release its report on the Soviet economy.'

This was unexpected news. I asked him: 'Have you seen the report?'

'No. But we have the guts of it. Disaster, Gil. There's grave fear of a total economic collapse. In spite of the fact that oil prices are going through the roof, the Soviet production is falling. Refineries, pipelines and transport are totally inefficient and getting worse. The whole economy is based now on a primitive barter system. I don't know where that leaves your project; but it scares the living daylights out of us.'

'When is the report due to be published?'

'Some time in January. But already the news is out. Already market confidence is being eroded. There's evidence that the Soviets may open their borders for a mass exodus before the end of winter.'

'All that and a Middle East war.' Jeannine Wylie set down her teacup

253

with a clatter. 'It doesn't bear thinking on. I know you two have to talk about it. I don't have to listen. I'm going to get my hair done. Forgive me, Gil. I'm not really the bitch I sound sometimes. It's just that I know too much and too little and I wish to Christ I could shut it all out and live in a little house in Vermont.'

'I'm trying to get you there, lover' said Max Wylie, and for that moment at least I believe he really meant it. When we were alone, he curled himself up in the corner of the peacock-blue sofa and told me: 'Don't be offended by Jeannine. When she's scared she gets prickly as a porcupine. She reads my mind, Gil. She knows I'm scared too. The Soviet débâcle will be slow but inexorable. A Gulf war will be a sudden horror. I'm afraid we're going to get both. There's a sick joke going round Israel that a syndicate is selling folding chairs and gas masks on the plain of Megiddo where Armageddon will be staged.'

'How do you read the latest reports: mediation by the European Community, offers of aid from Japan if Hussein is ready to withdraw his troops?'

'I think it's window-dressing, designed to persuade the Muslim world that the West is reasonable and well-intentioned and Saddam is a bloody-minded fanatic. It's also a useful sop to Congress so they'll leave the business of war to the President.'

'And what's your personal opinion, Max?'

'I think war's inevitable, and probably desirable, to break Hussein's power completely. A simple withdrawal now solves nothing. In fact, it's the nightmare solution. It leaves the Iraqis with their military strength undamaged, a constant threat to Saudi Arabia and the Gulf Emirates. On the other hand, if we win a war, we lose the peace. Islam has a new honour roll of martyrs and the West gets a new wave of terrorists.'

I said nothing. There was more to come. There had to be more than doomsday talk to justify his pressing invitation. I waited, sipping my tea and nibbling on sponge cake. Finally, Wylie found voice again.

'Back in Tokyo I gave you an assurance that I would not use Marta Boysen's thesis on Haushofer as a weapon against your project. I've honoured that. But other people have got hold of it and they're about to launch a series of attacks in the world press.'

'What other people, Max?'

'Mossad.'

'The Israelis? Why, for God's sake? What's their interest?'

'It's part of a pattern of reprisal.'

'For what?'

'For outbreaks of anti-Semitism in Germany, France, Middle Europe and Russia itself. We all know they've been going on: desecration of cemeteries, burning of dachas, graffiti on public buildings. This is part of the response: If you insult us, damage us, you will go hungry a little longer. That, at least, is how the story has been read to me. Knowing how Mossad works, it doesn't surprise me. So you'd better have your responses ready.'

'Thanks, Max. I appreciate the warning.'

'I don't believe it will make an iota of difference either way. I can't see you coming up with an agreement in two weeks, or even six months.'

'Frankly, neither can I, but I believe we should work through the agenda in the hope that we can salvage at least some of the groundwork we've done, and there is an enormous amount of it. Meantime, what other good news do you have for me?'

'The song and dance act: Hoshino and Cubeddu.'

'What about them?'

'Hoshino is in the entertainment business, which is also the flesh business. He exports women entertainers – and some male ones as well – all around the clubs he owns in South-East Asia. He's in the drug business, too, but he deals in amphetamines, which are a high-use item in Japan and can be dealt more easily through Asian pharmaceutical houses. So he's not a rival to the Thai and Chinese drug barons who deal in hash and heroin. All of that means he's on friendly terms with the Thai police and the big nightclub and brothel syndicates here. He flies in the tourists who spend the money in this country's sex markets.'

'And Cubeddu?'

'Is a loose cannon, a dangerous nuisance. He's trying to establish a Mafia connection for heroin and opiates. He thinks Hoshino's helping him to do it. Instead, Hoshino is keeping his bargain with Tanaka, holding Cubeddu under control until your conference is concluded.'

'And after that?'

'Exit Cubeddu.'

'How?'

'That will depend on how bright he is and how much he's prepared to pay to stay out of the river or out of a Thai Jail.'

'And you're sure of all this?'

'Absolutely. Cubeddu is under constant surveillance. His room is bugged and his favourite girl reports every day to the police.'

'It couldn't happen to a nicer guy.'

'True, but there is a complication.'

'Which is?'

'Tanaka's girlfriend, Miko. She had one meeting with Cubeddu in his hotel room. The meeting was monitored.'

'And?'

'There is a financial connection between them, a finder's fee and a million dollars in escrow, apparently related to this project.'

'We know about those transactions.'

'The monitored conversation takes them a little further. If Cubeddu is excluded from an interest in the Tanaka/Leibig consortium, Miko loses her million. She can, however, regain it if she agrees to work with Cubeddu on the Coast and in Japan and if she provides him with some personal hospitality on the side.'

'And Miko's answer?'

'That's on tape, too. She'll think about it. Tanaka is a sick man, she will do nothing to hurt him. Afterwards, the matter's open for discussion.'

'Did they have sex on that occasion?'

'Cubeddu wanted it. He didn't get it. The lady's a tramp, but she doesn't come cheap.'

'Who's holding the tapes?'

'The Thai police. Our people have copies. If they're leaked, as the Haushofer document was leaked, then your friend Tanaka is going to have a lot of egg on his face.'

'If the Thai police have them, Hoshino must know about them. He's the watchdog on Cubeddu.'

'I'd say that was a reasonable assumption. It means Tanaka must know too.'

'That doesn't necessarily follow, Max.'

'Why not?'

'Hoshino and Tanaka work different sides of the street, but there's a pact between them. One protects the other. Hoshino would never permit Tanaka to be blackmailed. He would also shield him from public shame, from loss of face.'

'In that case,' Max Wylie mused softly, 'in that case, the lady Miko could have a very short life.'

I had a sudden vivid memory of the warning Tanaka had given me in Tokyo: 'We are coming up to earthquake time, when the great rock plates shift and slide and buckle against each other and all our frail human edifices come tumbling down. People get hurt. You could get hurt.' Then out of the silence came Max Wylie's dry comment: 'I seem to have given you some problems, Gil?'

'You could say that.'

'I'll give you some advice, too.'

'I'm listening.'

'My old man was an FBI agent in the Hoover days. He used to say that the most economical solution to any problem was to let the Mob take care of it. That's exactly what Tanaka's doing. He's leaving everything to Hoshino. You shouldn't try to stir the soup. You're likely to get scalded. The best contribution you can make is to keep your hands in your pockets and your mouth shut.'

'You're probably right.'

'I know I'm right. They still shoot the bringer of bad news.' Suddenly, inanely, he burst out laughing. 'Do I hear you thanking me? Blessing me, because I've made you wiser than you were?'

Then, just as suddenly and inanely, I was laughing with him, as if all this talk of blackmail, betrayal, murder and the fall of empires were nothing but a Halloween story told to strike delicious terror into children at bedtime.

Fifteen

At five-thirty precisely, Kenji Tanaka received Leibig, Laszlo and myself in his suite. Miko served our drinks and withdrew. Tanaka made a brusque announcement.

'You are my friends. You are my collaborators on this and other enterprises. I wish to inform you about certain matters which affect our mutual interests. I will ask you to keep this information private until all stock exchange trading has closed in all world capitals on Friday of this week. Do you agree to that, gentlemen?'

There was a brief murmur of assent. Tanaka waited a moment and then, in the same brusque, impersonal fashion, set down the information.

'You all know that I am a dying man. I have, in the normal course of events, only a few months to live. I must look, therefore, to the speedy ordering of my affairs. I have already arranged, through a series of family and business transactions, an alliance between the House of Tanaka and the organisations controlled by my old friend Hisayuki Kobayashi. Each house will maintain its own identity and its own spheres of activities, but a family relationship now exists between them. The announcement of the merger will take place after the close of all stock exchange business this week. It will be obvious to you all that the new alliance creates a financial entity of enormous strength.

'However, I shall no longer be directing policy. Therefore, I have provided that each of you shall be free either to continue your present financial relationships with the Tanaka Group or to make other arrangements at a fair market price. In your case, Gil, our contract has always provided that if we wished to sell our interest in Polyglot Press, the first offer should be made to your present staff. You may inform them that our offer is now on the table and banking arrangements can be made for them to take it up.'

It was a gesture in the old, princely style and I was grateful to him and glad that he still had the magnanimity to make it. However, this was no time for speeches and demonstrations. Kenji Tanaka was writing his own obit.

'Now, to the business in hand, our negotiations with the Soviet Union. Our new associates have agreed that these negotiations should continue for the agreed period of two weeks. They are, however, convinced – as I am – that there is no possible hope of a resolution in that time. The whole apparatus of central government in the Soviet Union has broken down and there is no hope of restoration other than by bloody repression and ultimate dictatorship, or by the slow and painful process of consensus based upon common need. Either way, there is little hope of realistic commercial agreements in the immediate future. This diagnosis will, we believe, be confirmed in a forthcoming report by the International Monetary Fund.

'In practical terms, therefore, we should seek to preserve the goodwill which we have established, to capitalise at some time the investment we have already made in this plan and, at the same time, keep the goodwill of our bankers and investors. It is better that we should be known as prudent protectors of their funds than as profligate spenders of them. I would welcome your comments on this, gentlemen. Carl?'

Once again I had to give Leibig top marks. He was fully in command of himself and of the situation. 'Your personal news distresses me, Kenji. I will not embarrass you with sympathy. I respect your frankness and I have to say, with great regret, that I agree with your business assessment. A few weeks, even a few days, ago, I should have been prepared to go ahead alone, with a modified version of this plan, for the republics west of the Urals. Now I cannot see even that happening. I think we have to withdraw, but I believe we should do it with due respect for the difficulties in which the Soviets find themselves. We should not exacerbate those difficulties by untimely or intemperate announcements. In the end, I think we should agree a statement that the conference has been postponed while further studies are made by all parties. Would your colleagues agree to that, Kenji?'

'I'm sure they would.'

'I think we can do a lot better.' Pavel Laszlo was bustling and combative. 'This was a Soviet initiative, remember. They invited a proposal from Carl, Carl co-opted the Tanaka Group. Together, you put up an expensive and well-founded project on the minimal assumption that the central government could sign, seal and deliver binding agreements for the whole country. For the present at least, they can't do that. So, before all our work becomes public property, before this conference breaks up, we've got to lodge some formal demands: for compensation, for first and last bid if and when the market opens again and any other goddam shopping items you can dream up. To hell with their difficulties, Carl! They're self-inflicted. To hell with their goodwill. Of all the animals in creation, politicians have the shortest memories. We're not professional mourners. We're dollars and cents men, experts like plumbers and electricians. We give service, we expect to be paid. If we give free service, as we have done in this case, we expect to be called for the job that pays money. What say you, Gil?'

'I agree with you, Pavel, but I've got a couple of footnotes to make. All the Soviet delegates are bred to the same system: the hierarchy, the *nomenklatura*. So, at the end of the day each one is going to be covering his own arse, with his own set of excuses in his own collection of memos. In that operetta, we are cast, naturally, as the nasties. I don't think we should let it happen that way. We've begun with a very positive press release. We have to maintain that tone, while at the same time being very clear about the real difficulties that exist in Moscow, difficulties which we recognise may become insuperable. In short, our message is: the plan is great. There's money to make it work, but the Soviets have to put their political house in order before we can commit the funds of our investors. That's the first note. The second is about another matter altogether. I was warned today by Max Wylie that Israeli Intelligence, Mossad, has got hold of Marta Boysen's thesis and is preparing to launch a press campaign against what they are calling, "this new Berlin/Tokyo axis".'

'Do you believe that?' The challenge came from Laszlo. 'I don't. It's a fairytale, an anti-Jewish propaganda piece.'

'I take everything that comes from so-called Intelligence sources with a large grain of salt. Wylie's explanation is that this is part of a campaign of reprisals for anti-Semitic demonstrations in Germany and in Russia itself. On the other hand, it's possible that Wylie himself is the instigator. Whatever its origin, the campaign will begin very soon. We have to be ready for it.'

'In view of this new information,' Tanaka thrust himself back into the discussion, 'I ask why we continue to spend time and money on a cause we all know to be lost. Why not cut our losses now and get out clean, without having to answer to anybody? I know that's the solution my colleagues would prefer, although they have agreed not to force it upon us. You're the mediator, Gil. What's your advice?'

'Stick to protocols we've both agreed – open discussion, honest mediation. You spoke to General Popov this afternoon, Pavel. How did that talk go?'

'Well enough. He was reluctant at first to move beyond a formal positive statement. Then he loosened up and admitted that he's caught in a cleft stick between the military and the politicians. I think he was as open as he dared to be. For the present, at least, there's no way the military will release rolling stock or aircraft into civilian hands.'

'So let me talk to Vannikov. I'll give him the gist of what's been said here this evening, including our legitimate demands for a shopping list of compensatory items. I'll ask his opinion about the quickest and easiest way to disengage. Remember, it's his problem too. I'll see if I can take him out to dinner tonight. I'll report back to you before nine in the morning. Agreed?'

'Agreed.' It was a murmured chorus. Laszlo then faced me with a blunt question.

'Why did Max Wylie want to see you?'

'He said his wife was anxious to meet me.'

That raised a laugh, as I had hoped it might. It also prompted a tart little question from Carl Leibig.

'How do you cope with all these women, Gil?'

'Not well at all, Carl. But Wylie's wife is pleasant enough. She's number three and determined to have a long reign.'

'What was the real reason for the invitation?'

There was a barb in Tanaka's question that drew blood and made me irritated.

'He was delivering a warning.'

'About what?'

'About Domenico Cubeddu who, as you know, is here in Bangkok and still waiting for your word on his acceptance as an investor in the Tanaka/Leibig syndicate.'

'Which will soon be a dead letter.'

'But he doesn't know that and when he reads our first press report he will note that the Japanese funds are already fully subscribed. He will be insulted and vindictive. Meantime, however, he is using the good offices of Hoshino, who is also in town, to set up his own connection with the local drug lords.'

Tanaka gave a shrug and a small wintry smile. 'I wish him luck.'

'He is, I am told, under surveillance by the Thai police and his telephone is bugged. The DEA liaison office here has copies of the tapes.'

'And how is that supposed to concern you or us?'

'Marta Boysen's thesis on Haushofer was leaked. It is still an embarrassment to us. These tapes could embarrass all of us, you especially, Kenji.'

'Did your Max Wylie have any suggestion as to how we might avoid such embarrassment?'

'I asked him the same question. His answer was that I shouldn't stir the soup, because I was likely to get scalded; that I should keep my hands in my pockets and my mouth shut.'

'Sound advice.' Laszlo got up to leave. 'You owe us nothing. Why stick your neck out?'

'It is not our wish to put you at risk,' said Carl Leibig. He, too, was on his way to the door. I was just turning to follow them when Kenji Tanaka called me back.

'Do you mind staying, Gil? I need a few moments of your time.'

He was obviously embarrassed, so I tried to take some of the heat out of the occasion. I thanked him for his offer to sell his interest in Polyglot Press to my staff and told him I would put their response on the table as soon as possible. He made a small cautionary gesture.

'Don't delay, Gil. I'm not going to be around very long.'

'But you said a few months.'

'Much less, Gil. I am taking the shortest road possible to join my ancestors. I have no time left for bargaining and none for revenge either. So, whatever you have to tell me, I should like to hear now.'

'In that case, I'd like to have Miko here.'

For a longish moment I thought he was going to refuse, then he got up, opened the door to the adjoining room and summoned Miko to join us.

When she was seated, he announced in his brusque fashion: 'Gil has something to communicate to me. He insists you hear it too.'

'Why, Gil?'

'So that you will hear exactly what I am reporting in the words which I am using. How do you want to hear it, in English or Japanese?'

'You conversed with Wylie in English,' said Tanaka curtly. 'You should report in English.'

'This afternoon, I was invited to tea with Max Wylie and his wife. They are here on vacation, but he is obviously in touch with local colleagues. He told me, among other things, that Domenico Cubeddu is seeking to establish a connection with local drug lords. He is under surveillance by the Thai police and by local US narcotics agents working in co-operation with them. Cubeddu's phone is bugged. There is a record of a conversation between you, Miko, and Cubeddu. Copies of that tape are in the hands of the Thai police and US officials.'

There was no change in Miko's expression. She simply nodded and asked a bald question: 'Did Wylie say what was on the tape?'

'He described the contents. He didn't render them verbatim.'

'Tell me what he said, please.'

'He said the conversation dealt with the financial arrangements between you and Cubeddu: a finder's fee for the introduction into this current project and a million dollars held in escrow against a favourable outcome. If you lost the million you could recover it by agreeing to work for Cubeddu on the Coast and in Japan and by providing sexual hospitality to Cubeddu.'

'And my reply?'

'You had loyalties to Kenji Tanaka. You would do nothing to hurt him. When he was no longer here, you might discuss business.'

'Anything else?'

'Cubeddu wanted sex with you then and there. He didn't get it.'

'Did Wylie have any comment?'

'Yes. If the tapes were leaked and the Cubeddu connection became known, Kenji would be gravely embarrassed. More importantly, he suggested that you were in personal danger.'

'What sort of danger?'

'His exact words were: "The lady Miko could have a very short life." End of report, end of story.'

'Thank you, Gil.' Miko was very calm and composed.

'My thanks also,' said Kenji Tanaka. 'You have done us both a service. Now, if you will excuse us, we need to be alone for a little while.'

I let myself out of the room and went upstairs to call Boris Vannikov. Tanya answered.

'He's in the shower. Can I have him call you back?'

'What's he doing tonight?'

'He's taking me to dinner.'

'Tell him to cancel it. I'm taking you both.'

'If it's business, the answer's no.'

'It is business and if you're supposed to be reporting to Moscow, you'd better hear it too. Besides, I'll feed you better than Boris can.'

'Hold on a minute. He's just coming out of the bathroom.'

There was a murmur of talk in the background and then Boris came on the line. 'Gil. What's this about a business dinner?'

'The roof's falling in and the floor's collapsing. I'm commissioned to take you to dinner and report back to our people in the morning. If you want to bring Tanya, that's fine.'

'She'd better be there. She's an official monitor for Moscow. How serious is this?'

'Three days short of Judgment Day.'

'Where are we eating? What time? What's the dress?'

'Meet me on the landing stage at eight. We're going across the river. Dress is casual.'

'The food had better be good.'

'It will be.'

My next call was to Siri. She had just finished her business day. Would she be free to partner me at an eight o'clock dinner? She would be delighted. Would she call Madame Loi and ask her to prepare a dinner for four in her river room? It would be done. The guests? I explained who they were and why the occasion, for all its informality, was of diplomatic importance. I also explained that Boris Vannikov was a notable connoisseur of women. Siri laughed happily.

'Good. I love to be courted. Have you seen Marta today?'

'Not a chance. I'm about to call her.'

'Give her my good wishes.'

'I'll do that. We'll see you just after eight.'

'Come to my house for a cocktail. Then we'll all stroll round the corner to Madame Loi's.'

I was about to call the hospital when Laszlo telephoned me. He wanted to know whether I had fixed my dinner date with Vannikov. When I told him it was arranged, he grunted approval.

'Good. I'm taking the General for a meal with our local manager. I just wanted to be sure you and I are following the same script as we agreed with Tanaka.'

'Exactly the same. How is Leibig handling the decision?'

'Very well. He'd prefer to play the conference right out to the final session, but he's agreed to suspend judgment until your report is delivered. He is, however, enormously worried about Hoshino and Cubeddu.'

'He has reason to be. I'm hoping, however, that Tanaka will find his own solution to the problem.'

'Have you any idea what that might be?'

'None. I don't want to speculate. In fact, I don't want to know. I'd like to wake up one morning and find it's simply gone away.'

'Keep your fingers crossed, Gil.' There was a touch of gallows humour in his laugh. 'Touch wood and stroke your rabbit's foot. We're a long way east of Suez. Anything can happen.'

After that I called Marta at the clinic. She was feeling much stronger. She had walked about the room and down the corridors. They had taken her off the drip and were feeding her liquids and light nourishment. She hoped to be discharged the day after tomorrow. Franz had called to see her. He had brought the most beautiful orchids and entertained her with gossip and scandal. Miko had telephoned just before me. It was a goodbye call. She was flying back to Tokyo in the morning. She would stay there a week and then return to Los Angeles. She sounded strained. She was glad to be leaving Bangkok. The conference had been, for the most part, a bore, little groups of delegates huddled in technical talk. After all that had happened, this was the best way to say goodbye, yes? I agreed it was. I promised on my scout's honour to visit her the next day. 'Goodnight, *schatzi*, and golden dreams.'

My final call was to Tanaka. I made it on an impulse, because I was concerned at the news of Miko's imminent departure. However, I approached that subject walking on tiptoe by a roundabout route.

'Kenji? Gil. I thought you'd like to know that the dinner with Vannikov is arranged. He's elected to bring Tanya, who is also one of Moscow's monitors. I'm happy about that. Laszlo is taking General Popov to dinner. That will give us two angles on the same subject. I'd suggest an eight o'clock breakfast meeting to compare notes before the conference resumes. I think it best you call Leibig and Laszlo and set it up.'

'I'll do that, Gil. Anything else?'

'I spoke with Marta Boysen. She'll be discharged in the next forty eight hours. She told me Miko had called to say goodbye. Is this a sudden decision?'

'It's a prudent one, in view of your report.'

'What flight is she taking?'

'JAL. Why do you ask?'

'I believe she should be accompanied until she is ready to board.'

'Thank you for the thought, Gil. It is already arranged. Two of my staff will ride with her to the airport and see her through Immigration. There she will be met by a senior police officer and a male member of JAL service staff. She will remain in the VIP room until a few moments before departure.'

'Forgive me. I must have sounded very impertinent, but I've worked a long time in this town. Strange things can happen.'

'I know.' Kenji Tanaka was as bland as honey. 'I, too, have long connections here. I am glad you called. I did not have time to thank you this afternoon. You were in a difficult situation.'

'Not too difficult. Wylie gave me the information because he expected me to pass it on and because he couldn't prescribe protection for a non-national. Unless I gave it to both of you, I could have been rated by one or the other as a tale-bearer. Please give Miko my good wishes. Tell her I wish her a safe journey and a peaceful home-coming.'

'She's at the hairdresser's now. I know she will want to call you before she leaves in the morning.'

'And you, Kenji? How long will you stay in Bangkok?'

'Until our situation with Leibig and with the Soviets is resolved.' He gave a small, humourless laugh. 'I am not yet ready to bid farewell to Gilbert Langton. Have a pleasant dinner.'

One way and another, it had been a very busy day. I decided I had earned a drink before I showered and dressed for dinner. I poured myself a stiff bourbon and picked up the South-East Asian edition of the *Wall Street Journal*. Our story had made two columns on page one, which was a compliment to Alex Boyko and his team. His text had been printed verbatim, but it ended with an editorial comment: 'This news should lay to rest certain rumours which have been circulating in Asian financial circles, that the Tanaka Group has been in bad odour with the *keiretsu* and has been forced to seek maverick money to bolster its more risky enterprises.'

The italic type seemed to leap from the page. No one, least of all Domenico Cubeddu of the Palermitan Banking Corporation, could miss the import of the words. The shit had already hit the fan. Miko was

266

still in the fall-out zone. Kenji Tanaka himself was working very close to the wind.

At eight o'clock, showered, shaved and dressed in tropical cottons, I was waiting on the landing stage for Boris and Tanya. Boris embraced me in a bear-hug. Tanya kissed me with agreeable intensity. The boatman handed us into the narrow craft and we roared across the river, narrowly missing a rice barge and a sand scow and a floating restaurant. Conversation was impossible until we were decanted on the wharf at the other side and walked the two hundred paces to Siri's house on the klong. Tanya was goggle-eyed at the exotic interior; the rich teak, the antique tapestries in gold and silver thread, the cool stone of the Khmer figures. Boris stared at his hostess open-mouthed, like a frog-prince waiting to be made human with a kiss. It pleased me that I was the one to be kissed and ordered to make the cocktails. The children were not in evidence. This was a business occasion, they were absent about their own concerns. Finally, Boris found voice.

'Siri, I am your slave. You are the most beautiful woman in the world!'

'He was my slave when we were in bed at five-thirty.' Tanya was ready for a pitched battle.

'He will be again at twelve-thirty,' Siri told her cheerfully. 'As Gil will tell you, I never even kiss on the first date. The last Russian I kissed was Yuri Yevtushenko, and only because he was a fine poet, slightly drunk, in a fit of deep melancholy. You remember, Gil! He stood where Tanya is standing now and recited ten stanzas of "Babi Yar". What an actor!'

God bless the woman! She had Boris tamed and Tanya adoring her before we had finished the first martini. She told them the tale of Madame Loi, daughter of a Chinese warlord in the highlands, mistress of a prince, lover of an American diplomat, who had invested her savings in a house on the river and three godowns which she leased to the river traders and a small restaurant where she cooked and served the best Chinese/Thai food in Bangkok. It was a very private place. Big deals were done there. Marriages were arranged there. Certain noble love affairs had been consummated there. Once, according to ugly rumour, murder had been done in the river room. The truth, as Siri explained it in her calm fashion, was that the assassin and his victim had dined there; but the killing had been done twenty miles away in a banana plantation.

We strolled there in pairs, Boris and Siri in the lead, Tanya clinging

267

to my arm and firing questions at me in Armenian. Where did you meet her? Have you ever been lovers? How can you work so closely together and still be just friends? How old is she? Where did she get all that beautiful education? Fortunately I did not have to answer too many of the queries because Tanya ran them together in a kind of breathless monologue, all the time keeping a wary eye on Boris, who was playing the courtier as if he had just stepped out of the pages of *War and Peace*.

At Madame Loi's the miracle of food was performed, followed by another which never failed to amaze me: Siri effacing herself into almost total anonymity while the currents of business talk swirled around her. Yet her placid presence muted the harshness of the problems exposed in our talk. I set down the options as they had been discussed with Tanaka, Leibig and Laszlo; I asked Vannikov to give me his own version of the possibilities. His answer was simple.

'There is nothing in your documents which, in normal circumstances, we would refuse to accept. The principles are sound. The ways and means could be argued, plus or minus, in committee. However, our circumstances are not normal. The Union of Soviet Socialist Republics is fragmenting itself. The president has been vested with dictatorial powers to stop the fragmentation. There is grave doubt that he can succeed. Therefore, much as I regret to say so, our discussions here in Bangkok have become marginal, untimely and unreal.'

'Wrong words, Boris!' Tanya was a dominating presence in the quiet room. 'There are eight billion dollars of hard currency investment available. They are not at the exclusive disposition of the presidential council. They are a benefit to be shared with all the republics. That's real. And God knows, it couldn't be more timely. We have to make that clear at home.'

For a long moment, Vannikov sat silent, staring down at his plate. When he looked up, his face was sombre and there was in his eyes a tenderness I had never seen before. He addressed himself to Tanya.

'I wasn't going to tell you this until the morning. But, to the Devil with it! Before we came out tonight, I received a message from the Embassy. It was an instruction from the presidential council. Their own difficulties make it impossible to commit to the terms of this commercial enterprise at this moment. They now take the view that further debates and discussions in Bangkok will serve only to highlight the increasing problems in the homeland. Therefore we are recalled!'

'No!' It was a cry of pure despair from Tanya. 'They can't do that!' She fought back the tears of anger and frustration.

Vannikov's answer was curt and final. 'They've done it. We wear it.'

'Not without a fight.' Tanya refused to be silenced or mollified. 'You've got to hold them off a few days longer. We can't retreat from Bangkok like a defeated army. I refuse to be shamed by those bastards in Moscow.'

'They'll shame you more if they refuse to pay your hotel bill and your airfare.' Vannikov still managed to extract a drop of black humour from the situation. 'Unless, of course, you want to defect and take a job with Gil here.'

'Will you have me, Gil?'

'Any time, my love.'

'Good!' Vannikov was in control again. 'Now, let's be practical. If Moscow will consent to a tactical withdrawal instead of a full retreat, how far will your people co-operate, Gil?'

'Frankly, I don't know. It's your people who are pulling the rug on the deal. If you can persuade them to modify their attitude – to postpone, prorogue, pending further consultations – then the picture changes somewhat. However, if you're asking the investors to hold their money in place, you have to hold their rights and pre-emptions in place too. What we don't want is a repetition of today's situation, where the presidential council had agreed something and the army counter-manded it. We need assurances that the position we have established will be maintained, at least for a reasonable time.'

'Therefore we need time to frame the assurances.' Tanya was pressing hard. 'We also need time to explain our resolves to the press. We dare not break off abruptly. I think we have to sit out the whole session here. At least we have to leave a working committee for the full time. Don't you agree, Gil?'

'Tanya, my love, it doesn't matter whether I agree or not. I'm the mediator, not a voter. Let me show you what you're up against. Item: a lot of money which can't be kept idle. Item: Kenji Tanaka, a dying man eager to quit, his new and powerful associates sceptical of the venture anyway. Item: Carl Leibig, a solid man with steady nerves but dependent on his bankers; Pavel Laszlo, a brilliant entrepreneur but totally intolerant of bureaucrats and bunglers. Item: an underlying resentment that, having invited them to set up this consortium, you are not ready to meet your commitments. Add to that the prospect of war in the Gulf and the forgotten trade war which is going on between the United States and Europe and Japan – you've got a hell of a lot to contend with.'

'And you, my dear Gil,' Siri spoke for the first time. 'You have now said enough. In this place we are friends trying to help each other. Look out at the river. It is the lifeline of our delta people, but we have to adapt to it, live with its moods, rejoice in the food it nourishes, endure the parasites it inflicts upon us. You are all caught in the current of history whose headwaters rise in the dark mountains of the past. You cannot change it; you survive and help others to survive by adapting to it. Let us relax now. We are friends who trust each other. Madame Loi still has a few surprises for us.'

'My biggest surprise,' said Tanya in her forthright fashion, 'is that you and Gil work so closely together, you're so obviously fond of each other, yet you've never thought of getting married.'

Siri smiled, that slow, subtle Buddha-smile, and answered for both of us. 'Once, a long time ago, we thought about it and talked about it, but it didn't make sense to change the course of our lives so radically. We have each been married before, and very happily. Each of us has grown children. Gil, like his father, is at heart a gypsy. I am a very settled person, with many relatives of my own and a whole web of family connections on my husband's side. Those connections mean duties and pieties of one sort and another which, to a *farang* like Gil, would mean a total shift in the direction of his life. Neither of us demands that kind of sacrifice from the other. My children and I were brought up by Gil's father, so there is already a family relationship between us . . . What more do we need?'

'Gil needs a wife!' Tanya was getting high on Madame Loi's Chinese wine.

'I know he does, my dear.' Siri seemed to have a limitless fund of patience. 'But I'm not the woman for that role.'

'Would you consider a bid from me, madam?' Boris was elated but still sober. 'I'm not doing so well as a chief of delegation, but I do have other talents.'

'I know you have, Boris, but I'm not sure that I'd wear very well in a Moscow winter, or you in a tropic monsoon.'

'He'd probably end up covered with green mould.' That was Tanya's last contribution before Madame Loi presented the masterpiece of the evening: deep-fried duckling in pandamus leaves with a sauté of tropic vegetables and fruits.

270

We sat for another hour over the meal. Our talk lapsed into fragmented exchanges of reminiscence, old tales retold, opinions half examined, trotted out once more for friendly inspection. It was just after eleven when Madame Loi bowed us off the premises. It was half past when we said goodbye to Siri at her front door and strolled arm in arm down to the landing stage to pick up a water taxi for the short river crossing.

From where we stood, the Oriental hotel was clearly visible, the last late diners on the terrace, the glow of the barbecue area, the landing stage where the big river boat was moored, fuelled and ready for the next day's excursion to Ayutthaya, the upward thrust of the high block of balconied suites overlooking the terrace and the river reaches.

We were just settling ourselves into the narrow, rocking water taxi when we heard a hubbub of shouting and screaming. When we looked up, we saw the late, sparse crowd converging like a scurry of ants on the square of terrace just below the riverside suites. Then the scene was blotted out by a line of rice barges going down river. When we came finally to the landing stage the hubbub had died to a low, sinister murmur. The security guard who handed us ashore gave only a laconic answer to our questions: there had been an accident; we should not go along the terrace, but take the long way round, through the garden and past the swimming pool, thence into the foyer.

Once we were out of his sight, we slipped back on to the terrace and worked our way through the crowd of guests which was becoming denser every moment. As we moved, we gathered our information in snatches, but the final confirmation came from a young waiter whom I questioned in Thai. He pointed upwards along the lighted face of the residential block. A young woman had fallen or jumped from one of the topmost balconies. She died the moment she hit the ground, a terrible mess. The police were on their way. We could hear their sirens. We saw their first contingent thrusting through the crowd, forming a protective cordon around the victim, covered now with bloody tablecloths.

Suddenly I caught sight of Tanaka, flanked by two of his staff and led by the assistant manager, pushing his way through the crowd under the colonnade. I pointed them out to Vannikov and we, too, began to barge through the spectators towards the police cordon. Tanaka and his escorts got there before us. I saw them in hurried dialogue with the police. Tanaka stepped forward. One of the policemen lifted a corner of the tablecloths. Tanaka stared for a moment, nodded, then turned away and vomited on the pavement.

I turned to Vannikov. I read in his eyes my own unspoken thought. I told him curtly: 'Get Tanya out of here. Tanaka needs some help. I'll call you later.'

He moved fast, dragging Tanya out of the crowd and heading away into the shadows of the garden. I pressed forward to make contact with the officer in charge of the police detachment. Before I opened my mouth, he waved me away. Then, when he heard me speaking Thai, he became courteous, but made me pay a price: my own identification of the victim. I managed to control my nausea and confirm that it was Miko and that she was personal assistant to Mr Kenji Tanaka, one of the principals at the current conference. Then I had to explain my own role. After that the officer was amenable to the suggestion that I take Mr Tanaka away from the scene and hold both him and myself available for questioning after the forensic formalities.

We made our way back to Tanaka's suite in silence. Once there, he dismissed his two assistants and sat slumped in an armchair, staring into some private pit of despair. I made him a stiff drink. He gagged on the first sip and then downed half the glass at a gulp. Slowly the colour came back to his cheeks, but he found no words and his eyes were still focused on dark infinities. I had to begin the talk by telling him of the subtleties we might expect in a Thai interrogation. I warned him against any hint of brusqueness, impatience or irritation. I suggested that, unless the police officer spoke Japanese, which was unlikely, he permit me to act as interpreter from Thai to Japanese, from Japanese to Thai. I would undertake to read both the Thai and the Japanese transcripts. He should sign the Japanese version, while I certified the Thai version before he signed that too.

The exercise seemed to jolt him out of his torpor. He began to talk slowly and ruminatively as if he were totally detached from the events he described:

'You spoke to Miko and me in the suite. You told us of your talk with Wylie.'

Wylie! I had forgotten him completely. I muttered an excuse to Tanaka, reached for the telephone and asked to be put through to the Noel Coward Suite. Wylie answered. He sounded drowsy and distinctly unwelcoming.

'Who the hell is this?'

'It's Gil. What have you been doing for the last hour?'

'Sleeping, for Christ's sake! We were in bed by ten. What's going on?'

I told him. He was instantly awake and wary as a fox. I told him I had spent the evening on the other side of the river. He let out a long exhalation of relief.

'Good. Three-monkey trick: no see, no hear, no say.'

'That was my thought. The police will be here soon to question Tanaka. I'll be interpreting.'

'And you'll keep me posted.'

'You likewise, Max.'

'Of course, but, as they say in the army, never volunteer anything, even the time of day. I'm going back to sleep.'

'Apologies to Jeannine.'

'She wears earplugs and eyeshades. She didn't even stir. Good luck with the gendarmes.'

Kenji Tanaka was alert now, watching me with dark, mistrustful eyes.

'What was all that about?'

'A friendly exchange of news and views. Remember that Miko, Cubeddu and Hoshino are already in the police computers. Nothing that should concern you. Now, you were about to tell me what happened after I left you and Miko this evening. Imagine I am the policeman who will be here presently.'

'Nothing happened. We talked.'

'About what?'

'About the conference, whether it should be continued or post-poned. When I should return to Japan. Miko thought I should leave as soon as possible. I felt I should stay at least until the end of the week. I told her I did not want to linger in Tokyo, but go almost immediately to the country, to Nagano, because that is where I want to die. Miko thought it would be a good idea if she left early to prepare the place for my arrival. We agreed on that. She left to go to the hairdresser, saying she would have the concierge get her a seat on tomorrow morning's flight. While she was at the hairdresser's, I made all the other arrangements for her exit.'

'Why did you go to so much trouble?'

'You know why, Gil!'

'I am not Gil. I'm a police officer gathering information.'

'Miko is an important person on my staff and in my personal life. I depend upon her. It is only commonsense that I take care of her.'

'Good. So now she is back from the hairdresser. What time would that be?'

'You rang about seven-thirty. She was back shortly after your call. She mentioned that she gave the girls an extra tip because she had held them back.'

'It is now eight or thereabouts. Where did you go for dinner?'

'We had a light meal served here. Afterwards, Miko went to her own room to pack.'

'Her own room?'

'Whenever we travel, we have two bedrooms with a common lounge room. Look for yourself.'

It was a simple arrangement common to most hotels: three rooms in line, a bedroom on either side of a large salon. In this case, all three rooms faced the river and each had a separate balcony. I noted that Tanaka's room had a large king-sized bed while Miko's had twin beds. That was the extent of my examination. I was concerned to know the line of Tanaka's narrative and to guess how the police might attack it.

'Now, let's take this part very carefully. When I saw you on the terrace shortly after the accident, you were fully dressed, as you are now.'

'That's right.'

'So obviously you didn't go to bed. What were you doing while Miko was packing?'

'I was on the third floor, conferring with my staff, the two who accompanied me to the terrace.'

'Are you telling me you did not go back to your room?'

'Precisely that. When we had finished our discussions we went down to the foyer together. My boys were going to have a drink. They invited me to join them. We were on our way to the bar when the assistant manager stopped us and told us there had been an accident and a Japanese lady was involved. We went with him to the terrace and . . . the rest you know.'

'Had you and Miko quarrelled during the evening?'

'On the contrary, we were very tranquil in each other's company. More so than we had been for some time. The report of your conversation with Max Wylie was profoundly important to both of us. I knew about Miko's arrangement with Cubeddu, but only in the most

274

general way. I am impatient of such side issues, as you know. I told Miko that if Cubeddu were fool enough to pay her a success fee, she would be foolish not to take it. That's where the matter ended. I confess that her later meeting with Cubeddu raised certain suspicions in my mind, but your report was so clear and objective, it banished them instantly.'

'I'm glad to know that. I would also feel happier if you did not have to open the matter of Cubeddu and Hoshino with the police. If they themselves raise it, then you must be concerned only with the truth of your evidence.'

'Do you have any experience with the Thai police?'

'Some, yes. There is a wide range of quality in the force, but you will find, I think, that they will assign a top man to this case. This hotel is rated the best in the world. It is a key element in the tourist image of the country.'

'One moment, Gil. Why do you assume that there is what you call "a case"? All I can imagine is a tragic accident.'

'The police will begin with murder and work their way back to tragic accident which, of course, is exactly the label they want. However, with a foreign national, connected with an important international conference, they have to display due diligence. Besides, given all the circumstances of which you and I are aware – Hoshino, Cubeddu, Max Wylie – are you sure that murder should be ruled out?'

'I simply cannot conceive it.'

Watching him carefully, I was convinced that he was still in shock. He showed no evidence of grief, resentment, anger, any of the emotions that one might have expected after the violent death of a beloved mistress. Even his answers to my questions were mechanical, as if they had been constructed in a computer and intoned by a robotic voice. Then I perceived for the first time that I myself was in the same state.

I had identified the shattered body of a woman, whom I had seen only a few hours before living, breathing, talking in this very room. Now, ten minutes later, I was discussing the event in the bald terms of a police interrogation. I got up, went to the liquor cabinet, poured myself a large drink and offered the bottle to Tanaka. He waved it away.

'My head is full of cobwebs already. What the hell is keeping these people? Do they expect us to sit up all night for them?'

A few minutes later there was a knock at the door. When I opened it, two people entered the room: a uniformed lieutenant of police and an older man in civilian dress. The older man made the introductions, in English.

'This is Lieutenant Sarit. I am Captain Aditya. I know who you gentlemen are. I offer Mr Tanaka my sincere sympathies and to you, Mr Langton, my thanks for your helpful intervention. First, I should like Mr Tanaka to show me round the suite and then respond to some questions. Are you happy to work in English, Mr Tanaka?'

'For the moment, yes. When we come to depositions I should prefer to have Mr Langton translate from Thai to Japanese.'

Captain Aditya was too polite to show surprise. He bowed his acquiescence and then asked Tanaka to lead him on a tour of the three rooms. He suggested that I might care to sit and enjoy my drink in peace until they were ready to take Tanaka's statement. I was happy to do just that, but when I picked up the glass again my hand trembled violently, so that the ice rang against the glass and some of the liquor slopped into my lap. I drank, holding the glass with both hands, and felt the raw spirit burning my gullet. Finally, I was steady again, counting off the seconds and the minutes that Tanaka was absent with the police: three minutes in the master bedroom, a cursory glance in the lounge; ten, twelve, twenty minutes in Miko's room, with long silences punctuated by bursts of talk, too low-toned to be intelligible.

When they returned, I was surprised to hear Captain Aditya announce cheerfully: 'That will be all for this evening, gentlemen. I understand you will be in the hotel all day tomorrow. We'll talk again when you are rested, Mr Tanaka. As for you Mr Langton, perhaps you'd be good enough to ride down with us to the foyer and give us a brief account of your movements this evening.'

'Whatever you say, captain. Will you be all right, Kenji? I can call back before I go to bed.'

'No thank you, Gil. I'll be better alone. Thank you for your help. Our breakfast meeting stands. Goodnight.'

As we walked down the corridor to the elevators, Captain Aditya told me with a smile: 'You come up nice and clean on our computers, Mr Langton. Also, your friend Doctor Kukrit is doing the autopsy at his clinic. We, too, are old friends. He is working late to oblige me. Just to complete the formalities, would you give me a rundown on your evening?'

I gave it to him in sixty seconds flat. The elevator arrived and we rode down together to the lobby. The young lieutenant saluted and left us. Captain Aditya steered me to a quiet corner out of earshot of the few remaining guests. Then, without warning, he began conversing in Thai.

'This is an embarrassing business, Mr Langton, as much for you, I imagine, as it is for us.'

'I agree, captain.'

'Did you know the lady well?'

'I've met her many times in my association with Tanaka.'

'What precisely is your association with Mr Tanaka?'

'He is a partner in my Japanese publishing company, as Doctor Kukrit's sister is my partner in the enterprise here. I happen also to command a number of languages, so I function sometimes as a mediator, arbitrator, consultant at international conferences like this one.'

'To return to the lady. It would appear that, while her relationship with Mr Tanaka is of long standing, she runs an independent business in Los Angeles.'

'That's right.'

'Is it possible that in the course of that business she has made enemies?'

'It's possible in any business.'

'Even in yours, Mr Langton?'

'Even in mine. For instance, here in Bangkok we compete for contracts to produce school textbooks. Sometimes we win, sometimes we lose. When we win, someone else loses. So there is always a potential enemy.'

'Have you any reason to believe that the business carried on by this young woman was in any way drug related?'

'As I have always understood it, from hearsay only, Miko supplied commercial services to Japanese companies operating on the West Coast. I am speaking of legitimate business services. She was not in the escort or entertainment business. Drugs? I wouldn't think so for a very simple reason. It's a dangerous trade and she was not in need of money. However, if you're asking me whether any of her clients were drug-connected, I have no first-hand knowledge at all.'

'You obviously feel a need to be very precise in your answers.'

'A matter of training. Hearsay evidence is inadmissible in British and American courts. In a travelling life, I hear enough gossip to fill a dozen scandal magazines. Even in this project, we have had long debates on the origin of funds offered for investment. It was agreed that if the funds were offered through legitimate agencies, we had neither duty nor right to enquire as to their origins, though we might ultimately decline to use them. Does that make my position any clearer to you?'

'It does. I am not sure that it advances my case very far.'

'Are you able to say what your case is likely to be, captain?'

'I have no doubt at all, Mr Langton, that we are dealing with murder.'

Suddenly I had run out of words. I sat gaping at him like an idiot, while he waited, placid as a Buddha, his hands folded on his lap. Finally, with a singular gentleness, he said: 'You are shocked, Mr Langton. You should not be. We live in violent times, when rational solutions to human problems seem sometimes fruitless and often too tedious to accomplish. But let me make a confession to you. I believe we have a murder on our hands. I am not sure we can prove it. I am even less sure that we want to prove it. Can you understand that?'

'Yes.'

'A scandal solves nothing. It may do much damage to good people and important projects.'

That little ploy was like a needle jabbed in my backside. It not only woke me up, it made me very angry indeed. I was being asked to give tacit assent to two separate propositions: that I might well have access to vital information and that I might be prepared to conceal it to avoid a scandal. But remembering my long education in Thai manners, I could not show anger and I could not make the captain lose face by telling him I had seen the barb under the bait. My response was sedulously mild.

'I see your dilemma, captain. It's the problem we all face from time to time: expedient solutions or legal ones? I'm glad it is you who has to make the decision, not I. Be assured, however, of my fullest co-operation in your investigations. Now, if there is nothing else, I beg you to excuse me. I have a breakfast conference at eight in the morning and committee meetings after that.'

'Be assured I shall bother you as little as possible.'

I stood up, laid my hands palm to palm and offered him the goodnight salutation. He returned it with a graceful compliment.

'It is a pleasure to hear you speak my language, Mr Langton.'

'Thank you. My only regret is that we have such a sad subject to discuss.'

278

As I walked across the foyer to the elevators, I knew that he was watching me, counting my sluggard paces in case I faltered or stumbled. This was his bailiwick and however beautifully I spoke his language, I was still the *farang*, the foreigner, the outside man, who had always to mind his manners.

Sixteen

By the time I reached my room, I was rocking with fatigue, sour with indigestion. There were messages under my door from Leibig, Laszlo, Vannikov and Max Wylie. The tenor of each was the same: 'Call me, any hour!' I tore them up and tossed them in the waste basket. There was, however, one more missive: a note written on hotel stationary. It was in English.

Dear Gil,
   I am writing this under the drier in the beauty parlour. This is the last and only place I can be private now. You thought you were doing me a favour when you let me down so lightly over the Max Wylie report. When I heard you tell it to Kenji and me I was grateful. I had never been half as kind to you.
   Kenji, however, was enraged. I have never known him so cold and bitter and cruel. He ordered me instantly out of his life. Had there been a night flight to Tokyo, he would have put me on it. He called Hoshino and arranged to have me escorted to the airport and physically conducted on to the aircraft like a criminal. I am to stop in Tokyo only long enough to collect my belongings. Then I am to go back to Los Angeles for good – or for bad, who knows! Kenji has sworn to destroy my business. He can do it, too, simply by withdrawing his own patronage and putting the word about that I am no longer to be trusted. Then Cubeddu can move in and turn me into anything he wants, from whorehouse madam to coke dealer.
   Does that surprise you? It surprises me, too; but I've just learned something. When you've lived as long as I have under an invisible umbrella of protection, you forget how to come in from the rain. Silly and sad, but true. I don't know when I've ever felt so helpless. For the first time, I understand why Kenji wants to take what he calls the short way out.
   Long before we left Tokyo, he asked me to make a suicide pact with him, so that we could go out together. Part of me was

attracted to the idea. Part of me rejected it utterly. Kenji refused to understand. That was when he began to close me out and I began to make separate plans for my life after his death. Now the estrangement is total and all my plans are in ruins.

I've called Marta and told her I am leaving – just that; the rest of the story is too long and complicated. She is relieved, I think. She's another one with a foot in two worlds and not yet enough courage to choose between them. I didn't take her away from you, Gil. She never really belonged to you, though she could and would if you ever wanted her enough to reach out and lift her over the barrier.

Why am I telling you all this? You of all men, I of all women? If you hadn't been so locked into your loyalties to Kenji, you could have had me any time – no strings, no questions. Who knows what we might have done together? But that's all fairytale and illusion, like the legend of the fox-woman who destroys the men who love her. Not true, Gil. Not true at all. It is always the fox who is hunted and, in the end, destroyed.

I wish I could say I love you. It would be pleasant to dream that you loved me. At least believe I've never hated you. *Sayonara*, Gil-san.
    Miko.

I folded the letter and locked it in my briefcase. I opened the sliding doors that gave on to the river terrace and stood leaning on the metal railing, staring down at the tropic garden and the long vista of the river reaches, lined with new developments: hotels, apartments, warehouses. I changed posture several times, making macabre experiments. Could I fall if I stood like this? If I leaned thus, what kind of force would be needed to tip me over the rail? If I really wanted to jump, how would I do it? Somersault over the rail? Or climb over it and drop myself into space?

For one drunken moment, I was tempted to straddle the rail and test the sensation on the other side. I drew back, sweating and shivering, went inside and closed the door. It was time to sleep, if sleep would come. I stripped off my sweat-sodden clothes, doused myself under the shower, put in a wake-up call for seven in the morning and lapsed into a dead, dreamless slumber.

The phone rang at six-thirty. Max Wylie was on the line.

'What the hell happened, Gil? I was expecting a call.'

'Very little. A Captain Aditya interviewed Tanaka and me. The autopsy was going on at Kukrit's clinic. Nothing more will happen until this morning. We've been asked to hold ourselves available for further interviews. I gathered the police would like a tidy solution.'

'And that's all?'

'All we should discuss on the telephone. I've got a breakfast meeting at eight, a conference at nine. Why don't we meet for coffee in the Writers' Lounge at ten-thirty?'

'Done. Meantime, I've got something for you. Domenico Cubeddu shipped out of Bangkok at three-thirty yesterday afternoon – Korean Airlines to Seoul. That takes him right out of this picture. Interesting, yes?'

'Very. Do you know this Captain Aditya?'

'No, but I'll check him out before we meet. What's going to happen about the conference?'

'I'll know that by ten-thirty. *Ciao*, Max!'

Since I was awake, I saw no good reason why others should sleep. I called Boris Vannikov who, much to my surprise, was just back from an hour's exercise at the gymnasium and jogging track across the river. I suggested it would save time if he joined our breakfast conference on the terrace.

'We've all gone round and round the mulberry bush. A decision has to be made. As I read it, we could get a consensus to break off at the end of this week and announce a continuance after further study. The way things are in the Gulf, with war almost certain, it would make sense and save face for everybody.'

'I'll need time to clear it with Moscow.'

'You'll get it, Boris. But let's establish the general agreement, then we can go into conference at nine with a clear direction. By the way, we should open with a brief silence for our colleague Miko.'

'What news do you have?'

'Police investigations are in progress. Everyone is hoping for a decision in favour of accidental death.'

'Nobody more than we, Gil. I've just turned on the American news. We seem to be living in a chamber of horrors. Moscow has sent our black beret paratroopers into the Baltic republics, into Georgia and the southern Ukraine. I confess to you, Gil, I want to go home. I don't want to be stuck here, lusting after little Thai girls, while they're cooking up a new revolution at home. By the way, talking of Thai girls, your Siri is wonderful, and so was the dinner. It worked wonders for Tanya. I'm almost prepared to go on living with her. See you at eight.'

Leibig and Laszlo were both astir. I gave them a quick résumé of the night's events and told them that I had invited Vannikov to join us for breakfast. I had the impression that neither wanted to discuss the circumstances of Miko's death. She belonged to Tanaka. He should look to his own house. I was Tanaka's man; they expected me to keep the thoroughfares of business clean and tidy.

My final call was to the clinic. They told me Doctor Kukrit was resting in his office. He had been up all night doing an autopsy and writing a report. They asked me to spare him any calls until later in the day. I had them connect me to Marta's room. She told me, calmly enough, that Kukrit had told her the news of Miko's death, describing it as a 'one-in-a-million accident' and the police investigation as a 'necessary and quite normal routine'. She had cried for a while, but she was over it now. I told her I would be in to see her at lunch hour with an extended version of the news.

That was the last of my duty calls and it was with a real sense of relief that I put down the receiver. These days people did not kill the bad-news messenger, but they certainly did not thank him. Rather, they seemed to regard him as a kind of tax-gatherer, levying compassion and care that folk were no longer prepared to give freely. I found myself wondering about the last dark hour of Miko's life as she finished her packing, alone in her bedroom, and then moved out on to the balcony to see and hear the nocturne of the great river.

I found myself wondering, too, about Tanaka and the vast difference between his version of the night's events and the brief, poignant narrative in Miko's letter. I had no doubt at all that, by Western norms, Tanaka was lying and Miko was telling the truth. But it was not as easy as that to render the right judgment. It never had been, it never would be. Each one, the living Tanaka, the dead Miko, was making the same plea: *wakatte kudasai*, please understand; what seems is not what truly is; what truly is demands to be accepted, tolerated at least, because it cannot be changed.

I could almost hear the cogs and ratchets clicking inside Tanaka's brain: 'This is my woman. She has grown up under my patronage. She has been ennobled by my esteem. I have opened my heart to her. I have caused her to be respected among my peers. Now she has dishonoured me, disprized me, exposed me to public and to private shame. She has to go, and go quickly!'

He would say none of it, of course, even to me, his friend. It was my obligation to accept what he presented to me. I could not even suggest that the woman's story might be more acceptable than his own. I must know that honour in such a one was as rare as a square duck-egg. I must know, too, that only my acceptance would make the new circumstance tolerable to him. Came then the questions: how much was I prepared to accept, to what limits would my tolerance stretch? To murder? Conspiracy to murder? To suicide under duress or in a crisis of desperation? I had heard a long time ago of Tanaka's capacity for teasing cruelties. He had warned me himself that, given a choice between his interest or mine, I would be the one who went to the wall. I should have no illusions about what he could do. The question now was what he had done. In default of a clear answer, what was I going to do to a friend who already had the mark of death on his forehead?

I carried the thought with me to the breakfast table, where Tanaka sat, calm and composed, the elder statesman wholly dedicated to the business in hand. When the waitress had taken our orders he invited me to sum up the opinions of the group.

'As I interpret them, we all agree to continue until the end of this week, then suspend sessions until further notice. If members desire, working committees could continue during the second week, but this could complicate matters, since their reports and recommendations would not receive adequate study. For the press and public relations generally, a clean break is easier to handle: the danger of a Gulf war, the problems within the Soviet Union itself both dictate a temporary postponement. Boris here is aware of your requirement for protection of your existing interests. He sees that your control of existing funds is the best guarantee of Soviet compliance. And that, gentlemen, is about all I can usefully say, except that I think you should be agreed before you go into the conference room. It will save a lot of time and make it a lot easier to handle the press, who will be baying at our heels today.'

'For obvious reasons,' said Boris Vannikov, 'I have to bow out of today's press conferences. Can you handle it, Gil?'

'If you trust me, Boris.'

'I would trust you even with my own wife, Gil, only because she is a singularly disagreeable woman.'

'It's a tasteless question,' Laszlo addressed himself directly to me. 'But how do you propose to treat the question of Miko's death?'

'As far as we are aware, it was a sad and tragic accident. Unless the police pronounce differently, that's the word for the press, too. We refuse to speculate. I'll instruct Alex Boyko accordingly. They will, however, ask about funeral arrangements.'

'My people will take care of those.' Tanaka waved the subject aside. 'I myself may leave for Tokyo before the end of the week. There is nothing more I can do here and I am in urgent need of medical attention.'

I was tempted to remind him that the Thai police might have something to say about his departure, but I held my peace. Tanaka was rich enough and potent enough throughout South-East Asia to put up a hefty bond against his return and leave it as a charge against his estate when he made his final act of abdication. Suddenly I felt an enormous sense of anticlimax. The event which had been planned for so many months, for which astronomical sums of money had been pledged, was fizzling out like a firework display on a stormy night. The real lightnings and the real thunders, the torrential downpours, dwarfed and then doused the puny gunpowder games of our contrivance. We had so inflated the importance of our commercial enterprise that we had forgotten how fragile its foundations really were. We had forgotten that the whole world floated on oil and that, as old Haushofer had foretold, the fate of the nations, East and West, was being determined by events in the heartland of Eurasia.

Since we were now back to banalities, I asked my colleagues whom they would choose to make the announcement to the assembled delegates. Tanaka suggested I should do it, as a neutral spokesman. I refused. Leibig supported me. Vannikov saved the day by claiming the right for himself as leader of the Soviet delegation. His reasoning was simple: Moscow had invited the proposal, Moscow was entertaining it, Moscow had requested a postponement of decision. The consortium had graciously agreed. It would be Gil's job to carry and interpret that decision to the press. All in favour? So carried.

Since there seemed little likelihood that I would be needed for consultations during the morning sessions, I begged to be excused so that I could confer with our press people. I had also to call Tokyo to discuss a staff acquisition of Tanaka's holding in Polyglot Press. If anyone needed me, I would be in my suite for the next hour. I was glad to be free of them for a while, to begin at least to make sense of my relationship with Kenji Tanaka. There was all the more reason to do so because I knew it would be very brief now and I did not want it to end in enmity.

I went back to my suite and called Tanizaki in Tokyo. He was delighted with the prospect of buying into Polyglot Press and asked what I thought Tanaka would accept for his interest and what rate he would charge for loan money. I told him to send me an offer based on book value and three years' profits after tax and a request for a loan at one per cent over prime. I would try to set the deal before Tanaka left for Tokyo. Then I told him about Miko. He gave a long, doleful whistle.

'Sad, Gil, very sad. Also very strange. This is not a country girl dying of disappointed love. This is Nisei woman, running her own life and her own business. So her protector is dying; she is not going to climb into the grave with him. Take my advice, Gil-san, and stay always two steps away from the rest of that drama.'

It was good advice and I was only too ready to take it. However, there was no way to side-step the ladies and gentlemen of the press, so I called Alex Boyko and his cohorts and briefed them for the day's encounters. They had an extra problem for me: a carefully crafted piece in the *Washington Post*, linking German geopolitical theory with the long suppressed *Kokutai no Hongi*, Cardinal Principles of the National Entity of Japan, which had once been the prescribed textbook of the prewar imperialists. By linking the two themes the writer had raised once again the most sinister ghosts of the forties. His conclusion was cogent.

> There is a hard core of truth in the geopolitical thesis. Geography is still a major determinant in human affairs. Eurasia is an enormously large, diverse and rich continent. Germany, united again, is the natural land bridge to those resources. Japan, hungrier than ever for natural resources, controls the sea routes to Vladivostok. The world should beware of any bargains, such as that now being negotiated in Bangkok, which set the world spinning again on the Berlin/Tokyo axis.

This was Max Wylie's prophecy fulfilled. The immediate question was how to answer it or whether, given the short term which the conference now had to rum, it should be answered at all. Alex Boyko thought it should. However, he confessed himself ill-equipped in the subject. I suggested that if Marta were well enough we should take the article around to the clinic and have her outline the counter argument for him. It was still early enough to have the meeting and be back in time for the press conference at noon.

No sooner said than done. I called Marta and explained our mission. She was delighted to have something to do. Five minutes later we were on our way. I introduced Boyko and Marta and left them to their discussion. As I walked through the foyer, I came face to face with Captain Aditya, who had just arrived. He greeted me with warmth and enthusiasm.

'My dear Mr Langton. What a fortunate encounter. I have just come to discuss with Doctor Kukrit the results of his autopsy. After that, I intended to call on you and Mr Tanaka to go over some of the ground we touched last night. But since you are here and you are such a good friend of Doctor Kukrit, why don't we combine the two exercises? Do you have any experience of forensic pathology?'

'Fortunately, or regrettably, no.'

'Then you will find this session very instructive. Come!'

Kukrit was pleased to see me, but friend enough to warn me that a cadaver after an autopsy was not a pretty sight. He suggested we deal first with his report and leave the inspection of the body until the end. Kukrit's clinical explanation was brisk and lucid.

'We have established beyond doubt that she was alive on the balcony and that she died when she hit the ground. There are massive fractures throughout the whole bony structure and ruptures of internal organs. Details of the damage are listed in my report. There was no evidence of recent sexual congress. There was food in the stomach, consistent with Mr Tanaka's description of the light meal they had taken together. She was dressed in bra and panties over which she wore one of those silk dressing gowns supplied by the hotel to all the guests. The feet were bare; but I understand you found a pair of mules on the balcony – again, the type supplied by the hotel. There were no marks of gross violence, strangulation, beating, scratching, none of those things. However, violence had been used, of a particular and professional kind. That violence rendered her swiftly unconscious. She was then lifted and tossed over the balcony like a sack of rice. Let me demonstrate. Gil, would you stand up please. Now, move behind your chair and lean on the back of it, facing Captain Aditya. Hold that position for a few moments.' He touched both sides of my neck with a pencil, while the policeman watched intently. 'Here and here, we found bruise marks. Watch how they were made. Don't move please, Gil. The victim is standing thus, leaning on the rail. The killer approaches from behind, braces his knee in the small of her back and depresses both carotid arteries. The supply of blood to the brain is shut off, the victim becomes unconscious. It's one of the most dangerous holds in wrestling. It is called, obviously enough, the sleeper. That's how it was done.'

287

'When, and by whom?'

'Immediately before she was thrown off the balcony. Once the pressure is removed from the arteries, the victim returns fairly quickly to normal.'

'By whom then?'

'I don't know. There is no tissue under the victim's fingernails, because no struggle took place. Effectively, he was holding her at arm's length from behind.'

'Could she have cried out?'

'Possibly.'

Captain Aditya supplied the rest of the answer: 'From up there with the longboats roaring by, the clatter and buzz of the restaurant, who would have heard? Certainly no one would have seen, because the room was in darkness and the angle of light from the terrace precludes it. Nevertheless, doctor, you are sure it was murder.'

'I'm sure.'

'Two more questions then. Who did it? And why?'

'Both beyond my competence,' said Doctor Kukrit firmly.

'Mr Langton? Do you have any comment?' He smiled engagingly. 'You can sit down before you answer.'

'I presume you have checked Mr Tanaka's account of his movements that evening.'

'Most thoroughly. There is no doubt at all that at the relevant time he was downstairs with his colleagues.'

'Then someone else must have entered the room in his absence.'

'The room waiter came in to remove the dinner things. The maids came in to turn down the beds and tidy the rooms for the night. But all that was much earlier, before ten.'

'The floor staff saw no one else enter any of the three rooms?'

'No. They admit they do not see everyone who comes on to the floor; they never challenge anyone who has a key or who is known to them as a resident on that floor.'

'Suppose a stranger comes and knocks on a guest's door?'

'The floor staff will wait to see whether the guest admits the visitor. It is the guest's room, after all; he or she may receive anyone, except, be it said, professional prostitutes, who are easily recognised if they are locals.'

'But clearly someone did enter the Tanaka suite and that someone killed Miko.'

288

'You can't suggest who that someone might be, Mr Langton?'

'Regrettably, no.'

'Could you suggest a reason why anyone would want to kill this woman?'

'Captain, in a matter of such importance, I must refuse to speculate. You must not ask me to do so.'

'Does the name Domenico Cubeddu mean anything to you?'

'Yes. In Tokyo Cubeddu was introduced as a possible investor in the Tanaka/Leibig consortium. He is the President of the Palermitan Banking Corporation. It is my understanding that his offer was declined.'

'Do you know of any connection between Cubeddu and the deceased?'

'Miko had made contact with him about logging rights in South America. Then he paid her a finder's fee for an introduction to this syndicate. She was to have earned a much more substantial fee if Cubeddu had been accepted into the group.'

'So in fact she had already forfeited that fee?'

'Yes.'

'What else can you tell me about Domenico Cubeddu?'

'He came to Bangkok. We had a brief conversation last Sunday by the pool.'

'Do you know whether he met with the victim?'

'I believe he did. I am told the meeting was recorded by the police.'

His head came up like that of a cobra, ready to strike: He demanded: 'Who told you that?'

'A reliable and official source.'

'I would remind you, Mr Langton, that you are a guest in this country.'

'A law-abiding and profitable guest, Captain. I am therefore entitled to certain courtesies and obliged to certain privacies.'

He was obviously taken aback. He made a gesture of apology. 'Forgive me. I am, as you may imagine, under a certain stress. You and I, Mr Langton, must take pains to understand each other, to be friends if we can.'

'I know no reason to the contrary, Captain.' I turned to Kukrit, who had sat silently through the exchange. 'What time is Marta to be discharged tomorrow?'

'Nine-thirty.'

'What do I have to do?'

'You? Nothing. She will have a diet chart, a list of medications and a set of simple instructions: no liquor, no spices, no tobacco, minimal stress. The only permitted indulgence is sex.'

'You've explained all that to her?'

'All of it in great detail. See you, Gil.'

'I'll see you, too,' said Captain Aditya amiably. 'One of the things I miss in the crime business is stimulating dialogue.'

I went back to Marta's room to pick up Alex Boyko. He retired discreetly while I talked to Marta. I told her she would be discharged in the morning. Once again, there was the question of what clothes she would need. This time she wrote a list, which she folded into my breast pocket. As I kissed her goodbye, she clung to me for a moment and said: 'I shouldn't say it, to you of all people, but I have the strange feeling Miko is in the room with me, trying to tell me something.'

'I can tell you what it is.' The words were out before I realised what I was saying. Marta stared at me in disbelief.

'How can you possibly know?'

'Because she told me herself.'

'What did she say?'

'She said you'd never be happy until you decided what side of the fence you wanted to live on – and until someone wanted you enough to lift you over the barrier.'

'Why are you telling me this now?'

'Because it was her last message. Only you can judge how important it is. By the way, if you'd like a hairdo, I'll have the salon send a girl around this afternoon.'

'I'd love that. This time I'd like to make a decent entrance. The last one was very messy.'

'I think, my love, we'd better take your mother's advice and revise the whole act. See you in the morning.'

It was an odd, abrupt farewell and it shocked me almost as much as it did Marta. But murder was out now and in the end a lot of other ugliness would come out with it. Bluebeard's chamber was about to be opened. The key was in Miko's letter, locked in my briefcase at the Oriental. I still had to decide whether to hand it to Captain Aditya or fit it myself into the lock and open the fateful door.

On the short ride back to the hotel, Alex Boyko read me the notes Marta had dictated to him. She had made an almost surgical dissection of the *Washington Post* article and revealed it for what it was, a highly partisan piece which leaned heavily on the circumstances and psychology of another era and paid scant attention to the massive changes brought about by fifty years of global trade and communication. Boyko was confident he could turn the notes into a respectable and controversial rebuttal which would follow the original piece on its syndicated journey round the world.

When we got back to the hotel it was time for my morning tea with Max Wylie. He had already staked a claim to the most discreet corner of the Writers' Lounge and was impatient to begin his interrogation. I decided to short-circuit the whole procedure.

'I've spoken with the autopsy surgeon and the police, Max. It's murder.'

'God Almighty! Who did it?'

'Person or persons unknown.'

'Why?'

'No known motive.'

'Suspects?'

'None. Tanaka's in the clear. I'm clean. Cubeddu's out of the country – that is, if your information is correct.'

'It is. Triple-A plus. How was she killed?'

'She was put to sleep with carotid pressure, then tossed over the balcony. She was alive when she fell.'

'It sounds like a hired hitman.'

'Do you know anybody who works like that, Max?'

'Yes. But one's in Hawaii, the other works out of Hong Kong.'

'I'm guessing that this was arranged at very short notice, here in Bangkok.'

'This is your town, Gil.'

'It's one of many, and I don't work the dark side of the street.'

'But you're on it now, little brother. You'd better get some lessons in local geography.'

'True. You can give me the first one. Suddenly Cubeddu's heading for Seoul, eight hours before Miko is murdered.'

'More like ten, eleven hours, allowing for checkout time and the trip to the airport. But why would he kill Miko? That would mean ruining a good investment. He was going to take her over, use her business as a base. Remember what this guy's about. He's a banker looking for investment connections in areas of high risk but very high returns.'

'So why, suddenly, does he quit?'

'Because he's out of the Tanaka/Leibig sydicate. Your press release made that very clear. Because he suddenly realised that Hoshino was setting him up for a big fall in Thailand – which is a bad place to take a fall.'

'Why would it happen so suddenly, Max?'

'Isn't that the way it always goes, Gil?' Wylie was now the wise man of the East, relaxed and tolerant. 'You live for a long time with a certain framework of ideas and convictions, then one day you shrug, cough, bend to tie a shoelace and the whole damn structure collapses and you have to start building again from the ground up. It happens faster with a guy like Cubeddu because he's always got the smell of danger in his nostrils. But for someone like you, Gil, full of temperate scholarship, it happens much more slowly. When I told you about Miko and Cubeddu, what did you do?'

'Exactly what you knew I would do, what you wanted me to do. I told them both.'

'Together or separately?'

'Together.'

He stared at me for a moment in utter disbelief, then he shook his head violently as if to clear it of cobwebs. Finally, he said softly: 'I never believed you would be so naive, or so goddam dangerous!'

'That's our problem, Max. We are naive because we're vain and we think sometimes we hold the keys to the mystery of creation. When we find we don't, then we become dangerous. We try to kick the door in. You say Miko was killed by a hired hitman.'

'That's a guess.'

'Make another one. Who hired the hitman?'

'Hoshino.'

'On his own account?'

'No. For Kenji Tanaka.'

'Motive?'

'Long-time mistress turned reckless and greedy, consorting with scum like Cubeddu. And remember, his information was rock solid, from Hoshino on one side of the fence and you on the other.'

'So how do we prove it?'

'We don't. You don't. They don't. Hoshino's a big man in this town, he makes a lot of money for a lot of people. You'll never get within a shout of him. Even Cubeddu, with all that South American money to

292

spend, was scared off in the end. Tanaka's a big man in the other world, and he's going to be dead very soon. Your Captain Aditya is going through all the right motions so that he keeps his record clean and builds up some credit on the side for conducting a discreet burial of an embarrassing affair. Money will change hands, of course. Documents will be lost or altered. In the end, what does it matter? *Mai pen rai*. Give it up, Gil. Cut loose and go about your own scholar's business. It's good advice, believe me!'

'I know it is, Max. What sticks in my craw is that Tanaka was my friend.'

'He still is, Gil.' Max Wylie's tone was curiously compassionate. 'I believe he's guilty, but I haven't proved it. Under your rules and mine, he's still innocent. Under his own rules, he has no guilt at all. He has performed a necessary duty. He has removed an embarrassment and a threat to his family name, to his colleagues, to a whole complex of relationships in which his obligations are specific. He has done it with the same determination with which he will remove himself from the scene before he, too, becomes an embarrassment. What the hell am I going on about? You know all this better than I do.'

'Sure I know it. I'm not sure I believe it any more. God damn him to hell! I don't have to live by his rules.'

'So kick the door down.' Max Wylie threw up his hands in resignation. 'But don't come crying to me if you break your toes.'

My final ordeal for the morning was the noon press conference, which this time had attracted a whole battery of reporters and all the international television crews resident in Bangkok. Alex Boyko had them settled down before I arrived. The women had distributed the handouts and were working the crowd quietly, explaining that I would take questions in any language, but if I had to do that, then there would be a strict time limit for each questioner.

It would have been easier to conduct the whole session in a single language but, since there were three nations involved in the negotiation and I was, in effect, the servant of all, it seemed there was much goodwill to be gained by a polyglot performance. The first question came from Associated Press. This was the one with dynamite in it. The others followed like buckshot from all corners of the room.

'How, if at all, are these negotiations affected by the crisis in the Gulf and the unstable situation in the Soviet Union itself?'

'We are trying to put together a complex commercial deal with international capital. We're a bunch of experienced people, working with genuine goodwill. Of course we're affected by contemporary events, every event, even the bushfires and the floods in Australia. Money itself is a mobile element. Agreements have to be both acceptable and enforceable.'

'Can you see yourselves reaching agreement this week or next?'

'No, we cannot. There are too many issues which must be resolved elsewhere before we can go ahead here. At a meeting of principals this morning, it was agreed to end the first stage this week and resume discussions at a later date.'

'Was that agreement unanimous?'

'Yes.'

'That means the project is, to all intents and purposes, dead.'

'On the contrary, it is very much alive. It is an initiative which, in one form or another, is vital to the Soviet Union, who invited the submission in the first place. Its leaders clearly recognise the large investment which has already been made and the pre-emptive right of the Tanaka/Leibig consortium to a continuity of interest in the development.'

'When do you expect the conference to resume?'

'I wish I could say, madam; but at this moment none of us can see round corners. Perhaps it's just as well we can't?'

'How do you react to the suggestion which has begun to be circulated in the press, that this German/Japanese consortium is, in some sense at least, a model for a new Berlin/Tokyo axis which could in the end control both Eastern and Western trade with the Soviet Union?'

'It's obviously something we've all thought about. The Leibig organisation actually co-opted the distinguished historian, Professor Marta Boysen, to advise on geopolitical aspects. The Japanese government itself is involved in negotiations with the Soviet Union over the Kuril Islands. Obviously there are echoes of past history and questions about future relationships. It would be foolish to ignore them and irrational to try to deal with them in terms of another era.'

'What can you tell us about the mysterious and tragic death of Mr Tanaka's assistant?'

'Nothing, I'm afraid. We are all deeply shocked. The Thai police are investigating. It would be unwise and improper to pre-empt their findings.'

'One more question, Mr Langton. What do you know about "maverick capital"?'

294

'I know that you're quoting the words from the financial press. When I read them, I did not understand them. I still don't.'

Alex Boyko stepped in then and closed the meeting. I invited him and the women to join me for drinks and sandwiches on the terrace. It made an agreeable coda to my first and last public performance on behalf of Leibig and Tanaka. I still had to face some private ones and I was not looking forward to them at all.

At two I was back in my suite, dictating a batch of business memoranda to Eiko, who was downcast at the thought of leaving Bangkok and her young salary-man. He was an owl-eyed fledgling whom she had presented to me as if he were the handsomest juvenile lead in the movie world. I was tempted to tell her she could do a hundred times better; but love is blind and Tokyo was not that easy for a virtuous young women and what the hell would I know anyway? My own recent judgments in business, politics and love had not been the wisest.

Instead, I consoled her with the offer of an extra day in Bangkok if she could switch the air booking. For a moment, I thought she was about to burst into tears, then she tucked her papers under her arm and went out walking on air, invoking blessings on my head.

I called Siri and asked if we might postpone our dinner for a day or two.

'There's too much happening. I'm tugged this way and that. I want to be calm and comfortable with the children.'

'I understand. This is your house, Gil. Come when you please. Kukrit has told me about the Japanese woman. It's all so sad and wasteful. He also tells me Marta will be discharged tomorrow. You know she will be welcome whenever you wish to bring her.'

'I know, and thank you. I'm taking that one very quietly.'

'That's wise. Pity is the worst gift you can offer a woman and the most destructive indulgence for you, Gil.'

'My God! Now we have an aphorist in the family. Where did you pick that one up?'

'I wrote it myself. In my diary, last night. And I think it sounds better in Thai than it does in English. I was wondering how I could stop you making a mess of your life, which, in case you don't know it, Gil, is a very lucky, very rich one, important to a lot of people.'

'Do I sound sorry for myself?'

'No, sorry for other people. Some of whom don't deserve it.

Look after yourself. Remember, you and I have work to do before you leave.'

There was a knock at the door. A messenger from the business office delivered a fax from Tanizaki:

> All permanent staff prepared to make corporate offer for shares in
> Polyglot Press presently held by Tanaka Group or Tanaka
> personally. Our offer firm at book value plus goodwill calculated
> on three years of taxed profits. We have established that we can
> raise finance, outside Tanaka Group if necessary, at one per cent
> over prime. Thanks and salutations.

It was one less detail to worry about. I called Tanaka's room. To my great surprise, because he was usually heavily insulated from casual contacts, he answered the telephone himself. I asked when it would be convenient to see him. He answered comfortably enough.

'Captain Aditya is with me, let me ask how much more time he needs.' There was a murmur of conversation in the background, then he came on the line again. 'Give us fifteen minutes and then come up. I'd like to tidy all our business at this meeting. I leave for Tokyo in the morning.'

And there it was, cold turkey, no ifs, buts or maybes. The fix was in. Kenji Tanaka was getting away with murder.

Seventeen

In the brief respite before my meeting with Tanaka, I was overwhelmed by a flood of memories, still vivid after the lapse of decades. It was just after the birth of our first child, a year after Polyglot Press had opened its British office in Bloomsbury. My father was still alive, ailing, but sturdy enough to live alone in the small apartment over the office, active enough to meddle in any project that interested him, close enough to the university and the the British Museum to maintain a few academic contacts.

I was living in Hampstead, in an old Georgian house with a walled garden, a perfect nurturing place for a young family. In the very small hours of a winter morning, my father telephoned me with an outrageous demand.

'Get yourself dressed, Gil. Meet me at the office in forty minutes.'

'Are you drunk?'

'I'm stone cold sober; but I need you. I need you now. This is life and death.'

'Whose life, whose death?'

'Don't argue, for Christ's sake! Just get here!'

'Are you sick?'

'No! But you're going to make a sick call with me. Please don't waste any more time; just come.'

I went of course. I found him outside the office, muffled to the eyeballs against the biting wind, stamping his feet to help his sluggish circulation. As he climbed into the car, he stifled my objections before they were spoken.

'Not a word out of you, boy. Not a sparrow's chirp. I'm collecting a small instalment on what you owe me and your Maker.'

'Where are we going?'

'Holland Street.'

'Jesus! You could have taken a taxi!'

'I didn't want a bloody taxi! I want company. Now will you shut up please, and just drive!'

I could not, for the life of me, see why he needed company, because he was silent all the way to Holland Street and he left me freezing in the car outside a rundown terrace house with an overturned rubbish bin on the pavement near the front gate. He was obviously expected, because the door was opened a few seconds after his ring, though I could not see who received him into the house.

I waited. I waited thirty minutes, forty-five. A pair of policemen in a prowl car stopped and asked for my identification. They looked very dubious when I explained that my elderly father was visiting a sick friend, but the cold was too much even for them, so I was left alone for another fifteen minutes. When my father finally appeared, he was carrying a parcel wrapped in brown paper and tied with string. His only comment was: 'Sorry I took so long. Get me home and I'll make you an Irish coffee. You look as though you need it.'

I was too angry to give him the satisfaction of asking for an explanation. I would have preferred to cut my tongue out. Besides, he looked so drawn and doleful that I could not bring myself to bully him. When finally we reached the apartment, he tossed the package on his desk and, still mute, made very strong coffee laced with Irish whisky. Then, and only then, did he condescend to enlighten me.

'I suppose you're wondering what this is all about?'

'You might suppose that, yes.'

'I've been hearing a confession, a deathbed confession.'

'And since when have you been a minister of religion?'

'Longer than you might imagine, my son.' Much to my surprise, he quoted softly: ' "Religion, pure and undefiled, is this: to visit the fatherless and widows in their affliction and to keep yourselves unspotted from the world." Your mother, God rest her, used to say: "Religion is the good you do in the bad times." And tonight was one of the worst times. Here's an old man, a fine scholar, long retired, a fellow I've shared wine and pasta with sometimes – just that, we were never close friends. And he's dying and he doesn't believe in God but he's ashamed of stepping out into the dark with the load he's carrying. So he calls me and we talk and he hands me the burden and when I left he was asleep and probably won't wake again.'

'And that's all you're going to tell me?'

'If you'll bribe me with another whiskey you can have the rest of the story.' The moment I started pouring, he launched again into his narrative. 'It's a small tale really, a footnote to a subtext of history, overpassed and obscured long since by later researches. He was a philologist, you see, and his line of research was ancient Etruscan, of which we have a few decipherable fragments and many more undecipherable ones. Finally, he achieved a breakthrough which established his reputation as a scholar, gained him a doctorate and ultimately a tenured professorship. What he had done was establish a clear connection between the Etruscan texts and modern remnants of Illyrian languages, like Albanian . . . All very obscure stuff to the non-academic, but you know how important it is to the initiates. In that package on the desk are all his early papers, the foundation of a life's work. He wants me to edit and publish them.'

'And that's a confession? It sounds more like a final act of academic vanity.'

'He also wants me to publish the fact that he stole the original material and used it without attribution, as the basis of his own research.'

'Stole it from whom?'

'A junior curator at the Etruscan Museum in Rome, who made the original discovery but took longer to present and publish the material. By the time it was out, it was already superseded. He shot himself in a garret in Trastevere.'

'God! No wonder your friend needed a confessor. All that guilt festering inside him for so long.'

'That's the strange thing. I don't think it festered at all. I think it just popped up one day like a genie out of a bottle and then wouldn't go away. It wasn't a confessor he needed, but an exorcist. I was the only one he knew who would recognise the haunting.'

'So what are you going to do about the material?'

'That's why I got you out of bed, to have the benefit of your sage counsel. What would you do about it?'

'A plea from a dying man? I'd do what he asked.'

'You would?'

'No question about it.'

'Well now, let's raise a question or two and, if you need another drink, take it. You can buy me a fresh bottle tomorrow. Our dead penitent leaves a wife. She's an elderly lady, something of a scholar in her own right, a musicologist to wit. They have three children, two sons

299

and a daughter, all professional people launched on their own careers. There are also two grandchildren, not to mention a small extended family and a tribe of acquaintances, ex-students and friends in one academic discipline or another. The fellow he wronged is dead long since, probably buried in unhallowed ground or tossed in some ossuary because the lease on his burial place has run out. So who profits from this great penitential revelation? Nobody but me. It would be an interesting little end-piece for my own scholarly career. But who gets hurt? The wife, the children, the grandchildren, all those other innocents who never heard of plagiarism, probably wouldn't know it if they fell over it in the street. Am I going to be the one who inflicts the pain? No way in the world! Promises to a dying man? Rubbish! I sent him out in peace. He can claim no more rights over the living. I'm going to burn the stuff and you're going to help me do it, right now.'

If you've ever tried to light a fire in a Bloomsbury grate with a high wind howling across the rooftops and the draft funnelling down the chimney instead of up it, you will need no description of the epilogue. By the time the last pages were consumed, we were sooty, dishevelled and a little drunk with Irish whiskey and our own exceeding charity. Of the pair of us, I think I was the happier, because I had one more pearl to add to the chaplet of memories of my mother. For the first time, it seemed that I could catch the tones of her voice and the light in her eyes as she framed the motto: 'Religion is the good you do in the bad times.' It gave me courage enough for my final encounter with Kenji Tanaka.

He received me with a smile, seated me and offered me coffee, which I declined. I handed him the faxed offer from Tanizaki. He glanced at it and nodded agreement.

'Good! We'll settle at that. I'll deal with it as soon as I get back to Tokyo. I take it I treat with Tanizaki?'

'That's right. He'll form a corporate group for the purchase. When do you leave?'

'First JAL flight in the morning.'

'No problems with the police?'

'None. They have all the information I can give them. They still have no idea of the identity of the assailant or how entry was made into the suite.'

'What arrangements have been made for Miko's funeral?'

'The body will be released today. My people are arranging to have it shipped to California, where her assistant and her family will arrange the obsequies, at our company expense. The possessions she left in Tokyo will be packed and sent on in due course.'

'And that's it?'

He seemed vaguely surprised by the question. 'What else is there, for any of us? We drop out. The space we leave is cleared and made ready for the next occupant. It will happen to me very soon.'

'Have you made any plans?'

'For myself, yes. I have perhaps two weeks' work in Tokyo. Then I shall go back to Nagano. My doctor will accompany me. He is a good friend, he has agreed to facilitate my exit. My son and adopted son will be with me. At one time I had thought . . .' He shrugged off the unspoken thought. 'But that was an idle wish. I am ashamed of it now. So, for you and me, Gil, today is goodbye.'

'I have a farewell gift for you, Kenji.'

'And I have none for you. I am ashamed.'

'There is no need. We have been friends a long time. I believe we understand each other.'

I handed him the envelope containing Miko's letter. He stared at it for a moment then, punctilious as always, asked: 'May I read it now?'

'Of course.'

I watched him as he read the note, once, twice and again. It was an eerie experience, like seeing living tissue turn to grey stone. When he had finished, he refolded the paper with meticulous care and slid it into the envelope. He asked: 'Who else knows about this?'

'Nobody.'

'What are you going to do with it?'

'Nothing. It's my gift to you. Keep it.'

'I may choose to destroy it.'

'Your property. Your choice.'

I stood up, ready to take my leave. Tanaka obviously wanted to prolong the talk. He said: 'You place me deeply in your debt. How can I possibly . . .'

'All debts are cancelled, Kenji. We part here.'

He made a small gesture of surrender. 'So be it then. I thank you. I wish you well.'

'I hope you have a good journey, too.'

Then he said the one thing I had prayed he would not say. 'Gil, my friend, please understand . . .'

I turned away and left him standing there, with the letter still in his hand. Had I lingered a moment I think I might have killed him.

Hard on the heels of anger came a surge of new emotion – of exultation in a liberty I had lost a long time and found again in strange and tragic circumstances. I had not understood how long and how stringently I had bound myself to manners and customs that were not my own, how often, like that other voyager, Lemuel Gulliver, I had found myself on an alien shore, tied down with gossamer threads, or clod-hopping through tiny alleys, or dwarfed by gigantesque figures whose commands echoed like thunder.

Now I was free. Free enough to juggle a man's life in my hands and toss it back to him as the last tribute of a dead friendship, free enough to look at myself in the mirror and ask finally what more I wanted out of life and how much I was prepared to pay to get it. Kenji Tanaka had never been free. He had been born in fetters and had never struck them off. His only release would be the death he had contrived for himself.

Marta Boysen had been born to another kind of captivity, in an old city, in an old tradition of theatrical vagabondage, a framework of European scholarship which set the pupils in serfdom to the master and in the end pricked them to revolt, but left them small room for a change. I acknowledged her scholarship. I truly could not see myself accommodating to her moods, struggling always with the complicated logic of her divided psyche. Friends we could be, lovers no more and married never. Commonsense and decency demanded that I tell her so, face to face. With the high mood still on me, I decided to get it over and done with before she left the hospital, so that she could step out of the sickroom into a life of her own.

As we drove round to the clinic, I rehearsed my lines like an actor, testing the phrases, changing the emphasis, looking for the last felicities of expression. I should have known better. There are no felicities at the end of an affair. I had hardly begun to explain my untimely visit when Marta Boysen changed instantly into the Frau Professor Doktor, calm, imperious and dismissive.

'No explanations are needed, Gil. We are good friends. I hope we shall remain so but it has become clear to both of us, I think, that we are quite unready and, indeed, incompatible, for a continued relationship. You are older than I, a very settled man with many career demands. I have not yet found a mode of activity or an emotional life that satisfies me. Best we recognise that now and spare each other a later pain. You do agree, don't you?'

'I agree.'

'Then let's kiss and be friends and say no more about it.'

We did kiss and we were friends, but there was more to be said. Marta made me sit on the bed and imprisoned my hands in her own. She faced me with the blunt question:

'Was Miko murdered?'

'The police believe so.'

'And you, Gil?'

'I believe it, too.'

'Who did it?'

'Nobody knows. Nobody wants to know.'

'That's horrible!'

'It's also a matter of practical politics. In this city, at this time, with the rest of the world falling apart, nobody wants an international scandal. So take my advice. Don't gossip, don't speculate. Miko's dead. Let her rest in peace.'

'She knew she was going to die.'

'How do you know?'

'She wrote me a note from the hairdressers.'

'May I see it?'

'Here.'

She handed me a similar envelope to the one I had received. The note was much shorter.

My dearest Marta,
    I feel terribly alone, threatened by every shadow. You tell me
you want to be a straight. It is an ugly piece of jargon, but I
understand it and I wish you luck and love. If you can't, look at
this sometimes and remember. Miko.

'This' was an old ivory *netsuke*: two courtesans making sapphic love together. It was exquisitely carved and the two tiny bodies seemed warm and writhing to the touch. Marta's eyes never left my face. Her question was a challenge.

'Don't you think it's beautiful?'

'Very beautiful.'

'I prayed last night that wherever Miko is, she won't be lonely.'

'We can all use a prayer or two.'

'I said one for you as well.'

'And what did you ask for me?'

'Peace at your coming, peace at your going. Your father taught it to me. He said it was the prayer of friends. We are friends aren't we, Gil Langton?'

'At last we are, Marta Boysen.'

I left the hospital a few minutes after four. The day was almost over and I was at a loose end, with nothing I needed or wanted to do. I looked in on the committees. Their discussions were tailing off into repetitive exchanges, because the same questions kept coming up, with the same dearth of answers. Nothing could be settled in Bangkok, because in Moscow the President was fighting to stop the Soviet empire exploding, like an overheated mill-saw, into lethal fragments.

I was sorry now I had postponed my dinner date with Siri. I debated taking some exercise in the pool or taking my ease in the hairdresser's with a shave, manicure, pedicure and body massage thrown in for good measure. For once, virtue triumphed. I decided the exercise would do me more good than the pampering.

I counted off forty lengths of the big pool, then towelled myself and lay back on a lounger to watch the last poolside parade of the pretty girls and the predator males. It was a languid diversion which made no demands upon the mind and certainly no music on the heartstrings. Then Sir Pavel Laszlo, grotesque in a skimpy pair of swim-shorts, took possession of the lounger beside me.

'People have been looking for you, Gil. I'm supposed to pass messages. Vannikov wants you to dine with him tonight in the Soviet Embassy.'

I let out a theatrical groan. 'Not tonight, Josephine!'

'Alternatively, Carl and I can offer you drinks at seven and Carl will take you to dinner if you wish.'

'The drinks I'll accept. I'd like to reserve judgment on the dinner. I've had a rough day, one way and another. I might settle for an early night with a good book.'

'Safest diversion there is in Bangkok.' Laszlo made no bones about the follies of promiscuity in the Orient. 'Did you see Tanaka today?'

'I saw him. My business with him is finished.'

'He's damn near finished himself.'

'I know. He says he's spending only a couple of weeks in Tokyo, then he's going up to Nagano. He's decided that's where he wants to die.'

'I wasn't thinking of Tokyo.' Laszlo glanced around furtively to make sure no one was eavesdropping, then he switched to Hungarian for extra safety. 'He's getting out of Bangkok by the skin of his teeth. It's cost him the best part of a million dollars to buy his immunity and his exit.'

'But the police had nothing on him.'

'They had enough to put him in the griller, because of Miko's murder and of his connection with Cubeddu and Hoshino.'

'Why didn't they?'

'I've told you. Money. And monkey-shines with Hoshino's local Yakuza connections.'

'Have the police bothered you?'

'Why should they?'

'You've got connections of your own with Tanaka.'

Laszlo waved a pudgy hand, dismissing the subject as a trifle. 'Some of 'em are now embarrassing, others aren't. I'll try to unload the embarrassing ones as soon as the market hardens up.'

'And when will that be?'

'God only knows, Gil. The news gets blacker every day. War in the Gulf is almost certain now and that touches off a whole chain reaction, uncontrollable as a nuclear burnout. Look at me. I'm a refugee. I made a fortune in Australia; now I'm back trying to reconstruct the Europe I fled fifty years ago. As of today, that's a débâcle, too. The latest news is that Gorbachev has sent the tanks and the gunners into Lithuania to take the radio station. People have been killed. The man must be going crazy! This conference of ours is only a metaphor for much bigger and bloodier messes. Tomorrow? Who dares even dream it? I have nightmares in which I see the bodybags being loaded into my planes and my trucks. Only today, I was thinking Tanaka might have the right idea. Give up the game. Sign out.'

'And let the bastards inherit the earth?'

'According to the press, they already own it – and I'm one of 'em!' He gave a long, spluttering laugh. 'They're right, too. I am a bastard, but at least I'm a constructive one. I build things, I don't blow 'em up. I run a tourist industry, for Christ's sake! I provide the fullest service in the world for human generation, from conception in the honeymoon suite to a kindergarten for the kids on a reef resort. What are you drinking?'

'Bourbon on the rocks.'

'Let me buy you another. I'll have one myself. I need a drink to cry into.'

I might have known that if he was buying me a drink I would end up paying for it, one way or another. On Laszlo's tours, there was no such thing as a free lunch. He did, however, have a little surprise for me.

'Now that this little circus is folding its tents, what are you going to do, Gil?'

'Attend to my own business for a change. I've got to make my annual round of the companies. I'll complete the circuit, visit my kids in England and the US, then head back home. I've got more than enough to keep me off the streets.'

'What would it take to put you back on the streets for a while?'

'Meaning what, Pavel?'

'It's too early to be specific, but let me try to draw a picture for you. Right now, everyone's talking war. Everyone has the same picture of it, because it's the picture they get on television: the ravaged battlefields, mutilated bodies, the battle-weary men, defeated even in victory, the long lines of bodybags with the chaplain consigning them to the earth and to their Maker. But that's only part of it, Gil. The other part is a vast tide of refugees, displaced by war or famine or tribal retribution, ebbing and flowing across the continents. That's the horror I remember; and it lasts much longer than the war, its wounded take much, much longer to heal. There are teams in the field all the time: United Nations, Red Cross, Save the Children, Oxfam. Their work is heroic, but it's like trying to stem Niagara Falls with sandbags. We need an enormous effort to co-ordinate resources, break down cultural barriers, silence the clamour of the Tower of Babel, so that the voice of reason and compassion can be heard. You've got the talent for it, Gil. You've got the languages and the background of history and culture. You've got the organisation, too. That publishing group of yours can be a powerhouse for a cause like this. If I can show you that there is a new starting point and there is a clear focus and there are funds and you wouldn't just be flailing around in a vacuum, would you be willing to think about it?'

'Think about it, yes. But no promises, no commitments.'

'Understood, of course. Perhaps on this trip you could make time to talk to some people in Switzerland and London.'

'Pavel! You're hustling me.'

He was, too. He could talk the birds out of the trees and blood out of dead rocks; but at the heart of every dream he conjured up was a solid commercial nut, with 'Profit' engraved on it. Also, like every hustler, he could read thoughts and faces. He began to take the pressure off me.

'I'm talking too much. I always do. I sell too hard? It's because I'm obsessed with time, intolerant of those who waste it. Enough! You will simply send me your itinerary and I'll arrange the appointments. Agreed?'

'I'll think about it, but there's a condition.'

'What's that?'

'Answer some questions for me.'

'If I can, sure.'

'Do you know who killed Miko?'

He did not hesitate for a moment. 'Yes.'

'Who was it?'

'Hoshino.'

'How do you know that?'

'I called to see Tanaka about seven. We had a short conversation. I left. Hoshino passed me in the corridor. He was going to see Tanaka.'

'Why didn't you tell the police?'

'Two very good reasons. Nobody asked me and I assumed Tanaka had accounted for his own movements. It was only afterwards that I began to speculate but, as you know, Gil, speculation isn't proof and in Asia no one is invited to meddle in police business.'

'So why try to dazzle me with all that rhetoric about tides of refugees and the aftermath of conflict?'

'Because it's true. It's going to happen. It's a theme that even here runs through all our debates. Look, Gil. Not all of me is a bazaar huckster. I have memories and I have nightmares, even now. I've got a conscience buried under all this blubber.'

'I know, Pavel. I'm sorry. I never liked Miko. She managed to foul up a few passages in my life as well as her own. But she's dead, and the men who conspired to kill her are home free. We let 'em go, both of us!'

'And for the same reason. Tanaka's as good as dead. Hoshino may last a little longer; but I've dealt with Captain Aditya before. He's very ambitious. He's on his way to being rich. This deal with Tanaka will just about get him there. After that, he'll turn respectable and start eliminating anyone who can blackmail him. Hoshino is very high on his hit list.'

'And how come you know so much about him?'

'I've been freighting in and out of Bangkok for fifteen years.' Once again, he gave that strange, spluttering laugh. 'I told you I was a bastard, didn't I? The first lesson you learn in trade and politics is that if you want to get you've got to give. Captain Aditya is one of my local charities. It entitles me to remind him of his duty from time to time.'

It was that odd, off-key conversation that made me cancel out the rest of the evening and cross to Siri's house. All of a sudden I felt desperate, shamed and angered by the cold brutality of my world. I must have looked a wreck, because she made me strip off and shower and wrap myself in one of those sarongs of woven silk which the Thais call *pakomas*. They are cool and comfortable and, like an actor's costume, they conduce to a shedding of one's everyday banal identity.

The children, who were not children, but a beautiful young woman and a proud, handsome young man, greeted me first with careful respect and then with a sudden rush of affection that warmed my arid heart. We sat, family style, round the low teak table and nibbled small plates of food, spiced and bland, while Siri coaxed me through an account of my recent doings. She wanted me to be open. She wanted the children to hear. It was an important part of their education, and it was my duty as an elder in the house to impart it to them.

So I talked to them about the conference, the high hopes with which it had begun, the tragic collapse of its careful plans. I tried to explain the gerrymandered structure of the Soviet republics, with their transplanted ethnic groups; the ancient enmities, the entrenched privilege of the *nomenklatura*. The young man, bred to monarchy and an established Buddhist faith, was hard put to understand the scope and rancour of tribal rivalries in the rest of the world. He was, however, fascinated by the story of Leibig and his family, the old Baltic traders who had found a foothold in Japan so long ago and had held it ever since, as the Danes had held theirs in Thailand. My beautiful niece was more interested in the tragic tale of Miko, the fox-woman, run finally to earth and destroyed by stronger predators, and the unfinished drama of Marta Boysen, whom she characterised, with rare perception, as a half-built palace for which the plans have been mislaid.

When I told them about Kenji Tanaka, our long friendship and its abrupt end, they were suddenly caught in a flurry of family recollections: their grandfather, who had been active in the Free Thai movement and had been a friend of Jim Thompson; the half remembered, carefully suppressed tales they had heard about the infamies of the Burma railway, the experiences of their father, who had many times visited Japan and had never quite come to terms with it.

Vannikov fascinated them because they both remembered the big, dramatic occasion when Yuri Yevtushenko, in town for an Asian writers' conference, had stood declaiming his verses, singing melancholy folk songs and trying to thread his tipsy way through an aria from Eugen Onegin. Vannikov was made in the same mould, big and lusty and full of ready passions. They loved passionate people. They did not mind melancholy ones either, so long as they were sad in a placid kind of way, like the countryside under the monsoon rain clouds.

Then came a moment when everything fell quiet and the young ones kissed me goodnight and melted into the shadows of the old house.

Siri said gently: 'I'm so glad you came. You don't know how important you are to the children.'

'They and you are just as important to me . . . I felt like a fugitive tonight, panting for sanctuary.'

'The night is not over yet. You are staying here. Everything is ready.'

She took my hand and led me across the footbridge that spanned the klong, to the small detached dwelling where my father had lived during his sojourn in Bangkok. Although I, too, occupied it sometimes, I had never regarded it as mine, always as my father's. Everything in it was his: the books, the desk, the old Thai paintings, the small bronze Buddha perched on a wall bracket over the bed.

Siri peeled off her wrap and mine. Her body was smooth as old ivory, supple as silk. She made me lie down on the bed and sponged me with cool, perfumed water. She drew the mosquito net around the bed like a vast white tent, tucked it under the mattress, then turned out the light and slid into bed beside me. No words were spoken; none had ever been needed in this place. All argument ended, all dissension died, all doubts and fears and all the sadness of the world were left behind on the other side of the bridge. Here, there was only love; the giving of it, the taking of it, the high leap to ecstasy, the long, slow, languid glide into sleep.

This was the true gypsy's resting place, marked by secret signs, redolent of the magic of other happy sojourns. Here, the yellow moon shone kindly; the spirits who lived in the tiny gilded house in the garden were all friendly; the Buddha who smiled from the shrine above the bed told the same age-old message to an unheeding world: 'Nothing is permanent. Tomorrow the caravan moves on. The wheels turn. The flowers bloom and die. The good we do in bad times is a seed planted for others to harvest. Evil is a dark hole in creation, where good may once have flourished, where it may take root again one starlit night, when the wounded world murmurs in a healing sleep.'